Mother of Lies

Please see www.daveduncan.com for more information.

mother of Lies

dave duncan

a tom doherty associates book TOR® new york

MOTHER OF LIES

Copyright © 2007 by Dave Duncan

This book is printed on acid-free paper.

Edited by Liz Gorinsky

Maps by Ellisa Mitchell

A Tor Book
Published by Tom Doherty Associates, LLC
175 Fifth Avenue
New York, NY 10010

www.tor.com

Tor® is a registered trademark of Tom Doherty Associates, LLC.

Library of Congress Cataloging-in-Publication Data

Duncan, Dave, 1933–
    Mother of lies / Dave Duncan.—1st ed.
        p.   cm.
    "A Tom Doherty Associates book."
    ISBN-13: 978-0-7653-1484-0
    ISBN-10: 0-7653-1484-3
    I. Title.

PR9199.3.D847M68 2007
813'.54—dc22   2007004544

First Edition: May 2007

Printed in the United States of America

0 9 8 7 6 5 4 3 2 1

With thanks to
Cliff, Eileen, Janet, Robert, Tony
(and several others over the years),
who have read my manuscripts and
helped me make them better

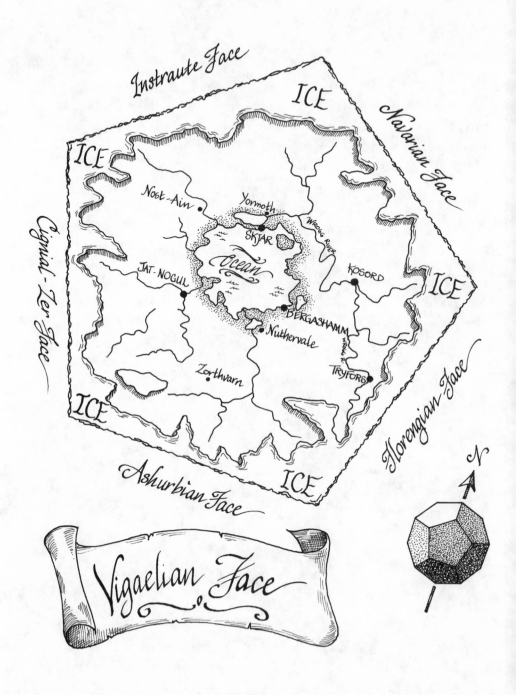

Instraute Face

ICE

ICE

Navarian Face

Nost-Ain

Yormoth

SKJAR

Wrong River

Ocean

KOSORD

ICE

Cignial - Zer Face

JAT-NOGUL

BERGASHAMM

Nuthervale

Zorthvarn

Tryfors

Morengian Face

ICE

ICE

Ashurbian Face

ICE

Vigaelian Face

N

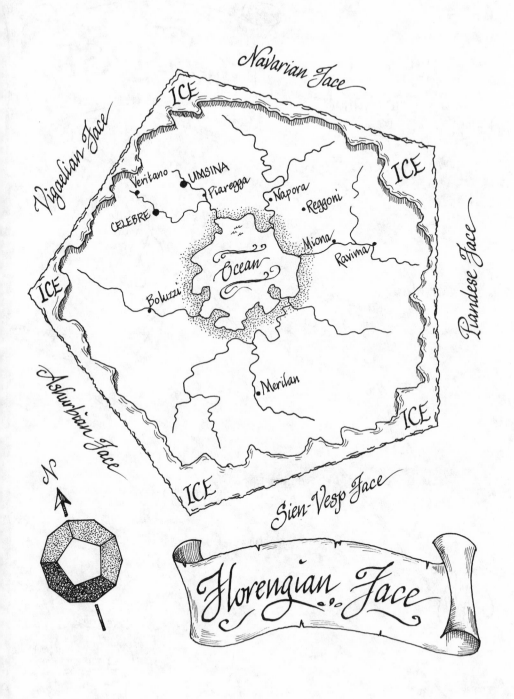

Navarian Face

Vigelian Face

ICE

ICE

Veritano
UMSINA
Piaregga
Napora
Reggoni

CELEBRE

Miona

Ravima

ICE

Ocean

Boluzzi

Randese Face

Ashurbian Face

Meritan

N

ICE

ICE

Sien-Vesp Face

Florengian Face

The EDGE

Milk
High Timber
Wrogg River
Tryfors
L. Stony
Nardalborg
MOORS
FIRST ICE
FIRST ICE
Mount Varakats
Florengia
Mountain of Skulls
Fist's Leap
N
FIRST ICE
FIRST ICE
N
Vigaelia
ALTIPLANO
Veritano
Nelina
Two Fords
Ruisa River
Celebre
FIRST ICE
Sturia
Tupami

Elisa Mitchell 2007

Mother of Lies

Preface

THE GODS

Anziel, goddess of beauty
Cienu, god of mirth and chance
Demern, god of law and justice
Eriander, god-goddess of sex and madness
Hrada, goddess of crafts and skill
Mayn, goddess of wisdom
Nastrar, god of animals and nature
Nula, goddess of pity
Sinura, goddess of health
Ucr, god of prosperity and abundance
Veslih, goddess of the hearth and home
Weru, god of storm and battle
Xaran, goddess of death and evil (known as the Mother,
    the Old One, Mother of Lies, Womb of the World, &c.)

PRINCIPAL MORTALS

Most of the characters in the story are initiates of mystery cults, meaning each has sworn allegiance to a single god or goddess. They are listed here with their loyalties and their locations at the end of *Children of Chaos*:

On the Florengian Face
Doge Piero, ruler of the city of Celebre, is reported to be near death.

Dogaressa Oliva Assichie, his wife, is reported to be acting as his regent.

Marno Cavotti, a Hero of Weru, is leading the Florengian Resistance, from an unknown location.

Stralg Hragson, bloodlord of the Heroes of Weru ("the Fist of Weru"), location unknown, is still fighting a war he began fifteen years ago.

On the Vigaelian Face

The Children of Hrag:

Saltaja Hragsdor, Stralg Hragson's sister and greatly feared regent—and a Chosen of Xaran, known as the Queen of Shadows—is asleep in the palace at Tryfors.

Horold Hragson, her youngest brother, a Hero of Weru and satrap of Kosord, is on his way to Tryfors to reclaim his fugitive wife, Ingeld Narsdor, because it is only his marriage to her that gives him legal claim to rule as consort of Kosord.

(**Ingeld Narsdor,** a Daughter of Veslih and hereditary dynast of Kosord, is in a boat heading downstream from Tryfors, but knows by pyromancy that Horold is heading in her direction.)

Cutrath Horoldson, son of Horold and Ingeld, a Hero of Weru, is in the fortress at Nardalborg, waiting to cross over the Edge to fight in the Florengian war.

Heth "Hethson," a Hero of Weru and bastard son of Therek Hragson, is commandant of Nardalborg.

The children of Doge Piero:

Eldest son **Dantio,** who is also a Witness of Mayn known as Mist, is driving a chariot cross-country in the Tryfors area.

Son **Benard,** a Hand of Anziel, is fleeing Kosord in the same boat as his lover, Ingeld, knowing that he will die if Horold's warbeasts catch him.

Son **Orlad** (formerly Orlando), a newly initiated Hero of Werist, is in the Tryfors area, having just killed Therek Hragson.

Daughter **Fabia,** a Chosen of Xaran, is traveling with Benard, fleeing a forced betrothal to Cutrath Horoldson.

Others:

Arbanerik Kranson, a Hero of Weru and hordeleader of "New Dawn," the Vigaelian rebels, is believed to have his headquarters not far from Tryfors.

Horth Wigson, a Ucrist reputed to be the richest man in Vigaelia, and Fabia's foster father, is with Fabia.

Deceased but relevant to the story:

Karvak Hragson, a Hero of Weru and satrap of Jat-Nogul, was slain in self-defense by Paola Apicella.

Paola Apicella, a Chosen of Xaran, originally Fabia's wet nurse and later her foster mother and wife of Horth Wigson, was slain by Perag Hrothgatson on Saltaja's orders in retribution for the death of her brother Karvak.

Perag Hrothgatson, a Hero of Weru, was slain by Fabia for murdering Paola.

Therek Hragson, a Hero of Weru and late satrap of Tryfors, lies dead on a hillside near the city, slain by Orlad Celebre.

Part I

✦

An Unwelcome Visitor

✦

ᴜᴨᴇ

MARNO CAVOTTI

was better known as the Mutineer. Bloodlord Stralg, the Fist of Weru, had promised years ago that he would buy the Mutineer's corpse for its weight in gold or pay six times that much for the man alive and fit enough to be tortured. The offer still stood. Any hamlet or city that gave him refuge would be razed and all its inhabitants slain—this offer was still good, too. The Mutineer was coming home, to the city of his birth, which he had not seen since his childhood. It was entirely fitting that he travel under the shadow and protection of a storm.

The storm's approach had been visible for days, for it was one of the great sea storms, born above the steamy waters of the Florengian Ocean. From there it had spun out edgeward, over coastal jungles and swamps, to wreak havoc in the Fertile Circle that made up most of the Face. Like most of its kind, it came at Celebre from the east. Day by day it rose higher over the hazy wall of the world, white at noon and black at dawn; bloodred at sunset, ruling the sky and looming above the landscape. By the time it reached the city walls its greatest violence was spent, but it could still lash with gales and drench with killer rains. It could lift roofs and fell trees, flood low areas, wash out bridges. Amid so much evil a little more would not be noticed, so the storm closed its black wings around the traveler and hid him from those who looked for him to slay him.

He splashed along the muddy track beside a small wagon laden with amphorae of wine, drawn by an ancient guanaco named Misery, whose persistent humming showed that it was, indeed, unhappy—justifiably so, although Cavotti was careful to stay on the upwind side, where he could protect the animal from flying branches and other debris. Delayed by fallen trees and swollen streams, he worried that he would not arrive before the gates closed at sunset. The day had already faded to a twilight gloom when the walls and towers of Celebre emerged from the mist, but the rules said that the gates must stay open until the curfew bell sounded, and rules were rules.

Head down, Cavotti plodded under the great archway into the narrow barbican, where the strident creak and rattle of his wheels reverberated from the walls and wind howled along the canyon, driving rain before it. This was the moment of greatest peril, when he must satisfy the guards, when the inner and outer gates could be swung shut to trap him. Sure enough, a man shouted and ran out from the guard room.

He was a skinny black-haired Florengian, a boy sporting a bronze helmet and sword, both too large for him, but he wore a baldric in the doge's colors slung across his chain-mailed chest, and the bull's horn hanging on it gave him authority. Armed or not, a mere extrinsic was no threat—Cavotti could break his neck before he even drew. Even if he blew his horn and summoned another dozen like him, the intruder would be in little danger.

"Snotty scum, the Foul One take you, dragging honest men out in this fuck'n weather!" The boy squinted into the rain. Only the most junior member of the guard would be sent out on such a day.

Cavotti hauled on Misery's cheek strap; the wagon rattled to a halt. He bowed respectfully. "May it please your honor, I am Siero of Syiso, bondman of noble Master Scarpol of Treianne, bringing produce from his estate to his palace here in Celebre, on the Piazza Colonna. And more fuck'n rain has gone down my fuck'n neck than yours, may it please your honor." All the names he mentioned were genuine, except that they did not apply to him. He kept his eyes humbly lowered.

"Pig filth!" said the boy with the sword. "What sort of produce?"

Then two more men emerged from the guard room, and the odds shifted drastically, because they were pale-skinned Vigaelians, with flaxen hair and beards cropped to stubble. They wore only leather sandals and striped cotton loincloths tied with a colored sash, but their brass collars marked them as Heroes of Weru. They moved around the wagon and out of Cavotti's view.

Awareness of the peril lurking behind him was almost enough to make Cavotti's hair stand on end. If it literally did so, it would reveal his own brass collar, and then he would die. It was to hide that collar on occasions such as this that he had let his hair and beard grow in. The collar was the reason he had timed his visit for this howling storm, as it was the only time he could reasonably wear a cloth tied over his head and a leather cloak with a high neck, instead of just the loose-draped chlamys that was young men's normal garb on the Florengian Face. The garments that disguised him made him vulnerable, for a Werist who tried to battleform with clothes on ran the risk of being entangled in them, and would certainly be distracted and hampered by them. The two near-naked ice devils could rip off their rags in an instant.

"Wine, may it please your honor," he told the boy. "The chalk marks on the bottles say that they are bound for my master's palace, not for sale." Writing might impress the guard, although he would not be able to read it any more than Cavotti could.

"Open the stinking cover, you diseased, ditch-borne progeny of a toad."

Cavotti obeyed, rain-chilled fingers fumbling with waterlogged ropes, but as he pulled back a corner, he could turn enough to take surreptitious note of the ice devils. They were just standing there, staring at him, arms folded, backs to the wind. Wearing only those wet wisps of cotton, they ought to be freezing in this deluge, but Vigaelians felt the cold less. The warriors Stralg had brought over the Edge fifteen years ago had worn massive garments called palls. Florengia's climate had taught them to wear as little as possible.

Stralg maintained a small garrison in Celebre, but his men normally left routine guard duty to the doge's Florengians. Why were these two on the gate today, and why would they bother coming out in the year's worst weather to stare at a solitary peasant?

"All of it!" shouted the boy, adding some salacious imperatives.

Cavotti unlaced more rope and the wind threw the cover up in his face, revealing that the wagon held only sealed clay jugs. But he had to fight the cover with one hand and control the guanaco with the other as Misery stamped feet and flicked ears.

"Don't go away." The swordsman helped himself to an amphora and staggered back into the guard room with it.

The Vigaelians said nothing, did nothing, just studied the imposter carter with colorless eyes. Their brown sashes denoted mere front-fang warriors. Surely their flankleader would have come in person if he thought there was the faintest chance of apprehending the infamous Mutineer? But Celebre had other gates to watch.

Very large Florengian male, twenty-eight years old, dark-skinned and dangerous—his description must be too vague to be useful. His size might give him away, but his face would not. Holy Weru had been kind to him— in ten years of battle, Cavotti had taken no serious wounds and consequently showed none of the bestial "battle hardening" most older Werists did. If the ice devils had any doubts about him, they need only demand to see his neck.

The guard emerged with another man, older and not so wet. They grabbed two more amphorae. "All right, you can go," the second man said. They departed with their prizes.

"Wait!" said the larger Werist, in a harsh accent. Leaving his companion, he began wandering around the wagon, ghostly eyes inspecting the rig. His stripes were hard to read in the gloom, but they seemed to be black, brown, and green—which meant nothing, because the invaders' horde was being so badly mauled these days that half their units were makeshift collections of survivors. His fair skin was scarred and peeling from sunburn, meaning he had only recently come over the Edge.

Cavotti suppressed mad thoughts of making conversation, professional small talk: Pardon my curiosity, swine, but have you heard about Napora yet? Me and my men butchered three sixty of your buddies there not two thirties ago. We did to your wounded what you used to do to ours.

The big Vigaelian came close, still silent. He probably did not speak or understand much Florengian; few of them did, no matter how long they had been here. Carefully watching Cavotti, he reached out and hooked a finger through the handle of yet another amphora. He lifted the bottle out at arm's length, a feat few men would be inclined to try. Cavotti displayed humble admiration, as any sensible peasant would. He would give five teeth to know what the one at his back was doing.

The big Vigaelian smiled and deliberately threw the bottle to the paving. Cavotti jumped back with a cry, clothes soaked by wine. Black eyes met pale blue. The next step in this sort of harassment was for the Vigaelian overlord to order the subhuman Florengian serf down on his knees to start licking up the wine. That would not only put him at an impossible disadvantage, it would expose the back of his neck to view. There were limits; he would rather die on his feet.

The final, fatal challenge did not come. The other Werist laughed and said something in guttural Vigaelian. The big one shrugged, spat contemptuously at the Florengian, and then they went back into the guard room, slamming the door.

Cavotti's hands were shaking as he wrestled the cover back in place, but apparently he had merely been a victim of Vigaelian humor, two bored young thugs having some fun with the oversized native. Probably they were being punished for some minor offense, required to go outside and inspect every traveler in person. So the test had been good news in disguise. If the Vigaelians had the slightest suspicion that the army of liberation was starting to move in on Celebre, these two would have made sure they saw his neck.

◆

He was home for the first time in fifteen years, and there was no one to see him. The inhabitants had fled the storm, leaving the streets to thrashing trees, leaping torrents, and a steady sleet of roof tiles, which exploded like thunderbolts as they landed. It would be a jest of holy Cienu if the war of liberation failed now because the partisan leader got brained by falling terra cotta.

Home at last! Incredible! In all the long years of war and struggle, he had clung bitterly to the hope that one day he would return, but only recently had he truly believed it would ever happen. His dream had been to return victorious, of course, to drive a chariot along this avenue waving to tumultuous crowds cheering *Cavotti the Mutineer, Cavotti the Liberator*. This skulking in dark corners was a poor substitute, but it was probably what he would have to settle for. If Stralg did not destroy Celebre before the end, the Freedom Fighters might have to.

Celebre deserved its fame; it truly was the finest of them all, the Admirable City. Cavotti had been everywhere on the Florengian Face in the last ten years. He had been hunted twice around the Fertile Circle, had swum in the warm waves of Ocean, and nearly frozen to death in the airless wastes of the Altiplano. He had visited cities so ancient that they had sunk beneath the waves, and others left high and dry when the sea withdrew or rivers changed course, but most of those he had seen had recently been sacked—usually by Stralg and his horde, but every once in a while by his own side. Neither group left much more in their wake than bones and stinking ashes.

Celebre, however, was still unscathed. Celebre was still wide avenues and stately facades, shapely towers and temples, spacious colonnades, piazzas, and gardens. It had weaknesses, yes. Some of the grandiose mercantile palaces were known to be barns inside. Conversely, the central piazza was an ugly, ill-shaped hole, and the Ducal Palace looked like a gigantic outhouse because Celebrians had never approved of ostentatious rulers. Its interior, though, Cavotti remembered as a feast of beauty, a treasury of resplendent art spanning a dozen generations.

It would be a nice place to die in if things went wrong tonight.

◆

Marno was not a sentimental man. Any romantic tendencies he might have once possessed had been beaten out of him eons ago, yet he felt pangs of nostalgia as he headed inward from Meadow Gate up Goldbeater Street. The last time he had run down this same avenue in the company of his childhood gang had been on the day the city fell.

One of his friends had owned an uncle whose house overlooked the walls, and from there the pack had planned to view the arrival of the Vigaelian monsters. Refused admission to the house, they climbed on the roof instead and from that sunbaked vantage point had watched as Doge Piero drove out with his family. They had booed when he knelt to kiss the blood-lord's feet, but had been shocked into silence when he was sent home alone, in humiliation, while the dogaressa and her children had been taken away as hostages. Cavotti had known Dantio, the eldest, who was a couple of years younger than he was, but a bearable sort of brat in spite of being heir presumptive. The children had probably been sent over the Edge to Vigaelia, as had many other hostages. The dogaressa had later been returned to her husband, but not until long after Cavotti had gone from Celebre.

✦

Bent into the storm, the Mutineer led Misery into Pantheon Way, which in turn reminded him of the day after the fall, the day his own fate had been sealed by a powerful hand grabbing his arm in this very street. He had struggled and screamed and been well thumped for it. Marched away to the Vigaelians' camp and informed that he was to be trained to be a Hero of Weru like the ice devils, he had retorted that his father was a councillor and councillors' sons could not be treated like this. For that insolence he had been beaten. Thereafter he had sulked in angry silence within the great weeping, suffering mass of boys who had been taken—a hundred and nineteen sons of artisans and weavers and shopkeepers. There he had waited for his father to discover where he had gone and come and claim him.

Two days later his father did appear, arriving with an imposing entourage while the young victims were being drilled in calisthenics. Young Marno was duly called forward and recognized. Instead of releasing him, the Vigaelian commander ordered him tied up and flogged until his father had run all the way back to the city gate. Councillor Cavotti had not been a fast runner. And so Marno Cavotti, who had dreamed of being a great patron of the arts, become a Werist probationer, then a cadet, and finally a sworn warrior in the cult.

✦

He had seen his parents just once after that, when he was a new-collared Werist, posted to the garrison in Umsina. They had come to visit him, but his brothers had stayed away, shunning him as a monster. His mother had wept, his father had asked penetrating questions about loyalty.

Cavotti had dropped hints about his plans. His mother had screamed at him not to; his father had smiled proudly and told him to go ahead. For that encouragement—revealed to Stralg by his seers—the bloodlord had later put the councillor to death and fined House Cavotti an incredible weight of gold. Marno doubted that his brothers had forgiven him even yet. If they learned that he was in the city, they would likely betray him to the Fist.

Just for nostalgia's sake, he led Misery along River Way and let the guanaco see the Cavotti Palace. It was not one of the really big ones, although it was not exactly small either. It probably did not impress the llamoid much, but it did remind Cavotti that life could be anything except fair.

✦

Any city, no matter how grand its public face, must have squalid corners somewhere. The Mutineer's destination was a small and stinking courtyard behind the abattoir, where rain hissed on an ankle-deep quag of blood and mire. Even in that downpour the stench was very bad, and no one ever lingered there after the morning slaughter. Anybody who now followed him in would not be an innocent passerby.

The partisans kept no regular agents in the city, because they could not be hidden from Stralg's seers, but Cavotti had stayed in touch with a few old friends over the years, exchanging innocent messages by roundabout means, and yesterday he had sent an urgent appeal for help to a man he judged trustworthy. If his messenger did not appear at this rendezvous, both of them were as good as dead.

After a few suffocating moments, the rough plank door in the corner creaked open. The man who emerged was heavily muffled against the storm and held a cloth over his face to block the smell, but he was still recognizable as Siero of Syiso, whose name Cavotti had used at the gate. He trudged across to the wagon and Misery brightened enough to sneer at an old friend.

"Said yes, my lord. Didn't hesitate. The brown door at the bottom of the steps behind the Linen Weavers' Guildhall."

The Mutineer nodded. "Well done."

Siero led Misery back out to the street and Cavotti departed by an alley on the far side. So far so good. Another river crossed.

✦

He found the brown door and stepped into a cavernous kitchen, shadowed and cool, tidy but dusty. Not recently used. Stale food odors, bronze tripods on bare hearths, massive chopping blocks, a pump and trough, and rows of clay pots on shelves defined its purpose, but obviously the homeowners were not presently in residence.

For a moment longer he just stood there, enjoying calm after the day-long buffeting. One small oil lamp glowed on a table in the far corner and the man who had chosen this meeting place was standing beside it, staring with understandable doubt at the bearded villain in squalid peasant garb. The Mutineer sank to his knees and touched his forehead on the flags.

"Oh, learned master, may holy Mayn bless the wisdom you impart today, may holy Hrada bless the skills you reveal, and may holy Demern guide me to be an obedient and conscientious pupil, oh most beloved master." He made obeisance again—the morning ritual.

"He never did before," the other man muttered dryly, starting forward.

"Times change. As you see, I have returned to complete my education. You still owe me a year." Cavotti scrambled to his feet and they exchanged formal bows. Most old acquaintances would have embraced after so long, but he could not imagine anyone ever embracing Master Dicerno.

The old man cackled nervously. "I certainly did not expect you to show up in person, my lord. I greatly doubt your sanity in coming, but you are a most welcome sight. All Florengia is in your debt." Last survivor of an ancient but impoverished house, Dicerno had spent a lifetime teaching sons of the rich all the things Celebrian nobles must know—respect for the gods, the laws of holy Demern, the customs of their city, its art and history, manners and deportment, dancing and music, etiquette and court protocol, agriculture, hunting, and finance, the driving and care of llamoids, and sixty-sixty other things. He had been Cavotti's preceptor from the time he was removed from women's care at the age of seven until the morning his arm was grabbed on Pantheon Way.

Dicerno scorned concessions to age. His hair was silver, his bony face crinkled like brown leather, but he was still erect and trim, soft-spoken, unfailingly courteous. It was impossible to imagine him ever marrying or fathering sons of his own, but far more impossible that he should ever be tainted by the slightest hint of scandal in his dealings with his charges—or in any other matter, either. He had probably not spoken an ill-advised word or made a clumsy gesture in his life.

In the present unusual circumstances, he did allow a hint of worry to crease his forehead. "Of course you are aware that the enemy has a garrison in the city, my lord?"

"I saw two at the gate. How many, and who is in charge of them?"

"Usually just a dozen, except when a caravan comes through from Veritano. The current keeper is Flankleader Jorvark, who styles himself governor." The old man pulled a face. "The sort of adolescent who gives youth a bad name. They seem worse even than they used to be, my lord—ill-trained, ill-bred brutes."

Cavotti shed his sodden cloak. "They are having serious recruiting problems back home. What news of the councillor?"

The doge had appointed Berlice Spirno-Cavotti to replace her murdered husband. Other cities marveled at the Celebrian custom of admitting women to its council of elders.

"Your honored mother is well, my lord, although she must feel her years, as we all do. She is currently in the city, so far as I know."

Dicerno returned to his corner and came back carrying a basket, from which he produced a towel. Cavotti accepted it gratefully, having by this time stripped down to his scars, brass collar, and two pelf strings laden with silver and copper twists. He dried his face.

"Will you take a message to her for me?"

"Um . . . of course, my lord." The tactful pause said more than the words.

"Has Celebre sunk so far that mothers betray their sons?"

"The Fist's methods are brutal beyond belief, my lord." *Remember, she was forced to watch your father die.* "If any rumor of your visit reaches his ears, she and all your family will be in gravest peril. She cannot lie to a seer."

Cavotti said, "And I am putting you at risk also. I will give you silver, master, and I want you to leave the city tomorrow to go and spend some time elsewhere. I know you have sixty-sixty friends you can call on. No, do not argue—it will not serve my cause to have you flayed in the piazza for aiding me. I need instruction in the present affairs of the city. What news of the doge? I must see him tonight and be gone by dawn."

"I do not believe that will be possible, my lord." The old man was emptying his basket of all the things Siero had asked for—more towels, scented oil, clothes, rope, food, a razor.

"Ah! Celebrian bread! I missed this more than anything." Cavotti added with his mouth full, "Without the beard."

"I am more relieved to hear that than you can imagine. My reputation would be ruined. But even without the beard, the noble lord will not receive you."

"Why not? Is my mother out of favor?"

Dicerno shook his head. "It is his health. The Mercies are in constant attendance. The lady Oliva is acting as regent, unofficially."

This news complicated matters. "Grievous tidings! I knew he was failing, of course, but not so far." The Mutineer had not known how hungry he was, either. He tore off a chunk of cold meat and chewed vigorously.

"Few in the city do, my lord," the old man said apologetically. "Even Bloodlord Stralg may not."

Deceiving your enemies was a good idea; confusing your friends was not—but that assumed Cavotti and his army of liberation were to be regarded as friends of Celebre, which was to be the topic of tonight's discussion.

"How often do the healers treat him?"

Dicerno frowned, reluctant to set aside his lifelong hatred of gossip. "The doge rallied markedly back in the spring. Thanks to holy Sinura, he even appeared in public a few times, but it is whispered that Her price for that remission was a healer's life. No Sinurist has attended him since, although this is said to have been the doge's decision, not theirs. As for your honored mother, if you have matters to discuss with her, then I shall advise her of your arrival. If you are merely seeking access to the lady Oliva, of course I can arrange that for you."

"You have pupils within the Ducal Palace?"

"I do have that honor." Even now he would tell Cavotti no more than he felt he must.

"Such as the boy, Chies?"

The silver head bowed in acquiescence.

"He must be . . . fourteen now?"

Again the preceptor nodded, but he was not smiling, and the lack of automatic praise was a crushing comment on the youth in question.

"And who will succeed Doge Piero when the Old One claims him?"

The old man said coldly, "You know that the council of elders makes that decision, lord. You should perhaps discuss it with your honored mother."

It would certainly not be an easy topic to raise with the lady Oliva.

"This collar of mine . . ." The Mutineer reached into the pile of garments Dicerno had produced from his basket of wonders and extracted a Nulist cowl of brown linen. There was a matching gown, too, and when he held it against himself, it was revealed to be very large. "Where in the world did you manage to obtain *these* on such short notice? You said you did not expect the visitor to be me? Master, did you not teach us that excessive modesty is a form of arrogance?"

The dark eyes twinkled inside their nests of wrinkles. "I also taught you that the poet Gievo sang, 'Those who hope greatly must love disappointment.' I was not disappointed this time, is all."

Cavotti assumed the singsong chant of a pupil repeating his lessons. "Master, holy Demern decrees: 'He who makes false claim to belong to a guild commits a crime, and an extrinsic who masquerades as initiate of a cult is guilty of blasphemy, and both shall be sold into slavery.' "

The smile that teased the preceptor's withered lips was an unusual outburst of emotion for him. "But this dogma is subordinate to the paramount duties, specifically the fourth. Would you not judge that if you visit the palace with your collar showing, then your life will be forfeit to the Evil One?"

"That and then some. I also consider that I visit the palace to serve my birth lord the doge—although he may not agree—and therefore the second duty also applies. See how well you taught me?"

"And the first duty?"

Cavotti laughed aloud. "Oh, the cunning of the man!" He reverted to singsong. "Master, it is decreed: 'A mortal's first duty is to honor and obey the gods.' " He grinned through his piratical beard. "First chapter, clause one. But when the mortal is a henotheist, then he must give precedence to the oaths and edicts of his chosen god. Also first chapter, I believe?"

"Clause five." Dicerno beamed at this escape into the unreal world of the scholar. "Far be it from me to pry into the secrets of a holy mystery, but the vulgar believe that the god of battle gives only one directive to His Heroes, and that is to win at any cost and by any means."

"So only a fool would trust a Werist," the Mutineer agreed. "If you start hinting that you may betray me, old master, I will break your neck."

"Being in my dotage, I am prepared to trust you."

More fool him! The play was wearing thin, wandering dangerously close to reality, for Cavotti's activities very well might kill the old man. He glanced across to the solitary lamp in the corner. "What were you doing that I interrupted?" He strolled over there, still eating and still unclothed, although he knew such boorish behavior must pain his old teacher like a robe of nettles. He had forgotten how much he had enjoyed provoking the old pedant. Evidently he still did.

As he had guessed, a branching trail of colored pentagons had been laid out on the planks. *"Tégale,* of course! And five-color *tégale* at that! What is the contention?"

"You still play?" Dicerno asked eagerly.

"I manage a game once in a while, but never more than three-color. Werists are not chosen for their brains, master. *Tégale* is a game for Demernists. What is the contention?"

The preceptor had been the best player in Celebre when Cavotti had known him. He rubbed his hands in glee as he explained. "It is a very old puzzle, my lord, shown to me many years ago by the present doge's father, when I was a mere lad. I don't believe it really has a solution. He knew of none. The contention is to obtain closure in two moves, against any defense. As you can see, the logical move is to revert that blue to a green, but then your opponent merely plays a white here, and you are lost. I expect I have forgotten the correct layout, or perhaps he did. It is impossible."

Cavotti said, "Perhaps. It will be something to keep me from worrying while you are gone—after I have removed the baneful beard, illicitly robed myself as a Nulist, scouted an emergency escape route out of this house, and generally made myself more worthy of your teaching. I will even clean up the mud I tracked in from the door."

"I did not teach you how to do that, my lord!" Dicerno was shocked at the very idea of a noble performing such labor. He could not have the slightest idea of the systematic degradation involved in Werist training.

"You did, you know! Don't you remember the time Pillono and I climbed out a window to visit the fair?"

"Ah, of course! It was climbing back in that gave you away."

"And the next year you didn't catch us."

"So what is the solution to the doge's problem?"

Cavotti frowned at the old man's bland smile. "Master, you have had years to work on it and you expect me to solve it at a glance?"

"I had six years to learn you, Hordeleader, and you know the answer."

Cavotti chuckled to hide annoyance. "True. Yes, I have been shown this problem before. In fact, it is known as Weru's Device, which is why you are showing it to me now, correct?"

Thin lips smiled. "I may have heard that name applied, yes."

"The trap is that it makes you think of classic problems like the Speaker's Dilemma or the Two Elbows Gambit, so you look for subtlety, master. What happens if I degrade this red to a white?"

Dicerno stared at the tiles in horror. "You would be sacrificing this entire branch, destroying all your major positions and leaving your opponent's intact!"

"But my opponent would have only one possible move—commuting this green to a blue—and I block that with a black. Then he has no legal move at all, so he loses. I do not obtain closure, but I win the game."

"It is monstrous! An inelegant, barbarous solution!"

"That is why it is called Weru's Device," the Mutineer said.

two

OLIVA ASSICHIE-CELEBRE

sat on her ivory chair alongside the doge's empty throne and made a valiant effort to attend to city business.

The ancient palace of the doge had been built on a vast scale for comfort in Celebre's tropical climate. When the noon sun blazed down, its high ceilings and wide concourses offered cool breezes and welcome shade, but such grandiose architecture was less effective against tempests. On that fearsome night, invisible storm giants stalked the galleries, rattling doors, swirling drapes. Even the Hall of Pillars, normally majestic and serene, was clamorous. The spaces between the columns that divided it from the river terrace had been closed off with massive shutters, but even they fluttered in the wind like aspen leaves, continually rattling and creaking. Periodically an especially massive gust would either suck all the air out of the hall and make Oliva's ears pop, or else push far too much air in and make her ears pop. Water trickled under the shutters to puddle on the polychrome tiles. Thunder rumbled petulantly in the distance.

Oliva's head throbbed and her ears pop-pop-popped. Her senior scribes, Gienni and Althuse, waited cross-legged at her feet, surrounded by the clutter of their profession—baskets of baked clay tablets, boards with soft clay rolled ready for inscription, pots holding sharpened reed styli. Two tiny oil lamps flickered in the wind, barely illuminating their work, and an apprentice lurked mouselike in the background, ready to attend to the needs of his betters. The rest of the hall was a restless, noisy darkness.

She did not trust either Gienni or Althuse. Gienni had served the doge and his own interests—not necessarily in that order—for many years. He was old and desiccated, a human pinecone wrapped in his official robes, whereas Althuse was newer and much younger, hiding his thoughts behind the compellingly trustworthy eyes of a gazelle. He seemed competent enough, but he had won his promotion to master scribe in Gienni's bed. They were both in the pay of the great houses, although such disloyalty was traditional and was normally kept within limits by fear of the doge. Regrettably, these two were well aware how little real authority Oliva possessed. She often wondered if some of the letters she dictated were ever sent, and how many other people read them first.

"A letter," she said wearily. "From our lord doge to Flankleader Jorvark. Usual greetings."

Althuse started poking the clay with his stylus, but Gienni looked up.

"My lady? Do you wish us to address the Werist that way or give him the state he claims—Governor of Celebre and so on?"

"As I said." It was absurd to write a letter to a juvenile hooligan who lived on the far side of a narrow street and could not read, but the last time she had sent a runner, the boy had been returned on a litter and had required the services of two healers. Jorvark would have to take the tablet to a public scribe, and they were notorious gossips. Her protest would do no good, but at least it would become public knowledge.

"Begin. 'The lord doge speaks: Since our last words to you, five sixdays ago, the offenses of which we complained have continued unabated. Hardly a day passes without your men committing rapes, beatings, and thefts, violating guarantees the bloodlord made when we put our city under his mercy, fifteen years ago.'"

She waited for the styli to stop moving. "'We shall send a full report of your offenses to Bloodlord Stralg and demand—'"

"My lady!" Gienni muttered.

"Write my words! 'And demand that you be held responsible.'"

She stopped with a sigh. She had no idea where Stralg might currently be, and he rarely acknowledged her letters. It was not impossible that Flankleader Jorvark would come storming back from the scribe and make her eat her words, clay tablet and all—but even that would shore up her crumbling authority in the city. "Usual ending."

In a moment the apprentice came to kneel at her feet and proffer the first tablet. She rolled her husband's seal across the clay just below the writing. Then the archive copy . . .

At the edge of the shadows, a herald was bowing.

"Yes?"

"Master Preceptor Dicerno, my lady. He craves audience on a matter of extreme urgency."

Oliva could not recall that most dignified of mummies ever using words like "extreme urgency" before. Whatever had Chies gotten up to this time? It was a good excuse to stop, though.

"Scribes, you may withdraw. We shall seal the covers tomorrow before the letters are sent." Perhaps a night's sleep would reveal a better way to deal with the odious Jorvark. "Admit the honorable preceptor." She sighed again. "And send our son to us."

◆

They went, leaving her alone on the ivory chair in near darkness, while her ears popped and the storm rattled the great shutters like some monster beast trying to break in. Piero, were he his usual self, would be planning to tour the city on the morrow, viewing damage, giving comfort, and organizing relief. She wondered if she dared try that. She feared that she would be snubbed, or ignored, or mocked.

Fourth daughter of an ancient but decayed mercantile house, Oliva Assichie had seemed fated to wed some prosperous apothecary or master artisan willing to accept noble relations in lieu of dowry. But by the mercy of holy Eriander, or perhaps holy Cienu, at fifteen she had caught the eye of Lord Piero, the widowed and childless doge. Her mother had fainted from joy. Her sisters had never quite recovered.

Four children Oliva had given him, three sons and a daughter, and their life had been an idyll of happiness until the Vigaelians came. Stralg had taken her and the children away. Later he had sent her back to her husband and she had borne a fifth child. Even in her youth she had never been sylphlike, and now she was nothing less than hefty. She was effectively doge of Celebre while her husband wasted away in the torments of the Dark One, but the council put up with her because it was seriously divided on what to do. As soon as it reached a consensus she would be gone.

Even so, running a city was easier than being a mother.

A pale robe shimmered in the shadows. The old man lowered himself carefully to his knees, then folded forward, forehead to floor, just on the edge of the puddle of light the two little oil lamps spilled on the tiles. Everything else under the high ceiling was darkness and the gigantic surging of the storm.

Oliva had several choices. She had once seen Piero leave an unwelcome petitioner crouching like that for half a day until the man must have been near to screaming from cramp. Or she could say, "Approach," which would mean he had to crawl forward like an insect.

Instead she said, "Welcome, Master Dicerno," and that was permission for him to rise and walk closer—bowing several times, naturally. They were alone and no one could eavesdrop in a hall so huge. "Well? What has my infamous son been up to this time?"

Chies was already taller than her by a fair amount and absolutely impossible. Master Preceptor Dicerno had the reputation of being able to turn the most obdurate adolescent animals into model citizens, but she would not be surprised in the slightest if he had come tonight to announce that he had met his match at last and must wash his hands of an intractable lout. Then all the tongues of Celebre would wag harder than ever. Blood, as they said, will out.

The preceptor looked blank. "To my knowledge nothing, my lady! I believe he is really trying now. Lord Chies is truly remorseful when he offends you, you know, even if he cannot say so; men of his age have trouble admitting to errors of judgment. If I may presume . . . a few words of praise from you now would be most helpful. I am very happy with his progress and his efforts."

Oliva breathed a silent prayer to some god or goddess. No, to *all* of Them. "I shall certainly congratulate him. That is very good news! But if you have not come about my son, why do you venture here in such weather?"

She was surprised to see the haughty old man glance around at the shadows. Paradoxically, he seemed both nervous and even more pleased with himself than usual.

"I come as envoy from an important visitor, my lady. He wished an audience with his lordship, and I explained how that would not be possible. So he begs that *you* will receive him tonight. Here. He specifically asked that the audience be here in the Hall of Pillars."

She hid an unexpected shiver of fear behind bluster. "Outrageous! To dictate where I will receive him? I doubt if even the Fist himself would presume so. Who is this arrogant knave?" Whoever he was, she was much afraid that she could guess who had sent him. For the last year, the war had been relentlessly moving in this direction.

Dicerno came a pace closer. His voice was soft as gossamer, almost inaudible under the rattling of the shutters. "A man who may now be greater than the Fist."

If all her blood were drained away and replaced by ice, she might feel like this. . . . "In person?" she whispered. "Here in Celebre?" Ice, ice! "Are you sure?"

"He was a pupil of mine, my lady. A little older than lord Dantio. I believe he can be trusted. He . . . he has a warrior's rough manner at times, my lady, but he is not the bloodlord."

No. No one else was Stralg. Utter evil could not appear twice in human guise. "What does he *want*?"

"He will not say."

"Tomorrow, when my advisers—"

Dicerno shook his head. "He swears he will be gone by dawn. My lady, I wager my soul that he can be trusted this far! He . . . he is a Celebrian noble, remember. My lady, you *must* receive him!"

Piero would not tolerate that word, and Dicerno would never use a word by accident.

Marno Cavotti himself? She could not imagine what Stralg would do if he found out, and few knew his cruelty better than she did. But what might the Mutineer do if she refused him? She was between millstones. His mother was a councillor, but no friend of Oliva's—and perhaps not of her own son, either.

Shivering, she nodded. "Bring him. I will receive him here, if that is what he wants."

◆

On this she must seek Piero's advice and instructions. As she hurried through the drafty halls, she prayed to holy Sinura that he would be well enough to give them. She went alone, bearing a single oil lamp on the palm of one hand and sheltering its tiny flame with the other. Two years ago she would have moved within an entourage of ladies-in-waiting and flunkies carrying lights, but as Piero's health had failed, their state had dwindled. That was mostly her doing. She feared all courtiers now, imagining their sneering amusement that Assichie-Celebre thought she could run the city, their hints that the council must appoint a regent in her place, or the bloodlord would soon impose a new doge of his own choosing. Convinced that the people were better off not knowing how near to death their lord was when all rightful heirs were still far away in Vigaelia, she had steadily shed attendants, as if the court itself was dying. At times she felt like the last inhabitant of the palace, or even of the city.

The official ducal sleeping chamber was spectacular, a treasure hall where doges were supposedly born, fathered heirs, and died, but Piero had never used it. It made him feel like an exhibit in a museum, he said. He and Oliva had slept in what were officially guest quarters, and quite opulent enough. One of the larger rooms had now been turned into a sanctuary of Nula and stank of the godswood being burned before holy images. Although at first glance it seemed almost deserted, it contained four Nulists, two nurses, and a trio of palace flunkies, several of whom were stretched out on the great sleeping platform, dozing. Obviously they had not expected the dogaressa to return tonight. The senior Mercy—a large, matronly woman distinguished by a white cowl—knelt in prayer before an altar of holy Nula. The rest were watching a *tégale* game; players and audience scrambled to their feet as Oliva entered. Without comment, she swept on through, into the short corridor that led to more intimate chambers, one of which had been converted into Piero's sickroom. He had always hated dying in public, he said.

Hearing her husband's voice, she stopped in the doorway, sudden anger flaring—she had repeatedly stressed that they were to summon her at once if he rallied. The chamber was small and simple, but all the banked flowers along the far wall could not hide a sour scent of death. The dying man lay on rugs on a portable cot, his face ochre in the spectral lamplight. Never a large man, Piero now seemed wizened and discolored like last year's apples.

Another Mercy, dark-robed and cowled, sat on a stool beside him, holding his hand, listening to his raspy whisper winding on and on. Oliva moved softly closer, straining to hear what state secrets he might be revealing. The words were not in Florengian. Nor, she realized, were they anything like the fragments of Vigaelian she had learned during her captivity.

"What?"

The Nulist jumped and looked around. Oliva was accustomed to Mercies being elderly people, but that might be because they usually sent only their most senior members to solace a doge. The face inside the cowl this time was that of a boy, startled by her silent approach. He looked barely older than Chies.

"What is he talking about?"

The youth smiled the typical sad smile of a Nulist. He had mastered that at least, even if he was only a second-string beginner given a try at night duty when the dogaressa wasn't around to notice. "Nothing, my lady. It is only babbling."

He murmured something to the patient and patted his hand. Piero fell silent.

Oliva did not know—probably no extrinsic knew—how much of the Nulists' comfort came directly from the goddess and how much the cultists themselves controlled. "Were you *making* him do that? How dare you!"

"Not *making* him, my lady. *Letting* him, perhaps. It seems to help him."

"Leave us. I will speak to your superior later."

The boy carefully laid the patient's hand on the bedding and rose. The light fell on his face for the first time and she saw that it was wet with tears, his eyes raw with weeping. Shaken by that, she took the stool he had vacated and put her lamp on the table. He bowed and withdrew.

"Where have they gone?"

Piero's quiet whisper startled her, it was so clear. His eyes were open, but still unfocused.

"Bring them back!" He frowned at her—puzzled, dazed.

"Bring who, dear?"

The Mutineer was in the city, but Piero could not advise her now. At first one brief Nulist treatment a day had sufficed to hold the pain at bay, but now he could only snatch a few lucid moments before it returned. She should not have come here to trouble him. Yet if she had not come, she would not have stumbled upon that *boy* engaged in whatever foul experimentation he had been up to.

"The children!" Piero closed his eyes for a moment, and when he opened them he was conscious, smiling at her. "Dreaming. I was dreaming the children were coming home."

Unlike the Nulist, she had no tears left to shed. "I'm sure they won't be long now, dearest. It must be a year since Stralg promised to send for them." Only an incorrigibly bewildered imbecile would trust a word that monster said.

"They are all grownup now, you know."

She nodded. Twelve have mercy! Fifteen years gone. Fifteen years lost. Even if they still lived, what would they care for Celebre? Or Florengia? Or her. "Fabia must be a young woman?"

"A beautiful one." He sighed.

"What did she look like—in your dream?"

"In my dream . . . very like you, my dear, at her age. Your fierce eyes. I always liked your eyes."

"That wasn't what you told me you liked."

"In public I said eyes." He smiled. "You should see Benard! So strong-looking." He smiled. "Just a dream, but vivid! They were coming in a boat, can you imagine? Over the Edge in a boat! Benard was always the artistic one. He's a sculptor now, got his shoulders chipping marble, he said. In my dream he did, I mean. Remember we used to say Orlando was the fighter?"

No, she just remembered the terrible day when they had been stolen—Stralg holding out his hands to the toddler and Orlando, too young to understand evil, going to him. Dantio had been staring in horror, Benard hiding his face in her skirts, Fabia fretting, wanting to suck. She could not imagine Fabia as an adolescent, nor even Dantio as a grown man.

"Brass collar," Piero muttered, frowning. "And Dantio . . . great sorrow there, my dear. Great wisdom. I always said he'd make a fine *tégale* player, remember? They were speaking with me. Asking . . ." He winced. His face was so shrunken and skeletal that it seemed to be all teeth and gaping eye sockets. He drew a deep breath. "Asking who was going to . . ." *Gasp!* ". . . succeed me."

"And who did you tell them?"

The dead man's vote, they called it. A doge's designation of his heir counted as one vote in the council, no more, no less, but only very rarely in the history of Celebre had the elders overruled the dead man's wishes. Piero had made no testament because he did not know which, if any, of his children still lived. He shook his head, unable to speak. His skull face shone with sweat. The pain was back already, tearing at him.

She rose and went from the room, almost running into the young Mercy in the corridor, waiting for the call. He hurried over to the bed, clasping the patient's hand even before he sat down. In a few moments Piero was sleeping peacefully again.

In a few more moments the Nulist was able to glance around at Oliva, who stood by the door.

"I am sorry I spoke harshly," she said. "Your name?"

"Luigo, my lady."

"Thank you, Brother Luigo. Whatever you were doing made him very happy. Please continue."

"I will try, my lady."

"Twelve blessings on you."

"He's not dead, then?" Stralg said.

The voice behind her was unforgettable—deep and sonorous, but also imperious, very masculine. Like a war horn.

She gasped with shock and spun around so hard she staggered.

She looked up. He seemed taller every day. Still bony, all feet and hands and a boy's loincloth like a linen flute. On his way to being *very* big. Gold bracelets adorned his wrists and a weighty pelf string laden with silver wisps encircled his neck. He had dark Florengian coloring, but the fierce eagle-beak nose was developing fast. Since his voice broke, Chies had sounded exactly like his father, and now was undeniably starting to look like him, too.

"You sent for me. I thought he must be dead."

"No. Come." She pushed past him and did not speak until they had passed through the sanctuary. She nodded approvingly to the senior Mercy and went out into the corridor with her willow-tree bastard slouching behind her.

They walked together with her little lamp throwing bizarre shadows on the high walls. Typically, Chies had not bothered to bring a light. Perhaps young eyes saw better in the dark.

"I wanted to tell you that Master Dicerno is pleased with your progress. He says you are trying very hard. I am happy to hear this, Chies."

Grunt. "That's all?"

Her mind groped for the right answer. Was there ever a right answer when dealing with adolescents? She had no experience. Dantio had been only a child when her first brood was stolen away. She was very old to be learning. Deep breath . . .

"It is a sign of maturity. As a reward, and as long as you continue to progress, I will let you wear a dagger. You can choose—"

"Why not a sword?"

You could never score when the target kept moving.

"Not until you know how to use one. You'd be a gift-wrapped prize to the first street thug you met."

"I'd still have my guards with me," he said sulkily.

"And if you run into trouble, you'll just stand by without drawing and let them defend you?" But apparently the absence of a dagger was no longer the most important thing in the entire world, no longer a source of eternal shame. It no longer justified suicide, as it had a sixday ago. "Is there something you would rather have?"

"Take girls to my room."

She needed several deep breaths for that one, but Master Dicerno's strongest advice had been "Be just, be fair, and encourage him any chance you get." Better his room than under a bush somewhere.

"Have you taken girls to your room already?"

Pause. "Maybe."

She knew he had tried twice and the guards had blocked him. But he had not told her a direct lie. *Encourage him,* the preceptor had said.

"As long as you continue to be discreet I won't mind. I'll give you a key to the private door."

She stole a glance. He was pleased. *Very* pleased. Probably quite pink, although it was hard to say in this light. How long before he started giving away palace silverware? How long before the first little hussy cried rape or pregnancy?

"You are almost grown up. At New Year, you'll start wearing a seal and I shall take Master Dicerno's teeth out of your leg. You may find your girl-friends' brothers and fathers coming after you with cudgels, but that will be your problem."

"By then I'll be doge."

"What!?" The echo of her cry rolled away along the concourse.

He smirked down at her. "It has to be a man of the royal house and I'm the only one. Who else can they choose?"

"Chies, Chies darling . . . I've never lied to you. You know that Piero is not your father."

"But you lied to everyone else." *Sneer.* "He accepted me as his. Didn't want to tell people his wife balled other men."

Piero could have handled this with a few quiet words. She couldn't. She warned herself not to start screaming. "Have you looked in a mirror lately?"

He laughed. "The Werists call me 'the Little Fist'!" Even more than dagger-wearing, his chumminess with the garrison had been a source of family friction. Practicing his Vigaelian, he'd called it. She'd thought they were just loose company. So now she knew better. If the ice devils saw him as the bloodlord's son they might even start taking his orders, and then Chies would be *dangerous.*

"It's the council that matters."

"Piero never denied me!" Chies shouted and stopped walking. "They won't!"

She turned to face him, feeling as if she were drowning. Why had she never guessed he would aspire to the coronet? Was that why he had been on his best behavior lately?

"The last time Stralg . . ." She began again. *"Your father* carried me away by force and kept me for seven sixdays as his prisoner and plaything. He raped me, abused me, even stole the babe from my breast. The day he released me he told me that the seers said I was carrying his child and it was a boy. He said he still had my four children as hostage and I was to carry you to term and Piero was to raise you as his own, or else he'd send orders and all four would die."

Stralg's son shrugged. "So he hadn't any choice."

Why should the boy be grateful?

"Piero? Yes, Piero had a choice, because I never told him what Stralg said. He knew you weren't his, but you were mine, and you were innocent of the crime, so he let you live. He reared you and loved you. When you were lovable."

At once she wished she hadn't said that last thing, but it was too late to take it back. If anything, Chies had been *too* lovable. With the others gone, he'd been all they had, and they had spoiled him horribly. Now their weakness was about to bear terrible fruit.

A stray gust puffed out the flame on her lamp.

"But you just admitted," Stralg's voice resonated in the darkness, "that the Fist made me because he wanted me. Obviously he wanted me so I can be doge and rule Celebre for him."

No. Stralg had just wanted to show his contempt for Piero by sending her home bearing his bastard, but she could never tell Chies that.

He said, "The council knows what's good for it. They'll do what my *real* father tells it to do, just like that milksop husband of yours always did." The hated voice suddenly turned squeaky. "My *real* father will tell them to elect me! And if you *really* try hard and *behave yourself in future,* I may let you take *men* to your room!"

While she was still floundering to find a suitable retort, *any* retort, she remembered that she was on her way to meet with Marno Cavotti. If Chies Stralgson caught the merest hint of a suspicion of a rumor that the Mutineer was in the palace, he would be across the road to the Vigaelian barracks to claim the notorious reward, faster than a thunderbolt.

Without another word, he turned and ran. She caught a brief glimpse of his gangling form against a glow at the end of the concourse as he ran around the corner into the Hall of Pillars.

✦

The storm was moving on. One of the great shutters in the colonnade had been unlatched and moved aside to admit glimmers of gray light and wafts of steamy air. The rain on the terrace outside had dwindled to a drizzle.

Forcing herself to move no faster than usual, Oliva swept across to join the three men standing there.

Silvery robe, silver hair—the one holding the lamp was Master Dicerno, and beside him stood Chies in loincloth and glints of silver. He was as tall as the preceptor, but he looked like a child alongside the third man. Werists were chosen for their size in adolescence and kept on growing—a little larger every time they battleformed, it was said.

As she arrived at the group, she was shocked to realize that the third man wore a Nulist robe. The cowl covered his head and shoulders leaving only his face exposed, so it was one of the very few garments that would hide a brass collar, but it seemed especial blasphemy for a Hero to pose as a Mercy. All three knelt to her, Chies just a fraction of a second behind the others. Correct protocol would have been for him to bow only, then present the newcomer.

Dicerno waited an instant for him before saying, "My lady . . . if I may have the honor . . . Brother Marno. Brother Marno is a renowned and skillful devotee of holy Nula."

Marno was a common name, but Oliva wished they had chosen another. One glance at Chies warned her that his mood had changed yet again. He was twitching, excited, unable to keep his eyes off the disguised Werist. *He knew!* She had no idea how he knew, but she was quite certain he did.

Life had become a nightmare inside a nightmare.

"Rise, please, all of you. You are very welcome to our house, Brother Marno."

"My lady, I thank the gods for giving me the opportunity and honor of attending lord Piero." The big man spoke in a harsh growl, very unlike Stralg's sonorous carillons, but his face was completely unlike her expectations of what a notorious rebel should look like—handsome, sensitive, aristocratic, with a strong resemblance to Duilio Cavotti, his long-dead father.

"You will be able to assuage my husband's distress?"

"Not I, my lady. The goddess."

"Of course."

He should have said *my* goddess.

"You are new to our fair city, brother?" Chies making small talk had to mark the dawn of an epoch.

Cavotti must be aware of his Celebrian accent, because he evaded the trap. "I was born here, but I have been away for some years."

"Since before I was born, yes?"

The fake Nulist waited a beat before saying, "*Much* longer than that, lord Chies."

Oliva chuckled, which was perhaps a mistake, but probably nothing would have stopped Chies now.

"Did you move that shutter, brother? It takes four men to put them up."

"Master Dicerno did it. As he will have told you, the gods give strength to the pure in heart."

Chies let out a surprised snigger.

"I have certainly told him that diffidence is a sign of good breeding," Dicerno countered.

The boy's eyes narrowed. "I saw my father just now and he's in such terrible pain that I feel very upset. Will you give me some comfort, Nulist? Just a touch?" He extended a skinny arm.

Cavotti closed a huge hand around it. "Better, lad, I will show you how to work off your own worries." He moved over to the doorway and out onto the terrace.

Chies perforce went with him, struggling, kicking, squealing. "Stop! You're hurting! Let me go!"

"You don't need holy Nula," the giant growled. "See there? An agile youngster like you can easily scramble over that balustrade and jump down to the river wall. Run twice around the city as fast as you can, and you will find that all your cares have given way to a glow of healthy well-being."

Released, Chies sprang away, rubbing the white marks on his arm and spitting anger like a cat. "I'll find better shoes." Without even a bow to his mother, he sprinted across the chamber and disappeared the way he had come.

The Werist came back in, chuckling. "Sorry, my lady, but I enjoyed that. I am a disgrace to Master Dicerno's training." He bowed again. "Marno Cavotti, at your service."

"You dare manhandle my son?"

His eyes blazed. "You are lucky I didn't break his neck, lady. At his age I was a prisoner at Boluzzi in compulsory Werist training. The only way to fail the course there was to *die* there. If you ran away you were run down— you know warbeasts can track like hounds? Ripped to pieces. Boys of thirteen, fourteen. They'd bring the scraps back to show us. No, my complaint against Stralg is even heavier than yours, my lady, and your precious bastard is lucky he's still got his balls on right now."

The preceptor moaned and was ignored.

"Boor!" Oliva had found a target for the fury she had been building all night. "It is you who may be lacking body parts very shortly. Chies has undoubtedly gone to ask the senior Mercy if she knows anything of a Brother Marno."

"And after that how long for him to reach the Vigaelians?"

"A few minutes only."

"My lady!" Dicerno squealed. "Cannot you send the palace guard to stop him? This is terrible!"

"We have time to attend to our business," the Mutineer said calmly. "But the less you know the better, old man. Leave us. I suggest you quit the city the moment the gates are opened in the morning."

"Do as he says, master." Oliva dismissed the preceptor by turning her back on him. "Be quick, Cavotti. I don't want you all over my clean floor."

The big man laughed and tucked his hands inside his sleeves as if he had worn Nulist garb for years. "We can start by agreeing that we share no love for Stralg Hragson. There were about four sixty of us to start with in the school, half of us from Celebre. In the five years we were there, earning our collars, we were joined by six or seven times that many—boys kidnapped from all over the Face."

"I know the history," she said, imagining Chies bursting into the sanctuary, yelling out his questions, then taking off along the corridor like a mad guanaco. "What do you want of me?"

"I'll get to that. We stayed and we worked and we won our collars. Stralg was dreaming . . . he's basically just a thug bully, as you well know . . . dreaming of setting up a second empire here, to match the one he had on the Vigaelian Face. He expected us loyal Florengian Werists to run it for him when he went home. Expected us to be grateful, I suppose. We were initiated, the first of us. We swore the oaths. He came to Boluzzi in person for the ceremony, and by that time he'd been all around the Fertile Circle, stamping out opposition. He ruled the Face then. Two Faces. Dream come true. We were part of his great plan, the first crop from Boluzzi, donning the collars we can never shed. We swore eternal obedience, cheered him, and went off to our postings, but we'd agreed to meet back at the school after Stralg and his guards had left."

"This was *your* plan, *your* mutiny, how you got your name." She thought Chies wouldn't come back through here. He'd go around by the west stairs. That would hardly slow him at all, not the way he could move those long legs. Yet the Mutineer was showing no signs of haste, almost as if he were dragging this out.

"I was one of the ringleaders. The others are all dead now. On the cho-

sen night we broke in and there was a fight. Oh, was there a fight! By the
time the blood congealed, all the instructors were dead and so were most of
us. There were twenty-four Werist survivors—me and twenty-three others.
About four sixty cadets threw in their lot with us, and some senior probationers too. The young ones we had to leave. We told them to scatter and
look out for themselves, but we knew Stralg would get them."

Oliva imagined Chies hurtling down the stairs four at a time, belting
along the arcade to the main gate . . .

"The Fist realized his mistake at once and ordered us hunted down,
every Florengian Werist killed on sight. We were trying to stay ahead of
him and train the cadets at the same time. Mutineers, fugitives, oathbreak-
ers, partisans, guerrillas—call us what you will. It was a year before we
were strong enough to double back and ambush one of his patrols. He lost
five times as many as we did, but in those days he could afford the losses.
That was how it went the first few years. But gradually we gained in numbers. We recruited, we trained, and *the more we had the more we could get*!
Understand?"

Dicerno had gone, taking his lamp. The palace seemed deserted and
very silent without the wind. She felt as if she were alone in it, standing chatting with a madman.

"Yes, yes! What are you getting at?"

Chies would have to talk his way past the men on the gates, who had orders to send guards with him when he went out. No, of course he'd go out
the bolt-hole from the laundry, the one he thought nobody else knew about.
That would save him a run around the stables, too. Twelve gods!

"Getting *to,* my lady. We are *getting to* the final payoff. Two years ago we
finally had as many collars as Stralg did and were training faster than he
could bring men over the Edge. That was the turning point. He's limited by
the Ice on the other side, you see. Their seasons are more extreme over there,
and—"

"So you think you can beat him?"

"He's beaten now. He knows it. The problem is to kill off the survivors
with as few collateral deaths as possible. You heard about Miona?"

She shivered. "Conflicting stories."

"Believe the worst of them," Cavotti said grimly. "Stralg billeted a host
in the town. We surrounded it and torched it. You know how peasants burn
the stubble and the vermin run out with their fur—"

"Please!"

"He lost seventeen or eighteen sixties. That was two years' reinforcements gone in one night."

"And how many civilians died?"

"All of them, basically. It was not a small town."

"Atrocity!"

"Regrettable. But for Stralg it was the beginning of the end. Hardly a sixday goes by without a battle now. Piaregga, Reggoni Bridge . . . two sixties here, three there. I am nibbling him to death, my lady! He cannot stand these losses. We can match him body for body and still get stronger."

Horrible! Horrible! "What do you want of me?" she yelled. Why was Cavotti talking so much? It was almost as if we were waiting for the Vigaelians to get there and kill him. Chies belting along the alley, almost at the barracks . . .

Cavotti pulled a face. "I want to stop Celebre becoming another Miona, of course. It's my home, too, and the smell of burning babies isn't something you ever forget. Look at your maps, lady of Celebre. His escape route to Vigaelia goes past your city. He's falling back as slowly as he can, but we're driving him, and very soon now he will have to make a stand. Where better than here?" The big man's raspy voice rose to fill the hall: "He has about three-sixty-sixty left. How do you feel about that many ice devils occupying your city, Mistress? For half a year while the Vigaelian winter has the pass sealed?"

Gods! "No!" A mere dozen was more than it could stand now.

Chies *must* be at the barracks by this time, yelling for the flankleader. Werists moved like birds. It was their speed that made them so deadly. They'd come straight over the walls.

Cavotti smiled, exposing more tooth enamel than humans should have. "Then join us, my lady! Give me the signal, and I'll slip my men into Celebre before the garrison knows what's happening. I swear that I can control them. They'll behave. They're patriots, Florengians all, and they despise the Vigaelian scum. They want to show they're better." He thrust out a great paw, like a bear's. "Shake on it! Sixty-sixty of my men in Celebre and we'll deny it to Stralg. We'll cut him off from his base and bleed him to death on the plains."

Shake? She would not touch his murderer's hand if she were drowning. Piero was dying reviled, childless, and detested. "Never! You would make this city a battlefield. Don't you understand that my husband has been labeled coward and lackey and lickspittle all these years because he gave up his own happiness and mine just to *save* Celebre from sack? It worked. This city survived when most didn't, although many people still won't admit he was right. And now you would have me throw that all away?"

The Werist glowered at her angrily, then paused a moment as if listening. "I must go." He hauled off his cowl, exposing Weru's brass collar. Below such classically perfect features it seemed even more of an obscenity than usual.

Would the Vigaelians believe Chies's fantastic story of Cavotti in the palace? But he didn't need to say the Mutineer's name, just that there was a Florengian Werist. They knew Chies, they'd trust him.

They *must* be on their way by now.

"Your husband did as he saw right, lady, to stop Stralg from sacking the city as he'd sacked Nelina. But I am offering you a garrison to defend you. *At your invitation.*"

"And who rules Celebre then? The dogs would be worse than the wolves." What of the hostages Stralg held, her children? "Stralg showed fifteen years ago that Werists can run up stone walls like rats."

"Not when those walls are defended by other Werists, my lady. I didn't dare storm Miona with him in there."

"No, you burned it! And he would burn Celebre. No! No! Never! Begone! If I weren't certain that Chies had gone to summon Stralg's men, I would do it myself. Leave!"

Somewhere in the palace something bayed.

The Mutineer snorted. "Oh, hear that! That's shocking! Take that beast's name, Packleader. Well, it's been a joy talking to you, sweet lady. We must do this more often. Put it to your council and send me a signal if you change your mind. The best landmark in the city is the canopy on the temple of Veslih. I expect it's all covered with bird droppings?"

"Go!" She could hear something coming, many things. "Go! Go! Go! Go!"

"Needs cleaning. If you change your mind, put up a scaffolding around the tholos as if you're going to clean it. That'll be the signal. We'll move in." The big man clasped her shoulders and moved her aside as if she were a child. "Now, I really must dash. Don't stand in the opening, woman; you'll get run over."

He grabbed her hand to kiss it and was gone, racing across the terrace.

Then she guessed where he thought he was going, but that way was blocked. "There are knives on the weir!" she screamed.

She turned to the noise inside. Three . . . four . . . great beasts bunched in the doorway of the presence chamber, snarling and spitting, claws screeching on the tiles. She caught a fleeting glimpse of brass collars half-hidden by silver manes as they flashed across the hall, out through the opening, going almost too fast to see, going so fast she felt the wind stir her robe. More scraping claws and bestial baying as they saw their prey, then they were all gone in flying leaps over the balustrade.

three

MARNO CAVOTTI

heard the warbeasts' fury as he dived from the parapet. He very nearly dashed his brains out on a floating tree trunk, which was not part of the plan. It must have blown down within the city itself, because the Puisa River entered Celebre through siphons under the north wall. Floating debris remained in the pool outside, while any would-be intruder who tried to swim through the tunnels would be swept against bronze gratings and drowned.

He surfaced, rolled over on his back, and floated. Even if the Vigaelians had followed him in, they would not find him now. The world was silent when his ears were submerged, but stars were starting to show through the clouds, so the storm had gone. If he could just pull off this escape, he could rank his trip a complete success. Hoodwinking an aging, pompous pedant and a terrified bereaved mother was no great feat to brag of, but news of his visit here, far behind Stralg's lines, would fan the flames of freedom.

The river left the city over a weir, dropping into a narrow, walled canyon. The current was very fast, and the lip of the weir was armed with bronze blades to discourage exactly the feat he was attempting. This defense was effective, but frequently claimed swimmers who ventured too close, usually young boys, who were either gnashed into gobbets or drowned in the gyre in the canyon. Cavotti knew all about the weir because it had killed one of his cousins.

The river that night was much higher, faster, and colder than usual, and turgid as soup after the storm. Very fast. There was the spire of the Temple of Cienu already. He began his change, sending prayers to Weru, asking the god of storm and battle to arrange that the rain had raised the flow high enough to carry him over the knives.

Weir gone. The sky tilted above him and he was falling. The gyre was vicious, turning faster than any man could swim, sucking people down and holding them at the bottom of the river, spinning helplessly. Cavotti was still mostly human when he went over the weir, but not when he reached the gyre. He broke free with a few strokes of his flippers and went on his way downstream, to rendezvous with Butcher.

✦

The current slackened at the irrigation lagoon, where the Puisa was dammed to feed canals, and there he surfaced to hunt for the signal. He saw it right away, two bonfires like blazing eyes sending wheel tracks of light across the ripples. Someone was jumping up and down and waving.

He struck out in that direction, and the next time he raised his head, the woman had sat down to wait for him. Since his black seal-shape would be invisible to human sight in this darkness, she must be a seer. Stralg, curse his bowels, could command the service of Witnesses he had brought over from the Vigaelian Face, whereas the Florengian Maynists would help Cavotti and his helpers only sometimes, when they wished, as they chose. They would never even explain how they decided.

On reaching the rushes, he began to retroform. Battleforming was usually done in haste; the reversal had to be achieved in cold blood and always hurt more. This one needed longer than usual, because he had not been his normal warbeast. He was still sobbing with pain as he scrambled up the bank.

Without a word, the woman offered him a raw steak in one hand and a cloth in the other. He took the steak first.

✦

The storm had faded to stray damp puffs like some monster's hot breath, leaving the trees weeping from its mauling. Only Butcher and the Witness had come to meet him. Their camp was a bag of food and a leather groundsheet in the long wet grass—no tent or lamp to reveal their presence. Two chariots were hidden in the bushes; four hobbled guanacos grazed nearby.

The Mutineer sat and gorged on more raw meat. It was not as fresh as he would have liked, but meat was essential after battleforming. This was the pattern of his life. Most of the last ten years had been like this—danger, hardship, hasty withdrawal—and today's nostalgia trip to Celebre had made him aware how incredibly tired of it he was. Surely there had to be more to life than violence and concealment, death and flight, sorrow and atrocity? But another half-year should do it. He had promised himself Stralg's hide, stuffed.

The cloth was big enough to serve as his bedroll by night and chlamys by day, when hung over his left shoulder and pinned under his right arm. For now he laid it across his lap where he sat, not bothering to dress. For once there were no mosquitoes, all blown away by the storm. The Witness had her back turned to him, but that meant nothing—Vigaelian seers wore bags over their heads. In Florengia Maynists settled for bandaging their eyes when testifying in court. This one was not young, nor old either. Butcher had given her name as Giunietta, but she had not spoken one word yet. Cavotti was much aware of her, though. Because she was there, his body was reminding him that a woman was a Werist's second most urgent need after raw meat. Seers must not be asked.

"I'm grateful for your help, Witness. You'd have been a lifesaver if I'd gone past the signal."

"And I'm a good watchdog in case of burglars."

Not a promising opening.

"That, too."

Butcher bulked large on his other side, arms wrapped around shins and chin on knees. He was big, slow-spoken, rarely made eye contact. He and Cavotti were the last of the original impressed Celebrians who had won their collars in the first—and only—graduation at Boluzzi. His name had begun as an insult directed at his father's trade and become an honored title. Butcher could not play even one-color *tégale*, but no one matched him at killing Vigaelians, whether it was ripping out their throats on the battlefield or entertaining the wounded after it. He was also fanatically loyal to Cavotti, which was becoming an issue as victory drew closer. Nobody was yet admitting that the defeat of the Vigaelians would not end the fighting. Florengia had been shattered, but who owned the pieces?

"It worked?" Butcher asked his toes.

Cavotti tossed the last bone away and wiped his mouth with his wrist. "Like a charm. The doge is farther gone than we thought, but his wife took it all—head, shaft, and feathers."

"She accepted?"

"With four children supposedly still hostage? I don't *want* it accepted, Butcher, remember?"

"Will the Vigaelians believe it was really you?" the seer asked without turning.

"Certainly. They saw me off." He chuckled. "They'll catch Dicerno and force the story out of him." He took another bite. "I was lucky. Stralg's bastard was there."

"Hope you killed it," said a low mutter on his left.

"No. He's just a dumb kid. Not stupid-dumb, though. He guessed I'd moved a shutter that needed a little more than the real me. He was so screamingly suspicious that I scratched my neck. The gown Dicerno had given me had fleas anyway, which gave me the idea, and I let the baby Stralg spot the shape of the brass under the cowl. He damned near wet his sandals! Took off like an arrow to find his Vigaelian buddies. I let them smell my feet as I dived off the wall. Never hurts to add a little drama."

"A Speaker would judge you criminally crazy," Giunietta told the darkness. "Why take such an insane risk for a mere bluff?"

"A big hook needs good bait."

"So what happens tomorrow?" Butcher said.

"Tomorrow you and I get busy." Cavotti yawned ostentatiously and lay down—too weary to explain it all again to Butcher and too wary to talk in front of a woman he'd never met before. He turned away from her and pulled the cloth over himself.

"Busy doing what?" Giunietta's whisper came from right behind his head. He had not heard her come to lie beside him. His heart skipped a beat.

"Sorry, can't say."

"A battle. Fighting, slaughter." Seers could read emotions, not specific thoughts.

"I'm planning a killing ground."

She snuggled against him. "Tell me."

He had flogged men who breached security by discussing operations, but the seer already knew enough to betray him and in his present condition the bribe was irresistible.

"The baby ice devils in Celebre must be in a screaming panic. They will send word to Stralg that I'm sniffing around. Warbeasts cannot run all that way, so they will have to use chariots, and that means the message will go via the Vigaelian reserves camped near Umsina. The commander there is Hostleader Franin. He's a greenhorn, too, because Stralg needs to keep all his experienced men active in the field. He will send the message on, of course. Stralg's been burned often enough to suspect a trap, but I'm gambling that Franin will decide to move his camp closer to Celebre without waiting for orders. So two or three days from now an entire host, more than twenty sixties, will set off at the double."

Her arm slid around him. "And?"

"And I'll ambush them." Unless Cavotti had totally lost his touch,

Franin would bivouac the first night in the eminently suitable campsite at Black Lake, with his troops exhausted by a day's forced march, ripe for slaughter.

"That's wonderful!" Giunietta pulled the cloth off him and he realized that she had removed her wrap. Oh, yes!

He rolled over, face to face, and whispered, "Thanks."

Seers must not be asked, because they knew what a man wanted as soon as he did, or sooner. This one was certainly not one of the chatty ones. Infected by his unspoken desire, she was just as urgent as he was, which was fine. She kissed his mouth fiercely. He cooperated with lips and hands, tongue. His body had already completed its own battleforming. The lady brazenly reached down to encourage it. Soon she rolled over and pulled him on top of her.

Apparently Butcher was still staring at the night and hadn't noticed what was happening nearby. "Who's going to be doge after Piero dies?"

The lovers paused. Cavotti felt her shaking with laughter in his arms.

He said, "Don't know, don't care. Chances are there won't be anything left to be doge of."

Butcher said, "Ah! Carry on then."

He lay down and turned his back.

Part II

♦

Escapes
and
Rescues

♦

Four

SALTAJA HRAGSDOR

awoke with a snarl. For a moment she was confused by chinks of daylight peering around shutters, by solid masonry walls and paneled ceiling. Then she remembered she was in Tryfors, lying under clean blankets on a level sleeping platform, not some lumpy riverbank. So why the oppressive mood? Ah, yes! She had been dreaming of Benard Celebre.

Benard Celebre? Jarred, she sat up and peered at her arm. Last night she had sought guidance from the Mother, offering blood. She had felt the power flow and the cut was already healed, so what sort of reward was a useless dream of Benard Celebre ambling along a Tryforian street like some amiable half-wit bear? She had not seen him on her way through Kosord in the summer, but she had no doubt that it was he that she had just dreamt, and here in Tryfors, too.

That was ridiculous! She had given Horold leave to kill him. Her brother was a pathetic relic of the fearsome warrior he had once been, but he should be able to dispose of one penniless hostage. And even if Ingeld had somehow smuggled her boy lover out of the city, the satrap's Witnesses should have reported where Benard was and Horold's Werists should have run him down within hours.

Saltaja yelled to waken Guitha, who was sleeping on a mat near the door.

Benard? Was this some doing of his sister? Was this the final proof that Fabia Celebre was indeed a Chosen?

Not for nothing was holy Xaran known as the Mother of Lies. She spoke to all Her children, but not always with a clear voice, lest they betray Her secrets to lesser gods, who were young and foolish. She was usually helpful to Her Chosen, although even they could never count on Her absolutely. If two came into conflict, She might aid both, or aid one and deceive the other. Or deceive both.

As she attended to her toilet, Saltaja continued to puzzle. Her problems never grew any less. Her brothers, especially Therek, had become dangerously irrational. She would have to waste several days here in Tryfors repairing him and might not extend his useful life by more than a year or two. On the way home she would have to stop off in Kosord to mend Horold also. At times she even wondered about Stralg himself. As a natural-born warrior, he had required far less Shaping than any of his brothers, but the steadily worsening news of the war made her wonder if he were decaying also. Then there was yesterday's news about Kwirarl, the last of her sons dead, and these "New Dawn" rebel Werists massing at Nuthervale. With winter coming on, they were the most urgent problem. Last night she had dispatched warnings to both Horold and Eide, telling them to prepare for a spring campaign before the traitors grew any stronger.

Her life's work was unraveling in front of her eyes.

"Brainless slut!" Saltaja swung a slap that almost knocked Guitha off her feet. "A *clean* shift, I said! From that box!"

Wailing, Guitha ran to obey. The girl was useless, incompetent even at helping her mistress dress now. She would have to be replaced soon, before she became incapable of even dressing herself. The Dominance Saltaja had used on her was quick Control, but it soon burned out the mind. It was not to be compared with the painstaking Shaping that Saltaja and Hrag together had used on his sons from their conception through to manhood.

She pushed dismal thoughts out of her mind and concentrated on dressing, in spite of Guitha's bumbling. Tryfors Palace was surely the most dismal, bleakest royal residence on the entire Face, and in all the years since Stralg terminated the line of local kings and installed his brother as satrap, Therek had done nothing to improve it. No matter; it was a joy to pamper herself, to be rubbed with scented oil, try on fresh clothes specially made since she arrived yesterday, and to admire herself in a reasonably-sized silver mirror while Guitha wielded a hairbrush with the subtlety of a peasant flailing grain.

Saltaja's hair was snowy white but had always been so. Her skin was unusually pale, even for a Vigaelian, and her eyes a startling dark blue—Hrag had claimed that he arranged that distinctive touch when she was an infant. Her face was too elongated to be beautiful, but beauty was much less useful than power. She could still pass for less than forty, although she was almost twice that.

"Now my wimple." Living up to her reputation as Queen of Shadows, she always wore black, even to the cloth that concealed her hair and neck, the long cuffs draping her hands. Nothing but her face was ever visible to anyone except the many Guithas who had served her over the years—and certain highly privileged men, in the past. She must find a replacement Gui-tha here in Tryfors before she left. She always named her current maid Gui-tha, after the one who had been her first experiment in Dominance.

A new Guitha would have to wait. The first item of business today must be to confirm that the Celebre girl was a Chosen of Xaran. To give her a fair chance, though, she should be moved to some lower dungeon where she could draw power from the Mother. Then send in the brute Werist that Therek had promised. Back in Skjar, Saltaja would have arranged to have the rape done in a cell with a spyhole, so she could watch how it went, but Tryfors had no such convenience.

No matter. If the thug came out satisfied, the girl was innocent and would just have to take her chances with her future husband. If he wan-dered out obviously Controlled or didn't come out at all, then it would be time for Saltaja to sit down with the filly for the confidential chat they had been unable to share on the river. To convince Fabia of the advantages of co-operation, Saltaja would begin by conceding that her nephew, Cutrath Horoldson, was a repulsive choice of husband and then go on to instruct her in means to put him to rights as easily a skilled seamstress could reshape a gown. More easily, in fact. Grain needed thrashing, grinding, kneading, and baking before it became usable; men were much the same.

A knock on the door disturbed her reverie.

◆

Profoundly.

◆

Blazing with fury, she swept along the stark stone corridors. Werists trotted at her heels and hurried ahead of her, their torsos wrapped in striped palls, leav-ing brawny arms and legs bare. She swept through the outer room, where more Werists pressed back against the walls looking scared. As well they might.

The room beyond was a barren box without even a sleeping platform. The girl's baggage and clothes lay scattered everywhere, as if the idiots had ransacked them looking for her. Saltaja strode over to examine the single window with its two bronze bars. Satisfied that they were still solid, cor-roded in place, ancient as the wall, she laid her hand on the stonework and detected only a frail trace of the Old One's power filtering up from the heart of the world. Even she, with sixty years' more experience, would never con-trive an escape from here. Supposing she could somehow trick the jailers outside into opening the door, she could not Control eight at once. Chosen or not, the girl must have had help.

Outside, a heavy drizzle was sending sheets of water coursing over the paving, making pedestrians hurry. Take away that rain and the daylight, and this was the street in her dream. So Benard Celebre had rescued his sister, had he? That had been the Dark One's message.

She turned to face the Werists. Her two Controlled bodyguards, Ern and Brarag, were standing close to her, keeping watch on the rest. Six of the incompetent jailers had packed in after her, another two were outside, peering through the door. She could not remember the name of their leader, but it mattered not at all and soon would matter even less.

"Guarding a slip of a girl is beyond your ability?"

The flankleader bared his teeth at her. "All of us spent the night in the outer room. There were no visitors, no coming and going—"

"Except the prisoner."

"We can't fight gods! No mortal let that woman out of here."

"Since when does holy Weru accept excuses? Track her!"

"We tried, my lady." His stubbled hair and beard were wet. "The rain . . . We could not pick up her scent at all."

"And the Ucrist, Wigson? I suppose he's gone, too? Did you send someone to look?"

Nod.

"I expect he bribed his guards," she said. "The Witnesses will get the truth out of them."

"The jail guards have disappeared." The flankleader obviously wished he could.

"The Witnesses will locate them, and him," Saltaja said confidently. Even if they had moved out of range already, the seers should be able to tell Therek which way they had gone.

She should not have expected the public jail to hold the richest man in all Vigaelia. Horth Wigson was important only as surety for Fabia's good behavior. He could have bought his way out even if he had to pay his jailers enough to let them flee the satrap's anger and make new lives somewhere else. It would have been cheaper to have them permanently silenced, but that was not Wigson's style. Clever people don't need to break laws, he said— they can bend them. But even he could not bribe Werists.

Saltaja headed for the door. "Lock this bunch of imbeciles in here until I have spoken with the satrap."

Suddenly the air reeked of murder and mutiny. Saltaja Hragsdor might be the satrap's sister, the bloodlord's sister, a reputed chthonian, but *no* woman gave orders to Heroes of Weru!

Except she. The six remained inside, the two outside reluctantly joined them, and Ern slid the huge bronze bolts. He looked around, astonished, sweat shining on his forehead.

"How long will it hold them?" she asked.

He shrugged helplessly. "Until they decide to rip out the bars or tear up the floorboards, my lady. Battleformed, some of them could get out *between* the bars, given time. You *can't* imprison Werists!"

"Then we must bring this scum to justice quickly. They are a disgrace to your cult. Stay here, let no one in, no one out. Brarag, go and find the satrap. Tell him to come to my room. At once!"

Warrior Brarag flinched at the thought of giving orders to the Vulture, but he could not refuse. He saluted and ran off.

✦

Alone, Saltaja stalked back toward her dreary room, thinking furiously. What god was meddling? *Anziel?* Thanks to the Mother's sending she knew that Benard Celebre was here in Tryfors, instead of tidily rotting in a pauper's grave in Kosord. The boy was a scatterbrained dreamer, but he was a Hand of Anziel. He was certainly not capable of springing his sister from that cell, but his goddess was, if She chose to answer Her devotee's prayers.

What of the other brother, the Hero? No, the only god who would answer a prayer from him would be Weru, and this was certainly not Weru's work. Young Orlad was due to die right about now, murdered so that Therek could gloat over a dead Florengian.

Last night's dream had not been trivial; it had been a very important warning, perhaps even a hint that Fabia Celebre was now in favor and Saltaja Hragsdor was not. Of course the girl's sacrifice of Perag Hrothgatson would have raised her in Mother Xaran's esteem, but if the girl thought she could outbid Saltaja Hragsdor in offerings to the Old One, she had another think coming.

At that point in her journey, the Queen of Shadows stopped to open a creaky little door in a cobwebby alcove and peer out at a small enclosure, a neglected jungle surrounded by blank stone walls. This weed patch was known as the herb garden, and no doubt some long-ago queen of Tryfors had nurtured herbs there as a time-out from her royal duty of breeding princes, but the moment Saltaja had first seen it, years ago, she had known it to be accursed ground, dedicated to the Old One. In today's gloom and drizzle it seemed more baleful than ever.

Yes, it must be done there.

Back at her room, Saltaja found clothes all over the floor and Guitha sitting staring at the wall because she had been given no specific orders to tidy up. She would not even eat now unless told to do so. Saltaja was still hitting her when Brarag arrived, panting as if he had run all the way up the tower and back.

"Hostleader . . . not presently in the . . . palace, my lady . . . drove off in his chariot, short while ago."

She almost blurted out a curse but caught herself in time—her curses worked better than most people's. Obviously Therek had gone to the hill because in this weather he could not watch Orlad's murder from his tower. *Death and corruption!* Was that a trap?

"*Bring me Huntleader Fellard!* Now! Right away! Tell him it's urgent."

✦

Huntleader Fellard Lokison, commander of Fist's Own Hunt, was young to be so senior, even nowadays, when Stralg had stripped the Face of older Werists. He was also an arrogant fool. Yesterday he had deliberately snubbed Saltaja, leaving her standing on the beach when he drove away in his chariot with Fabia. To insult his hostleader's sister like that would have been stupid even if the rumors of Saltaja being a Chosen were unfounded. Since they were not, he was about to pay dearly for his folly.

He strode in, offering Saltaja a mocking smile and a devil-may-care nod instead of a bow. He was tall and lean, typical Werist arrogance sparkling in typically Vigaelian blue eyes. With chiseled jaw clean-shaven and scalp gold-stubbled, he would have been winsome had his face not been marred by four vertical claw scars that had left his mouth twisted. Saltaja, perversely, found this model of beauty marred quite appealing. He folded his arms and watched with no visible alarm as she advanced to meet him, bare feet on stone floor.

"My lady? You asked to see me?"

"Good of you to come, my lord. Flankleader, wait outside, please. Allow no one in." Guitha was still there, but she would notice nothing. "I need your help, Huntleader." The moment she came within range, Saltaja immobilized him.

"You will obey me," she said, taking a grip on his arm.

No response, except eyes rolling in sudden terror.

"You will obey me!" She was pushing power into solid muscle and meeting equally solid resistance. A most determined young man! But she had no time for pity. "In the name of holy Xaran, I command you!"

The shock of hearing that forbidden name collapsed Fellard's resistance like a bubble. Mumble: "I will . . . obey you."

Better! "Kneel!"

Werists knelt to no one, not even to holy Weru Himself. Horrified to find himself obeying, Fellard sank slowly, like some forest giant toppling, but his knees struck the flagstones with a crack that made Saltaja wince. He stared up at her, eyes stretched wide, face white and slick with sweat.

She peered into his mind. It was hard to make out anything through the surging waves of terror, but she could not entrance him yet, not until she had found her way around. Fear . . . the source of fear . . . and the object of it, which must be she. This was probably his pain center . . . she jabbed and he responded with a gasp of agony. Anger? . . . a twist there and she had him shivering like a horse in fly season. And that must be his sex? Yes, a touch or two there and he moaned with delight.

Now she could put him into a trance and inspect the rest of his mind. Very tidy and precise it was, with motivations ranked like the onyx pillars of Jat-Nogul. She poked the most dominant.

"Speak! Who do you see?"

He gasped a few times, then began babbling, "Weru, god, Hero, Weru, warbeast . . ."

That was himself, his identity. She left it and tried another.

"Vulture . . . m-my lord? . . ."

Therek. She tried the one she thought represented herself.

"The hag . . ."

Hag, was it? He was going to pay for that. She tried another.

"Puss? Oh, Puss . . . love . . ."

Huntleader Fellard was a busy man. She discovered no less than four women in his life, with Puss the current favorite. There were three children, too, which she did not try to relate to mothers. Also parents and a couple of siblings or childhood friends. Those had all faded to background, dead or far away. She ripped them out, ignoring his whimpers of pain. Then the lovers, all four of them—snap, break, cut away. Therek she left, but much decreased. Her own identity she inflated enormously, tying it to fear and sex and his own self-image. This was far more brutal than the simple Dominance she had used on Ern and Brarag. When the conversion was finished, she was the only person left in Huntleader Fellard's life. He would be devoted to her, obsessed by her. There! She released him, and he crumpled to the floor, gasping and weeping.

She tottered over to a chair. She was shaking too, head throbbing. "Come here!"

He tried to stand, failed, and compromised by crawling to her on hands and knees, looking like a corpse escaping from a graveyard. When he arrived, he sank down to kiss her foot. He mumbled something of which only "My lady . . ." was audible.

Usually she managed to tamper with her subjects' motivations and leave their other mental processes intact, at least in the short term, but Fellard would not last long after this butchery. In a couple of thirties he would be a gibbering animal. Fortunately, she did not need him for long.

"What do you want?"

"To serve you. Always. To serve you." He looked up with a hound's glazed devotion.

"Rise." She waited impatiently while he struggled to his feet. "You will obey me and serve me, but you will forget what has happened since you walked in."

He shook his head a few times to clear it, then his pupils dilated and he gave her the same lecherous smile he had given the girl yesterday. He was Saltaja's, body and soul.

"How may I be of service, my lady?"

"The Celebre prisoner has escaped."

"I heard." He tried hard not to grin, but not quite hard enough. "That is extremely distressing, my lady! Apparently Hostleader Therek ordered that she was to be guarded . . ." The amusement faded into incredulity.

"Yes?"

". . . on pain of death. But . . ." He smiled grotesquely. "But that is only an expression! Werists can't be put to death. I mean who . . . ? How? I expect your honored brother will punish them severely, but . . . not put . . . to . . ."

"There are eight of them locked in the room. You know where I mean?"

"Yes, my lady." He was seriously worried now.

"Go and get them. Take them to the herb garden and kill them."

"My lady! They will resist. Innocent men will—"

"Think of it as a training exercise," she said. "Kill them. In the herb garden. You will obey me."

Face white as bone, Huntleader Fellard whispered, "I will obey you."

Five

FABIA CELEBRE

had never truly expected to be forced into marrying a Werist, but it was nice
to think that Cutrath Horoldson no longer lurked in her future. He could
vanish over the Edge and enjoy his military career without ever knowing
about the wedded bliss he had so narrowly escaped. She had other problems
to worry about.

Free Spirit was a typical riverboat—long and shallow, with two masts
bearing triangular lateen sails. She might rank a little older and smellier
than most, but Dantio knew her of old and had judged that she was speedy
enough to outrun any likely pursuit. Her crew and owners were an extended
family of around twenty people, ranging from babes to ancients. The boat
was their home and the heap of bales and boxes amidships their worldly
wealth. By custom, the passengers sat in the bow and the crew stayed huddled in the stern, swathed in red or brown burnooses, chattering in their
strange singsong.

The rain had stopped just as *Free Spirit* left the Wrogg and proceeded up
a tributary, the Little Stony. Now the world was steaming in watery sunshine
and a ramshackle ferry dock had come into view ahead. The banks were
marshy and the surrounding woods scrubby, but to the southeast the dramatic
cone of Mount Varakats shone hugely white against a sky of midnight blue.

Fabia was seated on the port shelf next to Horth Wigson, almost touching knees with lady Ingeld opposite. Ingeld was between Flankleader Guthlag and Benard, who presently had his arm around her quite shamelessly.
She was being as charming as ever, but she hadn't eaten anything all morning. Had her idiot brother gotten her with child?

No one was saying much, as they were all lost in their worries. They all
knew that Saltaja and Therek could not be written off yet, and Ingeld insisted that Horold was pursuing her upriver, so Hrag jaws might yet close on
the fugitives. Orlad had been condemned to die today and might already be
dead. Dantio had stayed behind in Tryfors to watch what happened—
Witnesses were notoriously nosey people, he admitted, but he would be in no
danger because no one could sneak up on a seer. And somewhere there were
the mysterious rebels, poised to strike at Tryfors.

Apart from their common concerns, they all had their own worries. Fabia and Dantio wanted to return to Celebre, but the pass might be closed already. Benard was being evasive about going to Florengia, because he could not leave Ingeld. Fabia did not want to abandon Horth, who was much dearer to her than the true father she could not remember. Ingeld must be worrying about Cutrath, on his way to a war that now seemed to be lost.

"How far is it to High Timber?" Fabia asked. "Father?"

"I don't know," Horth said in his customary soft tones. "I suspect the riverfolk don't, either. I'm not sure High Timber is a real place at all. It may be several places, or just an idea."

Guthlag snorted contemptuously. The gnarly old Hero had taken a dislike to the wizened little Ucrist. "You can't hide a horde of Werists in an idea. Men need food and shelter and training grounds." He snorted again. "And women."

"Dantio said our journey wouldn't be long." Benard grinned as though he would not care if it lasted forever.

On the river "not long" meant anything from an hour to several sixdays. Fabia did not see how the rebel encampment could be anywhere near Tryfors if Arbanerik Kranson had managed to keep it secret from the Werist garrison there for at least two years. Dantio was coming overland to join them; she hoped he was all right, because only the family seer knew how to find the rebel headquarters.

The boat tacked across the stream to enter a stagnant inlet. Sheltered from the wind by treed banks and hampered by reeds and bulrushes, it gently lost way and stopped. This must be the chosen rendezvous, and was obviously a good one, easily identified but hidden from casual view. A Witness like Dantio could find them there even in pitch darkness. Four male sailors rose to begin lowering the sails.

"*Free Spirit* ahoy!" Like a mythical wood spirit, Dantio appeared amid the shrubbery, a slender young man in the hessian shirt and long breeches worn by slaves in Tryfors. The shabby leather cloak he wore over them hung open, its hood thrown back to show a brown Florengian face and a gleam of white teeth. He waved both fists overhead in triumph. *"Therek is dead!"*

For a moment no one spoke. Fabia thought of his horde, twenty sixty ferocious Werists, coming screaming after whoever had killed him.

Then everyone, including most of the riverfolk, yelled "What?" or "How?" or "No!" in disbelief.

"Dead!" Dantio insisted. "Orlad killed him! Orlad's alive!"

He half-turned to indicate the young man pushing his way out of the bushes to stand at his side. Orlad was smiling, too, and that just proved that there was a first for anything, for yesterday he had been as sullen as a hungry boar. His torso was draped in a waterlogged woolen pall, and the brass collar of Weru shone like yellow fire around his neck.

"Orlad!" Benard's great bellow of joy set birds a-flapping on the river. He started up, as if about to leap overboard and go welcome his brother. Ingeld caught hold of him. "Orlad!" he repeated. "You changed sides!"

The riverfolk were yelling, also, but theirs were cries of alarm. They had no liking for Werists at the best of times—they had grumbled at allowing old Guthlag on board—and a Florengian Werist was an unthinkable freak, perhaps a sign that the war had spilled back over the Edge and Vigaelia was being attacked. Men jumped for the yards and sails. Others produced poles and oars and stabbed them into the water to push *Free Spirit* clear of the reeds. The boat jerked back the way she had come only moments before.

Orlad barked an order. Heroes erupted out of the woods behind him—Werists with palls and brass collars, but regular, fair-skinned, golden-haired, *Vigaelian* Werists. Like otters they leaped into the river and surged forward through the reeds, barely slowing as the water deepened. Seven of them, the astonished Fabia counted. By the time the water was up to their shoulders, their hands were clasping the gunwale and *Free Spirit* was free no more.

A couple of the boatmen raised their poles as if to crack heads or crush fingers. Instantly old Packleader Guthlag was on his feet shouting warnings, but it was shrill yells in Wroggian from the even older Master Nok, the boat's patriarch, that averted disaster. The sailors froze.

"We will pay!" Ingeld shouted in the silence. "We have silver."

"Hit a Hero and he'll rip you apart," Guthlag grumbled, sitting down.

The riverfolk understood more Vigaelian than they usually admitted, and the poles were hastily hidden away. On the bank, Orlad crouched, pulled Dantio onto his shoulder, and lifted him effortlessly. Then he waded into the water, carrying the seer shoulder-high.

"I can walk, you know," Dantio said, amused. "*It is known* that no one has ever seen a Werist acting as a beast of burden before."

"I can't get any wetter. You can."

Yesterday Orlad had been a surly, humorless churl, fanatically loyal to Satrap Therek and his brother the Fist. What miracle had produced this conversion? He almost smiled a second time as he deposited his load aboard the boat, then hauled himself in also. His seven followers scrambled over the side. Suddenly *Free Spirit* was very crowded.

Dantio warbled at the riverfolk in fluent Wroggian, accepted a weighty bag from Ingeld, and proceeded to negotiate an extortionate fare of two handfuls of silver for the additional passengers. Calmed, if not contented, the sailors set to work to pole the boat out of the rushes, and some of the women began rummaging through the cargo. It seemed Dantio had either bought or rented all the towels and spare clothes aboard.

He turned to the newcomers. "My lords! Pray meet the lady Ingeld, noble dynast of Kosord; her Hordeleader Guthlag Guthlagson; Master Ucrist Horth Wigson; my brother Benard and sister Fabia. And you, gentlefolk, please greet these splendid warriors, lords Waels, Hrothgat, Snerfrik, Namberson, Narg, Prok, and Jungr. Their fame will shine forever!"

Snerfrik was one of the largest men Fabia had ever seen. Despite his obvious youth, he had a mean look. Prok was the smallest of the squad, and even meaner. As they stripped off their rain-soaked palls, many of them revealed fresh red scars, and some still showed traces of blood at the roots of their stubbly beards. The one called Waels had a scarlet stain covering the lower half of his face, but she decided that was a birthmark.

Dantio sat down on the bench next her to explain the miracle. "You know that Therek was planning to have Orlad ambushed on his way back to Nardalborg. Orlad got away, so the assassins had to chase after him. They didn't know that the commander at Nardalborg, Huntleader Heth, had sent Orlad's flank to see him safely home. They met up with him on King's Grass and ambushed the ambushers! It was a wonderful battle."

Fabia had never heard of this Heth. He must be one of Therek's most senior officers, yet he had clearly saved Orlad's life. Deliberately or unintentionally?

"What odds?" Guthlag asked.

"Flank to flank. Only one of Therek's men escaped."

The old Hero cackled in delight. "A great victory, then!"

But a full flank was a dozen men and there were only eight here.

"But there's more. Therek couldn't see what was happening in the rain," Dantio continued. "So he drove out to King's Grass without waiting for his bodyguard!" He grinned wickedly. "That battle was much shorter, but much more important! His death is a crippling blow to the House of Hrag."

Glances were exchanged. Ingeld put the question.

"So what will happen now in Tryfors?"

Never mind Tryfors!—Now Fabia had all three of her brothers to compare: Benard beefy, amiable, scatterbrained; Orlad scarred inside and out, and, despite his current smiles, basically bitter and dangerous; Witness Dantio . . . She had not assessed Dantio yet. Clever, of course, and omniscient. And a eunuch. In his Witness robes and veils he had sounded like a woman and hence seemed tall; out of them he was a boyish man of average height, and appeared immature compared even to Orlad, eight years his junior. Werist husbands Fabia could do without, but a Werist brother would be a useful defender. A seer brother should be a perfect adviser. And an artist . . . perhaps Benard could redecorate the palace in Celebre for her when she succeeded their father as doge. Dogess?

Eight large young men toweling, laughing, and trying on clothes did tend to make the vessel seem rather *crowded*. More *interesting* than usual, perhaps, but Fabia had met similar Werist exhibitionism often enough on her journey up from Skjar, and she knew she was meant to keep her eyes averted even if the riverfolk were openly watching and commenting.

At a pause in the conversation, she murmured, "Dantio, what's the feminine of 'doge'?"

"Dogaressa. What do you think of the beef, darling? Go ahead and stare if you want. They like it."

Fabia said, "Oh!" with as much outrage as she could muster. She could feel her face warming up—because she *had* stolen a few peeks, and he must know that. "Father, this man is making highly improper remarks to me."

Horth awarded her one of his meek little smiles. "Brothers do that, my dear. Terrible creatures, brothers. That's why I always spared you the ordeal of having any." Dressed in rags, the wealthiest man on the Vigaelian Face looked like an aging domestic servant of no consequence whatsoever.

"I hope Orlad can keep his Werists away from her," Benard remarked solemnly, "or she may be screaming for her other brothers to defend her."

"Orlad must have had a very narrow escape," Dantio said. "He didn't have those terrible scars on his back last night. Oh, look, everybody! Fabia is staring!"

She swung a slap, which he parried easily. "If there is anything worse than a normal brother," she said crossly, "it must surely be a seer brother!"

"No, artists are the worst," Benard said. "They keep gazing at you, wondering how to capture your beauty in marble or bronze so that future ages can marvel at it."

"That's an improvement. Continue."

"I like the cut of your dress, but that blue does nothing for your coloring."

"Her underwear is just hideous," Dantio said.

Fabia wailed. "Not fair! I've worn the same old rags ever since I left Skjar, and I had no chance to visit the Tryfors bazaar. These are the best castoffs I could find in Sixty Ways. Mock me and I shall burst into tears! Then you'll be sorry."

Dantio said, "No, we shall be amazed. Personally I think Orlad is more likely to break down and weep than you are. I know I am."

"Me too," Benard agreed. "She's tough as granite."

"My lady!" Fabia howled. "Stop them! What do I do?"

Ingeld smiled. "You thank the gods, dear. I think it is wonderful that you four have been reunited after so long. They're just teasing you to show you that they love you."

"I'd hate to hear what they'd be saying if they disliked me. I'll get Orlad to defend me."

"I suspect Orlad's sense of humor needs work, too," Benard said. "What do you think, Dantio? Let's practice on Fabia for the next sixday or so, and then start in on him."

"No!" Fabia snapped. "Start with him and I'll help bandage you."

Ingeld laughed. "Well done! I award that round to Fabia."

As flankleader, Orlad had claimed first choice of the available clothes— linen trousers and a leather jerkin left open to display his shiny brass collar and a hairless, badly scarred chest. His seven followers were doing the best they could with what was left, but most of them were far larger than riverfolk and had to settle for makeshift loincloths. Leaving them amidships, he came forward to join what Fabia was already starting to think of as *the family*. Why not? Horth was as dear as a father to her; Benard and Ingeld were lovesick loons, and at a pinch Packleader Guthlag could be cast as Faithful Old Retainer. Moreover, the family had been purged of unwanted hangers-on, specifically Cutrath the Unknown Suitor. Gone and good riddance!

Dantio sensed Orlad coming and slid off the bench to make a space. Orlad accepted the seat as his right and Dantio went off to rummage in the cargo. The boat heeled as it caught the main current of the Wrogg.

Orlad bit into a peach and waited for someone else to speak. He was not smiling now, but he did wear a very satisfied, confident air. Fabia supposed it came from knowing he need fear nobody and nothing in the world except other Werists. And he had already changed the flavor of the world by killing Therek Hragson.

"I take it," she said, "that you no longer approve of my enforced betrothal to Cutrath Horoldson?"

He flashed her a dark glance. "No."

"Or command me to be loyal to the House of Hrag?"

"*Shut,*" he said, "*up!*" No sense of humor.

Benard said, "Last night Dantio told us about a place called High Timber. He says a lot of Werists have gathered there rather than go to the war. They're called the New Dawn and they intend to overthrow Stralg."

"Deserters!" Orlad munched more peach.

"If you say so, brother. I'd say they displayed good common sense. You have just killed a satrap, a hostleader, a Hragson. You need help, you need allies. You can't take that collar off, can you?'

"Don't want to."

"You going home to Florengia?"

"Haven't decided."

The conversation did not prosper.

"Don't pester the man, dear," Ingeld said. "He has to be careful what he tells and who he tells it to. If he and his men still want to go and fight for Stralg, the New Dawn Werists will regard them as enemies. If they want to fight against Stralg, they'll be mistaken for his men as soon as they cross the Edge."

Benard pouted, puzzled. "You mean they shouldn't go to High Timber?"

"I mean you should let them make their own decision."

Dantio returned with an earthenware bottle and a beaker. He laid them on the boards and knelt between his brothers, closing off the family group from the riverfolk and other Werists. He worked on the wax seal with his belt knife. "This is an excellent wine. I couldn't bear to leave it behind for looters. I dedicate it to the gods." Having poured some into the beaker and sniffed at it, he surveyed his audience. A Daughter, two Heroes, a Hand, a Ucrist, one Witness, and a Chosen masquerading as an extrinsic—the wine ceremony often called for tricky decisions about precedence, but rarely as tricky as that.

"My lady, will you begin?"

Ingeld smiled a dynastic smile as she accepted the cup. "I shall be honored. I give thanks to the Bright Ones for reuniting the four children of

Celebre and I pray for their future prosperity and happiness together!" She spilled a drop for the gods, then drank the rest.

The others chorused, "Amen!"

Dantio refilled the beaker. "Flankleader?"

Guthlag beamed with an old man's long fangs at being granted the honor of speaking second. "I never heard of a Hero killing a hostleader on his first hunt, but it's long past time someone sent Therek Hragson to the halls of our god, where he will be greatly honored. So I give thanks to Holy Weru for the favor He has shown my cult brother Orlad, and pray that the Fierce One will continue to exalt his name in glory." He, too, spilled a drop and drank.

This time the amens were less certain. Orlad frowned as if suspecting mockery, making Fabia wonder if his show of indifference, which she had taken for confidence, was really a mask for an aching lack of it. Once, on the long journey up the Wrogg River, she had teased Flankleader Cnurg by saying that Werists had no minds of their own. He had told her quite seriously that life was much simpler when someone else took on all your doubts and worries and gave you orders in return. How could Orlad possibly be as calm as he looked when seven young outlaws now relied on him to keep them alive?

Again Dantio filled the beaker. This time he looked to Horth, but Benard's great paw lifted it from his hand before it could be passed.

"I'll add to the flankleader's prayer. I joyously thank the gods for releasing my lady from bondage to Horold Hragson, and I pray that They send him to join his brother as soon as possible." He offered and drank.

Now the agreement was certainly muted and Fabia was quite shocked. To curse anyone was unseemly, practically a prayer to Xaran. It was also dangerous, in that the Old One might take the curser before the cursed, and for a man to curse his mistress's husband was utterly shameful. Yet Ingeld actually patted his thigh in approval!

Orlad raised a skeptical eyebrow. "You going to look to that job yourself, Big Brother?"

Benard scowled. "I'd break his neck if he weren't a Werist."

"Ah, there is that." The husky young Hero leered through his patchy black stubble. "I'll help collect your remains for burial, if they're not too widespread."

Maybe he did have a trace of humor?

Dantio passed the next draft to Horth.

"In my experience," the merchant said shyly, "one should always ask for more than one is prepared to settle for, especially when petitioning gods.

One usually has to compromise. Frena and I have been released from captivity, so I give thanks for this deliverance, and I beseech the holy ones to bear us safely home and recompense us for all the wealth Satrap Eide and his wife have stolen from us over the years."

"Home?" Fabia said. "You mean Skjar, but . . ." She saw the others grinning at her.

"This city of ours, Celebre," Orlad said. He kept pulling peaches out from somewhere, popping them whole in his mouth, then spitting the pits overboard. Fabia thought it was a disgusting performance, but Ingeld was watching it raptly. "It is ruled by a *doge*? What is a *doge*?"

"*It is known,*" Dantio began, reverting to Witness, "that Celebre is the grandest and richest city of all Florengia, especially now that the war has destroyed so many others. The doge is supreme magistrate, elected for life by the council of elders. The office has been vested in our family for many generations, but succession is not automatically to the eldest son. In the past they have selected brothers, uncles, even sons-in-law. Hence Saltaja's idea of marrying Fabia to her nephew. Then Stralg would lay his claws on the table, the council would elect Cutrath, all legal, and everyone would be happy."

Except Cutrath's wife. For Ingeld's sake, Fabia did not say so.

Orlad accepted the beaker from Dantio and raised it. "I thank my lord, holy Weru, for today's victory and beseech Him to show this council of elders that the Hero Celebre is the best one to rule their city."

Guthlag smirked. Ingeld frowned. Benard scowled. Horth was as noncommittal as the Wrogg. The sun went behind a cloud just then, sending cold tremors down Fabia's backbone. Orlad could not speak Florengian, Benard was unthinkable as a ruler, and what council would elect a eunuch? While her father's household was considerably smaller than a city, she did have managerial experience. Of the four of them, she was the obvious choice. Why not a dogaressa regnant?

Dantio smiled. "Don't make the sauce before you catch the fish, brother!" He refilled the beaker and studied the wine in it for a moment. "I have worked long and hard toward this moment. I have served as a resident Witness in the palace of Kosord, Bena, and knew the anguish you felt every time you set eyes on Ingeld. I watched you put my face on the mural in her chamber and wonder whose face it was. As Urth the slave I carried burdens through the streets of Skjar in the monsoon deluge while Frena Wigson presided over great feasts for Saltaja and other rich folk in Horth's palace. I even went to Nardalborg once, as an itinerant merchant's slave. There I watched Orlad being systematically beaten up by his friends and could do nothing to help him. But now the gods have rewarded my efforts and granted us reunion!"

He raised the beaker. "For this I thank Them; and I ask only that I may soon watch Saltaja Hragsdor die."

A chill wind caught the sail and made it flap. No one commented. The prayers were becoming grimmer, yet who could blame Dantio for cursing Saltaja? As he passed the refilled beaker to Fabia, his sly smile was a secret challenge: To which god would she pray? If she mentioned Xaran, she would be lucky just to be thrown overboard.

"My brothers are kind," she said, gaining a moment to think. "Orlad has already slain Therek, Benard wants to kill Horold, and now Dantio takes Saltaja. I assume you expect me to get rid of Stralg for you?"

Everyone laughed—Guthlag guffawed as if that was funniest thing he had heard in years. Even Orlad smiled, although mockingly.

She raised the wine. "I give thanks to all the gods for the start They have made in righting the wrongs done to the House of Celebre, and I pray . . . I pray that They will also lead us home and give the council the wisdom to choose the best qualified candidate for doge."

"Amen to that!" Orlad shouted.

Dantio said. "There is fighting in Tryfors!"

"Who?" Orlad snapped. "Who is fighting?"

"I can't tell at this distance. But it has started."

SALTAJA HRAGSDOR

emerged from her room and told Ern to stay there on guard. Humming happily, she set off in the same direction Fellard had gone. This was going to work out very well, advantage snatched from the jaws of adversity.

Fabia's escape required a change of plan. In retrospect, Saltaja should have taken the girl into her confidence sooner, but in all her long lifetime, she had never admitted to anyone that she was a Chosen—that was a quick way to a living grave. There had been no way of testing the girl on the river, and it was too late to unchurn that butter now, however helpful it would have been to have a second chthonian in the family. Stralg would have to do the best he could about Celebre without any of the doge's children—and if the war was heading that way, the city would probably not survive anyway.

No, Saltaja would have to summon Cutrath back from Nardalborg and shape him herself. A wife could have given him the years of care required, but the long journey downstream to Kosord would have to suffice. She chuckled, wondering what her traveling companions would think of a young Werist who sat so close to his dear aunt all day and every day. Cutrath should be happy enough at the change of plan; a Werist would have to be insane to prefer a posting to Florengia nowadays, and her nephew had never struck Saltaja as insane. Petty, mean, and nasty, yes, but not insane. The family was not done for yet—there was the unknown Heth bastard, whom Therek was hiding from her, and probably a few Stralg by-blows growing up in Florengia. Stralg never acknowledged his bastards, but he must have sired a host of them in his time.

She stepped out into the herb garden—sodden, waist-high undergrowth and rain dribbling from foliage overhead, an unmistakable sense of evil. By the time she had forced her way through the jungle to a far corner and found a secluded nook between two trunks, her clothing was soaked through. There she veiled herself, spinning darkness until the court faded into gray around her and no one would notice her unless they actually walked into her. She stripped naked, then knelt and dug her fingers into the soil.

By blood and birth; death and the cold earth. "Most unholy Mother Xaran, accept the sacrifice I bring You to Your glory." She felt the power flow, the Mother's attention focus on her. She remained crouched there, patiently waiting, indifferent to the cold and wet, warmed by excitement. The Old One would certainly enjoy this bounty She was about to receive. She would reward Her servant. The earth hungered.

The door opened to admit a dozen Werists in orange-red-black stripes, who proceeded to spread themselves all around the court and crouch down as she had. One of them came so close to her that he was probably heading for the same spot, so she applied Dominance to make him stop. He knelt behind some weeds, grinning with nervy excitement and almost close enough to touch.

Evidently conversation had been forbidden, because only the rain made any noise at all, and that was a fine show of discipline from men facing their first true battle. Saltaja tried to imagine the sound of thirteen hearts beating in unison, very fast. The orange in the men's palls showed that they belonged to Therek's host, the red that they were from the Fist's Own, Fellard's hunt. The next arrivals were eight men in orange-brown-blue, the incompetents who should have done a better job of guarding Fabia Celebre. Evidently they thought they were on punishment detail, for every one of them carried a shovel or pick and looked furious at this indignity. Fellard was smart enough when he chose to be. Few Werists would have lured their victims here so plausibly.

The ploy held only barely long enough. Not a pick had been swung before another flank in orange-red-blue came trotting in and the prisoners' anger flared into suspicion. Lastly came the huntleader himself, in his orange-red stripes. He slammed the door behind him. That seemed to be the order to attack, but the Heroes were above all fast, and everything happened instantly: the hidden dozen leaping up, the eight hurling down their spades, all thirty-three men dropping palls and battleforming. Thirty-three blond warbeasts in brass collars clashed in a savagery of claws and fangs and animal roars.

Saltaja had seen Werist battles before, but never at such close quarters. She had barely registered that the fight was about to begin before she was splattered by flying blood. A catlike thing fell writhing beside her, thrashing talons in its death throes, but two wolves leaped on top of it, going for its throat. Clawed feet blurred by her on the other side, something slammed into one of the tree trunks, releasing cataracts of spray. Everywhere men were screaming, dying, and bleeding torrents into the cold earth, sacrificed to Mother Xaran. Through the fingers she kept hooked in the soil, Saltaja felt a huge surge of joy and gratitude, like cold fire blazing up from the ground. The sheer power of it was stunning. Rarely had she known the presence of the Old One so strong.

Hero battles never lasted long, and this one was already over. One by one the cats and hounds and bears reverted to naked young men, panting and blood-soaked. Soon only four wounded warbeasts remained, howling in pain and struggling to heal themselves. One was identified as one of the condemned and dispatched; the other three were comforted and encouraged.

"Take no honors!" Fellard shouted—he had blood around his mouth and angry red scars across his chest. "They redeemed themselves by dying well."

The response was an angry growl of agreement. He could equally have said that his own men had not fought well, for their advantages of surprise and odds of three-to-one had not saved them from heavy losses. Although Saltaja heard no open expression of shame at the murder of friends, the screaming jubilation that normally followed a Werist battle was strangely absent. When one of the wounded had retroformed and the others been borne away on palls to be cared for in more pleasant surroundings, the last man to leave closed the door on fifteen corpses.

Also on Saltaja Hragsdor. The herb garden was a trampled, bloody ruin. Two of the fallen had died from broken necks and one had been brained against a wall, but most had bled to death or been disemboweled. Fifteen healthy young men had been murdered to the glory of the goddess of death, and She rejoiced in Her feast.

Drunk with her mistress's joy, Saltaja laughed aloud, scrabbling in gory dirt, smearing handfuls of the red muck on her breasts, licking blood from the corpses, kissing their wounds. Power blazed through her. With such blessing she could repair Therek and perhaps even make something useful out of Cutrath. She would certainly not have to put up with further trouble from those Celebrian hostage nuisances.

◆

Having donned her soaked and soiled clothes and scrubbed her face with wet grass, Saltaja left the herb garden just in time to miss a gang of Florengian slaves coming to remove the bodies. Still veiled, she stepped into a doorway and they went grumbling past her along the corridor without noticing. A hot bath was definitely required, and after so much excitement, she was hungry.

Alas, back at her rooms, she found her two bodyguards in high agitation. Flankleader Ern might be senior, but Brarag was louder.

"The satrap, my lady, dead!"

"Murdered!"

"Up on the hill—"

She paced the length of the chamber three times before she wrung a clear story out of them. In the fog and rain the ambushers had themselves been ambushed so effectively that only one survivor had come running back to report. His packleader had led out his other three flanks and found Therek dead beside the ruins of his chariot.

It took time for all the rocks to land. Saltaja collapsed on a chair as the impacts registered.

The implications were . . . were shattering.

Was this the start of the rebellion she feared? Even if it weren't, the deserters would certainly strike as soon as they heard there was no Hragson hostleader to rally the defense. The fire would spread. Far away in Kosord, Horold could not even hear of their brother's death for a thirty or two. Winter was almost upon them, closing the pass and bringing the seasonal wind reversal that made upstream travel on the Wrogg close to impossible. Horold could not bring up an army before spring or early summer. The rebellion would have sunk deep roots by then.

And Orlad *Celebre* was involved. That dewy, newly collared Werist she had met yesterday had not been the dutiful idealist he had pretended. He had been bait! For the second time that morning, Saltaja caught herself on the verge of hurling a curse, and only sudden caution stopped her. She must think this out before she wasted any of her good standing with the Mother.

Those accursed Celebrians! Paola Apicella, Fabia's wet nurse, had killed Karvak. Now Saltaja had lost a second brother because of those same iniquitous hostages. They were everywhere, like vermin. Benard Celebre had somehow released Fabia from her cell. Orlad Celebre had murdered Therek. Saltaja had always had doubts about the death of the eldest, Dantio. The Witnesses insisted he was dead, but she had never seen his body. Even the Old One, Who certainly knew the dead, had never given her a clear account of what had happened to him.

Meanwhile, who should she appoint as replacement hostleader?

"Fetch Huntleader Fellard," she told Brarag. "And who are the other . . . *What* did you just say?" She had not been listening. Why were they both looking so terrified?

"I said you must flee, my lady!" Ern shouted. "They're saying . . ." he gulped nervously. ". . . saying terrible things about you, my lady! They're talking about . . ." He peered over his shoulder at the closed door.

Saltaja could guess what *They* were talking about, whoever *They* were. They were talking about her being a chthonian, about safety in numbers, about coming to get her. They were talking about burial facedown in the cold earth. That was what they did to Chosen—no trial, no testimony by Witnesses of Mayn, no divine judgment from Speakers of Demern, no delay. All her life, almost, she'd had Werist brothers around to defend her, if not the terrible Hrag himself. She shivered—because she was frightened, not because she was smeared with mud and blood under rain-soaked clothes. All her great powers could not stop a mob.

"Fetch Huntleader Fellard! At once! At once!"

✦

He came so quickly that he must have been very close. His earlier nonchalance was gone, and it was clear that Fellard had not had an easy morning. He had cleaned himself, yet he still smelled of blood and his face twitched with discordant emotions—hatred for what she had made him do, shame that he had done it, the overwhelming compulsion to please her that she had imposed on him . . . and fear. Incredibly, Fellard was afraid of something. A man in command of five packs of Werists, four sixty, *afraid?*

She stood by the window, the light at her back. "I understand my brother has been slain?"

"Apparently so, my lady." He did not care.

"It will be necessary to appoint a replacement—subject to the bloodlord's confirmation in due course. Who are the Huntleaders in Therek's Host, apart from yourself?"

Fellard put his fists on his hips and stared at her with what seemed to be disbelief. "Karrthin of Tryfors Hunt, Heth up at Nardalborg. My lady."

"Only three?"

"That's all we have. The Cullavi Hunt and the Fiends were disbanded, and the men sent over the Edge. I believe Nardalborg Hunt is at full strength, but I'm down to two sixty, and Tryfors has three. That was before this morning, you understand." Shame blazed up in his face. "Several sixty in transit are billeted at Nardalborg, but those men are not truly under Heth's command."

Therek had whined about being under strength and she hadn't listened. The unknown deserter horde must outnumber the forces in Tryfors handily, and she had sacrificed fifteen men to the Mother. *Wait a moment!—*

"Did you say 'Heth'?"

"Heth Hethson, my lady."

"And who was his father, really?"

Fellard looked puzzled. "Gossip says the satrap, my lady."

Mother of Death! Heth was quite a common name. She had been thinking of Therek's missing bastard as a child, but she must have presumed wrong. Therek had been slyer than she thought. He would have given Nardalborg to his most trusted deputy. The family still controlled the pass!

And shaping worked best on blood relatives.

"Heth's work at Nardalborg is too important to interrupt. Bring me this Karrthin."

Fellard chewed his lip. "He's not here. I'm told he drove out to inspect his herds. His mistress, more likely. Runners are on the way to him."

"And what will happen when he returns?"

"It will be interesting." Now his fear made more sense.

So men of the Fist's Own Hunt, on her orders, had slaughtered men belonging to Tryfors Hunt, which outnumbered it handily. Revenge was a powerful motive in itself, but ambition always came first with the Heroes, and there was a promotion to be claimed. Small wonder Fellard was nervous, facing an unequal battle with his troops already made restive by the massacre.

"Karrthin will naturally accuse you of arranging my brother's death because you were here, and you will accuse him because he was not. Is there any evidence who did do it?" Not that evidence would matter.

"The witnesses reported discarded orange-green-red palls."

Yesterday Orlad Celebre had been wearing orange-green-red: orange for Therek and green for Nardalborg. So Heth was prime suspect in the murder of his father. Did Heth know who his father was? Fellard had known of Therek's plans for Orlad—had Heth? Had he deliberately set a countertrap? Or had it been a horrible misunderstanding?

She said, "At the moment you have effective control of the city. Under the circumstances, you had best arrange to have Huntleader Karrthin met on his return, preferably at a narrow place on the trail with poor visibility."

"You think his packleaders are so stupid they would stand aside and let me try?" Fellard's face twisted in torment. "My lady, there is a lynch mob brewing!"

She knew she was not disguising her own fear as well as should, so she flaunted it in poor-little-woman mode. "But you will protect me!"

That was an order. "I will try, my lady. They're talking of digging a grave in the herb garden and throwing you in it." Facedown, of course.

Rumors about her being a Chosen had seethed for years. Yesterday she had suggested the pain-of-death order; today she had made Fellard carry out the execution. Sometimes a mob got things right. She shuddered. Fear was a new and strange experience for her, although she had always found it amusing in others. She was surprised how much it muddled her thinking, like trying to run in deep mud.

"If I appoint Karrthin as the new—"

"Lady, anyone you appoint to anything will die very soon."

"Then explain how you will defend me."

"We must flee, my lady. I'll send men to seize all the boats they can, and we'll head off downstream before Karrthin returns."

No! That felt impossibly wrong. She would be fleeing inward, away from the Edge, abandoning Stralg. The rebels would close the pass, divide the Children of Hrag. "Let me think!" she barked, and began to pace. There was something not right about this. She needed to sleep on it to obtain the Old One's guidance. Impossible at the moment, of course.

The lynch mob was the most urgent, but blood would be shed over Therek's disputed succession, an army of deserters was waiting to pounce, and the Florengian war effort must be sustained somehow.

Therek, Orlad, Fellard, Karrthin, Hethson, Orlad, deserters, Nardalborg, Fabia, Orlad—

Rain! That was what was wrong. Heth could have planned Orlad's rescue, but not the satrap's death, which had been caused by the rain. Without rain, Therek would have watched the murder from the safety of his tower.

Heth commanded the largest hunt and Nardalborg controlled the road to the Edge. If she could Shape Heth, she might bring some order to the situation yet. Fellard was fidgeting, repeatedly shooting nervous glances at the door.

"You will escort me to Nardalborg," she said.

"But—" Fellard turned to the window. The rain had stopped. "There will be fresh snow up—"

"Don't argue. We leave at once."

He bowed hastily and turned.

"Wait! I need more guards on these rooms. And do you know a girl called Puss?"

"I think there's a kitchen maid by that name."

"Send her to me. And on your way out . . ." Saltaja looked with disgust at Guitha, who was staring at the walls again. "Take *that* to the herb garden. Make sure you're not observed. Say aloud, 'Beloved Mother Xaran, your servant Saltaja sends you this.' Then cut her throat."

Ivory pale, Fellard stared hard at her, seeming at a loss for words.

"You will obey me!"

"My . . . lady . . ." His voice failed him. He took Guitha by the wrist and led her out.

ſeven

DANTIO CELEBRE

huddled by himself next to the foremast, chin on knees, struggling against madness. Too much joy! He was crumbling under the sheer load of emotion, his and others. Holy Mayn granted Her Witnesses all knowledge, but the corban She required was that they must never use it. They must observe and never participate, excepting only that they might testify for Speakers of Demern in criminal trials. All this Dantio had sworn at his initiation. Yesterday he had broken his oath, and for that he must die.

Of the five divine senses the Goddess had given him, "sight" was the least of his problems. The fighting at Tryfors was out of his range now, and he could see nothing of importance, only a peaceful passing landscape of pasture and some orchards, fading back edgeward to the gloomy forests of the Hemlock Hills with the glint of the Ice beyond. Seaward he could see to a hazy height of land two or three menzils away. The Wrogg was already a wide river here, a braid of streams twined between shoals and bushy islands, so the crew was busy with sweeps, keeping the boat in the best current they could find. "Doldrum weather," they called this near the Edge, and it heralded the seasonal wind reversal. Upstream traffic had tied up to wait for a change. Poppy and the other Witnesses had fled Tryfors at dawn, heading downstream, carrying word of Witness Mist's catastrophic meddling.

When the news reached the Eldest at Bergashamm, she would anathematize him and he would die. That was the price of his victory. He had accepted it; it was a problem for another day. At the moment he was overwhelmed by the sheer concentrated emotion aboard *Free Spirit*. He could not ignore it, as Witnesses generally could, because he was personally involved, trapped in impossible conflicts, with fear, love, anger, and hate beating on him like hailstones. He had kicked a rock and started a landslide.

He was tormented by "feeling," which let him sense others' emotions. The riverfolk were arguing in their singsong Wroggian about the dangers of having so many Werists aboard. Nok was insisting he would cut loose in the night and leave the ruffians on the bank, although then he must forfeit the silver promised him and abandon all the boat's camping equipment. Others were arguing that these warriors were deserters and would fetch a handsome bounty if delivered to the rebel recruitment post at High Timber. It was typical sailor bickering, whose like Dantio had heard uncountable times on his travels, and in the end the crew would do nothing. Meanwhile he had to endure their emotional chorus. *(anger—greed—fear)*

The eight maligned young men sprawled amidships on and among the baggage were emitting an emotional storm sixty times stronger than the sailors' as they adjusted to the morning's stunning victory and their uncertain new status. *(triumph—fear—love—fear)* The seven's devotion to Orlad was intense, almost sexual, and sex baffled Dantio, an irrational hunger he would never share.

Other conflicts roiled among the passengers in the bow: Horth, Ingeld, and Guthlag all anxious to go home but fearing revenge from the Children of Hrag *(heartache—dread)*; Fabia cherishing impractical dreams of strolling over the Edge to Celebre and being acclaimed ruler. *(greed)* And Benard, sitting there with his arm around Ingeld? Often the lovers' emotions were a sexual firestorm that Dantio found repugnant, although he was happy to sense Benard so happy. *(lust—hunger—adore)* Moments later they would be children together *(covet—tease—make-believe)* or mother and son. *(guide—cherish—obey—protect)* There was still a rejected orphan hidden inside the hulking sculptor and the hereditary dynast of Kosord had endured two loveless political marriages. He was hiding misgivings about becoming a father; she had seen frightening auguries in the fire last night. It was small wonder they clung hard to each other.

And if feeling was not enough, Witnesses also had "hearing," which told them the recent history of things or people. Orlad and his Werists had fought a battle not long ago, and the carnage screamed at Dantio like trumpets in his ears. He knew which of the youths had actually killed, and how. He could, in a sense, *hear* the bloodstains they had washed away in the Stony.

Another of his divine senses badly overloaded was the one the Witnesses called "smell," which detected the inner nature of people or things. *Free Spirit* carried many complicated, confusing people. Most of the Werists were naturally violent bullies, a few were misfits forced into an unnatural mold. Orlad was one of those, but it would be folly to tell him so. Fabia was not naturally greedy. She had modeled herself on Horth, who absolutely reeked of avarice. Her basic instinct was to mother her brothers, gather them under her wings.

It was all too much! Dantio needed to hide under a Witness's veil. He needed a distaff and spindle to calm his thoughts and spin out the thread of events.

"Seer!"

Dantio looked around. "Lord?"

"Come here," Orlad said. "Mist, or Dantio, or whoever."

Dantio scrambled in among the baggage to join the Werists. Although he had about ten years on most of them, he felt like the new sapling in the forest. Orlad alone was a fair oak, although he was almost the smallest.

As Dantio settled in between Prok and Namberson, they scowled and wriggled aside to open space. Most of the eight were uncomfortable even looking at a eunuch, let alone touching one, although a couple of them were curious enough to make Dantio squirm. Earlier, when Orlad had shown off his manly brawn by carrying Dantio out to the boat, Dantio had learned that his brother was still a seasoner. "Taste" was the only one of the Witnesses' five blessings requiring physical contact, and most seers went through life never using it, for seasoning was very rare. Orlad had not lost his by killing a son of Hrag. Both Benard and Fabia still had theirs, so the doors to greatness stood open to at least three of the Celebres. Dantio could not judge if his own seasoning had survived his meddling. He might have done all he ever could to alter the flavor of the world.

Orlad said, "Tell us about this horde at High Timber."

"*It is known* that Hordeleader Arbanerik Kranson was a hostleader in Stralg's army on the Florengian Face and lost an arm in battle; that he returned over the Edge three years ago and began to gather a horde of his own, calling it New Dawn."

"How many men does he have?"

"I have never visited his camp. He must have more than twenty sixty." Saltaja had been quoting larger numbers than that and so had the Wisdom, the last time Dantio had been in Bergashamm.

The Werists exchanged glances. *(excitement—approval—relief)*

"And what is he going to do," Orlad demanded, "this Arbanerik? He is opposed to Stralg?" His own motivation was vehement. Fanatics who changed allegiance kept their zeal. From being the Fist's most dedicated supporter, Orlad had become his worst enemy. *(hate—hate—hate)*

"I cannot read thoughts, but I can witness, lord, that his detestation of the bloodlord is as great as yours."

"How—" Orlad began, then scowled as his men chuckled. "I see."

Waels, the one with the birthmark, said, "He bribes the riverfolk to recruit for him, to subvert new Werists on their way to Tryfors?"

"He does, lord."

"So who supplies the silver?" *(curiosity—suspicion)* "Who feeds New Dawn?"

Waels was the smartest of the eight and that insight made Dantio smile—to his own annoyance. He felt naked without his veil.

"Others who support his aims."

"The kings Stralg dispossessed? I thought they'd all died in failed revolutions years ago."

Dantio said, "He may have a few of those around, but would they have wealth?"

One by one, with Waels first, the Werists picked up the hint and looked to where Horth Wigson was now talking with Benard. One did not have to be a seer to know from Benard's animation and hand-waving that they were discussing art, but no extrinsic could have guessed that Horth's polite air of bemused interest belonged to one of the shrewdest collectors on the Face.

"Did my brother really rescue Fabia from the satrap's cells last night?" Orlad demanded. "How did he do that? An *artist*?"

"I don't know!" Dantio snapped with less humility than Werists expected from extrinsics. "My blessing does not allow me to spy on the actions of gods, and he must have had help from holy Anziel. Even those shoulders could not budge bronze bars." He had watched Benard go to the palace and return with Fabia, but he had not seen how the miracle had been done. He had asked her later, and she had not known. Benard had just mumbled about cult secrets. It was very annoying!

Orlad scowled. "How do you *think* he did it?"

How to explain art to a mob of Werist louts? "I *think*, my lords, that an artist sees the world as it is, but displays it as it should be. Benard sees a figure inside a block of marble and releases it so the rest of us can see the shape he saw."

"He didn't chisel a hole in the wall, though!"

"No. I am guessing, but I *think* he is such a superbly great artist that his goddess sometimes lets him just shape the world itself as it should be. Fabia said there were no bars on the window when Bena pulled her out. They were back there this morning."

The warriors did not like that suggestion of personal miracle-working.

"I do not trust Werists," old Nok warbled at the stern. "We must escape in the night and leave them."

"Urth vouches for them," said one of the women.

Fifteen years ago, at just about this point on the river, young hostage Dantio had decided that honor forbade him to learn Vigaelian, the language of his enemies. Instead he would learn the riverfolk tongue, so that one day soon he could escape and sail back up the river. By the time he reached Skjar, he had been almost fluent. His escape attempts had never prospered, and of course he now spoke Vigaelian like a native, but his Wroggian had proved very useful during his years as an itinerant Witness when he wanted to be Urth, the slave.

Orlad said, "If we go to High Timber, would we be allowed to leave?"

"Possibly not," Dantio admitted.

"We would have to swear fealty to this Arbanerik?" *(distrust)*

"That seems likely, lord."

"We might have to join in an attack on Nardalborg," said one of the others, provoking an eruption of emotion. *(hate—fear—disgust—outrage)* Many of them were Nardalborg bred; all must have friends there, and some would have family also.

Orlad was registering joy. "But if Stralg loses Nardalborg, he will be crippled."

"We might have to invade Florengia," Snerfrik said.

This comment brought a roar of denials and argument—

"We've gone over that, Hrothgat!"

"Arbanerik would be crazy to try it."

"He can shut Stralg out of Vigaelia and let the Mutineer finish him off."

"He'd still have to hold Nardalborg against Horold and Eide."

"Hold Tryfors, you mean! They'd starve him out of Nardalborg."

When the argument wound down, Orlad said, "Where is this High Timber, Dantio? And why are you smirking?"

Again Dantio wished he had a veil. "Because that's the first time you ever spoke my name, Orlad."

Scowl. "Back in Celebre I must have."

"No, you called me, 'Anto.'" Orlad had been a beautiful baby, but to say so now would be suicide. "I am under oath not to reveal the rebels' location." Dantio winced at the resulting surge of anger and suspicion. "Near the Wrogg, but not on it. We can probably arrive tomorrow."

"Anto?" sneered Snerfrik, the huge one. "Well, little Anto, suppose we decide we want to go over the Edge with Orlad and help him take power in this city of his—we have to get past Nardalborg?"

"No, lord. There is another pass, Varakats Pass." Dantio sensed a breathtaking rush of interest in his listeners. "Indeed, Varakats was originally the easier of the two. Nardalborg Pass has been much improved, as my lords are aware."

"So it would be possible?"

No, it was impossible, but Dantio would have to guide them to that conclusion gently. "The passes may stay open a short time yet. The problem would be on the other side. With respect, my lords, my skin and Orlad's are not so very much darker than yours, but our hair is black, while yours is mostly pale gold, and it is hair color that determines warbeast color, yes? The opposing forces in Florengia are like pieces on a game board, black and white. If Orlad sets foot over the edge, he'll be one of Cavotti's. All the rest of you will automatically be Stralg's, whether you like it or not."

They did not like it. *(fury—frustration)* They were young, immensely powerful, had recently won a stunning victory, and why shouldn't they see their hero elected doge?

"Where are we going now, today?" Orlad demanded. *(worry)*

"I must go to High Timber to inform the seers and Hordeleader Arbanerik that I have abrogated the compact between the Witnesses and the bloodlord. I will also pass on the news of your noble victory, of course."

"But if we come with you, we will be recruited?"

"Seers cannot prophesy, but I expect so."

"Or killed?"

Dantio sighed. "Detained, possibly. You will be hailed as great heroes, but the rebels must use extreme methods to keep their base secret."

The Heroes were displeased. *(anger—arrogance—belligerence)*

Waels put it into words. "Or we could stop you going there. We could make the boat sail on down the Wrogg."

"That is so, my lord," Dantio said humbly. "But to where? Who else will give you refuge from the bloodlord's wrath?"

They could hide their fear from his eyes, but not from his seer's feeling.

One of the sailors said, "The Werists are talking about High Timber. Will we camp at Milk tonight?"

"If this wind holds," Nok decreed. "The slave wants us to."

"Saltaja told Fabia you were dead," Orlad said suspiciously. "The seers must have told her."

Dantio shrugged. "No Witness ever said that. It wouldn't be true, would it?"

eight

ORLAD CELEBRE

was sorely perplexed. For years his course had been laid out for him. He had no experience making decisions, but now his choices would be matters of life and death. Seven men expected him to lead them somewhere, anywhere, and also see that they were clothed and regularly fed from now on. Yet he did not know the world outside Nardalborg or how to deal with people, even on the most trivial levels. He was repeatedly reminded of his ignorance as the day wore on. People kept shifting around the boat for variety, and sooner or later he found himself in private talks, one-on-one, with all his new-found siblings.

The dark-eyed, self-important sister he had suddenly acquired, for instance. He did not understand her at all.

"I will trade you," she told him pertly.

"Trade me for what?"

"I mean I need someone to escort me home to Celebre. There can be no finer protector than a Werist, yes? You defend me and in return I will teach you Florengian."

"You speak it?"

"Fluently."

It was maddening that he was the only one of the four who couldn't. "How? I mean who taught you?"

"My foster mother. I grew up speaking Florengian with her and Vigaelian with Horth. Now, do we have a deal? Language lessons for protection?"

"Why not ask Benard to protect you?"

She laughed, running hands through her black mane. "Benard couldn't guard a river from a duck, and Ingeld is in no state to tackle the Edge."

"What's wrong with her? She's no kitten, but she looks healthy."

"She is with child. I think she is. Even if she isn't, she'll have to go back to Kosord soon, and she has Benard by a ring through his nose."

That was obvious. "Your old man, then?"

"Horth is far too old."

"Dantio?"

"I love your dry sense of humor! No, it's up to you to escort me safely home, brother, and in return I will teach you the language. You were three years old, for gods's sakes! You must have known lots of words. You've just forgotten them."

Orlad ran a hand over his stubbled scalp. "I don't understand. If you want a Werist to take you back to Celebre, why didn't you agree to marry Cutrath Horoldson? He has the appeal of a dead toad, but he's bigger and stronger than I am. He also has an army guarding him and you'll have sex every night."

His sister pulled a face. "Brawn may impress other men, but not women. You cannot seriously expect Celebre to accept a Stralg nephew as doge? You really—"

He just did not understand her. "Why go at all, then? Horth is rich, I'm told. You're his heir, aren't you? Why don't you stay in Vigaelia and buy yourself whatever husband you fancy?"

"Duty!" She glared at him. "Don't Werists know that word? Our family has ruled Celebre for centuries. It is my duty to go back and see if I can help the people."

Did *help* mean *rule*? "My duty too?"

"That is what I have been trying to explain, Hero."

"If I decide to go, I'll let you come."

She pouted. "How much do you know about the pass?"

"I don't remember any more of our crossing than you do," he admitted. "But I do know Nardalborg Pass as far as the Fist's Leap. I helped rebuild the bridge there."

"Then you're hired," she said.

That was probably a joke.

◆

Fabia might be too devious ever to trust, but Orlad thought he could grow to like her, given time. Benard, on the other hand, was historically weird. Conversations with him made no sense at all.

"Orlad?" the big man said. "Or do I still have to call you 'my lord'?"

"I suppose not."

"Good. You used to call me Bena. That man with the birthmark?"

"Warrior Waels."

"Would he take his clothes off for me if I asked him nicely?"

"He had them off earlier."

"But I didn't get a good look at him."

Orlad mulled the query for a while, then asked, "I thought you were humping Ingeld, Bena?"

The artist promptly turned redder than Waels's chin. "That wasn't what I had in mind!"

"What did you have in mind, then?"

"Holy Cienu! He has such a wonderfully cute smile."

Orlad gave up. "It isn't worth the risk, Bena. Snerfrik plays that way sometimes, but if you suggest it to Waels he will disarticulate your skeleton."

Benard frowned in annoyance.

Orlad said, "Did you really get Fabia out of a Werist dungeon last night?"

"No. It wasn't a dungeon and I didn't do anything you could understand."

✦

If Benard was bizarre, the Witness was downright spooky.

"Fabia wants me to take her back to Celebre, so she can wear the crown," Orlad told him.

Dantio said, "Coronet."

"Whatever. We'll need permission from this Arbanerik oath-breaker?"

The seer gave him a wistful boy-girl smile. "I am sure the hordeleader will be happy to assist you. Anything that confounds Stralg is fine by him, and Cavotti can surely make good use of both of you, although perhaps not in ways you will like."

Orlad wondered if he was being mocked. "You will be coming with us?"

"I'd like to, but it's getting very late to start over the Edge. Every snow flurry will delay you. If you can't make it in a thirty you won't make it at all."

"Nothing ventured, nothing won."

"Spoken like a true Hero. Trouble is, I may not even have a thirty."

"Because you lied to Saltaja? You're serious about the curse thing?"

The seer stared at him with eyes as dark as his own. "It will take a thirty or longer for the news to reach Bergashamm, but as soon as Eldest LeAmber hears that I broke the compact, she will pronounce anathema on me. Then I die."

"Right away?"

"Within a few days."

"You drop dead, just like that?" Orlad asked skeptically. Holy Weru was known to strike men with thunderbolts, but not on request.

Dantio laughed oddly. "Dropping dead would be easy. You really don't want to know the details."

"Heroes don't shock easy."

"No? Well, then, *it is known* that when the Eldest pronounces anathema on a False Witness, the Goddess withdraws all the transgressor's senses. I will be struck blind and deaf, unable to taste, smell, or feel anything. I will soon go mad, of course, locked up alone inside my skull. I will scream a lot, but I won't hear my screams. I will thrash around and not know when I hurt myself. Eventually I will die of thirst, unable to know when to swallow."

"That's horrible!"

"This penalty keeps us from abusing the Lady's gifts to us. Absolute wisdom is absolute temptation."

"And you deliberately risked this punishment?"

"I invited it. It is not a risk. It is certain execution."

Orlad decided he had to believe this. Holy Weru took his Heroes' lives if they stayed in battleform too long at a time.

"You will die for revenge?"

"For justice, Orlando!" The eunuch's face no longer seemed weak or effeminate, in fact his smile was as terrible as Weru's. "For justice on all of them, the whole vile Hrag crew. For what they did to me and you and all of us and a million others. Given the same chance I had, would you find the price too high?"

"No, but I would rather die in battle."

"Who wouldn't? But families must hang together. If you will swear to kill me as soon as it happens, I will gladly come over Varakats Pass with you." After a moment he said, "Well? Will you?"

"Break your neck, you mean?" Orlad would certainly want someone to do that for him under those circumstances.

"That will do nicely. Or just choke me. I won't know the difference. Will you?"

"Yes. I promise."

"Spoken like a true brother. Thank you."

Weird.

✦

The old man in the brass collar, the one they addressed as a packleader although he wore civilian clothes—he was obviously an oath-breaker. So was

Orlad, of course, although his liege had broken faith with him first. They were all oath-breakers, even the mysterious Arbanerik. But old Guthlag did know some good stories. He joined the other Heroes amidships for a while and told them about the fall of Kosord and the coming of Stralg; and how Ingeld had been forced to marry Horold Hragson.

Yes, talking with other Werists was easier, and his flank-mates were best of all. Waels was Tryfors born, so the next time they were close, Orlad asked if he'd ever heard of High Timber. He knew Waels well enough by now to guess from his smile that something interesting was coming. *Cute,* Benard had called that smile; Waels would kill him if he knew.

"No, my lord. It doesn't sound like a real name. But the seer said it was near the Wrogg. Not on it, he said. Riverfolk can go there. And it's near Varakats Pass."

"So?"

"Then it can't be far away." Waels pointed Iceward, to the conical peak peering between the trees, Mount Varakats. "We'll come to Milk pretty soon, the first village down from Tryfors, where the river splits between lots of islands. The mouth of the Milky River is there. The Milky is a major tributary of the Wrogg—good hiding for boats! I'd guess that High Timber is a short way up the Milky."

"Well done!"

Waels looked pleased at the praise. "Your brother the seer has been holding out on you, my lord." His smile was even cuter when he explained what he meant by that.

◆

Sure enough, although the sun was still well above the hills, when *Free Spirit* entered the maze of brush-covered islands, the riverfolk steered into a minor channel and, after some argument, tied up to the island of their choice.

"Not like I'm trying to give anyone orders, flankleader," Guthlag said, "but boats have been known to untie knots in the night." He leered long yellow teeth.

"Appreciate the warning, packleader," Orlad said. "Hear that, Jungr? The boat stays here. You and Narg take first watch."

The rest of the passengers were jumping ashore, glad to stretch their legs. Orlad put Namberson in charge, telling him to see the palls spread on bushes to dry. Then he went exploring, as a leader should. The islands were less secure than they looked, for an agile man could wade, swim, or sometimes jump from one to another, and all of them were wooded more or less heavily with spindly trees and high shrubbery. Those would make good cover, but the ground was thick with twigs and dead leaves, so nobody should manage to sneak up on anyone in the night.

He found himself a small, sunny glade, where he could stretch out and do some serious thinking. Or perhaps he just needed to be alone, after his tumultuous day. He clasped his hands under his head and stared up at a cloudless sky through a weave of canes and bare branches. The girl had tried to lecture him about duty. Duty to whom? To what? He certainly owed no allegiance to a bloodlord whose deputy had tried to murder him. Nor any to Arbanerik. Did he owe anything to a father who had given him away? His oath was to Weru, of course, but he owed his life to his followers, his flank, and he certainly couldn't lead them over the Edge to be mistaken for Stralg men and slain in the upcoming massacre. If Cavotti eventually chased Stralg back into Vigaelia, then Orlad would be the odd one out on this side, liable to be killed on sight. Under Cavotti or Arbanerik, he would be just one more front-fang Werist. As the doge's son, he would be unique. He certainly couldn't let the eunuch outdo him in raw courage or the girl in duty. It was confusing.

A shift in the wind brought him a whiff of bungweed, and that provoked a rush of unhappy memory. As the only Florengian child around Nardalborg, he had always been appointed the Mutineer, so all the rest of the boys could be Stralg's Heroes, who would then hunt him down and beat him up. Bungweed grew in the moorland bogs where the best hiding places were, so its scent whispered of long hours of shivering in concealment, waiting for the inevitable ordeal to follow. He had taught them to do their hunting in groups, though. He had become very good at ambushing the strays.

Lost in reminiscence, he started when he heard footsteps rustling, then realized they must belong to a Werist. An extrinsic would make ten times as much noise. In a moment the celebrated Waels smile appeared above him, more diffident than usual.

"Am I intruding, lord?"

Orlad said, "No." He wasn't, surprisingly. "Sit down and talk, Hero."

Waels dropped, folding his legs on the way down. Orlad smiled—smiling was something he had to remember to do, not something that just happened. After that he was content just to contemplate the sky again.

Eventually Waels grew fidgety. "Talk about what, lord?"

"Anything. The battle? You were great! Or explain people to me. Yesterday I discovered I had family. Today I found friends, too. I've never had either before. Don't know how to handle them."

"You've been doing amazingly well . . . if you don't mind my saying so?"

"Have I? Life is complicated, suddenly." Why, for instance, was he pleased to have Waels as company?

"Um . . ." In another rustle of leaves, Waels stretched out beside him and leaned on an elbow. "It could be even more complicated." His eyes were bluer than the sky behind him.

"How?"

"Suppose you had a lover, too?"

That should have been a surprise, but it wasn't. Waels wasn't blushing or smirking, and Orlad was certain he wasn't, either. He remembered their intimate, face-to-face confrontation on King's Grass. His own reaction had puzzled him. He considered his memories of Musky, last night, which felt like a lifetime ago now. This was not that. Similar—some of the reactions were the same—but more complicated.

"I know even less about love. Nothing at all."

"Doesn't matter." Waels touched a finger to Orlad's collar and studied it as if he had never seen one before. "Remember the morning you chose me as your buddy? That was the happiest moment I'd known since my brother died."

"You had a brother? What happened to him?"

"Died in cadet training. He was a spare. I'd been watching you all through the testing, admiring you, and when you appointed me your buddy, I knew that you wouldn't let them do that to me. I almost wept, my lord."

Orlad mumbled, "Understandable." Never forgivable, though.

The smile that Benard admired flashed again, spoiled by the scarlet birthmark. "I've known ever since then . . . Orlad?"

Smile. "Waels."

After a while Orlad smiled again, this time without meaning to. "This morning, up on King's Grass—I have never been so glad to see anyone as I was when I found myself looking down at you." Lying on top of him, in fact. "I'd so nearly torn your gullet out! Glad I didn't."

"Me too." Another pause. "Just wanted you to know." The blue eyes held challenge. "How I feel about you, I mean. Sorry if I offend . . . *Orlad*."

"No," Orlad said. "You don't offend me, Waels. Not at all." He caught hold of Waels's collar and yanked him close. "How does one begin?"

Big smile. "Like this, I think . . ."

nine

FABIA CELEBRE

and her companions had camped on one of the Milk Islands on their way upriver. This one was more wooded, but the trees concealed a level, secluded campsite with a well of sweet water and a fire pit surrounded by tree-trunk benches. Luxury! She and Horth found a sunlit bench where they could sit while the riverfolk pitched tents, and were soon joined by Ingeld, Benard, and Guthlag. Later she saw Dantio playing slave, barefoot and stripped down to breeches, spreading the Werists' palls over bushes to dry. She persuaded him to come and sit beside her to tell the others what he had told her about the day Celebre fell, fifteen years ago.

"You are the only one of us who remembers it," she said.

"And I would happily forget."

Four Heroes gathered around and sprawled on the grass to listen, still wearing riverfolk castoffs, so that only their stubbled heads and the glint of sunlight on their collars showed their allegiance.

It was not a happy story. "Mama carried you into the farmhouse," Dantio finished. "That's the last I saw of you for years."

"What happened to her after that?"

"I don't know. We cannot see what happens beyond the Edge. I heard extrinsic reports that she was still alive earlier this year, caring for Father."

Fabia knew more than he did, then, but she was not going to admit that she had been shown a vision of her infant self being given to the wet nurse and her mother being abused by the bloodlord.

"I remember the parting," Benard said. "I remember screaming my head off, but almost nothing after that until I was living in Kosord."

Dantio described the harrowing journey over the Edge, and how the brothers had been forcibly separated. The Witness would have been a very handsome man, Fabia decided. Cropped ears and ragged haircut ruined his overall looks, of course, and she could see white whip scars on his back. But his face was lean and intense, shrewd-looking and refined by suffering.

Every now and again his attention would wander for a few moments. "Just riverfolk," he explained the second time it happened. "They like to overnight in these islands."

The biggest Werist growled, "You'll tell us if any Heroes arrive?"

"None so far, but I saw two boats of them going by a while ago, heading upstream. Their palls were purple and red, with either green or red flank stripes."

"Purple means Horold!" Ingeld said.

"'Fraid so. And red means Wrogg Hunt, which has all his best men. I doubt they're on their way to Florengia."

"Then he's close behind them!"

"Not necessarily so, my lady," old Guthlag said. "He never goes any nearer Saltaja than he must. He's sent his best man after you, Huntleader Loki Nargson. The satrap himself will have stayed home in Kosord to go duck hunting."

Ingeld looked unconvinced. Ducks would be safe from Horold until he had hunted down his wife.

A couple of the Werists sprang to their feet. "Must tell Orlad!"

Dantio squeaked "No!" in his treble, but so vehemently that they obeyed him. "They're gone upstream. They're no threat to us. Orlad's resting right now. We can call him if he's needed. His whole world has turned upside down, my lords. You went hunting at King's Grass. He was the prey! He needs some time to, um, make plans."

The two sat down again. "Can't hear anyone getting murdered, anyway," muttered the one they called Namberson. Fabia noticed fleeting grins and wondered what was funny.

"There was no huntleader in the boats I saw," Dantio said, "nor even a packleader, so that likely means there are more of them on the way. They may be days away, though. Some boats are faster than others; convoys get separated. And there are lots of islands here."

Fabia knew that most riverfolk would have made camp by now, so the chances of Horold arriving were fading. The sky was a blaze of red as the sun sank behind the wall of the world. Whatever its faults, Tryfors did have spectacular sunsets.

"Do you really know everything?" she asked.

"Within my range. The Wisdom knows everything, but it's back in the Ivory Cloisters."

"Tell us why Saltaja was so certain you were dead."

Dantio looked away. "It hurts to talk about it."

The riverfolk were laying out the evening meal on the ground near the

fire. The four Werists had begun showing interest. They would certainly insist on being served first.

Then Dantio said "O-oh! We have company!" and instantly had everyone's attention. "Three boats . . . more . . . They're going to make camp."

"Orlad!" The Werists all jumped up.

"Orlad's on his way back here," Dantio said. "There's no danger at the
moment. They're three bowshots downstream. I can't make out much detail."

"How many of them?" Snerfrik asked.

"A full hunt, maybe. Packleaders . . ." Dantio looked at Ingeld.

She sighed. "And Horold."

He nodded.

"How many in a full hunt?" Fabia asked, certain she would not like the
answer.

Many voices told her, "Four sixty."

The odds were impossible. The sailors had noticed the alarm and were
watching. Two more Werists emerged from the shrubbery—one fair, one
dark. They, too, saw that there was something amiss. They came at a run.
Everyone started telling Orlad about the danger.

"We should leave?" he asked his brother.

Surprisingly, Dantio laughed. "Leave? *Leave?* What sort of wimpy talk
is that? I thought you brave fellows *enjoyed* a good fight?"

Fabia winced, half-expecting to see her eldest brother massacred by the
youngest, and some of the Werists growled angrily at the slave's mockery.
Orlad did not, although he did not join in Dantio's laughter. "So it's true.
You've been holding out on us! You sent word to Arbanerik already?"

"Oh, well done, Little Brother! Did you work that out or did Hero
Waels?" Dantio's grin flickered back and forth between the two Werists.
"Mmm, thought so. Good man to have around, yes?"

Orlad scowled menacingly. "Get on with the story!"

Fabia wondered what was being hinted here. Seers could not read
thoughts, only emotions, but if Orlad and Waels had been plotting something together, Dantio probably knew what.

"Yes, lord. High Timber is a couple of menzils up the Milky. When we
camped in these islands three nights ago, Saltaja sent runners to Tryfors, but
I swam across to Milk and spoke with New Dawn's agent there. So, yes, a
tablet was baked that night to be sent upriver in the morning."

"Telling Arbanerik he could catch Saltaja if he attacked Tryfors?"

"Well done!" Dantio repeated. "He would have known she was coming, of course, because some of the men she lost on her journey passed through Milk a few days earlier. He should be ready by now. You've got the same idea I have. I don't know his plans, but my hope is that he moved his army into position yesterday. The battle may have started already."

"Not likely," Orlad said.

"Why not?" For once the Witness was surprised.

It was Orlad's turn to smirk. "Because nothing's happening here yet. Even a Werist host cannot just leap into battle on a moment's notice. It needs time to gather rations, make plans, issue orders. And think tactics! Arbanerik will certainly send a force down the Milky, to seize these islands and block off any escape by either Saltaja or Therek. There can't be many places where Werists can close off the Wrogg. Also, if he has enough men, he'll try to seize Nardalborg at the same time, and close that way out. So right now he's either still on the move or he's resting his men before hitting Tryfors, and perhaps Nardalborg, tonight." He turned his hard, dark stare on Waels. "But how many will he send here, you suppose? A full hunt? More?"

Waels murmured, "Depends how many men he thinks he can spare, lord."

"Can you see them, Witness?"

Dantio said, "No. But some of Horold's men went upriver earlier. If they discover trouble in Tryfors, they'll turn tail and come back to warn him. We certainly don't want him to escape back to Kosord, and we don't want him hitting Arbanerik from the rear."

Tactics and strategy were flying almost too fast for Fabia to follow, and some of the Werists seemed to be laboring also. She dared not look at Ingeld, whose son and husband were going to be on the wrong side of the coming battle. The riverfolk had noticed the discussion and were drifting closer, hoping to eavesdrop.

Dantio sewed it up. "It would be very tidy if the forces of virtue and vengeance could hit Satrap Horold here before he strikes camp in the morning. Please arrange that, Flankleader."

Orlad scowled. "If this New Dawn horde is on its way here, why don't we sail up the Milky to meet them?"

"The riverfolk won't try it in the dark. But you Heroes can see in the dark, can't you? And run in the dark? Not you, brother. We need you here, and your skin would take too much explaining."

Fabia expected Orlad to argue, but he just glanced over his men, who were all leering excitedly now.

"Namberson, Snerfrik, go and relieve Narg and Jungr at the boat. We'll bring you some chow shortly. Hrothgat, Prok, you're the best night runners. Witness, where do they go and what message do they deliver?"

Dantio said, "Cross to the east bank and head upstream to the junction, a bowshot or two. You'll know the Milky by its color. Follow it upstream until you're challenged—if you aren't, you'll reach High Timber itself before morning. The first password is 'At night the gods weep blood.' That should get you to the commander. Tell him 'Dark eyes see farther than you can hear.' That means you come from me."

Hrothgat repeated the passwords. "And then tell him to shift his ass down here soonest?"

"Even faster. Tell him about Therek being dead. If they can catch Horold here and Saltaja in Tryfors, then the Stralg tyranny is ended on this Face. Remember that Horold is camped at the downstream end of the islands. We're well upstream—we don't want any mistakes."

The eunuch was showing an astonishing ability to give orders to Werists, but now his eyes wandered, staring downstream again. "Even if he has seers with him . . ."

Orlad said, "What's wrong?"

Dantio took a moment to answer. "I suggest you recover your palls, even if they're not quite dry, then roll them up and hide them. Very few Witnesses have the range I do, but if Horold does have seers with him, he may ask them if there are other Werists nearby, and those stripes are distinctive. Otherwise, I still don't think we're in danger. They're lighting fires, unloading supplies. No one's scouting."

His voice had changed, though. Fabia noticed that Horth, who could smell an untruth two menzils away, was studying Dantio narrowly. So was Benard. The disconcerting thing about Benard was that he was not scatter-brained all the time. She still dared not look at Ingeld.

Orlad nodded. "Waels, see to it. Any more, er . . . advice, Witness?" He actually smiled, too! Fabia thought of a flower bud opening to the sun.

"Just to remind the commander that the satrap usually travels with seers."

"Hrothgat and Prok, proceed as instructed."

Cloth ripped. Leaving a trail of rags behind them, two *somethings* plunged into the shrubbery and were gone, leaving Fabia with a vague impression of huge golden beasts running on all fours.

For a moment nobody spoke. The war had begun. By morning a major battle might be raging through this campground, and other places too.

Fabia moved around the group to sit by Ingeld and offer what solace she could.

"Remember what Dantio said about Cutrath being more valuable as a hostage than a corpse. That's still true." It sounded weak even to her.

"But it will be much less true if my husband is killed tomorrow."

She was as rigid as a tree trunk. Benard, who already had one arm around her, added another and pulled her into a crushing embrace, muttering lover's comfort.

Fabia went back to sit by Horth. "Exciting enough for you, Father?"

He was frowning. "I have a strong impression of huge jaws closing while I am trapped between two of the teeth. And you beside me! I cannot imagine so many Werists spending a night here without scouring the islands in search of women to molest."

Dantio leaned over them. "I'm sentimental, I suppose, but I'd very much like to hold a little family dinner—just the four Celebres?"

Witness Mist was many things, Fabia thought, but *sentimental* was not the first adjective she would apply to him. *Devious, implacable,* and *ruthless* suited him better, and *mendacious* just at the moment. He was certainly lying, and making little effort to hide the fact, but Ingeld and Horth would humor his fancy, and the Werists would do whatever Orlad told them.

◆

As evening retreated into night, the four Florengians went off by themselves, carrying their meals to a far corner of the clearing. There they huddled in long grass, cross-legged and knee-to-knee. For a few moments they ate in silence.

"This is getting to be a habit," Fabia said flippantly. "These family conferences. Last night and again now."

Orlad said, "A lot has happened since last night. Do all families keep this busy?"

Dantio was not amused. He spoke with his mouth full. "I'm almost certain Horold does have a seer with him. I think only one, which is worrisome. She may not be able to see us, unless she's who I think she is, in which case she has an incredible range. She won't mention us unless he asks her, of course."

"Why worrisome?" Fabia asked.

"Because when he leaves Kosord, he usually orders all the Maynists in town to go with him. The Mother may not obey him exactly, but she would never send less than three."

"If he has a full hunt with him, or nearly," Orlad said, "why should he care who else is around?"

"He won't ask about you," Fabia said. "He'll ask about Ingeld. It's Ingeld he wants."

Dantio nodded, chewing mechanically, his mind elsewhere.

"Or me," Benard said.

"Wait until he hears about Orlad!" She grinned at the resulting glare from her Werist brother.

It folded into one of his so-rare smiles. "Let's tell him soon!"

"But in private."

"Right." The seer laid down his platter and licked his fingers. "Anyway, don't worry about Horold yet. His hunt are minding their own business and I can keep watch on them while I talk. I'll know if they start coming, and we'll have time to run. In the meantime . . . you have all been asking me why Saltaja was so sure I was dead."

"The Witnesses lied?" Benard asked.

"No! Maynists do not lie. We may mislead you, but we will never utter an actual untruth. I broke that rule in Tryfors, for which sin I will be expelled from the mystery and harshly punished. I'll tell you my story, but I want you to swear never to reveal it."

"I swear by my Lady of Art."

"And I by holy Weru."

Fabia could invoke any god she fancied—the Mother of Lies would not care about perjury. She briefly considered swearing by *Blood and birth; death and the cold earth* and decided it would be unkind. Dantio had already guessed her allegiance, but Benard would be horrified and frightened. Orlad might battleform and go for her.

"I swear by all I call holy."

Dantio gave no sign that he noticed the ambiguity. "I was present for some of this. Tranquility herself told me more, and the rest I learned from the Wisdom after I was initiated. That is very strange—seeing yourself from the outside. Some things I cannot speak of, even yet."

Fabia laid a hand on the cold earth for comfort. There was much more going on here than Dantio admitted. He had refused to tell this story until Horold arrived in the islands. He had Witnessed something that he was as yet unwilling to admit. Even Benard was looking suspicious.

Dantio continued, *"It is known . . ."*

ten

LONIA LARSDOR

was heading home one winter evening, returning from a visit to a nephew she had not seen in many years. With dusk fast fading to night and upper stories overhanging on either side, very little light reached down to the street, but this did not bother her. The bustling crowds respectfully avoided jostling soberly dressed matrons such as she.

As she was crossing High, one of the upstream islands of Skjar, she was surprised to observe a youth hurrying in her direction. He wore a long robe and a hat pulled down low on his head; he dangled a sack in one hand. Few boys his age wore anything more than a breechclout, and most would carry such a load draped over a shoulder. He had the black hair and dark skin of a Florengian, which were still extremely rare in Skjar. All those things were curious, but the most remarkable thing about Dantio Celebre was that he was scurrying along the crowded alleys of Sheeplick, almost halfway across the city from her. Very few seers in the cult could see as far as she could, but she had never in her life recognized anyone at such a distance. He must be extremely important! She recalled now that the Witnesses on duty in the palace a sixday ago had been able to locate this same stripling when he was well outside their normal range.

His efforts to appear inconspicuous were only making him seem furtive, and another escape attempt would put him in terrible danger. Although a Witness should never meddle in events, surely a word of caution to a child would not incur the wrath of holy Mayn.

She crossed the bridge to Milk Yellow and he to Limpet Bend.

As Sister Tranquility, Lonia was one of the most senior and most respected members of the Maynist cult, and commonly regarded as a possible future Eldest. She was a native of Skjar. She loved the horrible old city, crammed between its canyon walls, even when it was insufferably hot or unbelievably wet, which was almost all of the time. She knew every one of its sixty-sixty islands and innumerable bridges, all its splendid buildings and imaginative vice hovels—and, as a Witness, was even aware of what was going on inside, activities that varied from the frightful to the farcical.

She had recently been appointed Mother of the Skjar lodge, a posting that gave her enormous satisfaction, recognition of her long service to the cult. She could no longer deny her white hair, her wrinkled exterior, and sagging interior, but she still had all her faculties, thank the goddess. The thought of becoming Eldest one day held no appeal. Her new duties were quite challenge enough.

As she set foot on Snakeskin, Dantio began crossing to Egg.

Tranquility was one of the most outspoken critics of the infamous treaty the current Eldest had made with the bloodlord a decade ago. Although Stralg and his brothers were certainly Werists, Tranquility and her support-ers maintained that their sister Saltaja was a Chosen and probably their fa-ther Hrag had been one, also. It was written in the laws of holy Demern: *Thou shalt not covenant with the Evil One.* It was true that the Maynists had no proof to back up their suspicions, but if Stralg had accepted help from Xaran, the Eldest's compact with him was invalid and always had been.

Earlier that year, the bloodlord had lost two-thirds of his horde crossing to Florengia, but he himself had survived and was reputedly meeting almost no resistance there. His brothers and brother-in-law could not match him as warriors, but the Witnesses would prop them up and help them suppress any revolution before it became dangerous. Saltaja was going to continue ruling Vigaelia in Stralg's name for some time to come. Skjar was her capital, and when Mother Melody died, the Eldest had sent Tranquility to replace her, with orders to keep an eye on the Queen of Shadows. In other words, she was to prove her case or shut up. There never could be proof in the Maynist sense, because the Ancient One veiled Her followers from the sight of the All-Seeing, but there might be ordinary, extrinsic eyewitness evidence of chthonic actions.

Dantio crossed to Snakeskin.

Tranquility adjusted her route so that eventually they must meet face-to-face. She waited in a doorway as he dodged ever closer, then stepped out in his path.

"Dantio?"

He yelled in terror, dropped his burden, and fled off into the crowd. She watched him doubling around through alleys and courtyards until he went to ground under a wooden doorstep, wriggling down in the filth like a hu-man worm. She took the shortest route there and laid down his food sack at the end where his head was.

"Dantio," she said, "the seers in the palace see you. When you are missed, Satrap Eide will ask where you are and they will tell him. They don't want to, but they have no choice—they must answer any question a hostleader asks."

He was trying very hard to keep his weeping silent. He had opened some of the half-healed welts on his back.

"Then the lady Saltaja will have you flogged again. I heard her threaten you with double next time. I know she meant it."

"You're another!" said a muffled whimper.

"Yes, I'm a seer, but I'm not on duty just now. I am trying to help you. Why not come out and we'll talk about it?" This was outright meddling. She made a mental note to reprimand herself severely.

After a moment he began to wriggle. She reached down to help him and the moment their hands touched, she learned that he was a seasoner. She had never encountered seasoning before. It was so rare that the instructors at Bergashamm could only describe what they had been taught themselves. The only known living seasoners were Stralg Hragson and Saltaja Hragsdor. Now much more than compassion fueled Tranquility's interest in the hostage.

She walked Dantio back to the palace while explaining about the wicked compact and why he would always be caught if he tried to run away. She did not mention that she had been present in the palace during his last flogging, enduring his agony and terror.

"I promised my brothers," he said, over and over. "Benard and Orlando. I *promised* my brothers I would go back for them."

"Saltaja is a very evil woman, Dantio. She never makes an idle threat. If you continue to defy her, she will keep increasing the punishment until she kills you."

He said he believed, but she could feel the untruth. Racked by homesickness and imagined guilt, the boy was so desperate that he truly did not care.

That night she sent an urgent message to the Eldest, in Bergashamm.

✦

Tranquility was in the duty room the next day when Satrap Eide sent a summons for a Witness. Guessing the problem, she looked and saw Dantio already on the far side of Triangle. She sent Ember to answer the satrap's call because her range was not great, but Ember found the boy anyway. Her dismay when she had to report where he was moaned through the palace like eldritch funeral horns. Eide sent Werists to bring him back, and Saltaja sentenced him to a dozen lashes, four on each of three days.

Sick with horror, Tranquility fled to the Home of Holy Nula to consult the Senior Mercy, Mother Dolerian, who was a distant cousin of hers. Dolerian was tall and spare, but wore her years well. Her hair was silver, her face unlined, and not a wrinkle marred the fall of her brown robe. So great was the calm she projected that even to sit in the same room with her was to feel one's burdens grow lighter. She was sympathetic in this case, but not cooperative.

"Punishment is never pleasant, Lonia dear," she said. "But obviously the brat is stubborn and will have to learn his lesson."

"Lesson? You call that a lesson? She started with a leather belt, went on to a stick and now she's using the plaited leather whip they use on adult criminals! Wielded by a Werist! It cuts his flesh to the bone. And three separate floggings! Flogging unhealed cuts hurts *much* more. This is inhuman!"

Dolerian sighed and nodded. "But if the trollop finds out that we have been easing his suffering, Lonia, won't she simply increase the punishment?"

That was a very valid argument, for almost nothing happened within the palace without Saltaja hearing of it. Nulists were the kindest, most sympathetic of people by definition, but Mother Dolerian was stubborn, and nothing Tranquility could say would change her mind, not even angry sneers that she must be afraid of the Queen of Shadows. Defeated, Tranquility crawled back to a palace aflame—it seemed to her—with a boy's torment.

For a thirty after his ordeal on the whipping post, Dantio was kept in solitary confinement. Typically, when Saltaja eventually sent for him, it was in the middle of the night. As always she wore black, even to a black wimple and black cuffs covering her hands. She sat on a black throne in a black room lit by a single lamp, so almost nothing was visible except her corpse-pale, strangely elongated face. This treatment had been known to reduce strong men to gibbering terror, but the boy kept his poise. He was too young to see that such courage just increased his danger.

"If I release you, will you run away again?"

"Honored lady, I have learned my lesson. I swear I never will."

The seers eavesdropping in the duty room felt his duplicity like a slap in the face.

Saltaja was skeptical, too. "That is good," she said. "From now on you will report to the guard four times a day, and if you fail to do so just once, boy, I will have you gelded and your ears cropped. You believe me?"

The boy said, "I do believe you, honored lady," but his reservations were obvious to the watching seer. *First you will have to catch me.*

♦

The Eldest responded to Tranquility's report by agreeing that seasoning had never before been detected in one so young. She directed Tranquility to be *extremely diligent*, which meant that meddling would be overlooked, within reason. She also ordered that a Witness be assigned full-time to study this Dantio Celebre. Tranquility took on that job herself, and set out to win the boy's trust. She invited him repeatedly to her tiny home near the palace, talking endlessly with him and listening while he poured out his troubles. He had a great curiosity about Vigaelian history, customs, and—ominously—geography. He was clever, gentle-mannered, and impossibly stubborn.

Tranquility had written to the Kosord and Tryfors lodges, and early in the new year they replied with reports that Dantio's brothers were surviving or even thriving. She passed on this good news, of course. Amazingly, both had turned out to have seasoning also, and the entire Maynist cult was soon buzzing over this discovery. More hostages and slaves arrived from Florengia, so that dark skin became a less freakish sight in Skjar.

In the spring, Dantio broke his parole. Knowing more geography now, he went downstream to Ocean. By the time the hue and cry was raised, he had stowed away aboard a ship and the ship had weighed anchor. The satrap had to send another in pursuit of it.

Tranquility hurried to the sanctuary of Sinura on Broom Creek. There was a minor sanctuary within the palace, but Broom Creek was the Healers' headquarters and the senior Healer in Skjar was Ferganfar Narson.

She had known Ferganfar since childhood, when they had been neighbors in the potters' quarter. As a youth he had been godlike, a handsome giant, and if he had shown any romantic interest in little Lonia next door, holy Mayn would have had to have gotten by without Sister Tranquility. From those humble origins he had risen far. Now he dressed in silk and dwelt amid fine rugs and amberwood furniture, looking out on vistas of cataracts and lily ponds. The icon of his goddess on the wall was inlaid with jade and seashell. Physically he had not fared so well—stooped and almost crippled, a shrunken remnant of what he had been. Life had written suffering on his face as scribes inscribed clay

They talked briefly of old times and longer of newer, harder times. They discussed the possibility that the Queen of Shadows was a Chosen. Tranquility explained why she had come.

His first reaction was incredulity. "But the boy is a hostage, you say? No one treats hostages like that!" He spoke in painful whispers.

"Saltaja will. Who will ever carry word back to his father and what could he do about it if he knew? I overheard her threats and I swear that she meant them."

"But, Witness . . ." The old man shook his head in dismay, and his jowls flapped. "You know that our goddess will never restore missing parts. If the boy is mutilated, we could halt the bleeding and heal the wounds, at some cost to ourselves, but we can never replace what has been lost."

He gestured with a cruelly misshapen hand. Tranquility had heard about that hand many times, how a block of marble had fallen on a young stonemason, crippling him when his wife was great with their first child and leaving them facing starvation. Such a patient could pay no fee, but Fergan-far had entreated Sinura for him anyway. The goddess had restored the stonemason's hand, but the Healer had never recovered all the function in his. There were many similar stories about him.

"Your sympathy does you great credit," he said, "and I agree the woman is evil personified. If she really goes so far as castration . . . the Healer would have to be male, and even the elderly hesitate to treat such injuries."

"The boy is terminally stupid," she admitted. "His courage is rank in-sanity. What are the chances that he will die of shock and loss of blood?"

"That is quite likely. The slavers do not bring their victims to us to save, because the gifts we should require of them in return would be worth far more than the slave. Even if he survives the first day or two, the wound may well become poisoned."

She told him about seasoning.

He was shocked, but he believed her. "You think this child is destined to overthrow the bloodlord's tyranny?"

"You know we never prophesy. Seasoning is only a warning that one day the world may either curse or celebrate his name—provided he lives long enough. Knowing Dantio as I do, I am convinced his fame will not be noto-riety like that woman's."

The Healer took a while to think. Then he heaved himself painfully to his feet. "We must see that he survives the ordeal. Where is he now?"

✦

Dantio was delivered bound to the palace and taken before Saltaja, who struck him, hurling him to the floor. "Fool!" she said. "You were warned. You know I never make a vain threat, so you've forced me to do this. It is your own fault. Take him away."

He was handed over to the waiting slavers. They marched him out and led him on a tether down to Blackstaur, where slavers' barns were confined between dyers', tanners', abattoirs, and other malodorous premises.

Tranquility watched it all from the nearest Sinurist sanctuary, which was on Handily, two islands away. Although not as grand as the Broom Creek temple where the rich went for treatment, it was still a very splendid timbered hall, overshadowing the stores and tenements around it. It even had a small park of its own, and there she sat on a bench, feeling very untranquil indeed.

Her sight was barred from the interior of the consecrated building, but years earlier, in Nuthervale, she had broken an ankle and experienced Sinurist ritual firsthand. The Healer had bound her injured limb to his own healthy one; then he and his helpers had chanted prayers to the goddess. Tranquility had walked away with barely a limp, while the Sinurist was carried off on a litter. He had recovered in a couple of days, much faster than his patient would have done without help, but the Healers' mystery demanded true dedication.

Tranquility saw Dantio being carried screaming into the squalid little courtyard where the slavers did their butchery. She watched two men lash him to a grating and a third pump bellows at the furnace. While the monsters were waiting for their implements to become hot enough, a team of three white-clad stretcher bearers arrived, announcing that they had been sent to make sure the hostage survived the operation. The sanctuary had sent them, but the slavers assumed that the palace was keeping an eye on its property.

A brown-robed woman sat down beside Tranquility and clasped her wrist with a cool hand. "Try not to worry, honored lady. You will only give the Healers more work to do."

She was a Mercy. Nulists hung around the Healers' sanctuaries, providing their goddess's comfort to those in distress, and her influence calmed Tranquility's pounding heart. Because she was not dressed as a Witness, the Mercy misunderstood Tranquility's presence there and urged her to talk about her husband? son? daughter? and what malady had brought him? her? to the temple of healing? Tranquility's resisted the babble of questions, but was sufficiently distracted that she missed seeing Dantio actually being mutilated. When she forced her sight back to Blackstaur, he had already gone.

The healers—all large and powerful men—had not even bothered to put him on their stretcher. Instead, the largest was running flat out, carrying Dantio wrapped in a sheet. The other two were racing ahead, ringing handbells and clearing a path through the crowds by brute force when necessary. Tranquility shook off the Mercy's grip and leaped to her feet. Before she reached the sanctuary door, a novice opened it and Ferganfar came limping out, began to say something, and saw the answer already in her face.

"Where?"

"Just crossing Nig."

"They will be here very soon then. We are ready."

Shouts and bell clamor announced the healers' approach, and in moments they came racing along the street. The sanctuary door swung open to receive them, but as they plunged into the dimness within and vanished from Tranquility's sight, she began to weep.

The Mercy embraced her. "You must not give up hope, dear. The goddess is very merciful. The powers of Her Healers are boundless."

But they did not include resurrection. Not only Tranquility—every Witness in Skjar had seen that the seasoner was not breathing, that the bloodstained bundle the big man had brought contained a lifeless corpse. Tranquility sobbed for a long time, despite the Mercy's continuing comfort. When, at last, an elderly Healer came looking for her, it was not Ferganfar. He thanked the Nulist and led the Witness inside.

He took her through to one of the treatment rooms, and there, sitting on a bloodstained bed, clutching a steaming beaker in both hands, sat a very pale and subdued, brown-skinned boy. He had no tops to his ears. He stared up at her with wide dark eyes.

"But he was dead!" she whispered.

"Perhaps not quite dead," the Healer said softly. "Or perhaps She made an exception for Her dearly loved servant, Ferganfar."

Tranquility looked up at him in alarm. "How is . . . ?"

The man shook his head. "We urged him not to make the attempt. We all insisted it was too late. He knew. As I said, holy Sinura loved him very dearly, or She would not have granted his prayers in this instance."

Or else the gods loved Dantio even more.

✦

Later the chief slaver came looking for the palace's boy and was told he had been dead when he arrived. Justifiably apprehensive, the man went and reported to Saltaja, who ordered him flogged to the doorknocker of death for carelessness. She made Eide question a Witness, who confirmed what the slaver had said: Dantio had died.

By that time he and Tranquility were at sea.

No one pursued them or came looking for them. The voyage to Bergashamm never took less than two sixdays and she spun it out to two thirties, dallying at sun-dried fishing ports around the coast. Dantio soon recovered from his ordeal. With the resilience and ignorance of youth, he was more annoyed by the mutilation of his ears than worried over what else he had lost.

At first Tranquility worried that the Eldest would anathematize her for interfering, but eventually she realized that the gods had saved Dantio by a miracle and mortals must not argue with gods. Besides, the cult had reported that the boy had died, so how could it change its story without denying its own claim of infallibility? As long as Saltaja did not notice the difference between "died" and "is dead," she should nevermore be a problem for Dantio.

Unless he chose to become a problem for her, of course. Children do grow up.

◆

What was Tranquility to do with this ward she had so unexpectedly inherited? Try to smuggle him home over the Edge? See him apprenticed to some trade? Dantio answered that question for her one night.

The ship had been beached, as usual. Crew and passengers were asleep ashore under the sky, in a world deliciously cool after the daytime heat, scented by teasing breaths of salty sea-wind, lulled by the splash of waves. She wondered what had wakened her—the lurid phantasms of a dreaming sailor? Not predatory marauders approaching . . . No, the source was right beside her, staring up at the stars. Dantio was registering true happiness for the first time since she met him.

"Go to sleep," she whispered.

(surprise—joy) He grinned. "You know everything!"

"Only the goddess knows everything. Seers just know more than most people."

(worry) "My mama won't mind that I love you too, will she?"

"Of course not. And my goddess does not mind that I love you."

Tranquility felt the boy's adoration whenever he looked at her, but until then she had not realized how much she returned it. Few Witnesses ever managed enough self-deception to fall in love. Bergashamm was full of aging spinsters, with many sixty more of them scattered in retirement all over the Face.

"You will send me home, won't you?" *(anxiety, homesickness)*

Tranquility rolled over to face him, resigned to a serious discussion. The sailors snored on. Would the Eldest tolerate even more meddling than she had done already? "That may be possible, dear, but it will not be easy. I'm sure I cannot rescue your brothers. If we try to do that, we will put them in great danger. And you, too. And me."

(distress—resentment) "Why? I will not go without Benard and Orlando!"

It seemed to take half the night to convince him, but he accepted the situation at last. "Then teach me!" he said, frowning at the stars.

"Teach you what?"

"How to know the things you know."

His motivation was suspect, but she had long recognized his bright, questing mind. "I can try," she said.

"You can, but will you?"

She chuckled. "I will try, when we get to Bergashamm."

He was too young to be even a postulant, but he became a sort of mascot—and also a teaching aid in the lectures on seasoning. Later that year the Maynists located the Celebre daughter, who had vanished with her wet nurse during the sack of Jat-Nogul, and now turned up in Skjar as putative daughter of Master Merchant Horth. Some furtive prying soon confirmed that she was another seasoner. Four of them!

✦

Rather than return to Skjar, Tranquility accepted a roaming commission to investigate other Florengian hostages scattered around the Face. She established that most were being well treated, and that none had seasoning. Accompanying her on her travels, Dantio saw his brothers from afar and was comforted. He learned a great deal about Vigaelia, the way the Werists were ruling it, and the subtle art of snooping without being noticed. When he was sixteen, they returned to Bergashamm, and he was accepted as a novice, although he was still younger than all other novices and even most postulants.

He put up with the discipline for four sixdays. Then he came calling on Tranquility one evening and brazenly asked her to sponsor him for initiation. He was tall, slender, with the perpetual restlessness of an adolescent, but he was still a child. In one sense he always would be.

"You are insane!" she said. "At your age? The elders will never approve you. They would laugh me to shame if I put you forward."

He had a confidence far beyond his years, and he grinned at her doubts. "They won't, you know! Half of them are convinced that the goddess has chosen me to avenge the harm Stralg did to Her cult in the year I was born. The other half can't stand the sight of me and will rely on the All-Knowing to throw me out on my ear, what's left of it."

Holy Mayn rejected about one candidate in five. The discards were sent away, and it was known that few of them ever prospered afterward—how could they, when She did not want them and they had forsworn all other gods? But Dantio's confidence was as solid as rock, and Tranquility could not fault his logic. Ordinary rules did not apply to him.

The council agreed to consider his application, and even that was a surprise.

By tradition, examinations were held in the crypt below the chapel, in pitch darkness. Tranquility led him in, whispering a warning to watch his step, for a thick layer of black sand covered the floor. When they reached the center, she told him to kneel. The Eldest sat on a tall stool in the center like a mummified monkey, her twisted fingers clutching her staff. Eight elders stood on either side of her, in a crescent facing the applicant.

Darkness and silence. Tranquility had never known a mere initiation to raise such emotions. The chapel seemed to shake with them, and her own doubts rang as loud as any. She expected a refusal. He was the youngest novice ever put forward and the first Florengian to apply to the Vigaelian mystery, but his age and color barely mattered. Everyone knew that he was a brilliant student. What concerned the examiners was his history, and that rubbed salt into the gaping wound dividing the cult. Half the elders wanted to abrogate the Werist compact; the rest supported the Eldest, who was adamant that it must be preserved. The old crone did not like it, though, and she played fair in her appointments to the council. It was as evenly divided as the mystery itself.

She began the ritual without preliminaries. "Who seeks the goddess?"

"Honored mother, I bring Candidate Mist."

Hearing his new name for the first time, Dantio grinned in the darkness, unaware of the others' smiles and frowns. His own, joking, suggestion had been Garlic, but the choice was Tranquility's and she thought she had chosen well. He could pass for man or woman; he was fluent in Florengian, Vigaelian, and Wroggian. His dark complexion and cropped ears made him extremely visible, yet slaves were so unimportant that few people noticed him.

"Surely," whined the bitter voice of old Agate, "a Witness with seasoning is a contradiction of all the cult stands for?" She had been primed to ask this as the first question, to resolve the matter right away.

"Flavor is merely a potential," Tranquility said. "It may never be expressed in action, or it may act entirely by accident, with no intent on his part. The All-Knowing may even accept him and negate his seasoning—we have no precedents to judge by."

(doubt—relief—anger)

Also *fear*, because a seasoner Witness might change the flavor of the cult itself. The Eldest was already very old, so Mist-Dantio was too young to be her direct successor, but a generation after that . . . ? Aging childless spinsters do not accept change easily.

"How can he possibly be impartial?" Vihuela demanded. "After what that woman did to him? Can he take the oaths without reservation?"

Not completely. Tranquility knew that from their rehearsals, and her own emotional reaction to the question was an instant answer—there were no secrets in Bergashamm. "I have known candidates be less certain," she said. "If the goddess is not satisfied, She will not accept him." That argument sounded weak even to her.

Limpid agreed, though. "If holy Mayn cannot accept a seasoner into Her mystery, She will refuse him."

Carillon said, "Irresponsible thinking! We are supposed to stand behind the candidates we submit. Any time the All-Knowing refuses one of our candidates, we are disgraced!"

There were more questions about sincerity, integrity, dedication, until Ember asked, "It is customary for new-sworn Witnesses to be posted to obscure, faraway places. Is he reconciled to spending the rest of his youth at the back of beyond?"

(alarm) from Dantio.

"I have not asked him that," Tranquility admitted, "and the matter seems to trouble him. May the candidate speak to the question?"

(shock—disapproval—indignation) were gradually overruled by (approval) as this outrageous suggestion was considered. The Eldest nodded her little skull head.

Tranquility said, "Speak."

"Honored Witnesses," Dantio said softly (resignation), "it is my intention, if accepted, to apply for posting to Zorthvarn."

(bewilderment) flowed into (amusement) . . .

"The novice shames us," Ember said. "Where is Zorthvarn and why does he care?"

"Honored Witnesses, it is a very small settlement in the south. It is rumored to have been the birthplace of Hrag Hragson, the Fist's father, although I am told that this is not recorded in the Wisdom. At Zorthvarn I would hope to discover who Hrag was, where he came from, and where he has gone, for his death is no more recorded than his life."

Implications rolled like thunder through the crypt. *(amazement—distaste—anger—jubilation)* The split yawned open.

Outspoken Carillon said, "We should know these things!"

Thou shalt not compact with the Evil One.

"Sisters," mumbled Starfire, who was almost as shriveled as the Eldest. "You see how this candidate might do his duty to the goddess as She requires and yet change the flavor of the world? What can he tell us of the death of the saintly Healer Ferganfar?"

Dantio's silent scream of agony filled the crypt, making every elder cringe. He was no longer the callow child who had failed to appreciate the old man's sacrifice. Tranquility squeezed his shoulder in warning.

"That question is improper!" The Eldest never spoke at this stage of an initiation, but rules were for breaking, she often said.

"But it is most relevant!" Starfire said. "If it was nothing else, that event was a message to us."

(shock—outrage—jubilation)

Painfully, leaning on her cane, Starfire plodded forward through the sand to stand with Tranquility. Soon others followed. The silent movement continued until a clear majority had lined up behind the candidate. Would the goddess accept the verdict?

When the movement ceased, the Eldest whispered, "The candidate may offer allegiance. Is he ready?"

Unnecessarily, Dantio said, "He is," in a shaky voice.

This was the moment of truth, holy Mayn's truth. This was when the goddess would either grant him the powers of a Witness or refuse them. The elders would all know Her decision from his reaction, and if he had been refused they would banish him from the lodge instantly and forever.

The Eldest administered the oath, Mist repeating the words after her. When he pronounced the final 'Amen,' his amazement exploded through the crypt like a thunderbolt. He cried out in joy . . . blinked a couple of times . . . smiled widely . . . then leapt to his feet and turned to bow to his supporters.

Part III

✦

Dark Night
and
Darker Dawn

✦

eleven

FABIA CELEBRE

could hear the hunter's breath behind her. Not literally. She was still sitting in the grass with her three brothers, but with her fingertips dug into the cold earth she could sense the Old One sending her warnings. She knew now why Dantio had told her all this. He was clever, her eldest brother, and she was being hunted.

She said, "And what did you discover at Zorthvarn?"

On other islands, riverfolk were singing. They would not be doing that if they knew how many Heroes were camped nearby, or that a horde might be on its way.

"Not much." Dantio had talked himself hoarse. "I found some old-timers who remembered an evil man called Hrag. He was suspected of being a Chosen, so the village drove him out, him and his daughter. No one remembered her name, or knew where they went." Even in the darkness, his bitterness showed sometimes, in a quaver of voice, a tightness. His prayer that the gods would let him watch Saltaja die seemed very reasonable now.

The night was windless, very quiet. Voices murmuring around the campfires at the far end of the clearing seemed scarcely louder than the whine of insects and the occasional plop of a fish jumping.

"No wife? Hrag had no woman?"

"No."

"And what happened to Hrag in the end?"

"Nobody knows. He may still be around."

"Is Saltaja the satraps' sister or their mother?" rumbled Benard, a human boulder in the darkness.

Dantio said, "Possibly both. I heard old gossip that it was indications of another child about to appear that resulted in their banishment."

That felt right to Fabia. Incest was horrible enough to make sense in this grim, chthonic situation.

Ever wary, Orlad said, "And why have you been entertaining us with all this?" He could sense the prowler too.

Ever wary, Orlad said, "And why have you been entertaining us with all this?" He could sense the prowler too.

"I'll tell you why," Fabia said. "Because Horold is camped downstream and the seer he has with him is Tranquility, or Dantio thinks she is."

"It is known," Dantio said sadly. "It is she. She did not come with him willingly, for she is the only Witness there and she is not veiled. She stayed in the boat tonight, did not go ashore."

"She must be chained, then." Benard was plodding his way through the mental thicket. "She was at Kosord when you left?"

"Yes."

"Horold has a vile temper. If he forced her—struck her, say—the others would know, and flee, yes? Without their veils they would just be women of the palace. Hmm! And he couldn't round them up in advance, because they would know his men were coming? So he just got one."

Orlad made a scoffing noise. "Our Hand is a tactical genius. My darling Fabia, the family seer is hinting that we owe him a good turn or two. He wants us to go and rescue the old bag-head."

The riverfolk finished their song. Another started farther away and was picked up by closer camps in unison.

Dantio said, "I must try to rescue her, yes. I have no choice, brother. Even a half-man like me cannot deny the sort of debt I owe Tranquility. How can I leave her there when I expect Arbanerik's men to attack before dawn? Abandon her to die in the massacre? If any of you will help me, I will be very grateful. I do not deny that the attempt will be dangerous."

"Suicidal you mean," Benard growled. "I decline. I understand your debt, brother, but I have a lover and unborn child to consider. When Horold finds out your seer is gone, he will overrun the islands looking for her. Then he will find Ingeld."

"And find you," Orlad said. "Ah, the wages of adultery! And the wages of sympathy. Let's hear the plan first and collapse in mirth after."

Paradoxically, Dantio said "Oh, you wonderful, adorable brother!" as if the Werist had already promised to help. He must be reading the inside of Orlad's head. "Their camp's spread over three islands. The boats are beached, eighteen or twenty of them. Tranquility's in one near the middle, with two Werist guards. I have to assume they'll be asleep. It's a dark night, isn't it? We slip aboard, cut two throats. Launch the boat, then push it *up*-stream—the channels are shallow enough to walk in. When it's missed, Horold will assume it's drifted downstream."

Benard snorted. "No, he won't. He looks like a pig, he stinks like a pig, but he thinks a little better than your average hog. He'll see where you pushed the boat off. Riverfolk pull boats high enough that they *don't* just float away."

"Well said, Bena!" Orlad said. "Our seer is talking wind. You prayed Fabia out of the dungeon last night. Can't you pray one old woman out of a camp full of Werists tonight?"

"Don't blaspheme."

"You avoid the question?"

"No. The answer is no. I can't."

The Werist still mocked. "Dear Dantio, even our rock-basher brother can see that you are gibbering mad. How many sentries overall? You really think that the two guarding the prisoner will be asleep? Then you don't know Heroes. You really think you can cut their throats without making any noise? The best two cuts out of three? Or push a boat off unnoticed and unheard? You're *not* that stupid! What god do you pray to, Fabia?"

Benard grunted, "Huh?"

"What do you mean?" Fabia said, more shrilly than she intended.

"It wasn't Dantio's *brains* they cut off," Orlad said. "He needs a couple of strong-arm men. That explains us, but why are you here? Why include you in this conspiracy? Answer!"

She had distrusted the eldest brother and underestimated the youngest. He was more than just brute carnivore. She felt a chill of panic. "No! No, I won't!"

"Thank you for that answer." Orlad sounded very smug. "Bena can't help. He's got his doxy to comfort and he makes more noise than dueling thunderstorms. I'll go with Dantio if you'll come too."

"Me?" Her voice cracked.

"I might even vote for you as dogaressa."

Dantio laughed.

Benard had his penetrating artist's gaze locked on her. "Are you?"

"If I were, would I tell you?"

"You just did," Orlad said. "How powerful are you? Can you curse? How's your evil eye?"

"Stop it!" She scrambled to her feet and looked down at her three brothers, six eyes in the gloom. "You mustn't say such horrible things about me! People might believe them."

"You could be a big help to us. Or not."

"Leave her alone," Dantio said. "Saltaja stinks of evil. Fabia doesn't."

"Not yet, you mean?" Benard muttered.

She fought for calm. Orlad was threatening to denounce her. She had escaped from Satrap Therek's dungeon and that would be enough evidence to rouse a Vigaelian mob against a woman with black hair and brown skin.

She said, "I'll sleep on it. If any of you do decide to commit suicide, I hope you'll wait until just before dawn, so the rest of us can escape before the satrap gets here. Just before the rebels arrive would be even better."

Trembling, she stalked away. She had not handled that well. If she was to serve the Mother of Lies, she must learn to lie better.

twelve

SALTAJA HRAGSDOR

stood in the great cavern and breathed deeply of its ancient essence, the majesty of sanctified death, the power that vanquished all others: love, hate, ambition, hope. This cave was the temple of the Dark One in Skjar and she knew it well—the altar stone, the inscribed image above it that was older than any of the upper gods, the bottomless chasm that Hrag called the Mother's Bowels. Many had gone to meet the Old One down there with the help of Saltaja Hragsdor.

The vision was as sharp as a skull's smile. The offering she had made in the herb garden had been rewarded with increased power and favor. So why had she been brought here now? And when was now? Night, she thought, and yet there was some light filtering down from the chimneys. Ah, that was lightning! A great storm, and with the instant certainty of dreams she knew it was the tempest that struck the city just before she left, back in the spring. There was the proof she had wanted—the girl, kneeling before the altar with her arms raised. Naked, naturally, and about to give blood.

Blood fell from her hand like drops of fire . . .

Could this be her actual dedication, that very day? A seer had confirmed that Fabia had made her dedicatory oaths then, but Xaran might have blinded the seer as to which god had received them. Alone? Well, why not? Formal rituals were games the little gods played, but the Mother scorned them. She could accept a solitary dedication if She wanted. No doubt the Apicella woman had instructed the child . . . Was that to be all? A minor self-inflicted scratch?

Ah, there was another person present, a man emerging from the shadows, gross, repulsive, shining evil, tumescent. Punar? Pukar? Some name like that.

One of Her minor servants around Skjar. Saltaja hugged herself, savoring the game. Celebre tried to flee, he caught her, dragged her struggling to the altar. Watching this unequal contest took Saltaja back to her own youth, her own ded-ication in the hills above Zorthvarn. Hrag had not told her what he planned or why she must accompany him down into the odious crypt. Once in there, he had stripped her without a word, ignoring her pleas and screams. He had thrown her down on the altar and repeatedly forced her. With terror, disbelief, and pain he had introduced her to the worship of the Mother. As one began Her worship, so one continued it, he said later, and Saltaja had come to understand what a fine and fitting initiation it had been. She owed her ruthlessness to it. The Ancient One had given them Therek as a reward for that first dramatic coupling.

But this might not be the same. The girl was using Dominance. Clumsily, but effectively enough. How had she learned that? From Paola Apicella, no doubt. That was amusing, too, watching that whale of a man retreating, lust turning to terror, the sudden detumescence. Not quite enough power, though. The girl had used up her pathetic smear of blood. He was rallying. Rape it would be . . . Then, a quick shove by the girl and a wonderful scream of horror as he went down into the chasm, to the Ancient One's embrace.

All death was Her service and deliberate death Her worship.

Saltaja clapped. "That was beautifully done, girl. I wondered how you had come by the power to dispose of Perag Hrothgatson."

Celebre turned to scowl across the cavern at her. "This is your playroom, I suppose? Where you dump the bodies?"

"Bodies alive or dead. Are you seeking a moral high ground, child?"

"Like Paola's bodyguards, the two swordsmen who disappeared?"

"One was a body before. The other became one here, to Her glory. You are a fool, you know. Together we could have done wonderful things. You should have confided in me."

The girl showed her teeth. "You killed Paola. I will see you die for that."

Oh, the folly of youth! But also the firm breasts and tight belly, the thick hair and smooth skin of youth. She was still a virgin! By the Mother, a virgin and a Chosen! That must be very rare.

"Apicella died because she slew my brother. Your threats are ludicrous. Who let you out of that cell last night in Tryfors?"

"I will not tell you. Your reign is over, Queen of Shadows."

Saltaja laughed, thinking of the sacrifice she had made in the herb garden that morning. "Not by a menzil! Tell!" She forced an answer.

"My brother Benard and his goddess. Stop it! How did you do that?"

Saltaja was an old hand at manipulating dreams. She willed and instantly closed with the girl, so they were nose-to-nose.

"And where are you now, child? Your spirit roams the dreamland, but where do you sleep? Take me there."

Celebre's shout of protest was useless. The cavern melted and shifted. It became a place of grass and leafless trees, of stars peering between low clouds, a smell of the river. And there they were, all four of them, the accursed Celebres, sitting together, brown faces barely visible in the darkness, leaning forward, conspiring. They did not know Saltaja was there, of course, because she wasn't. This might not be happening right now, but they could not have fled very far from Tryfors yet. She could probably strike at them—but that would be a serious waste of power. They no longer mattered. One day she would hunt them down and enjoy their deaths at leisure.

The Dantio one was a temptation, though. How had the Witnesses managed to deceive her for so long? He had not died in Skjar that day, but he must have gone to the slavers', because the tops of his ears were missing. "Stand!" she said, and he was on his feet, facing her, but blank, unaware of her. The rest of the vision had gone, there was only him. Yes, she could remember that soft, unformed face. She willed away his covering and confirmed that he had been emasculated, too, as she had ordered.

"Turn!"

He turned his back. She smiled at the scars, recalling how he had screamed and begged for mercy when he was being flogged. But the familiarity was more than that.

"Look at me. I know you. Answer!"

He smiled, flashing white teeth. "I was a slave on the river, all the way from Skjar. For half a year I hid from you in plain sight! I stayed out of your boat, but you must have caught glimpses of me."

That voice! The Mother veiled him for her, shrouded him in white.

"So that was you, too," she said. "Yesterday in Tryfors, the seer?"

"It was me." He laughed aloud. "I lied and you believed." Flames of revenge and triumph blazed up around him like green wreaths.

She kept her rage in check, for now. "Not Nuthervale, then? You told us Nuthervale. So the rebels' camp is not near Nuthervale! Where is it?"

His eyes widened in shock as he felt her control. "Near Tryfors, of course, on the Milky River. Why would anyone put it near Nuthervale?"

"Speak on!"

"I sent word," his image said. "The night before we reached Tryfors. I told

them to strike soon, so they can catch you as well as Therek." He began to fade,
but his eyes burned bright with hate. "The jaws are closing, monster! They are
coming for you. The gods will have revenge."

◆

Saltaja started awake with a pounding heart and a sour taste of pursuit in
her throat. It was many, many years since she had been hunted and the sensation was distasteful. After leaving Zorthvarn, Hrag and she had been har-
ried from place to place. Producing four sons in seven years, they had needed
enormous amounts of power to Shape them. Too many unexplained disap-
pearances soon made neighbors suspicious.

She was lying on the flagstone floor of Halfway Hall, in a corner walled
off by three upturned tables. Her new Guitha was curled up nearby, snuffling
unpleasantly in her sleep. The rest of the upland shelter was packed with sleeping Werists, most of them forced to sit upright, leaning against the walls or one
another. The place reeked of male bodies and throbbed with massed snoring.

Halfway to Nardalborg, and so far so good. She had made Fellard bring
his entire hunt, although that was less than two sixty, and so far they had
obeyed him. She had ridden in a chariot at first, and after that on a sled that
Fellard had thought to bring, but the men had been run to exhaustion. By
the time they had staggered into the shelter, well after sunset, they had been
past thinking of mutiny. Huntleader Karrthin, back in Tryfors, had more
men, but not many more, and he would not strip the city of Werists. He was
much more likely to wait and see what happened than he was to come after
her. No, her present escort was the greater danger. In the morning, rested
but hungry, they might have a change of loyalty.

But what the Old One had just told her was worrisome. The accursed
Dantio had tipped off the rebels! Until now she had not considered the deserters an immediate threat. She knew that the Milky River was only a little
way downstream from Tryfors. Curse Therek for not knowing that mutiny
was festering practically outside his windows! How many rebels? She had
accounted for at least thirty sixty deserters over the last three years or so, and
the brass-collared Heroes were so hard to conceal that they could have been
concentrated in very few places. Even if all Therek's host stayed true to their
oaths—and she had few illusions about that improbability—they would be
outnumbered five to one. The rebels would seize Tryfors, then Nardalborg,
close the pass, leave Stralg cut off in Florengia. It might take two years for
Eide and Horold to clean them out.

If they ever can, whispered a cold breath of cowardice.

The traitors have enough men to storm Nardalborg and Tryfors at the same time, countered another.

She shivered and opened her eyes. The candles had gone out, but faint chinks of light seeped around the shutters. She sat up, aching and feeling her age. She had forbidden Huntleader Fellard to sleep, ordering him to sit on the only stool in the shelter, keeping watch just outside her barricade. He heard her move and peered around, although he probably could not see her. He looked haggard, twice the age he had seemed just a day ago.

"Is it dawn?" she asked.

"No, lady. That's the aurora, the Veils of Anziel."

"But we could travel by its light?"

"Probably, but the men are exhausted. So are the animals."

"Warbeasts can run."

"Not as far as Nardalborg, my lady! It would cripple them to go that far without meat."

"Waken Flankleader Ern. Tell him to rouse his men. I will go on ahead with just his flank as escort. You and the rest will remain here in case Huntleader Karrthin comes after me. Or anyone else, for that matter."

He took a moment to answer, eyes struggling to stay in focus. He was already close to the end of his usefulness. "Lady, we have no more food. The animals have no fodder."

"Slaughter the onagers. Throw a couple of haunches on my sled, so my escort can eat as we go. They will pull me." She glanced at the snoring Guitha and decided just to leave her. There were women at Nardalborg. "You have your orders, Fellard!"

There was no chance of getting lost. They could follow the trail the mammoths had left two days ago, and she would be in Nardalborg before noon if she had to kill the whole of Ern's flank getting there.

thirteen

FABIA CELEBRE

had shed a few drops of blood on the cold earth before she lay down to sleep. She had prayed the Old One to send her wisdom, to show her some way she might help rescue Tranquility. "Perhaps," she had suggested, "you could show me Horold's sentries exchanging passwords?" Knowing those, Orlad could send his men into the camp.

Suddenly she could hear voices. The dream was dark, but she recognized the cavern, the temple of the Old One under the Skjar pantheon—faint tendrils of light far overhead, shiny rock faces, some moss. This was where she had sworn loyalty to Xaran. She was standing unpleasantly close to the edge of the chasm. Why had she been brought here? Who was talking?

A man loomed out of the dark . . . very large, very ugly . . . bald and bloated, yellow-toothed. His face was too long, not improved by the dirty yellow beard dangling to his belly. He was holding the ankles of a naked girl, who must be still alive, because she was moaning as he dragged her behind him. He dropped her at the edge and rolled her closer with a shove of a bare foot.

"Holy Mother of Evil," he said. "Accept what's left of her." Another shove and she went over with a faint cry. He stood staring after her, leering as if he could watch her bounce from ledge to ledge, tooth to tooth, all the way down.

Behind him came Saltaja, equally naked and carrying a slab of rock as if it took all her strength to do so. Her hands were bloody halfway to her elbows.

The man spoke without turning. "You want to do the boys?"

Saltaja said, "Of course." With a great effort she raised the rock and slammed it against the back of his head.

The blow should have flattened his skull, yet somehow he saved himself from toppling forward into the abyss. He buckled to his knees, began to slide, then twisted and grabbed hold of her ankle. His other hand clawed at the crumbling brink, seeking purchase.

Saltaja staggered. "Take him, Mother!" She dropped the boulder on his head and he was gone. The rock rattled and crashed down into the chasm. The Queen of Shadows did not bother to stare after her handiwork, as he had. She just laughed and began picking her way back to the great altar rock, moving gingerly on bare feet. Two youths were kneeling there, gazing up at the image of the Mother, and apparently in some sort of trance, for they were paying no heed to the slaughter.

"That was Hrag, I suppose," Fabia said.

Saltaja turned to sneer. "Of course. He is no longer needed." She was younger than the Saltaja Fabia knew. This was a dream of the past.

"What are you doing?"

"Making sure Stralg wins the bloodlordship tomorrow. A major sacrifice is needed."

"Will Weru let you interfere in His rituals?"

The Queen of Shadows laughed harshly. "What a sweet innocent you are! Even He cannot resist Death Herself! My boy will find his opponents strangely lethargic."

"Stralg is both your brother and your son?"

"They all are, dearie." She limped forward, closing in on Fabia. Smiling.

"And you molded them into warriors from the day they were born?"

"It's called Shaping. It works best when there are blood ties, but you could have Shaped Cutrath into something bearable. There were sixty-sixty such things I could have taught you!"

Fabia did not want such skills. Paola Apicella had been a Chosen and a fighter, but not a monster wallowing in horrors. "This is happening before I was born."

"What does that matter? Dreams are no respecters of time. I know who you are, slut."

"Then you know that my brothers have defeated you. Therek is dead. Horold is trapped and doesn't know it yet. Stralg will be cut off. You are finished, spawn of Hrag!"

The Queen of Shadows chuckled throatily. She was very close now. "You think so? Let me give you another lesson, child."

The cavern shimmered and flowed and became somewhere else—a damp jungle in misty gray daylight. High walls enclosed it, but everywhere was damp and rank and neglected, and it stank of evil. Fabia recognized Tryfors stonework. Saltaja was a vague naked wraith at her side.

"Watch!" She pointed a bloody hand at a door in the corner. This was only a dream of course, so it flew open instantly. A line of Werists came trotting in.

Even more dreamlike, they were carrying spades and picks. "Your guards from last night."

"They didn't guard me very well."

"No, they didn't. They are about to suffer for their error."

Belatedly, Fabia wondered if she had any clothes on and decided it did not matter because this was only a dream. The men could not see her, or her companion. More Heroes came running in, the last one being that rakish huntleader she had met . . . Fellard. Suddenly dream became nightmare. As he closed the door, yet more men sprang up all over the courtyard and all the Heroes battleformed, so the place was instantly full of fighting warbeasts.

"No! No! Stop them! That's horrible." Fabia screamed and covered her eyes, which did no good at all, because she could still see. She heard Saltaja's coarse chuckle very close to her and backed away quickly, unwilling to come within reach of those gory claws.

"No, it is beautiful! It is an offering to the Mother, our lady. Look again, child!"

Fabia obeyed reluctantly. The living Heroes had departed, leaving mangled bodies everywhere—some human, some bestial, some both. And blood! Everywhere blood. The only living thing in the wasteland was Saltaja herself, rolling and wallowing in the gory mire, spreading it on herself, eating it.

And Saltaja was also at her side. "Do you understand now, foolish child? They were my gift to the Ancient One! You gave her Pukar, yes? And Perag. But I have given her multitudes in my time, and just this morning these fifteen strong young men. There was a girl, too, later. You cannot win, Fabia Celebre. I am stronger. I will always be stronger. Come and serve me!"

Her eyes—very dark eyes for a Vigaelian—seemed suddenly to blaze. "You will obey me!"

"No!" Fabia twisted away from her clutch and dove into the cold earth of the garden, down into the realm of the Mother. Like most Skjarans, she was a strong swimmer, and she swam swiftly through the darkness. The rock felt like water, offering no more resistance. This is a very odd dream, she thought, but I expect it means something. She saw the dead, standing like pale water weeds, rank on rank, watching her, rippling as she went past, but never trying to block her. Nor would they ever help her. They were dead and nothing mattered to them now, deep in the abode of the Most Ancient. Groves of them, a forest of wraiths, watched her pass through; they knew she was there, but they

did not care. When she felt she was a safe distance away from Saltaja, she turned on her back and let herself float upward until she was back on her sleeping rug.

✦

Shivering, she tried to force herself awake and rid her mind of the lingering taste of horror. It was hard to believe that even the Queen of Shadows could be as evil as she had appeared in the nightmare, but it had not been a nightmare, it had been a vision, a sending. Would the Mother of Lies lie about one of Her own? Had She been warning Fabia of the depths of Saltaja's evil and the strength of her powers, or had She been explaining that murder was a necessary part of Her worship and Fabia would have to start behaving like a faithful devotee? No! Fabia would not become another Saltaja. She would be like Paola Apicella, who had been a loving, caring foster mother and wife, not a murdering monster! Yes, Paola had killed Karvak Hragson and at least one of the assassin gang that slew her, but only in self-defense, yes?

How can you believe that? whispered a scathing inner doubt, a fading echo of Saltaja's mockery. *You think you know these things only because She told you so. She never showed you how Paola was initiated. She never explained how Paola's own baby died, did She? Can you blame the poor woman? She had lost her husband while she was giving birth and both she and the child were sure to starve to death, since the Fist's men had taken all the food. Much better to give the babe to Xaran right away.*

"No!"

Certainly. The Old One rewarded her with another child and a new life. Why do you suppose She is called the Mother of Lies? She tricked you into swearing allegiance and now She is calling for her due.

Trembling with doubt and terror, Fabia hugged herself in the darkness. Had she been a fool when she chose to follow her foster mother's goddess? Was she destined to descend from horror to horror? Must she be a Princess of Shadows, following in the Queen's bloody footsteps?

No! Feeble though her powers must be by Saltaja's standards, Fabia would use them for good, not evil. Rescuing Witness Tranquility would definitely not be an evil deed. So, had the vision contained any guidance? If it had, then Xaran was willing to help her in doing good. In her prayers earlier, she had asked to overhear the satrap's passwords, thinking that this might be the sort of help she could give Dantio without blatantly declaring her allegiance. What she had received instead had been very horrible. *Why?*

Why that impossible illusion of swimming through rock? If Chosen could do that, people would not bury them alive.

The poky cowhide tent the riverfolk had set up for her was as black as the depths of the earth had seemed in her dream, but warmer and smellier. And quiet. The camp was asleep, so the satrap's men had not invaded. The night was running away and the seer remained captive—unless those crazy brothers of hers had already tried something and gotten themselves killed.

She reexamined the conclusions she had reached before drifting off to sleep. Orlad, bitter and confused, was trying to adjust to a new world, to the mere idea of friends and family—poor Orlad! And poor Benard, facing responsibilities for the first time in his life with the knowledge that no Hand could ever be practical or responsible. And Dantio, who could never marry, never have family of his own, still trying to play big brother to all of them— Dantio plagued by the debt he owed his foster mother Tranquility. And Fabia herself, wanting to mother them, because she was a devotee of the Mother, the goddess who would eventually gather them all to Her bosom. That still seemed like her duty, though. She must encourage this fragile family cooperation by helping out with the mad rescue.

She unlaced the door and peered out. The fire pit was a faint glow of embers, the only landmark, because clouds had covered the stars. Extrinsics would be effectively blind. The seer would not be and probably not Orlad if he battleformed. Even Benard, when he had rescued her in Tryfors, had been very sure of his way through the dark streets, so his gentle goddess might help him see in the dark, too. The bright side of the darkness was that a Florengian would need very little veiling to be completely invisible to sentries, both Horold's and Orlad's. A reconnaissance should be in order, or at least a preliminary look at what a reconnaissance would involve. It would be horribly easy to get lost in a maze of scrubby little islands with no stars to guide her.

Oh! So *that* was what the dream had been telling her!

She whispered a prayer of veiling, cloaking herself in darkness more impenetrable than any she ever had tried before. Then she slipped out of the tent and picked her way carefully through the prickly undergrowth to where *Free Spirit* had been beached. If Orlad had posted sentries, none of them would see the naked Florengian moving through the night.

The water was cold, but not impossibly so. She stepped in, treading squishy mud and weeds, until the channel was deep enough to swim. Even then she kept her head above water and floated in a sort of crouch, propelling herself with her feet. There was just enough current to tell upstream from down even with no stars visible. If she was detected, she could vanish into the dark waters just as her dream self had escaped from Saltaja. Werists could not track in water.

They could probably turn into seals or lobsters if they had to, though. And finding her way back was going to be a lot trickier than she had expected. She had forgotten just how many islands and channels there were. Sometimes she found open water, wide and deep, and had to swim. At other times the branch she was following twisted around or died out in a tangle of weeds and mud, forcing her to backtrack. She passed a score of beached or tethered boats, many of them solitary and easily mistaken for *Free Spirit*. Then suddenly both sides of the channel were lined with them and she knew she had arrived at the Heroes' camp. She put her feet down and paused to consider the problem. The boats had been beached along one side, tied up on the other, where the bank was steeper and the water deeper. But which one did she need?

Why had she been such a fool as to come alone? She should have gone to Dantio and Orlad and told them her brainwave about swimming. Then she could have gone back to bed and left them to handle the heroics. But obviously they had thought of it for themselves, because there they were—under some shrubbery at the deep side of the channel, chin deep, four eyes and four rows of teeth gleaming in the night. They were staring across at the far bank, obviously balked.

She was equally stymied, because she did not know which boat contained the prisoner. Dantio would. She considered revealing herself and decided to investigate first. She slid away into the water, across to the shallows, then floated, walking on her arms, until she came to the boats. They had been pulled up in a herringbone pattern, sterns still in the river, bows ashore. She sat down between the first and second, with only her head above water. Now what? Four sixty Werists within half a bowshot were not good odds. And the sky was starting to brighten in what must be the east.

She thought back to her vision. *Control works best when there are blood ties.* But it would work with strangers, too. She had Controlled Pukar. She had watched Saltaja Control sentries in Therek's palace. Those doomed boys kneeling in the cavern had been under Control. Fabia could deal with the guards if she could locate them. Well, the Mother of All must be able to find Her children.

Guide me, I pray You, holy Xaran. Show Your servant where the . . .

Where the what? Guards? Or victims? Perhaps her brothers had brought knives with them, but she had not. Paola had not gone around cutting men's throats. But if Witness Tranquility escaped from her captivity, there could be no doubt what would happen to any Werist set to guard her. The vision had shown her how the Hrag spawn dealt with negligence, and she could not expect Horold to be more merciful than his mother-sister. Fabia would be killing two men just as surely as she had killed Master Pukar by pushing him into the chasm.

On the other hand, they *were* keeping an old woman chained up. That was an evil act. Besides, they would almost certainly die in the morning, when New Dawn arrived. Were those arguments strong enough to justify murder?

And if Dantio and Orlad tried to rescue Tranquility on their own, they would both get killed. That felt like a better argument. Fabia had to help her brothers. She shivered in the chill air.

Holy Xaran, my goddess, I dedicate their deaths to Your glory. Show me, I pray You, where to find them.

Ah! Now *there* was a familiar river sound! A faint shape was standing upright in the stern of the fourth boat, watering the water.

"I vaguely remember that this thing has other uses," he confided to the night air. "You suppose Eriander has a temple in Tryfors?"

Fabia lay down and floated, pulling herself closer.

"A garrison town?" said a voice from the bow. "Streets will be full of cuddlies. I'm planning to set a world record the first night."

"Follow my arse," said the man in the stern. " 'Tween you and me, Truk m'boy, I'm not too happy at getting so close to Nardalborg. Got a feeling the satrap may not take all of us home with him."

Fabia floated close in under the stern, below the first Werist. When he finished his business and was about to sit down, she stood up and let him see her. He started. He blinked and peered uncertainly at a hazy shape, dark on dark . . . Then he found her eyes and she had him.

There is nothing here. Sit down and sleep.

It was easy. He was already drowsy and would see no need whatsoever to stand guard over a chained, frail, elderly female prisoner. In a few minutes he was fast asleep. *Deeper!* She waited.

The man in the bow yawned. "Soon be morning. Wonder what time we'll get to Tryfors?" Then he said, "Mogranth?"

Deeper, Mogranth! Sleep deeper than you ever have.

"Mogranth?" Truk repeated. "Leader'll have your balls for knuckle-bones. Moggie! Wake up!"

Silence.

Grumbling, Truk rose and worked his way aft, stepping around cargo and the prostrate seer. "Moggie!" He bent to shake his friend's shoulder and Fabia scratched the gunwale with her fingernails.

Huh? He looked to see, found two eyes in the darkness . . .

Sleep!

He grunted, registered a mild alarm . . .

Sleep! Sleep! Sleep!

Truk settled like an autumn leaf alongside Mogranth. She drove them both down deep into coma and then drifted away to hide behind another boat, knowing that Dantio had been watching from the far side of the channel and must have seen what had happened, even if he could not be certain why.

"You're sure?" That was Orlad, who did not know how well even whispers traveled over water.

"You could cut their ears off and they wouldn't waken."

In a moment two pairs of eyes came floating over, predatory water beasts stalking prey. The brothers waded ashore between the third and fourth boats. Fabia stood up to watch. They climbed in over the gunwale and Dantio knelt to waken the woman beside the mast. She was white-haired and seemed very small alongside the two men.

"What? Mist, Mist! This is wonderful! I was frightened you might try something like this." She spoke softly but obviously had no worries of being overheard. "And you are a close relative, so you must be Orlando."

"Orlad!" Orlad said. "Give me room, Anto." He took her chain in both hands and strained.

"Where's Benard? And your sister?"

"Benard's looking after Ingeld, of course," Dantio said. "Fabia is around here . . . somewhere." He was probably thinking *quite close.*

Brother Orlad's shoulders grew steadily larger until a bronze link snapped with a sharp crack. He chuckled and lifted Witness Tranquility in both arms as if she weighed nothing. With two quick steps he jumped over the side of the boat to land silently on the grass. "You will have to get wet, lady," he said, wading into the river.

"You think I mind that, Hero? I am so grateful to you both!"

Dantio followed them into the water. "And New Dawn is on its way."

"Yes, I know," the woman said. "Can't you see them?"

A seer had no trouble finding the way back to *Free Spirit*'s camp, and all Fabia had to do now was follow. The mission had been a complete success, and yet the fruits of victory left a sour aftertaste.

She had killed Master Pukar in self-defense when he tried to rape her. She had killed Perag Hrothgatson in an act of justice for his murder of Paola Apicella. Now she had doomed two men to certain death in order to rescue an abused old lady. Each time the rationale grew weaker. Where would it end? Was she fated to become another Queen of Shadows?

Fourteen

HETH HETHSON

was awakened by a faint tap. He had been sleeping soundly through a barrage of much louder raps, squeaks, wails, and creaks as a moorland wind howled around Nardalborg, but this was business. He was off his sleeping platform and across the room before he was truly awake. A dim predawn light showed around the window shutter. He opened the door a finger-width. Inevitably, the caller was Frath Thranson, leader of white pack, which had the guard tonight.

"My lord, perimeter patrol reports a sighting. Seven warbeasts pulling a sled, my lord. Approaching Cleft Rock."

Heth said, "Wait." He recrossed the room, shivering now, and by touch found the stool on which his pall lay ready folded. His wife Femund had not moved, but he knew from her breathing that she was awake. Aided by a lifetime's practice, he wrapped himself while pushing his feet into his shoes.

He had instituted perimeter patrol very soon after being promoted to lead Nardalborg Hunt. Hostleader Therek, who disapproved of anyone else's ideas on principle, had sneered: "Who are you afraid of?" That was back in the years when the family had stamped out the last opposition in Vigaelia and the Florengian Mutineer was still no more than an annoyance.

Heth had said, "Only holy Weru, my lord. But it keeps the men on their toes and exercises the stock. And if we ever do have concern that some enemy may try to sever our communications with your noble brother, then we shall not have to seem weak by introducing such precautions at that time."

The satrap had walked away and never mentioned the subject again, which was his way of giving approval. Every night since then, except in truly lethal weather, a team of twelve men and three mammoths had patrolled the environs of Nardalborg.

The door pivots squealed as Heth opened it, and louder as he closed it. Frath handed him a fur cloak.

"When did this wind get up?"

"Very suddenly, my lord. Less than a pot-boiling ago."

No sane enemy would launch an assault in such a gale, but there might have been no way to recall it once it had started. The two men strode the gloomy corridor with Frath's lantern dragging their shadows along the stonework.

"You did say a sled?"

"Yes, my lord. Four pulling it, he said, and the others escorting."

Heth had known his sins would come home to roost eventually. He had just not expected them this soon. It was only two days since he had bundled Flankleader Orlad's former classmates into a makeshift flank and sent them off to Tryfors to back up the boy if the satrap tried to carry out his mad threats. That had not been the official purpose of the expedition, of course, but the brighter ones had guessed what was required of them. Strictly speaking, Heth had not been disobeying orders, but he had certainly exceeded his authority and sought to frustrate his commanding officer's intentions. The timing was tight but possible. Counting Orlad, twelve warriors had departed. Only seven returning? The sled might hold wounded, but a Werist either died or healed himself. If he needed to be carried, he had been maimed for life. Heth would have to justify five men lost, not counting casualties on the other side. Therek would have his liver for breakfast. He might find himself leading Caravan Six over the Edge, leaving Femund and the children forever.

His shadow led him up the stairs. Frath followed with his lantern.

Whatever was making them traverse the snowbound moors at night and in battleform? Such a suicidal overexertion could only be justified by a foe breathing on one's collar. Therek's men in hot pursuit? The future looked seriously uninviting.

"What flank?"

"Rear, my lord." Frath's voice raised hollow echoes in the staircase.

That was good. Flankleader Verinkar was an excellent youngster, first choice to be promoted the next time Nardalborg Hunt needed a packleader. He would keep his head no matter who or what he had met out there.

Because another possibility was that Heth's old pessimism might be justified at last. For the last two years, he had been picking up rumors of desertions among forces being posted to Florengia and this summer the losses had become blatant. Men had arrived grumbling about whole packs disappearing.

One flank coming overland from the south claimed to be the only remnant of
an entire hunt that had failed to reach Tryfors. Heth had listened, questioned,
and had his tallyman tally for him. Whenever he had tried to discuss the matter with his father, Therek had refused to listen. Heth had even considered
sending a letter directly to Saltaja, in Skjar. He might do so yet, as soon as the
downstream winds began to blow. That would be a second act of insubordi-
nation, but this was his problem more than anyone's. Desertion on such a scale
required an overall conspiracy, a revolution brewing, and in the past rebels had
often chosen to start by trying to cut Stralg's supply line through Nardalborg.

So had a new revolution started? If it had, the rebels' timing was bad.
Not only was Nardalborg Hunt up to strength, but there were another four
sixty packed into the fort, waiting to move out in Caravan Six. Heth could
put up a good fight.

The night air was waiting for him outside the door like an ocean of ice
water. Shuddering, he stepped out on the wall. Eastward the solar corona
was rising in a black and star-salted sky, blazing silver, breathtakingly beautiful. Red and green auroras danced silent minuets overhead, while to the
west a pinkish wall of cloud with brighter towers and battlements told of
doldrum weather seaward. Behind him stretched the frosted roofs of the
fortress. The open ground between it and the town was washed by billows
of blowing snow. Almost anything could creep in under that blanket, except
it would freeze to death on the way.

A well-muffled picket saluted.

"See anything?" Heth growled. Another warbeast should be on its way
from Verinkar by now.

The boy pointed. "My lord is kind. A mammoth approaching, my lord.
Flankleader Hrankag ran down to report."

What? Heth's neck prickled. Had Verinkar gone crazy? The drill was
that the patrol leader would send back a warbeast to report a sighting. If the
intruders seemed peaceable, then he had authority to make contact and establish their identity before sending a second warbeast to Nardalborg.
Breaking up the formation by detaching a mammoth was a flagrant breach
of standing orders. Breath smoking, Heth turned to Packleader Frath.
"Sound general quarters."

Frath gaped. Then his training asserted itself and he vanished down the
stairs, leaving the door wide.

"You'll have company in a moment," Heth told the sentry. "Meanwhile, keep your eyes skinned. We may be under attack." He headed for the door.

"My lord is kind. Two more mammoths following, my lord. Just coming into view."

Heth's eyes were watering too much for him to see such detail at that distance in that light. Baffled, he stared into the night. "You sure?"

"Not *certain,* my lord. Think so."

"Well done! You understand that either those are not our mammoths, or the wrong people are riding them?"

"My lord is kind. Rear flank is all dead, my lord, you mean?"

"We must assume so." If Flankleader Verinkar was not, Heth would have to kill him.

◆

When the sun's edge blazed up over the horizon and the sky abruptly turned indigo, every Hero in the Nardalborg Hunt was at battle stations, meaning that most of them were lining the walls. The men of Caravan Six, under Acting Huntleader Zarpan, were on standby. Heth had ordered two more mammoths sent out, but they had not yet left the pens. Lacking time to evacuate the town, he had sent right flank of gold pack over there to misinform the civilians that the alert was merely a drill.

In fact, it was obviously a false alarm. If a horde of warbeasts were to come racing in over the snow it would have done so before now, but Heth was not about to order the recall sounded until he understood what was going on. No problem that required him to put a man to death could be dismissed as trivial.

Perversely, the wind had dropped as suddenly as it had arisen. Heth stood on the wall and watched the three mammoths approaching, one in front, two a long way behind. He could recognize Rosebud, the bull in the lead, and the Nastrarian mahout astride its neck, but mammoths' backs sloped so steeply that the howdahs were not visible. However, the scouts he had sent out had identified Rosebud's passengers as Rear Flankleader Verinkar and two of his men, plus an unknown man heavily wrapped in furs. Heth spoke a prayer to Weru that it be Satrap Therek, the only man with authority to override his standing orders.

And now another scout was returning, streaking across the snow with sunlight flashing on his brass collar. He skirted the bull at a safe distance and stopped directly below the great gate. He shimmered and stood up as a naked young man with his face screwed up in the agony of retroforming.

Frath, his packleader, glanced at Heth for permission and then shouted, "Come on up, Tukrin."

Extruded talons on his hands and feet, the lad scrambled up the timber gate, sending splinters flying. He worked his way over the overhang of the lintel, and then up the stonework above it. A moment later he was on the battlements, fully human again, puffing and sweating. He would have had an easier climb if he had bypassed the gate and climbed straight up the vertical wall, but it had been a good chance to show off.

"Report, warrior." Frath handed him back his pall, so he could wrap up.

"My lord is kind. The rest of rear flank is riding on Strident. Dungheap carries seven men I do not recognize. I saw three brass collars and assume the other four are Werists also, because none of them have any clothes on. They are sort of *heaped,* my lord. For warmth?"

Frath said, "My lord?"

Heth nodded. "Well done, Hero. Anything else?"

"I do think the strangers are in a bad way, unconscious."

Hardly surprising if they had traveled far in battleform.

More diffidently, the boy added, "My lord is kind . . ."

"Yes?"

"I saw the civilian aboard Rosebud, my lord. She looked at me as I was coming back and I think I know her."

Her? Heth said, "Go on," but he had guessed the answer.

"I believe it is the lady Saltaja, my lord. I saw her some years ago when she visited Tryfors."

She had been pointed out to Heth there too, perhaps on the same occasion. She had visited her brother in the city three or four times in the last fifteen years, but had never come on to Nardalborg. What was she fleeing now that she would run men to death to outdistance pursuit? Had she fled all the way from Skjar? From Kosord? Or just from Tryfors? Therek had not mentioned that she was coming. Where was Therek now? Was he besieged in Tryfors? Or perhaps falling back on Nardalborg?

Heth said, "Very well done. Frath, you and your men may stand down, but you remain on alert." He beckoned his other packleaders forward and addressed Ruthur, who had first day watch. "Sound the recall."

"My lord is—"

"We remain on high alert. Put your men and black pack on extended perimeter patrol. Concentrate on the Tryfors road, but don't neglect other approaches. If they see anything unusual, anything at all, they are to report by warbeasts in pairs. I'll have Caravan Six men take over battlement watch. Blue pack will evacuate the town. Move all the people into the fort, and as much livestock as you can. Irig, red pack is to stand down but remain on call. This is not a drill! Dismissed."

The officers ran to obey. Eldritch howls announced the recall. Heth turned to stare at the mammoth lumbering up the road to the gate. He was tempted to leave it shut and send his aunt away. Hostleader Therek rarely confided in his last surviving son, but sometimes when seriously drunk he mumbled and maundered about Saltaja and his childhood. He feared her more than Weru. He muttered darkly that she was a Chosen and his mother, not his sister, although sometimes he said she was both. He thought she had murdered Hrag, his father, and the only reason he refused to acknowledge Heth was to keep him out of her clutches. So he said.

Alas, Therek was not the man he had been.

"She got Hrag, Stralg, and Nars," he would say, naming his three dead sons. "You stay away from her!"

The two relief mammoths had left the pens at last and were striding over the snow toward Dungheap and Strident. Soon there would be a patrol out on the perimeter again, and that was a relief. Heth trotted down the stairs. He must warn Femund that she would have company to entertain. He must have meat and blankets made ready for the Queen of Shadows' escort, those that had survived their ordeal.

The thought of dealing with Flankleader Verinkar made him feel ill. The lad was not stupid enough to think that his huntleader's standing orders could be ignored to satisfy some whim of the satrap's sister. He had taken an appalling risk when he broke up the string with only one Nastrarian on his patrol. So far the two cows were following their bull home out of habit, but they might easily change their stupid minds before the replacement Nastrarians reached them. Then they would make a run for freedom. Heth had seen it happen, and sooner or later the brutes would roll to get rid of their howdahs. That also disposed of the passengers.

Verinkar was guilty of flagrant dereliction of duty. If he were crazy enough to enter the fort, he must be put under arrest, but no Werist would submit to that on a capital charge. There would have to be a bloodbath.

Fifteen

BENARD CELEBRE

needed only a few seconds to dress—tie one loin cloth, grab two sandals—before he could wriggle out the door of the tent to see who was dismantling it and who was doing all the shouting. The sun was just rising in a narrow streak of sky between mountains and a roof of cloud. The island camp was in chaos.

"Wait a moment!" he shouted at the two sailors pulling up the tent pegs. "My wife isn't—"

But she was, if only just. The tent was whisked away and there was Ingeld, kneeling while wriggling into a dress, her copper head just emerging from the top of it. People were yelling and running in all directions. Benard dropped to his knees and began stuffing things in the clothes bag. Even a dumb Hand could guess that the boat was about to leave.

"Don't pack that yet! I need it!" Ingeld snatched back her comb. However gorgeous, long hair became a notable eyesore when badly tousled.

Dantio came staggering past carrying a rolled tent. Benard leaped up and blocked his way.

"What—"

"—is happening?" His brother grinned widely. "Horold's tribe of goons has discovered that Witness Tranquility got stolen away in the night. He is spitting blood and bones. He's ordered the islands searched. We think it wiser not to be here when he arrives." He tried to slip past and met the same wall of brother again.

"You mean you rescued her? You and who else?"

"Orlad kept me company, telling jokes."

Benard growled, unamused. "Where's this New Dawn you promised us?"

Dantio glanced eastward. "Close. Not quite close enough, unfortunately. If you want to help, brother . . ." He heaved his massive bundle at Benard, who foolishly caught it and was left holding it.

He ran to the boat with it, tossed it in, and came running back.

And met his sister carrying her clothes bag.

"So you did it!" he said, hugging her. "Congratulations! That's wonderful."

"Me?" Fabia's eyes were deep tarns of innocence. "Why do you think I had anything to do with it?"

"Your hair is damp and you smell of Wrogg."

She practically spat at him. "You are an absolutely infuriating man, Benard Celebre! One moment you are totally obtuse and the next you are sharper than Horth."

He spread his big mouth in a grin. "It was Orlad who saw that Dantio wouldn't be asking for your help last night unless he needed it. You're not worried I'm going to start boasting about my sister the Chosen, are you? Other people might not understand."

"And you do?"

He didn't, but he would trust her motives until he had reason not to. "Remember the day we met? Ingeld asked which goddess I would model on you?"

She raised two perfectly shaped eyebrows. "You told her Hrada."

"I had to say something."

"You guessed even then?" she asked skeptically.

"I suspected. I knew it wasn't one of the Bright Ones."

"I look evil, do I?"

"No, no, no!" He raked fingers through his hair. "I'm no good with words. The Bright Ones' cultists are . . . monochrome. Orlad is all ferocity. Dantio is pure nosiness. Love or war or law . . . I couldn't tie you down like that. You're a rainbow, a *dark* rainbow, all indigo, maroon, olive, walnut . . . But you're not, um, *dull* enough to be an extrinsic. I can't *tell* you. I'd have to paint it." He was happy to see her smile return. "It's wonderful, Fabia! There's an old saying that two gods are better than one. We have four!"

She kissed his stubbled cheek. "Then I won't blast you with my evil eye. We can talk on the boat. I'll talk, you draw."

"Benard!" Ingeld was calling and beckoning from the fire pit benches.

He remembered that Horold was coming and trotted over to where she stood alongside a seated woman—elderly, small, and disheveled. Her dress was tattered and one side of her face had been badly scarred since he had last seen her. Ingeld started to introduce him.

"Mistress Lonia!" He dropped to his knees. "I was horrified when my brother told us of your plight."

She smiled with grace. "And I worried about you, Master Artist. I was most relieved when I saw last night that you and the dynast were both alive and well."

"You know each other?" Ingeld seemed surprised, as if Benard did not know every face in Kosord.

"Well, I didn't know until last night that she was a Witness, but Mistress Lonia gave me one of my first commissions."

"Not quite, my lady," the seer said. "I asked young Master Artist Benard to make a mural in my home. When I told him I couldn't afford the gift of silver he asked in return, he said he would do it anyway and I could give him whatever I liked."

Ingeld chuckled. "Yes, you do know Benard."

"In the end she gave me even more than I'd asked," Benard countered. "I can tell an honest face."

"So what did you do with it? No, don't tell me."

"It's all right, I don't remember."

A Werist ran by. "Time to go, ladies! The monsters are coming." It was Waels, the beautiful one.

"Benard," Ingeld said. "Witness Tranquility is somewhat frail after her ordeal, and she still has a length of chain attached to her ankle, so I wondered—"

"My pleasure!" Benard scooped her up, chain and all, and strode off across the clearing. He grinned down at her. "You need fattening up, Witness!"

She laughed. "I feel like a child who has been lost and found. You Celebres don't lack for brawn, I must say."

"Orlad cheats," Benard said. "I'm the real beef. Dantio has the family brains." Fabia, he suspected, was more dangerous than any of them. "What happened after we left Kosord? How long was the satrap distracted by Nymph Hiddi?"

The old lady simpered, almost smirked. "She kept him very busy for two days and three nights, then took fright. I think she worried that his men would kill her. So she ran away—actually, she jumped on a boat going downstream, but only we Witnesses knew that. Horold regained his wits, discovered, er, um, the dynast's absence, and came charging into the duty room. Sensing his anger, I had sent everyone else away. When I said I didn't know where you were—which I didn't, because you were out of my range by then—he struck me." Her fingers touched the fading red scars on her cheek.

Benard said, "Monster!" The satrap must weigh four times what she did.

"In a way," the old woman said. "In another way it was a good thing. We've been hoping for years that something like that would happen."

"Horold broke the treaty?" asked Ingeld, who was hurrying along at their side, hard put to keep up with Benard's pace.

"Yes he did! If any of us had lied to him, we would have been anathematized, but the moment a Werist knocked me down, the pact was shattered."

That ought to mean that Dantio was now safe. Horold had broken the compact first.

The boat was in sight now, beyond shrubs and spindly trees. It had been launched; crew and passengers were boarding. Other riverfolk had taken alarm, and two boats were heading upstream, being rowed in the calm.

"So the satrap beat our destination out of you?" Benard asked.

The Witness sighed. "I am afraid he did, because I had seen you go off downstream and did not know you had doubled back until I saw you here last night. Trying to lie, I told him the truth—praise the All-Seeing."

"Then holy Demern was rendering justice!" Benard said firmly. "Today Horold meets his doom."

"How close is he now?" Ingeld asked.

"About halfway from his camp," the seer said. "He has his men spread out in a line, all the way across the islands, so they cannot move very fast."

"And New Dawn?"

"There's several sixty sweaty men coming down the Milky, but they won't be here for at least a pot-boiling. We can get away, but I'm very much afraid the satrap will, too. If he takes fright and heads downstream, then he'll have a fast run back to Kosord."

Benard thought, *Ridiculous! A Werist running away?* Then he recalled that the boar was a cunning beast. Horold must believe he was very close to his dread sister, and to turn up at Tryfors without orders, chasing a runaway wife he hadn't found yet, would be a major provocation. Worse, he certainly would not want to confess to Saltaja that he'd broken the precious compact with the Witnesses. Having done so he had effectively blinded himself, so he could never hope to find Ingeld. He might see Tranquility's escape as a face-saving excuse to run back to the safety of Kosord. Yes, Horold might well give up and go home.

And that would be a disaster!

The path narrowed between tall trees and for a moment Ingeld fell back out of earshot. "Do I still have seasoning?" he asked quietly.

The old seer twitched in surprise. "Mist told you about that?"

"Do I?"

She nodded.

He said, "Thanks," but he wished she had said no.

Free Spirit was a roiling mass of confusion. All the gear had been thrown in higgledy-piggledy. The sailors were burrowing under the heap to find the sweeps, which they then hauled out and swung around to set in the thole pins, narrowly avoiding braining bystanders. Most of the passengers were trying to stay out of the way, but a couple of Werists were holding tight to the shrubbery to keep the boat from drifting. As Orlad was helping Ingeld board, Benard stepped between two bushes and passed Tranquility across to big Snerfrik, who had to release a branch to take her.

Benard slipped back and sank down prone behind the bushes. He hid his face and lay very still. Most people never *saw* what was right in front of their eyes, and the simple trick worked perfectly. In the confusion of departure, his absence went unnoticed even by the Witnesses. The last two Werists boarded and the boat pushed off without him.

Overall the river was very quiet. Angry voices, the squeal of the thole pins, the coxswain's attempts to call a stroke—all soon faded into the distance. Dantio and Tranquility would see him the moment they looked, of course, and then there would be a battle royal between the passengers wanting to come back and get him and the crew wanting to escape from Horold. It was very doubtful that Orlad and his warriors could work the sweeps, so the sailors would probably win.

Benard was normally the least suicidal of men, but Ingeld would never be safe while Horold lived. She must go home very soon, because she had a duty to holy Veslih to let Oliva be born within the city she would one day rule. Now Horold had wandered into a trap and must not be allowed to wander out again before it was sprung. *A good trap needs good bait.*

Benard still had seasoning. He might yet change the flavor of the world.

He raised his head and confirmed that the over-long oars had already carried *Free Spirit* out of sight around a bend in the channel. He could hear another boat coming upstream. He rose and took off at a run, back to the clearing and on beyond it, heading downstream. When Dantio saw him, he would guess what his crazy brother was doing, but Benard would be hard to catch once he got a good start.

He reached a channel, paused to make sure his sandals were tightly tied, then plunged in and swam across to another island. And so on, across the maze of water and pathways. Whenever the way was clear he ran or trotted. And all the time he prayed to Anziel.

. . . great Her majesty and in infinity the realm of Her blessing . . . She is the sun, the candle, and the stars . . .

I know I'm not a good liar, my lady, but You could make me seem like a good liar, just this once. I'm not brave, either, but You could make me seem brave. He visualized his face all serene and earnest. *Make me look like that today!* Just today would be quite long enough. He might not live until noon, and if he did he would likely wish he hadn't. Horold could be incredibly spiteful.

When Benard judged that he was safe from pursuit, he found himself a ramshackle bench in a wide clearing and sat down to recover his breath and prepare a plausible story. He had done the first and was making progress with the second when a couple of Heroes came into sight through the trees. Then others. They saw him waiting and ran forward.

Yes, this was going to be bad. The blue-sashed flankleader was Vars Varson, who had been a cadet in the Kosord palace guard the last time Benard saw him and was even nastier than his friend Cutrath Horoldson. By the time he and half a flank of warriors arrived, Benard was on his knees, head humbly bowed.

"Looks like our lucky day, lads," Vars said. "Where's the woman?"

"I'll tell the satrap," Benard said and was slammed to the ground.

The flankleader licked his knuckles. "Nork, you've got a good bugle. Tell Big Pig."

One of his men screwed up his face as if he were doing something painful, and released a howl that could not have come from any normal throat: *"We got the mudface!"* He followed it with a series of trumpet blasts to help Horold locate him. He might have been audible in Tryfors.

Vars kicked Benard. "On your feet, vermin!" Then he said, "Now try and stay there!" and went for him with a blur of punches. Benard's efforts to parry, dodge, and retaliate met with no success at all. He could have broken Vars over his knee like a twig if he would have stayed still for it, but a Werist was a trained fighter. A Hand was not. He found himself lying on the grass, hurt and bleeding.

Vars said, "Your turn next, Ranthr. Just don't kill him, quite."

His men laughed at the sport. They took turns kicking Benard until he got up, then seeing how many hits they could get in before he went down again. When he could no longer stand, they just kicked—kidneys, belly, head, face, groin. A really good scream earned extra points. *He was going to die. Ingeld! Ingeld!* . . . His ordeal seemed to go on long enough to boil every pot in Vigaelia, one at a time, but eventually someone locked fingers in his hair and hauled him up to a kneeling position. He found himself peering blankly up at the tusks and snout of Satrap Horold.

"Where is my wife?"

Benard mumbled, "At a farmhouse on the Milky River, lord." He kept his eyes on the satrap's killer hooves.

"And what are you doing here?"

"I came to tell you, lord." Benard no longer worried whether he looked truthful or not. Nothing was going to show on the bloody pulp of his face. He had lost several teeth and could not see straight.

"Why?"

What was the story now? Oh yes . . . He spat out more blood. "Because she's pining, wasting away. She has to go home to her city or she's going to die!"

"You do know you are going to die, don't you?"

"My lord is kind."

"Not so as you will notice." Horold laughed. The day was looking up for him, after a bad start. "Did you get her with child?"

Benard vaguely remembered deciding that a straight denial would not be believed. "Yes, but she lost it. She said her goddess rejected it." Horold would like hearing that.

The satrap laughed again. After a season away from his palace bathtub and scent bottles, he reeked like a burning manure pile. He turned to a follower. "Packleader, summon the boats." The result was another flurry of long-distance howls, answered from afar.

"Who raided my camp last night and stole the seer?"

Through shattered teeth, puffed and bleeding lips, Benard mumbled, "Lord, I do not know."

Horold probably kicked him then, for he found himself flat on the ground again, with the world spinning overhead. His mouth was full of blood and broken teeth.

"Bring him," Horold said. "Don't hurt him any more or you won't leave any fun for me."

✦

There were no riverfolk in the satrap's boat. Either he had just seized it and thrown them out, or they had taken fright and fled. After a lifetime of campaigning all over Vigaelia, Horold was quite capable of fending for himself on land or water. Being no stranger to ambushes, either, he had sent six boats on in line ahead and had another six or more bringing up his rear.

The pallid Milky was a winding stream and the gusty wind kept changing direction also, but he had no need to raise sail or run out the steering oar.

He had lots of manpower available. Sixteen Werists walked alongside, hauling the boat. When they set out the Wrogg had been shoulder-deep, so they had stripped, leaving their palls and shoes aboard. Now they were having trouble moving the boat over the Milky's shallows and were pale blue with cold, whole-body goose bumps. Horold didn't care.

He lounged in the stern. Benard sat amidships, tightly bound to the mast, fading in and out of consciousness and in too much pain to pay attention anyway. That last blow had jangled him completely, so he was seeing double and hearing waterfall noises. He was also sitting in a scarlet puddle, copiously passing blood. Yesterday he had asked the gods to send Horold to join his brother, now it looked as if Benard himself would lead the way. That was traditionally what happened to those who cursed.

"Prisoner!" Horold roared, for the third or fourth time.

Benard managed to lift his head and half open one eye. "Lord?"

"I said that if this is a trap, I will kill you first. Understand? I'll rip your balls off and tear the rest of you into little pieces."

He would probably do that anyway.

Benard peered around at the fuzzy, blurred, and duplicated landscape. It had been farmland the last time he looked, and now it was bulrushes and swamp, with patches of willow, dogwood, and bungweed. The little town of Milk had come and gone. There was still no sign of the New Dawn rebels, but at least the satrap's flotilla had not run into *Free Spirit,* which had been his greatest fear.

"How far to this farmhouse?" the satrap demanded.

Benard's mouth was so swollen he could hardly speak. If he waited any longer he wouldn't be able to say what he wanted to say. It would doubtless kill him, but this folly had already gone on too long. Life hurt too much.

"There is no farmhouse," he mumbled. "This's an ambush. Your reign is ended, monster. My brother Orlad killed your brother Therek yesterday. Him and a few others to help." He vomited more blood and the world spun again. "There was fighting in Tryfors later. Don't know if your sister got her deserts yet or not. But she's going to. These woods are stiff with rebels. New Dawn, they call themselves."

"You're delirious!"

"I lied about the baby. My daughter will rule Kosord after Ingeld."

The giant uttered a deep roar. He rose to his feet, enraged and enormous, raising a hand armed with massive claws. "Florengian trash!" He took two steps forward.

The warriors splashing along beside the boat had been listening to Benard's mumbled diatribe and were curious to see how their hostleader would dismember him. They were less attentive than they should have been to their surroundings, so many of them failed to battleform soon enough when a hundred warbeasts erupted out of the rushes. Men hit by two or more warbeasts apiece died quickly. Up and downstream, the attacks came moments later, but those crews had seen what was happening and had time to react, so those battles went on longer. The results were the same in the end, though.

Guthlag Guthlagson had long maintained that Satrap Horold would never dare battleform again unless it was a matter of life and death. That day had now arrived. His warbeast was more like an eight-foot bear than a boar, armored in yellow fur and wielding claws like meat hooks, but it did have two dagger-sized boar tusks. He disemboweled his first two attackers, then toppled under a pack of them. The boat fell apart when the mountain of flesh hit the side, but the water was too shallow for it to sink. The mob had to tear him apart to kill him.

Benard watched it happen. The gods had granted his prayer. Now he could die happy.

Part IV

◆

The Race
to the
Edge

◆

ſixteen

HETH HETHSON

had never put much stock in old Therek's ravings about Saltaja being a Chosen. He barely believed in Chosen at all—how could anyone worship death and evil? Now he was not so sure.

Nightmare made real, Rosebud lumbered in through the fortress gate, a hairy walking mountain, peering around with clever, hate-filled eyes. He was old, so his huge curved tusks were worn and broken at the ends, but his strength was prodigious. Treb, his Nastrarian, ducked prone to avoid being smeared against the lintel and muttered in the mammoth's hairy ear to bring him to a halt. Men ran forward, pushing the wheeled ladder.

The howdah was shaped like a staircase up the long sloping back, a set of six benches each wide enough for two men or three at a pinch. Rosebud could carry such a load all day. Two young Heroes sat on the lowest seat, both hunched small and looking terrified, but whether they feared the woman, Heth's rage, or simply the gods, could not be determined. Perhaps all three. At the top, near the Nastrarian, sat the Queen of Shadows and Flankleader Verinkar. He was the one who ought to be terrified, ashen-faced and gibbering, but he was smiling. When Saltaja rose to her feet and moved to discard her fur cloak, Ver jumped up and graciously lifted it from her shoulders like an awestruck boy fluttering around his first love. That was when Heth decided that he did believe in the powers of evil, and if he had had a bow in his hand, he would have let fly and nailed the hag. How *dare* she pervert one of his best warriors and turn him into a performing loris like that? She had effectively murdered the man.

The two warriors jumped to the ground and made themselves scarce. Black-clad Saltaja began a dignified descent of the stair with Ver close behind her, paying no attention whatsoever to Heth waiting at the bottom of the ladder, or Packleader Frath and his death squad, miserably holding the bronze manacles they had no reasonable hope of using. Verinkar was a powerful fighter, sure to take one or two of them with him. Inevitably the entire fortress knew what was in the offing. All around the courtyard, at windows, even the sentries on the walls—hundreds of eyes were watching the unfolding tragedy.

The Queen of Shadows paused a few steps up. "Huntleader Heth!"

He bowed very slightly. "Welcome to Nardalborg, my lady."

She eyed the posse and then turned to whisper a remark to Verinkar. He nodded. She resumed her descent. He followed close.

At ground level she held out a hand to Heth. Feeling sudden revulsion, unwilling to touch her or even let her come close, he backed away and ordered a nearby Werist to lead the lady to the guardroom. She stepped aside to let Verinkar clear the bottom of the steps, but then went no farther.

Restraining a Werist malefactor was no simple task. He must be arrested by members of his own pack, for he would be less willing to harm them than he would others and they, in turn, would be less likely to leap to his defense. With a visible shudder, Frath took one pace forward. The manacles he held were massive enough to give a mammoth pause and they would be followed by fetters, chains, and stone weights, unless by then the detainee was already dead.

"Flankleader, you are charged with gross dereliction of duty and must be confined until your case is judged."

"My lord is kind." Ver turned around and held out his wrists behind him to be shackled.

Heth felt the shock like a physical blow and heard a collective gasp from the audience. He turned his fury on Packleader Ruthur. "Weru's balls! Haven't you anything better to do than stand around with your tongue hanging out? Are those men or owls? Put them to work shoveling snow if you have nothing better to do." The courtyard erupted in meaningless activity.

It might have been better to have them start digging a grave. Heth nodded to the Queen of Shadows. "Come with me, my lady."

◆

The guard room was small and poorly lit, furnished with one battered table and benches along two walls. It had a distinctive musty male smell, but a pile of glowing peat on the hearth made it cozy. Saltaja headed straight for the fireplace. Heth closed the door and remained standing just inside it.

Warming her hands and not looking at him, she said, "I bring serious news, Huntleader."

"I assumed as much from the manner of your arrival."

Now she did look around at him. Her face was flushed by the cold, framed by a black wimple. He saw no resemblance to Therek, but he could barely remember what his father had looked like when fully human. That same high-arched, arrogant nose had arrived in Nardalborg just two days ago on Cutrath Horoldson. On the cub it had been bent out of shape by successive fists and merely looked ridiculous. On her it was striking. Her eyes were large and curiously dark for a Vigaelian.

"I regret to tell you that Satrap Therek has returned to the womb."

That was no surprise, somehow. It was not even a cause for regret. The real man had died years ago. But it did change things. Who now ruled Tryfors?

"He will be honored in the halls of our god."

She noted the lack of regret. "He was slain by your men."

Oh! Heth had expected her to start complaining about rebels. That did complicate matters. If Therek Host now had no hostleader, Fellard and Karrthin would be circling like bull mammoths in musth. One of them was probably dead already. *Weru's balls!* Heth still had Caravan Six available. His loyalty to Stralg required him to—

To Xaran with Stralg! Abandon the brute! Cut him off and let the Mutineer have him. This was a chance to end the war. No more endless lines of young men heading to destruction, a new life for himself and his family in a decent climate . . .

"My men? Are you sure?"

His aunt the Chosen pursued her lips in distaste. "He tried to murder the Florengian, Orlad, and got ambushed himself."

"Many other casualties?"

"Tryfors Hunt lost eleven men. You lost four, I understand. Did the rest not return here?"

Heth barely restrained a smile. Brilliant! An incredible victory! Orlad was a born leader, a Hero's Hero. Now he must be an outlaw, of course, poor kid, he and his seven liegemen. "No, my lady. He was not acting on my orders. And may I ask why you came here?"

He had no need to ask. Heth stepped to the window and stared out, so she wouldn't see his face. The Queen of Shadows had fled to Nardalborg because Therek was dead and his men had started digging a deep hole in which to store his sister. Wasn't that a *good* idea? After what she had done to Verinkar, perverting him from his duty, there was no need for further evidence, surely. The ground wasn't frozen yet. Bury the bitch at last? *Yes!* He had better summon reinforcements before he tried it, though. He turned toward the door . . .

He found himself looking into those strangely dark eyes. So close! He had not heard her approach. *My lady . . .*

ѕeventeen

WAELS BORKSON

sat on a stump outside the sanctuary of Sinura in High Timber, gnawing his way through a rack of pig ribs. He had eaten about half a hog already and would finish the rest if given the chance. Dogs lying in the shadows watched enviously as grease ran into his stubble, and waited to see where he would throw the next bone. Some faint sounds of chanting drifted through the rough plank door behind him, but the sanctuary contained only one suppli-cant at present, because Werists had to heal themselves. He was almost dis-appointed that he had not earned the chance to try. He had broken two necks in the Battle of the Milky—perhaps one and a half necks, since Hrothgat had helped him with the second one. A battle scar or two would have been a nice souvenir. Orlad had added some to his collection.

On the far side of the muddy, rutted trail that served as a street stood an-other solid log building, the temple of Veslih. It was making noises also, be-cause Ingeld Narsdor was in there with some local women, rededicating the sacred fire. High Timber did not possess a resident Daughter, although it was a sizable town. Three years ago it had been primeval forest. Three days ago it had held more than *forty sixty* Werists, plus uncounted civilians, a lot of whom were Nymphs. Today it was notably empty, with most of the resi-dents away attending to their bloody business at Tryfors and Nardalborg. It would probably be burned before winter, whichever side won.

Around the corner to his right came Namberson and Snerfrik and two other people, whom Waels needed a moment to recognize. Horth Wigson and Orlad's sister had acquired new clothes, surprisingly fine-looking gar-ments to find in a temporary hill settlement. Fabia had her hair dressed in long black ringlets, trailing down to her sable wrap, which hung loose on her shoulders—broad shoulders ran in the family. The top of her gown was cut low to reveal the top third of a pair of nicely plump breasts. She was easy to look at, if not as winsome as her brother. It was a pity she had not found lighter colors to show off her brown skin, but there could not be much choice in High Timber.

The merchant was grandly attired in a many-colored robe and a fur-trimmed mantle, with gold bands glittering around his neck and wrists, all of which somehow made him seem even less imposing than he had done in his previous rags. Having two great muscular Heroes skulking along right behind him did not help, of course. He looked old and unhealthy by comparison, not to mention worried, shrunken, stooped, and mousy. How could a man so wealthy seem so insignificant? Was there a lesson there?

Snerfrik and Namberson were not happy at being assigned to keep their leader's sister from being hassled by drunks. They wanted to go and join in the victory party, which was already audible, even at this distance, and would be a real roof-raiser by sunset.

Fabia accosted Waels as if the state of the world was all his fault. "He's still in there?"

He waved the pig ribs expressively. "The last they told me was that they needed another pot-boiling or so." He did not mention that the sanctuary had sent out for another three healers. In all, they had said, about eight Sinurists would be needed to assume all of Benard's injuries, and he had been extremely lucky to have reached High Timber alive—which he had done only because relays of Werists had carried him in on a litter at warbeast speed. That was not an honor Werists *ever* accorded to extrinsics, other than a few mythical characters in ancient legends.

"You tell him I need to see him right away!" the girl said. "We'll be in Panther Hunt's gold barracks."

Orlad, Dantio, Ingeld, and Huntleader Nils Frathson also wanted to see Benard as soon as possible. Revengers and Thunderbolt Hunts both wanted to carry him around the town shoulder high.

"I promise." Waels gave her a big smile, hoping to win one in return.

He didn't, so he waited until she and her companions had moved along the road, then set the dogs on them by hurling a pig rib over their heads. The curs exploded after it, racing by them and between them, yelping and barking, almost knocking Horth over. Even the two Werists jumped. Snerfrik looked back and made an obscene gesture. Waels waved cheerily.

He had time to gnaw one more rib before the door behind him creaked open.

An elderly Healer peered out. "Are you waiting to guide Master Artist Benard?" His seriously bruised and swollen mouth gave him trouble speaking.

"I am. Can he walk?" Waels thought he could carry the beefy lad to the Orlad flank billet, but would prefer not to have to try.

"Of course." The old man smirked toothlessly and pushed the door wider.

Out came Benard, blinking in the sunlight, then smiling at Waels. His face was still puffy and multicolored . . . no, *all* of him was puffy and discolored by either bloodstains or fading bruises, but he did not seem to be in much pain.

"Good of you to wait for me, my lord." He slurred the words. He had lost half his teeth and Healers could not replace those.

"A pleasure."

Waels tossed the rest of the pig ribs to a fast-looking dog and watched the entire pack streak off after it. He licked his fingers. "I wish you would just call me Waels, Master Artist."

"Every Hero I ever met insisted on being called 'lord.'"

"But you're special. You're a hero to us Heroes. You trapped the Kosord boar! There's nothing we admire more than really suicidal courage."

As much as a badly bruised Florengian could, Benard blushed. "Thanks. Where's Ingeld?"

"Playing with fire over there." Waels pointed across at the temple with its Veslihan symbols. "I have orders to lead you to our quarters and feed you. The rest of us have all eaten."

"Sounds promising, but I need a wash first."

"This way, then. The bathhouse is this way."

As they started along the street, Benard said, "Tell me what happened. I don't remember much."

"That's a shame! It all went just as you'd planned. Dantio and Ingeld wanted to go back and catch you, but Orlad wouldn't hear of it. He said you were probably going to be killed whatever we did and the least we could do was make your sacrifice worthwhile. He told Namberson and the rest to make sure the boat carried on up the Wrogg, out of harm's way, and then he and I set off to fetch New Dawn." Waels did not mention that keeping up with Orlad on the run had just about killed him. That went without saying. "We met Huntleader Nils coming down the Milky with Revengers Hunt and most of Thunderbolt Hunt. Nils set up the ambush."

Waels remembered Nils from years ago, for they were both Tryfors born. Nils had even remembered him, because of his birthmark. It could not hurt an able youngster to be known to a man three ranks above him.

Benard pulled a face. "I vaguely remember seeing Horold battleforming."

"I missed that. We were two boats upstream from you. He died well; took three Heroes with him. But it was a *beautiful* massacre! The Milky ran strawberry."

The Hand did not comment. They turned at the temple of Weru and scrambled down the bank, all mud and exposed roots. The streambed at the bottom was a morass, trampled by innumerable feet, which hardly mattered on the way to the bathhouse. Regrettably this was also the way back, which made the journey seem self-defeating.

Waels paused outside the bathhouse door, in case there was someone inside. "Orlad said you want to ask a favor of me."

"He did?"

"He did. Said he wasn't sure what it was, but he asked Ingeld and she laughed, so he's decided it's not what he thought it was at first. Whatever it is, go ahead and ask."

The Hand said, "You won't get mad?"

"*Mad?*" Waels laughed aloud. "I won't get mad at you if you tell me to eat mud. You're so brave you're insane, even by Werist standards. You're also the brother of my, er, flankleader, and, I mean, why would I get mad?"

Benard smiled shyly, showing gaps and half-healed gums. "If I tell you I love your smile?"

Waels felt his fists and jaw clench. Blood pounded in his throat. He was a Werist now and didn't have to take that from anyone, not ever again.

"If anyone but you said that, I'd *eat* him."

Benard seemed truly puzzled. "Said what? You worried about that mark on your face? I don't even see it when I look at you. All I see is *shape*. I have a commission to carve some gods. The marble is Vigaelian color. You think I'd paint that mark in? All I want is *shape*, and you have one of the finest male bodies I've ever seen. Gods must be as beautiful as possible, obviously, and your proportions are perfect. Your muscle definition is superb. And your smile is incredibly cryptic."

Oh? Waels said, "Thank you," awkwardly.

"My brother must think so too, judging by the way he looks at you."

Annoyed again, Waels said, "Are we so very obvious?"

"No, I'm very observant. Your flank-mates know, you know?"

"They don't matter." Whatever Orlad wanted was fine by them. Fortunately he wanted Waels.

"Now, are you going to strip in here?"

"I s'pose another dip won't hurt me."

"That's all I need—to get a proper look at you."

Starting to feel flattered, Waels said, "You're welcome. Admire anything you want." He tried to look cryptic.

◆

The bathhouse was large and dim, just a log shed built over a creek, full of dank odors of mud and wet timber. Water entered by a trough about thigh height, splashed onto some flat stones, then fed into a pool that took up most of the interior. Some attempt had been made to provide benches and flooring, but mud had spread over everything. There was no one else there—to Waels's intense relief—but the Revengers had churned the pool to a black wallow.

"The idea is to get yourself dirty in that," he said, "and then crawl under the dribble to get clean again."

Benard waded into the wallow, loincloth and all, and sat down with only his head showing. He sighed with delight. And looked expectantly at Waels.

Who said, "It's very dark in here. Wouldn't you rather wait until . . . I mean . . ."

The artist chuckled. "I can see very well. Get it over with. I won't laugh."

"There's nothing to laugh at!" Waels said angrily, and stripped to prove it. Funny—he'd been naked around men every day for years and never felt embarrassed like this before.

"Feet a little closer together," Benard said. "Bend your left knee just a . . . not so much. Now imagine you're holding a heavy wine jug against your thigh. A little higher. Oh, yes! Push that hand down with the other one so I see how your muscles would take the weight. Wonderful! Turn around. Thank you. You're going to be holy Cienu, except you'll be wearing that gorgeous smile of yours instead of looking like a virgin on her wedding night."

Waels responded to that remark by jumping into the pool ass-first and throwing a monster wave into Benard's face. He spluttered and laughed.

For a moment they just sat there in the muddy water and grinned. Benard himself had a mammoth-wrestler's physique. Orlad did not, but he was much stronger than he looked, able to do wine-jug-at-arm's-length tricks that even Snerfrik couldn't.

Waels said, "You're going back to Kosord now, to finish your statues?"

"Hope so. Ingeld has to bear Oliva there—our daughter. Horold is no threat now. What are you going to do?"

What Waels *wanted* to do and what he *could* do were very different. "Don't know," he said miserably. "Thanks to you Celebres, Stralg's brothers are both dead. His sister should be by now. But who's going to rule after them? Heroes won't be short of work in my lifetime."

"Seems wrong to kill for a living."

How could such a hunk of a man be so unmanly? "You don't want to be doge of your father's city?"

Benard guffawed. "Me? You're joking!"

How could a man with such incredible courage have so little ambition? Pause.

"Waels . . ."

"Mm?"

"You love Orlad?"

Any other man who had the cheek to ask that would learn not to very swiftly. "What's it to you?"

"Just that I'm very happy about it. Orlad's been hurt more than any of us, even Dantio. He reminds me of castings I do sometimes—a coating of hard bronze outside and a clay center. Of course, in the casting the clay is baked hard, but I think there's still some human softness left deep inside Orlad. I hope you can find it. He loves you?"

Waels debated breaking another neck, but three in one day seemed excessive. The alternative was to trust this bewildering, tangled sculptor person. "He says he thinks he does. He says he'd rather be with me than with anyone else, and he will never do anything to hurt me."

"Then he's being honest, and that's rare in love affairs. You can't expect more from him yet. Ask Ingeld. She knows more about love than Eriander, who just peddles lust. Her goddess does, I mean. She'll advise you. No, I mean it. Talk to Ingeld."

After a moment, the sculptor shrugged, raising ripples. "I don't know if this would help . . . I can't promise anything. If that birthmark bothers you, I can ask holy Anziel to remove it. She sometimes does favors like that for me. Often she won't, of course, but you would be incredibly beautiful without it. It would be a sort of present to Orlad."

Great murderous, frightful, wonderful Weru!

Waels had not really believed Orlad's account of how his sister had escaped from the satrap's palace. But . . . He looked down at his paler limbs, glimmering under the muddy water. Benard's were almost invisible. He was a black-stubbled brown face floating above nothing.

Trying hard to keep his voice steady, Waels said, "If you can do that, can't you change all of me?"

Benard looked startled. "What? Why?"

"Because Orlad's going over the Edge to win back his city and he won't let us go with him! Fair-haired Werists die on sight over there, he says. I've told him I don't care, but he insists."

"You love him that much, that you'd go and fight for him?"

"And die for him if I must."

"You're sure, absolutely sure . . . ?"

"Oh, yes!"

"That's beautiful too," the artist said. "Be quiet a moment."

He stared at Waels and for a while his lips moved. Then just a stare. At last he frowned in annoyance. "This is harder than I thought it would be. Look, grab a couple of handfuls of mud and rub it in your hair."

"Why?"

"Shut up and do it."

Waels hesitated. An extrinsic telling a Hero to *shut up?* If this was a juvenile joke . . . If anyone came in . . . He pulled up two handfuls of black muck and did as he was told, rubbing it into his stubble.

"Now your face," Benard said.

The *mudface* said! Admiration of a man's courage only went so far. Either this artist was gibbering crazy or he was trying to sucker a Hero and ought to be dismantled. But Waels thought about losing Orlad and nothing would be worse than that. He spread more of the revolting ooze over his face.

"And your ears. And neck. Down to your collar. Then either cover your shoulders too or put them under water where I can't see them. And be quiet again."

Any moment now half a dozen men would come storming in and start laughing their guts out.

Benard sighed. "All right, wash it off now. I'm sorry. I must be out of favor today. I'm not supposed to meddle in wars."

Waels ducked under the surface and rubbed his hair and beard clean, or so he hoped. The water went up his nose. He emerged spluttering. His hands were still dirty. He rubbed them. They stayed dirty, didn't feel dirty, arms the same color . . .

Benard nodded happily. "Seems I am in favor after all. Praise the lady!"

Waels erupted out of the pool and confirmed that he really was brown all over, the exact shade Orlad was. Miracle! Palms and nails pinker . . . *Black hair!* Even the hairs on his arms.

"Oh . . . Hero?" Wearing a stupid grin, Benard waded out and thumped him on the shoulder.

The new Florengian had to try twice before he managed to croak, "What?"

"I love that baby brother of mine too! Look after him for me, won't you? Wherever you two go and whatever you do together, you keep him safe!"

eighteen

HETH HETHSON

—or Heth Therekson, as he must now call himself—said, "Now that my father has gone, of course I am happy to claim his name and acknowledge my membership in such a distinguished family, my lady. To be related even just to you alone is a wonderful honor, a cause to boast."

He walked across the guard room to a bench and sat down. He felt as if he had been standing a very long time and yet that couldn't be, because—

Saltaja delicately licked fingertips. She had eaten almost everything on the tray, which had been a meal fit for a Hero in training. She pushed it to the far side of the table. Heth suddenly realized that he was starving. He couldn't recall eating anything since—

"And what do you think of your cousin Cutrath?" she asked, with one of her wonderful little smiles.

"Honest opinion, my lady?"

"You will always answer my questions honestly."

"Of course! I think he is a thoroughly spoiled brat, but he does not lack courage or self-confidence. A few years of life's rough-and-tumble could turn an overgrown child into quite a decent man."

"Then we must oblige him! You are certain we cannot leave today?"

Heth glanced at the sunlight falling through the window. It was a little shy of noon. He slid off the bench and dropped to his knees. "Forgive me, my lady! I did not know that there would be this terrible urgency. The last supply train is not due back until this evening, and we must not leave without those mammoths."

"Get up! Men go past that window all the time. You must not kneel to me when there is the slightest chance that anyone else will see you. You may do so when we are quite alone, if you wish."

He scrambled to his feet. "Thank you, my lady." He did not resume his seat, feeling it was disrespectful to sit in her presence. "But I fear that the few hours' advantage we might gain by setting out today would be wasted or even harmful, my lady. The first campsite—"

She stopped him with a dismissive wave. "Dawn it shall be, then. I depend on you to see me safely to Florengia. How long to reach the Edge?"

"At least twenty days, my lady, but it depends entirely on the weather. Thirty would be good going at this season. The descent on the far side is reputedly easier, but at least another ten days to Veritano, I understand."

"I should send a letter to my brother advising him that I am coming." She sensed his alarm and smiled again. "No?"

"We do not know what is happening on the Florengian side, my lady. If the Mutineer intercepted your letter he might bring up enough forces to intercept you also." To be responsible for her safety was a terrifying responsibility. "And now we even have the problem of traitors on this Face. They could try to stop us from reaching the pass, or might even cross over and ambush us on the far side, since you tell me that they are concentrated near Varakats." She had not said how she knew that, but he did not doubt her word for a moment. "And then there is the uncertain situation in Tryfors. Your plans should be kept secret."

She sighed. She did look a little tired, but then she was older than Therek and must be close to sixty, so it was amazing that she had withstood her journey as well as she had. "Yes," she said. "Now, about those men from Tryfors who were escorting me when your patrol appeared—they all know about the satrap's death. I don't want them chattering."

"No, indeed, my lady! No one else in Nardalborg should know about that. I imagine they are all still unconscious, recovering from their exertions, but do you want me to . . . to . . ." To do what? She wouldn't ask him to put them to death, would she?

"I will have a word with them," she said.

"Flankleader Verinkar, my lady? He was quite right to bring you in by the fastest means possible, but technically he was disobeying—"

"Do whatever you judge best, Huntleader. Kill him or pardon him and say it is a favor to me. It doesn't matter. He is of no importance."

"Of course not, my lady. Forgive me for wasting your time." It would be best to put Verinkar to death, in case he babbled things that might imperil the lady.

She said, "I am a little weary. I shall lie down for a while. I know you have duties to attend to. How many children do you have, Huntleader?"

"Three, my lady. A daughter and two sons."

"How old?"

"Ten, seven, and three, my lady."

"Ah, then the boys are too young to be warriors. But the girl might make a good lady's companion. Send her to me. If she seems promising, she can accompany us to Florengia."

"That would be a great honor, my lady." Heth knew that Femund would complain at not being consulted, but he had always been considerate of her wishes, and she would have to understand that a man sometimes had higher responsibilities.

"I shall require a room on the ground floor with a good bolt on the door and a squad of—Ah, that must be my other nephew at last."

Heth did not recall sending for Hero Cutrath, but he barked, "Enter!" and the face that peered in was indeed that of his parboiled young cousin.

"I said, 'Enter!,' not 'Play peekaboo!'"

Cutrath jumped in like a startled coney and slammed the door behind him. He looked terrified out of his wits—such as they were—which was perverse of him so soon after Heth had praised his courage.

"You may greet your aunt, boy!"

Saltaja rose and held out her black-draped arms. "My, what a fine, upstanding warrior you have become since I saw you last! Come and give your old auntie a kiss, Hero."

Cutrath made a choking noise, fumbling behind him for the door latch. Heth took him by the arm and marched him across the room. Cutrath went reluctantly. Something in the air suggested that he had a urinary problem.

nineteen

FABIA CELEBRE

and Horth Wigson arrived back at their quarters, still escorted by their two grumpy Werist bodyguards. Huntleader Nils had assigned them a long barnlike building knocked together out of great undressed tree trunks, reeking of pine. The crude painting above the door showed that it was normally home to the men of gold pack, Panthers Hunt. Although daylight shone through the roof in places and there were no shutters to keep rain from blowing in the window slits, it was certainly roomy enough, and Fabia would not be staying long. That was another problem—time was desperately short. She must have a serious talk with Horth, and Orlad, and Benard . . . and just about everybody else.

The rest of the clothes she had bought had not been delivered yet, but her brother was waiting for her—her youngest brother, the dangerous one—accompanied by six gangly boys armed with cudgels. They wore peasant garb and unsightly hemp collars that must signify something to Werists.

Orlad bore a satisfied air. He was a seasoner. In the last two days two sons of Hrag had died by his hand, more or less. War was easy, wasn't it? He had added a new scar, a jagged line, still red, from the corner of his mouth almost to his ear, as if a claw had ripped his face open.

"You can go," he told Namberson and Snerfrik, and they vanished along the trail while still telling their lord that he was kind. He indicated the newcomers and rattled off some names.

"Probationers," he told Horth. "They will look after you."

The boys were regarding Fabia with interest, as if Florengian women were rarities thereabouts. She could see nothing in them to interest her.

"Are you sure?" she asked.

Her brother shrugged. "You want to hear what I've promised to do to these maggots if you get molested, or insulted, or even annoyed?"

"No."

"I warned them that I always carry out my threats. Didn't I, maggots?"

They chorused nervously that their lord was kind.

"I must talk with you," Fabia told him. "Come in here."

She marched into the barracks, and continued along the narrow walkway that ran the full length of the building, between two raised platforms of packed earth. A thick litter of blankets and other personal gear on them suggested that Panther Hunt's gold pack had left town in a hurry, no doubt right after Dantio's letter had brought the news that Saltaja was entering the trap.

She turned. Orlad had chosen to sit down just inside the door, and Horth was perched on the edge of the platform opposite. Angrily she stalked back to them.

"I don't want those boys eavesdropping!" She remained standing.

Orlad shrugged. "You think they haven't noticed the windows?"

"Will they listen?"

"Certainly. Will it matter?"

That would depend on what was said. "You are going to Celebre?"

He nodded.

"When?"

"Soon as Arbanerik gives permission. Nils has sent him my request. Tomorrow if we can." Orlad was very sure of himself now. Yesterday's outlaw had become today's warrior leader. He killed sons of Hrag. He was on first-name terms with huntleaders. He needed practice smiling, but he could smirk.

"You don't speak the language!"

"I can learn it faster than you can become a man."

She scowled. "You think you can be doge?"

"Certainly. Benard isn't going, he says. Dantio can never produce an heir, and that's one of a ruler's duties."

"I'm coming with you!"

Orlad smiled for the first time. It was not much of a smile, and it was directed at Horth, sharing amusement at Fabia's performance. "Dantio insists Celebre has never had a female doge. They're hardly likely to want one at a time like this."

"But Stralg may," she said.

His eyes narrowed. "After you have sold us to him, you mean—me and Dantio?"

"Of course not! But I am coming with you."

Orlad rose to his feet, surprisingly tall at close quarters. Her eyes were not much higher than his brass collar.

"It's no journey for a woman."

"I crossed as a babe in arms."

"You don't understand the dangers, kitten."

"Of course I do!" In fact she knew the Ice better than he did. She had seen a vision of her infant self almost dying there. She must not lose her temper.

"Do you?" He put a knuckle under her chin and raised it so they were eye-to-eye. "Only twice has Nardalborg sent out a caravan this late in the season, and neither one arrived. There's death and frostbite out there, also rock boar and catbears. At the Edge there's no air, no water. You can't sleep, can't breathe, your skin cracks. Rivers of dust will swallow you whole."

"You know all this personally, I suppose?"

"Yes I do." Nothing fazed him now. "I worked on the bridge at Fist's Leap. Also, when we get to Florengia, if we ever do, we will have to avoid Stralg loyalists guarding the far end. The Mutineer and his men will have their own ideas about who's going to run Celebre after Father. We may find when we get there that the city does not even exist any more. Are you still sure you want to risk your pretty little neck?"

Ignorant, arrogant boy! Saltaja was out there, bloated with evil and a much worse danger than any he had mentioned.

"Yes!" she shouted. Remembering the probationers, she dropped her voice to a whisper. "You need me!"

"Of course we do." Orlad pulled her to him and kissed her, full on the mouth. It was definitely not a brotherly kiss, and yet somehow it did not ring true.

She struggled free, still angry at his mockery. "That means you give your permission, my lord?"

"It means we both need you and want you, tigress! We're going to discuss it with the huntleader in the Panthers' mess at sunset." He headed for the door.

"My lord!" Horth said softly.

Orlad stopped, turned. "Master Merchant?"

"You know Nardalborg Pass, you say?"

"The first part of it. Not the Edge itself."

The Ucrist smiled diffidently. "I know both passes, but only by hearsay. Nardalborg Pass is well signposted. Varakats is not. You have no hope of finding it without a guide, no hope at all. Anyone will tell you that. Have you spoken with the Pathfinders?"

Orlad shook his head. "No, but I will, right away. Thank you."

The door banged and he was gone.

Fabia slumped down on the edge of the platform beside Horth. "This is awful, just awful! The family has been reunited just one day and already it's splitting up—Ingeld and Benard going back to Kosord, Orlad and Dantio rushing off into the war. And I must go with them, even if it's just to say farewell to my dying father, who deserted me, although that means deserting you, who have always been my father."

Horth patted her hand diffidently. "Orlad and Dantio will not be rushing off anywhere, my dear."

"What? How can you say that?"

"Because that man I was speaking to while you were buying your new gown was Pathfinder Hermesk. I have known him for years."

She knew what that subtle little smile meant and her heart dropped. Here was a complication she had not foreseen. She should know better than to underestimate Horth Wigson.

"I confess I don't know what pathfinders do. A guild?"

"No, no. The Pathfinders are a cult of holy Hrada. Hermesk is head of the local lodge. You could say he is the light of Hrada on High Timber, but that seems a little pretentious."

Hrada was goddess of useful skills and crafts, like pottery and writing, but those were regulated by guilds. Offhand, Fabia could not have named a single Hrada mystery. "And you bribed . . . I mean you discouraged Pathfinder Hermesk from supporting any further travels over Varakats Pass before spring?"

"Not at all!" Horth said cheerfully. "He volunteered the information. He mentioned that the pass was now closed for the season. All the traders and all his cult brothers have already gone seaward. Pathfinders are restless folk, never staying in one place for long. And they cannot be bribed, my dear, any more than Werists can. If Hermesk says he is not going, then he is not going, and that is that."

"Oh." She huddled small while she brooded over this news. "Why can't they be bribed?" she asked suspiciously. Bribery was one thing Horth could do better than anyone.

"I told you! They never stay anywhere long. They had to keep moving. Wanderlust is their corban. Wealth is just useless baggage for them to carry and real estate would tie them down." Horth put an arm around her, an unusual intimacy from him. "So you need not worry any more, my dear. Spring is a long time off, and we shall have each other until then. In summer we shall know more of what is happening in your homeland. And if you still feel that you should accompany your brothers . . . Perhaps separation will not seem as hard a blow when we have had time to prepare for it."

He had had half a year to prepare for it already. He was refusing to face facts. Go all the way back to Skjar just to turn around and come back here?

"You're overlooking something, Father."

"What?"

"Saltaja. Saltaja has escaped. I mean *if* Saltaja has escaped, then Arbanerik will never catch her. No matter what the risk, she'll make a run for Florengia. Saltaja is the power behind the sons of Hrag and if she can link up with Stralg, then she may manage to turn the war around. Even if all she does is hold off the Mutineer for a while, that delay will increase the danger to Celebre." Once Saltaja reached Nardalborg she would have Cutrath to work on—Shaping worked best on blood relatives, she had said—and who could tell how many monsters Stralg had spawned?

Horth smiled blandly. "I fail to see the connection." He was denying the unpalatable again.

"Orlad and Dantio can't handle her. It takes a woman to deal with a woman." Even if the boys outside were listening, that was innocent enough.

"Fabia!" Horth said sternly. "The lady Saltaja can be harsh, I admit, but I refuse to countenance those foul slanders about her. If she were what you are hinting, she would have been brought to book years ago. I certainly fail to see that she is any business of yours. Lord Dantio and lord Orlando are much better equipped to deal with her, whatever her talents or loyalties or gender. *Even,*" he insisted when she tried to interrupt, "if you were a Chosen yourself and wished to oppose the lady, instead of aiding her and her Ancient Mistress, your powers and experience would be so much less than hers that you could not possibly hope to prevail against her."

That was as far as he could go to admitting the truth he had guessed. And what did Fabia tell him now—that she had already slain four men? That it was she who had made the seer's rescue possible last night? He would not hear what he did not wish to hear.

"Whatever happened to Quera, Father?"

He jerked away from her. "Who?"

"Quera, the woman who nursed Mother after Saltaja's men beat her. I have heard rumors that you had her impaled."

"*Impaled?*" he squealed. "Fabia, how you could you possibly suspect me of such an appalling thing? I threw her out the door myself. In fact, I recall that you were there. You saw me do it!"

She nodded sadly. She was convinced now that he was lying, although that did not necessarily mean that Verk had known the true story. Horth himself might not. He paid other people to do his dirty work for him, so he need never know the details. Had Paola helped him that way? He would certainly never say just what services his Chosen beloved had performed to forward his career. Loving support or outright murder or something in between? Xaran might tell, if asked, but Xaran was the Mother of Lies.

When Fabia did not speak, Horth said, "It is starting to rain again. We must invite those fine young men inside. They won't do much of a job of guarding us if they have to keep stopping to sneeze." He rose and shuffled over to the door. The discussion was over.

✦

At sunset, Fabia and Horth set out for the Panthers' mess with their escort of juvenile strong-arms. She reveled in the sensation of being clean and well-dressed again, even if the muddy, root-infested roadway forced her to wear clumsy boots. Another light shower seemed to justify trying out her sable cloak and hat, but they were much too warm for the weather. They were Ice wear, originally intended for merchants heading over the Edge and cut down to fit her.

Sounds of drunken singing floated through the town, and she saw several exuberant Heroes staggering along the road, most supported by women in Nymphs' red wraps. Once something streaked across the trail a few paces ahead of her—two somethings, giant cats, pale gold. Before she had time to scream, they vanished around a corner. They had been wearing brass collars. Her probationer bodyguards yelled "Runners!" and began gabbling about messengers from Hordeleader Arbanerik bringing news of the battle.

✦

The mess was a circular building, large enough to seat four sixty men. A fire crackled on the central hearth of undressed boulders and a ceiling of white smoke hung just about head height, moving in uneasy swells like an inverted ocean, dribbling out through the thatch reluctantly, as if it would rather stay and attend the meeting. The floor was packed dirt, booby-trapped with tree roots, and the windows were open slots. There were no tables and the benches were merely split logs lashed on to stumps, so they were located at random and most had a slight slope—everything about High Timber was temporary.

The only people present were Dantio, Orlad, and the man Fabia had seen earlier, whom Horth had named as Pathfinder Hermesk. From their stiff postures and the way they were spread out around the center, they had not been engaged in a cozy chat.

Wearing a pall of green, blue, and red, Orlad scowled at Horth, but told the probationers. "You can go, maggots. Give my thanks to your herder, and when you wake up dying, remember I told you not to drink so much." The boys buzzed out the door like bees from a hive.

Dantio remained tactfully inscrutable. He wore a scuffed jerkin and well-worn linen trousers too short for him.

The Pathfinder looked like an elderly woodsman or farmer, tall and spare, with a face well-weathered, almost haggard. The tip of his nose was missing, as was the top of one ear. When he spoke, his mouth twisted to one side. As a cultist, he had high status and wore a seal on his wrist, but his clothes were shabby leathers. Horth introduced him to Fabia.

He did not stand up. "I am honored to meet the daughter of Ucrist Horth. I have often had the privilege of serving him."

"He speaks highly of you, Pathfinder." Fabia spread her robe on a bench for Horth to share with her.

"I brought the Pathfinder along," Orlad said, "in the hope of convincing him our mission is urgent."

Hermesk's smile was dangerously close to a sneer. "Brought me by the scruff of the neck! Perhaps you, young lady, can convince your impetuous brother that urgency is irrelevant when no one will be crossing the Edge now before spring? In fact I am here because Nils Frathson asked me to be here. Otherwise I would have already left High Timber. My canoe is packed, ready to go. We Pathfinders have restless feet, always eager to walk new roads."

Anyone who addressed Fabia Celebre as "young lady" was taking unnecessary risks. "How about the other pass? If Saltaja has escaped as far as Nardalborg, can she cross the Ice from there?"

"She can certainly try, of course. Whether she succeeds will depend on holy Weru, Who is god of storms. I do not predict His whims." The Pathfinder sighed with exaggerated patience. "Holy Hrada guides me. I never lose my way, but I cannot move through snow or quicksand any faster than you extrinsics can. I can freeze or starve like other mortals." He held up his hands, displaying a total of six fingers. "I know the Edge as well as any, and it is deadly. I have lost most of my toes, also, and this sinister leer of mine was another brush with frostbite. I am sympathetic to the flankleader's impatience, but I decline to commit suicide."

Fabia now understood why Orlad looked so grumpy. "Nardalborg Pass is well furnished with shelters, I understand, and the shelters are provisioned."

"Then the lady Saltaja may win her gamble."

"Would it be possible for us to slip past Nardalborg before she sets out? Could we get ahead of her?"

Orlad said, "Never! That's stupid! Nardalborg was built where it is to guard the road. There are bogs on one side and a canyon on the other. I suppose you might find another way over the moors, but it would take you days. You would need good weather; and then the patrols would see you."

So much for her efforts to be helpful. "And there is no one in High Timber except you, Pathfinder, who can guide us over Varakats Pass? No merchants?"

This time it was Horth who smacked her down. "I told you the merchants have all gone seaward, dear."

"Packed their boats and gone," Hermesk agreed.

Fabia had her back to the door and jumped when a man moved in silently around the end of her bench. He was a brass-collared, pall-wrapped Werist, but a Florengian. He sat down beside Orlad.

"Any luck?" Orlad asked.

The newcomer shook his head.

Then came the shock of recognition. Waels had a whole new skin. His birthmark had gone. His close-cropped beard and hair were jet black.

"Have you been *dyeing* yourself, my lord?" Horth asked.

"No." The changeling beamed. "Aren't I beautiful? Orlad thinks I am, don't you?" He flinched at Orlad's glare and muttered, "My lord is kind."

There were a lot of emotional breezes eddying around this evening.

"How did you do that?" Fabia demanded.

"I didn't. Benard did."

"Should have guessed!" Nobody produced random miracles as casually as Benard seemed to.

Dantio had been leaning forearms on knees, glumly staring at the ground. Now he looked up. "Our brother is on his way here from the bathhouse, with six angry Heroes in pursuit."

Waels laughed. "All still the same pretty pink?"

"But with mud in their hair. Ah! Lady Ingeld!"

All the men rose and bowed to the Daughter. Even the Pathfinder did.

She was introduced to him and chose a nearby bench to share with her usual shadow, old Packleader Guthlag.

Fabia asked, "Is Benard completely recovered, my lady?"

"Yes, thank holy Sinura! He is still badly bruised. The Healers admit that they did not think their goddess would save him. Witness Tranquility is resting, but insists that she feels no ill effects."

"And you are planning to return to Kosord?"

Ingeld smiled wistfully. "I have no choice, my dear! I must go home, just as you must follow your destiny and head for Celebre. And Benard will not abandon his unborn daughter."

"Will not abandon you, you mean. I have rarely seen a man so in love."

Dantio rose and stepped over to Fabia, holding out a hand. Puzzled, she responded. He merely touched her fingers, went to Orlad, repeated the gesture; then resumed his seat. "There is something you should know, both of you. You will respect our confidence, Master Pathfinder?"

"You wish me to leave?" Hermesk asked stiffly.

"No, I rely on you to be discreet." Dantio looked around the group. "I congratulated Benard on his recovery tonight, just before Orlad's horde carried him off to the bathhouse. When I hugged him, I learned that he has lost his seasoning. I don't know when the change happened, but I suspect it was when he snared Horold. Or it may have been in the bathhouse with Waels. He still had it when we left Tryfors."

There was a puzzled pause until Ingeld appointed herself spokesperson. "What does it mean, though?"

"I don't know," the seer said. "I honestly do not know. Seasoning is very rare, very mysterious. I *think* it means that Benard has done everything he ever can to change the world. He had his chance at glory and he took it. I don't think it means he is about to die." He shrugged. "But even that I don't know. Seers do not prophesy. Orlad and Fabia still have theirs."

"And you?" Orlad barked.

"I can't taste my own flavor, brother."

"So what does Witness Tranquility say?" Waels asked softly.

Dantio's chuckle sounded forced. "A Werist with brains is against nature! Yes, mine has gone also. It's up to Orlad and Fabia from now on. Ah, listen!"

Orlad frowned suspiciously. "Cheering?"

"Certainly cheering! Two runners arrived in town a little while ago, probably from Arbanerik. They reported to Huntleader Nils and he went over to Revengers' Mess, where the remains of the celebration is collapsing into a collective stupor. Whatever his news is, they have stopped heaving long enough to cheer it."

"You could hear what he said, couldn't you?"

The seer smiled. "Well, yes, but I'll let him tell you. He's on his way. Have you met him yet, Fabia?"

She shook her head.

"Nils Thranson and Hordeleader Arbanerik are lifelong friends. They trained together, were initiated together, crossed the Edge in the same summer. They were even disabled the same day, in the ambush at Merilan, which was the Mutineer's first big victory. Arbanerik's arm was torn off, and Nils lost half his face. Orlad will tell you that one-eyed Werists and one-armed Werists are equally useless. Both men were invalided back to Vigaelia. They founded New Dawn together. And here comes our sculptor. No more miracles, brother?"

Benard loomed in from the gathering dusk and went straight to Ingeld's side. He was soaking wet and scowling ferociously.

"No! They wouldn't believe me when I said I didn't *do* anything to Waels, the goddess did it, and all I could ever do was *ask*, and he was special. They made me ask Her for each and every one of them!"

"Why is Waels special?" Fabia asked.

"Ask him. Or ask Orlad. Stupid, bone-headed . . ." Benard's growl faded into angry muttering as the rest of Orlad's men trooped in. They were all still Vigaelian pink, apparently unhappily so.

Before anyone else could speak, Dantio warned: "Nils is here."

The current ruler of High Timber was small for a Hero, and younger than Fabia had expected, no more than middle twenties. He wore a two-colored pall and a curiously tied head scarf, one end draped down the left side of his face and tucked into his brass collar. He marched straight to the hearth and turned to survey the group with a menacing one-eyed stare. Knowing or guessing who everyone was, he dispensed with formal introductions.

"Heroes . . . Daughter Ingeld . . . Ucrist Horth . . . Herm . . ." He nodded to each in turn, ending with Fabia. The half-face smiled. "The news is good, as you probably heard. Tryfors has fallen. The Hordeleader confirms that Satrap Therek is dead, as you already knew. His successor, Huntleader Karrthin, has sworn allegiance to New Dawn. There was almost no bloodshed at all at Tryfors."

Orlad's Heroes raised a cheer, but it sounded halfhearted. Bloodless victories were in poor taste.

"Saltaja?" Fabia asked.

The solitary eye swung around to regard her coldly. "Escaped. Yesterday she fled upcountry with Huntleader Fellard and the Fist's Own. By now she is almost certainly at Nardalborg. Two of our hunts, the Fangs and Weru's Sons, set off in pursuit. At Halfway Hall they met considerable resistance from Fellard and his men. Heavy losses on both sides." No cheers. "The hordeleader feels no great urgency about this. He can starve Nardalborg into submission if necessary. If the woman escapes over the Edge, she will no longer be our problem."

But she would certainly be a problem for Florengia and Celebre. Fabia opened her mouth and Horth laid a warning hand on her arm. She closed it again—Orlad was watching them suspiciously.

Nils Thranson said, "So the Hragson tyranny has collapsed, and much of the credit goes to the sons of Celebre gathered here. Witness Mist has been a tireless supporter of our efforts for years. Flankleader Orlad and his Heroes disposed of Therek Hragson by seizing a god-given opportunity with commendable courage and resolution. Hand Benard displayed incredible, legendary courage when he led Horold Hragson into our ambush."

Pause for more cheering. Benard looked bashful. Ingeld kissed him.

"For the first time," the hostleader said, "I am free to acknowledge the vital contribution of Ucrist Horth, who unstintingly financed our revolution. Without his gold and his courage, there would have been no New Dawn."

Gasps of surprise turning into wild cheering. Horth smiled shyly. Fabia hugged him; others flocked over to shake his hand.

When order had been restored, the huntleader said, "Now we must consider the future and your rewards. Hordeleader Arbanerik has ordered me to extend any assistance within my power. At Daughter Ingeld's request I asked our resident Speaker to join us. He will also witness any other oaths that may be required."

Fabia wondered why a backwoods rebel cantonment would need a resident Speaker at all, then decided that every Werist who had enrolled in New Dawn must be already sworn to another loyalty. Speakers spoke the laws of holy Demern, but they also knew loopholes in them, ways to undo inconvenient oaths.

Benard eyed Ingeld suspiciously. "Why do you need a Speaker?"

The dynast somehow managed to look arch and supremely innocent at the same time. "Because Horold's dead, dear. Don't you want to make an honest woman of me and give your daughter a legal father?"

"Er. Yes. Course. But you're a Daughter. Can't you marry us?"

Dantio was grinning. So was Huntleader Nils. Everyone else seemed as puzzled as Benard.

"No Daughter can marry me," Ingeld said. "As dynast of Kosord, I must be married by a Speaker, who will administer the oath to my husband."

"Oath?" Benard was thoroughly alarmed now. "What oath?"

"Oath of office, darling. A dynast's husband is city consort."

His howl of horror was audible even over the massed laughter of everyone else. The Werists were convulsed.

"*Me*? I can't rule a city!"

Ingeld wrapped an arm around him and laid her head on his meaty shoulder. She was clearly sublimely happy. "Why not? You can just order other people to do all the work!"

"But . . . I can?"

"Yes, you can. Everyone in the city knows you."

"That's what I mean. You can't make Kosord accept me as ruler!"

"Watch me!" she said.

"Then that's settled," Nils said. "Flankleader Orlad?"

Orlad's new scar made his scowls more menacing than ever. "Dantio and I are going home to Celebre. Waels wishes to accompany us. So does Fabia. Pathfinder Hermesk refuses to guide us."

The hostleader frowned. "That so, Herm?"

"It is not a matter of refusal, Nils. It is a matter of impossibility. I thought Heroes understood campaigning." The Pathfinder turned a world-weary look on Orlad. "Listen, lad. You must carry your own food, because you cannot live off the land. You must also pack clothes and at least a bedroll, if not a tent, and even weapons until you reach the real Ice, where nothing else lives. The bigger and stronger you are, the more food you need. At the very most, you can carry about ten days' rations, and when you reach the Edge itself, any burden at all seems impossibly heavy, even your own body. Understand now?"

The Pathfinder obviously enjoyed lecturing, but he would not dare use this tone to a Werist if he were not a friend of the huntleader. "At Nardalborg, you start with mammoths. On Varakats Pass the merchants use canoes to carry provisions up the Milky. Either way, you cache food upcountry before the caravan proper even leaves. Huntleader Heth has spent years building shelters and bridges. In either case you come to an end. Neither mammoths nor canoes can climb First Ice. From there you must use human muscle. So you set off from the trail head and after ten days you run out of food. No? Of course not. You build a pyramid. You start with thirty men, say, and after four days twenty of them drop their loads and head back. The other ten carry on, taking the extra rations the others left. They can go another ten days before they start to starve, which is still only fourteen days from the trail head. So you really needed to begin with sixty men, didn't you? Or twice that? Or four times? In the end a very few have enough food to complete the journey. Nardalborg has tallymen who can work it out, allowing for bad weather and men dying of Ice sickness. Understand? Nardalborg has done all that work ahead of time on the Nardalborg Pass. You have not provisioned Varakats Pass and therefore it is not presently passable."

Orlad was flushed with fury. "We have the men! Didn't the hordeleader say to give us all the help possible?"

"I can't command the Pathfinders," Nils said unhappily.

Hermesk smirked as if the quarry had just stepped into his trap. "Men, yes, but you have no canoes. The merchants took them when they set off seaward to trade their goods. Even if you did, we do not have time. It takes at least a thirty to set up a caravan, and by then winter will be upon us."

"The witness speaks the truth," Dantio murmured.

Orlad bared teeth at him in a silent snarl.

"There has to be a way," Fabia said. They *must* catch Saltaja before she linked up with Stralg!

The Pathfinder laughed. "Do tell us."

"I'm just the pretty little woman. You're the expert. You tell me. Or you, Orlad. You say we cannot go around Nardalborg. The Pathfinder says we cannot go over Varakats. Suppose New Dawn takes Nardalborg, or surrounds it—"

"Puts it under siege?" Orlad said.

"Yes. Couldn't we *follow* Saltaja over Nardalborg Pass?"

Orlad rolled his eyes to indicate that women should not meddle in manly matters.

Dantio said, "If Saltaja does attempt the pass, she will close it behind her, to prevent pursuit. She will leave no supplies. She may even tear down the bridges and burn the shelters. Here comes the Speaker."

Fabia turned to watch the newcomer stride in the door. Night was falling fast and he was muffled in Speakers' black, from his hood to the hem of the ankle-length robe swirling around his boots. She had met more than enough Speakers in Skjar. Without exception they had been sour, joyless, literal-minded people who would win any argument with a quotation from the Arcana, usually expressed in a tongue so ancient than no one else could understand it. A Speaker's only virtue was absolute incorruptibility, which was both his blessing and his corban. In theory a Speaker would even sentence himself to death—but only in theory, because he would never be guilty of a crime.

"Speaker Ardial Berkson," the huntleader announced, and even he gave way, stepping aside to let the newcomer take the place of honor beside the fireplace.

Only then did Ardial throw back his hood. Unsurprisingly, his face was narrow and bony, scored by deep lines. Also, he was tall and lean. Speakers always were, because holy Demern forbade gluttony. This one was elderly, with a striking mane of white hair. He would be handsome if he could seem just a little more human.

"Good of you to come, Speaker," Nils said. "Daughter Ingeld, dynast of Kosord, wishes you to conduct her marriage to—"

"That is not possible, Huntleader." Predictably, Ardial spoke with a sonorous orator's voice. "The years have been kind to you, Ingeld."

Ingeld's face was stark with horror and pale as bone.

Benard said, "What? What's wrong?" and started to rise. She clung to him, pulling him back down.

"What's wrong is that she is already married," the Speaker said. "Release my wife, young man."

Orlad stood up. *"Is that so?"* Instantly seven other Werists sprang up also and menace echoed through the mess hall.

"That is so," the Speaker said calmly. "Sit down, boy. All of you boys sit. I am still her husband and rightful state consort of Kosord. Are you incapable of speech, wife?"

Ingeld moved her lips several times before she produced an audible sound. "You ran away! When Stralg came you ran away!"

"On, no, wife." Ardial smiled bloodlessly. "You misstate the facts. The bloodlord's brother, Horold Hragson, swore by his god that he would kill me if I did not leave the city directly, or if I ever returned to Kosord. You know that the fourth paramount duty is to preserve one's own life, subject to the first three duties. Furthermore, *it is written* in the laws of holy Demern, chapter two, clause eighteen, that a man should prevent a crime even if a lesser crime may result. I will quote you the exact text if you wish, but it is quite long, listing numerous crimes in their rankings. Faced with the promise of death, wife, I asked you if you would satisfy Therek Hragson's carnal demands, on the premise that he had been imposed in my place as consort of the city and your person. You said that you would, having no reasonable choice. I obtained from him a promise that he would use no violence upon you as long as you were obedient and true to him only. Thus I had assurance that the result would be adultery, not forcible rape, and that is a lesser crime than my own murder would have been. I therefore left the city in obedience to the law."

"Murder?" Benard still had an arm around the Speaker's alleged wife. "Suddenly I appreciate the brighter side of murder."

"Let the professionals handle it," said Orlad, stepping forward with a commendable awakening of family solidarity. His men began to move in unison.

Hostleader Nils roared, *"Silence!"* He glared around, one-eyed. "Sit down, all of you! You know the penalty for injuring a Speaker."

The Werists sat down, glowering.

Ardial said, "Thank you. I ordered you to unhand my wife, Florengian."

"No." Benard had paled, so that bruises stood out as blotches all over his face. "I killed Horold Hragson for her and she is *mine*! Now and always. And her child is mine, also."

"Child? Was the babe conceived according to the rituals of Veslih's holy mystery, Daughter?"

Ingeld nodded mutely.

Ardial shrugged. "Then she will be your legitimate heir and I will see she is raised accordingly. Under chapter seven, clause forty-nine, your sacred duty to provide a successor in my enforced absence excuses your adultery. I will accept you back as my wife once you have undergone ritual purification. The man, however, is guilty of adultery and usurpation. I hereby sentence him to death under chapter one, clause seven, also chapter three, clause fourteen. Huntleader, arrest that man."

Orlad's flank growled like surf in a major storm

Dantio chuckled and stood up. *"It is known* that I am a Witness of Mayn."

The Speaker frowned at him. "You are not dressed as one. Establish your claim."

Dantio's smile turned frosty as the Ice. "It may be legal, but I find it unseemly for a man to accuse his alleged wife of adultery when he has two Nymphs of Eriander in his quarters."

Ardial's shrug was barely perceptible. "It is both legal and irrelevant. I acknowledge your credential but not your relevance to this situation. I was present at the events I described, so I know them to be as stated. Did my wife just give perjured testimony?"

"*It is known* that she did not. A Witness may ask a Speaker to rule on the holy laws."

"She . . . I mean *he* may."

Dantio clasped his hands behind his back and rocked a few times on the balls of his feet, but then spoiled the solemn effect by winking across at Benard. "*The Witness asks*: If a man does not lie with his wife, after how many years may she have their marriage nullified?"

"In chapter one, clause eight," the Speaker declaimed, "it is written that she may make application to a Speaker to have her marriage nullified after seven years. But," and now Ardial displayed his first faint hint of human emotion, triumph, "has any Speaker set foot in Kosord since I departed?"

"*It is known* that none has, prior to her departure."

"Then she cannot have made such application, and if she makes such application now, I shall refuse it under the clause subsequent to the aforementioned clause because our reunion here tonight is a significant change of circumstance."

Dantio bowed. "The Witness thanks the Speaker for this determination of the holy Arcana. *The Witness further asks*: Is it not permitted, when legitimate or traditional authority—which in the case of Kosord would be the dynast's consort—has been evicted or overthrown by force, for the people to accept and obey edicts of the hegemonic power as if they were legitimate?"

"It is so written in chapter seven, clause ninety-five," Ardial conceded, and now he was definitely frowning.

"*It is known,*" the seer said blithely, "that seven years and seven days after the city of Kosord was bereft of its most recent consort, namely your learned self, Speaker Ardial, Satrap Therek celebrated his marriage with the dynast, Daughter Ingeld Narsdor, having publicly declared her previous marriage nullified. *It is also known* that no protests were lodged against his proclamation within the time duly allotted."

Ardial looked at Ingeld, who was glowing in the twilight, then at Benard, who now had both arms around her, and finally at the half-grin of Huntleader Nils.

"Then my initial ruling was based on incomplete information and it is possible for me to marry this woman to this man."

"And you will!" Orlad said, loud enough to be heard over the cheering. "*You most certainly will!*"

twenty

DANTIO CELEBRE

sat down, having achieved his purpose. He usually avoided weddings. Partly he disliked the absurd extravagance, the inevitable waste of more wealth than families could afford. A party was always a good idea, certainly, but why did a wedding need anything extra except a bedroom near at hand? Mostly he hated the surging cross-tides of emotion, ranging from lechery to suppressed terror.

He could not complain about extravagance tonight. The hereditary ruler of one of the greatest cities of the Face was marrying her penniless sculptor in a barbaric backwoods shed without one solid gold saltcellar in sight. A few candles would have helped. Even the usual lecherous remarks from the onlookers were subdued when the bride was older than all but two of the guests. Both bride and groom were bubbling with happiness, so Benard must have decided that the burden of being a dynast's consort was not so very terrible. Ingeld had been nominal ruler of Kosord since before he was born, and in practice she had run it alone for long periods when the satrap was away on campaign. A Hand would probably perform ceremonial duties beautifully.

Still, there was enough emotion loose to make a seer feel he was being pelted with snowballs and hot coals at the same time. Ardial Berkson was a predictable pillar of ice in the center, but all Speakers were like that. To the extrinsics present, Horth Wigson would seem another human fish; only a seer could sense the blazing exultation the Ucrist was hiding so well. Poor, lonely old rich man! His glow of triumph must mean that he believed he had blocked Fabia's ambition to leave him and return to Florengia.

The Speaker began administering a complicated oath to Benard, who stammered and floundered in the archaic language.

A scorching anger approached Dantio's left shoulder—Orlad, of course, seething with the frustrated bloodlust of a hunter who sees his prey escaping.

Glaring down, he said, "Well, brother?"

Back to that problem . . . "Well what?" Dantio said.

"How do we get to Florengia?"

The other source of rage in the hall was Fabia, but she was more frustrated than angry. Perhaps her chthonic powers let her detect a little of what

Dantio himself knew—that there was a way past the impasse if they could only find it. At the moment she was intent on the ceremony.

"You want me to meddle some more, do you?"

Orlad flashed *(alarm)*. "Not if it brings on that anathema thing you were frightened of earlier."

Dantio turned to face him. "That I am still frightened of."

(dismay) "I thought you were safe now? Didn't Horold break the compact before you did?"

Yes, although Dantio had not known that at the time, so he had been guilty in spirit. "I did worse. I could have broken the compact just by refusing to answer Therek's questions. But I lied. I gave False Witness, and that is a breach of the laws of our cult. The Eldest will have no choice but to rule against me, so our bargain still holds, brother." He winced at Orlad's surge of horror and forced himself to smile. "But I am not certain that her anathema will be effective on the Florengian Face, so I want to cross the Edge even more urgently than you do. There is a way. I just don't know what it is, exactly."

His baby brother bared fangs at him. "Oh, very helpful! You said the Pathfinder was not lying."

"I did. And he is genuinely afraid of the danger. But when Fabia asked about following Saltaja over Nardalborg Pass, and I said that was impossible, he reacted with panic. He saw a solution! Then the Speaker arrived and we talked of other things."

(fury) Orlad clenched his fists and—to a seer's vision—half the muscles in his body as well. "So what did he see?"

"I don't know. I suspect Horth Wigson does, though."

Orlad stared angrily across at the little merchant. "Hermesk told me that Pathfinders cannot be bribed."

"I expect they can be threatened. Nobody wants to antagonize the world's richest man." Who was still feeling disgustingly smug.

The room broke into cheers as the ceremony ended and Benard kissed his bride. Even as he did so, Dantio felt a sudden surge of satisfaction, which he recognized as coming from Fabia. The night had not done with surprises.

"I think," he whispered, "that you can stop worrying. Our sweet and deadly little sister has just solved the mystery."

Orlad chuckled. "Ah! Know something? There are times she scares me more than Stralg does!" He plowed into the press of people and benches, heading for Fabia. A moment later, his feelings welled up in satisfaction also. Dantio followed him into the throng, intending to give Benard his congratulations—and farewells, too, because it seemed as if the way to Florengia was about to open. Sure enough, even before he reached the newly-weds, Orlad's head appeared over the crowd and his powerful voice boomed out above the chatter.

"Pathfinder!"

Hermesk had been just about to slip out the door. He turned reluctantly. "My lord?"

"Small parties travel faster than large ones, don't they?"

(caution—deceit) The Pathfinder was wary, fearing a trap, wanting to hide something. "Not necessarily. Any party goes at the pace of its slowest member."

"How far apart are the two passes over the Edge?"

(fear) "It varies."

"In places they are quite close? Less than a menzil apart?"

(resignation) "Yes."

(joy—triumph) "So if we set out at dawn tomorrow, we might be able to cut across from Varakats Pass to Nardalborg Pass and *get ahead* of Saltaja?"

Well, of course! Dantio should have seen that. If they could get ahead of the Vigaelians—and stay ahead—then they could live off the enemy's food caches.

The spectators had fallen silent. Hermesk began protesting the dangers again, but Orlad would not concede. He won an admission that the early stretches of Varakats Pass were slightly easier than the start of Nardalborg Pass and that the two came close before they reached the High Ice.

The Pathfinder took refuge in outright refusal. "It is absurdly dangerous! I refuse to be involved."

Huntleader Nils intervened. "Oh, come, Herm! It isn't winter yet. The Milky is still running. The rain's washed away the snow."

Hermesk set his jaw. "It is still a risk. What fee am I being offered?"

The huntleader said, "Where is our Ucrist? Master Horth, you have contributed so much to the overthrow of the Hrag tyranny, you will help the cause some more, I hope?"

The little man's bland smile did not waver. Nobody but Dantio would sense his internal torment. He shifted his ground—slightly. "If brave Hero Orlad is adamant on taking the risk, I will happily finance his expedition. But Fabia will not go with him. She will be returning to Skjar with me."

"No!" Fabia pushed between two Werists to reach him.

He looked up with bland stubbornness. "Frena, my dear child! The journey is a ridiculous risk, and the war in Florengia is a worse one. Why go there, for the gods's sake? Your parents are nothing to you now, nor you to them. Here I can give you anything you can possibly want. What can Celebre offer you that Skjar cannot?"

Seers knew how deceptive some people's appearance could be, but even Dantio marveled that such a predator hid behind Horth's ovine exterior. His protest was logical, and it hurt Fabia. *(love—pity—sorrow—anger—determination)* She truly loved him. He was her father in all but blood, and to wound him in any way must be the worst sort of ingratitude. He was old and unwell. He had no one but her. He could reasonably demand her company until she married.

Alas, he was fighting destiny. Fabia knew about seasoning. She could see, as well as any mortal could, how the gods had set the House of Celebre against the House of Hrag. Horold and Therek were gone. Benard and Dantio had played their parts. Only Orlad and Fabia were left, against Saltaja and Stralg. Why else had she been Chosen, if not for this purpose? She probably could not resist her own grim goddess; it would be great folly to try.

"If I stay, will that make you happy, Father?"

Oh, brutal! Horth recoiled in dismay. Happiness was his corban. Nothing in the world could ever make Horth Wigson happy.

He rallied. "I am sorry, my dear, but I insist. An unmarried woman is subject to her father, or foster father in your case. If you do not believe me, ask the Speaker. I cannot possibly let you embark on such a perilous journey."

"Very well, I will ask him," Fabia said angrily. She called through the crowd. "Speaker Ardial? If a woman is unmarried and her true parents are unavailable, who has authority over her—her guardian or her brothers?"

"Guardian?" The Speaker made the word roll like a carillon. "Was she given into the keeping of this guardian by her father according to procedures set forth in the Arcana, chapter six, clause eighty-two?"

Of course not, she had been stolen. Only males over the age of ten could legally be taken hostage. With a few deft quotes and citations, Ardial Berkson decreed that under the third duty and various obscure clauses, Fabia belonged to Benard Celebre—not her eldest brother, to Dantio's relief, because he had forsaken the world when he joined the Witnesses.

Dantio would not gamble a stale crust on Fabia being any more obedient to Benard than she was to Horth.

Benard clearly thought the same. "You want to go with Orlad?"

"Yes, I do."

The Hand grinned. "Then I put you under his authority. Put that in formal language, Speaker. Good luck, brother."

Fabia grabbed Orlad in a hug. He lifted her and spun her around.

But Pathfinder Hermesk promptly hurled another rock into the emotional pond, sending ripples surging. "I still want to know my fee! What am I offered to risk my neck traveling upcountry at this time of year with a bunch of crazy children?"

"You could keep it unbroken," Waels muttered on the sidelines, but even he must realize that violence was not an option when the Pathfinder was a close friend of Hostleader Nils.

The room fell quiet. Pathfinders could not be bribed.

Fabia detached her Werist brother and returned to Horth. She took his hands in hers.

"Father? You have given me so much! Will you not grant me this last gift of freedom? That is a parent's last sacrifice. Let me grow up and fly away?"

She might be using chthonic powers to change his mind, but all Dantio detected was rank ingratitude. He felt the entire room squirm. If she had learned her ruthlessness from the Ucrist, the pupil now surpassed the teacher. Horth had met his match.

(resignation) "Name your price, Master Hermesk."

(surprise—greed) "Another ten years on Yeti Pass."

All that meant to Dantio was that Pathfinders could apparently be bribed after all.

The Ucrist understood, though. "Agreed."

"So we can leave at dawn?" Orlad shouted. *(jubilation)* "Fabia and Dantio and Waels and me? You won't mind if I put a guard on your canoe overnight, Pathfinder, will you? You will provide supplies for us, my lord?"

Excepting Waels, his Werists started shouting that they wanted to come, too.

"No room in the canoe," Orlad said. "But I can suggest honorable employment for all of you now. The new state consort of Kosord is not a Hero, but he is worthy of Heroes' service. Lord Benard, can you use some tried and true, well-blooded young warriors?"

Benard had been gazing blissfully into his wife's eyes. He looked around and said, "What? Oh, I'm sure we can. I have to win back my wife's city, my lords. The odds will be at least two sixty to one, none of this easy stuff Orlad has been giving you." He grinned, showing his shattered teeth. "As consort of Kosord, I hereby appoint Guthlag Guthlagson my hordeleader. Speaker, will you administer whatever oath he has to swear? Then he can start recruiting."

"Told you it wasn't difficult, dearest," Ingeld said.

twenty-one

HETH THEREKSON

had not slept all night. That was not unusual for him on the eve of a caravan departure, but it was poor preparation when he would be leading the caravan himself and would need all his wits in the day ahead. Obviously an elderly woman could not be expected to keep up with young Heroes trained to razor sharpness for the ordeal, so the addition of Saltaja to the roster had required innumerable changes and additions—a prefabricated carrying chair, a stove to warm her tent, and so on. Around midnight a runner from Halfway Hall reported rebel troops moving up from Tryfors, so Nardalborg would probably come under attack very shortly. Having appointed Frath his own replacement and Zarpan leader of white pack, Heth had been forced to spend time instructing them in their duties, stressing the need to defend the fortress. As if all those worries were not enough, Femund had gone into screaming hysterics when she learned that Filukena was to go along as Saltaja's lady's maid. In the end Heth had been forced to order her confined.

Now dawn was near. When he rapped on Saltaja's door, it was opened by Filukena herself, already dressed. She blinked uncertainly at her father, as if she barely remembered him.

"You're up early!" he whispered. He had assumed she was fast asleep in her own room.

She smiled uncertainly. "I sleep on a mat on the floor beside her ladyship now, so I will be within call whenever she needs me. And I must never tell anyone anything I see or overhear. Not even you."

He swallowed an inexplicable lump in his throat. "It's a great honor to serve her! You must try very hard to please."

"Yes, I know." Filukena lowered her voice. "Father, what's a guitha?"

"I have no idea. Why?"

"Her ladyship calls me that. I am to be Guitha from now on."

"Well . . . that's a pretty name. Good morning, Guitha! Is her ladyship awake also?"

"Yes she is!" said another voice. The door was hauled wide, revealing Cutrath Horoldson, unarmed, barefoot, with his pall untidily wound around him like a blanket, as if he had just awakened. "Do come in—*cousin!*" He smirked.

Heth noted the insolence for later adjustment and walked past him. Saltaja sat on the edge of the platform, fully dressed and eating from a loaded tray beside her. She had insisted on a ground floor room, which in Nardalborg meant a very small one, with little space for more than a narrow sleeping platform. If all three of them had spent the night in there, two must have slept on the floor and would have been crowded even so.

She looked at Heth with very little interest. "Good morning, Huntleader."

Heth bowed. He told her of the news from Halfway Hall.

"So when do we leave?"

"In about a pot-boiling, my lady. We have started loading the mammoths, as you can probably hear."

She nodded. "Ah, yes, the mammoths. Cutrath was telling me about the mammoths. How many do you have? How many will we take with us?"

Cutrath's stubbled face looked inexcusably smug. If that young prig thought he could appoint himself military adviser to lady Saltaja, he was going to meet a painful lesson very soon. The fact that she had two nephews in Nardalborg did not make them equals.

"We will take almost all of them, my lady. You will ride on a howdah, of course, but the rest of us will walk, except when we have to ford rivers and cross boggy patches. Wading through shoulder-deep ice water will kill a man very quickly. Mammoths also carry victuals and the clothing we will need for the Ice itself."

"What else do they carry? How far do they take us?"

Again Heth glanced at his cousin, but this time the young oaf kept his face respectful. Heth had been running these caravans for ten years now. All Cutrath knew about crossing the Edge he had learned in the orientation lecture that Heth gave the transients when they arrived. He had not noticed young Horoldson being particularly attentive.

"They mostly carry their own fodder, my lady." Had Cutrath remembered that detail? "This late in the season, they have stripped the grazing all along the road. Each night we feed them and stockpile enough for their return. If the weather holds, the fifth night will see us at First Ice. That is where we have to leave the mammoths. The going is too steep for them beyond that."

Saltaja looked expectantly at her other nephew.

"If we took all the mammoths and less fodder, couldn't we get there faster . . ." The word *cousin* hung in the air unsaid. ". . . my lord?"

"Perhaps, but they would not have enough to eat on the way back."

Cutrath's eyes glinted. Heth's confidence wavered under a strong suspicion that he had just stepped in something even nastier than mammoth dung.

"And if you had not stockpiled any fodder on the road home," the boy said, "what would the mammoths do?"

"They would scatter to find fresh grazing, of course. The Nastrarians would bring them in eventually."

"And if they had no Nastrarians to guide them?"

Heth gasped, as if at a physical pain. *It had taken years to build up that herd.* "They would just wander." He admitted. "Go feral."

Cutrath shot his aunt a triumphant, I-told-you-so smile. "Without the burden of return-journey fodder, the brutes could get us there faster and carry additional equipment, as well?"

"What sort of additional equipment?"

"Axes to destroy the bridges. Oil to burn the shelters and food stores."

Heth's life's work . . .

Cutrath shone with joy. "And the river crossings would go faster if the mammoths were less burdened?"

"What is the purpose of this harangue?" Heth barked.

"We don't want to leave anything for the traitors, do we—my lord? Surely your duty is not just to see her ladyship safely over the Edge, but also to make certain her enemies do not pursue her?"

Of course. This murderous scheme was probably a mixture of Saltaja's ruthlessness and the boy's local knowledge, but it did make sense. No cost was too great to secure the lady's safety. "You are right. We can release those we don't take with us. They will likely follow for a while and then scatter. We destroy everything we can on the road. And at the Ice . . ." He had to stop and swallow a few times.

"We kill all the Nastrarians, my lord? Is that what my lord was planning to say?"

Heth nodded miserably. Nastrarians were cold fish, unable to befriend other people, responsive only to their animal charges. Nardalborg employed fifteen of them, men and women. He knew every one of them and he cared, even if they did not. So there was another task to do—delegate some assassins. They would have to be newcomers, not Nardalborg men. "Yes."

"My lord is kind."

"Please attend to it, Huntleader," Saltaja said. "I think warrior Cutrath deserves a promotion for offering this insight, don't you?"

Cutrath had evidently not expected that, because he flushed. The idea was ridiculous. From what Heth had seen of his nephew so far, he would rather promote one of the kitchen roaches. But he must not offend the Fist's sister.

"If it was his doing, he certainly does, my lady." He forced himself to offer Cutrath the customary handshake. "You are advanced to flankleader." He could not resist asking, "Do you have any special flank in mind?" *Is there one that will tolerate you?*

The boy pouted, hearing the silent insult. "Couldn't I just be your military attaché, Aunt?"

That would save him from pulling his weight in the grunt work. It might even keep him from being hassled to death.

"An excellent idea!" Saltaja said.

If he must play such games, Heth would make it obvious that games they were. "Then you are promoted two ranks, to packleader, and assigned as special aide to her ladyship. Inform your previous flankleader of your new posting. Draw a red sash from the quartermaster's."

Cutrath's smile was a leer. "My lord is kind."

"Huntleader," Saltaja said, nibbling a roll, "how long can the men you leave behind here defend the pass?"

"Depends on the size of the attacking force, my lady."

"You have instructed the garrison that they must fight to the last drop of blood?"

Heth nodded, throat suddenly dry.

"Good. Another little pep talk will not hurt, though. Send the packleaders to me now. One at a time."

twenty-two

ORLAD CELEBRE

so distrusted the grumpy Pathfinder that he borrowed Namberson and
Snerfrik back from Guthlag and set them to guarding Hermesk's canoe. He
did not doubt that canoes, like river boats, could launch themselves in the
dark.

Far from objecting, the Pathfinder promptly put all three Heroes—and
also Waels, who never left Orlad's side—to work unloading his personal
goods and moving them to safekeeping, then requisitioning and loading
supplies needed for the journey. He agreed with them when they grumbled
that common porters could do such labor, but pointed out that one ballast
stone dropped through the canoe's fragile bark skin would force time-
consuming repair. Orlad was in a hurry, wasn't he?

Yes, he was, and quite prepared to drag people off their sleeping mats
and keep them working all night if necessary. At first light the wayfarers
were ready to go. With luck they would steal a head start on Saltaja.

Having never experienced farewells, Orlad found the cold predawn
parting much sadder than he had expected. The rivals he had defeated in the
testing half a year ago had become his team, then his friends, and finally his
battle-tested brother warriors. Several of them wept; he had to blink a lot.
Benard openly sobbed, that amiable bear who had seemed such a puffball
when they first met, yet had turned out to be a man of suicidal courage. How
could long-lost brothers have become so close in so little time? Orlad even
felt moved just watching the Ucrist taking leave of his foster daughter. The
greedy little man would have to find consolation in his farms and houses and
his sacks of gold. Fabia was still weeping when she stepped into the canoe.
So was Dantio, steeped in the others' emotions as well as his own.

The canoe was narrow enough for each paddler to work both sides, but
not quite long enough for five people and the baggage. Hermesk repeatedly
stressed how fragile it was. It must be lifted in and out of the water, he said,
never allowed to touch the shore. Tipping it over in the wilds would result in
them all freezing, drowning, or starving to death. He put himself in the
bow, then Waels, Fabia in the middle—she promised to take a turn with the

work if the men wanted her to—followed by Orlad, and finally Dantio in the stern because he had canoed before and could help with the steering.

By the time the sun was fully up, the tyros had stopped soaking everyone with every stroke and Orlad was confident he would enjoy the next few days. Paddling was pleasant exercise. The Milky ran lovat green under the trees and ultramarine under the sky. Strings of noisy birds flew seaward, to lands where the winter would be warmer, if no shorter.

By the time the sun cleared the peak of Mount Varakats he was starting to consider blisters, the uncomfortable bundle he was sitting on, and how cramped his legs were getting—not to mention what a whole day of this was going to do to his arms and shoulders. No one had spoken for some time, except when Hermesk shouted "Change!" and they switched their paddles to the other side. The Pathfinder looked old enough to be a grandfather, but he had been doing this sort of thing all his life. He flapped along like a home-bound crow, never tiring.

It was going to be a long day.

Fabia peered around and said, *"¿Co sofo lattie par tenziale paludio u Florezou?"*

"Huh?"

"Co!" She shrugged. *"¿Sofo?"* She pointed at herself. *"Lattie."* She waggled her tongue . . .

"Can't you just tell me what the words mean to start with?"

"Nyb!" Head shake. Her eyes gleamed with amusement.

He sighed. "How do I say, 'Start again!'?"

With both hands busy he could not even seek help in gestures and he must keep paddling in time with the others. It was going to be a *very* long day.

◆

Soon the forest disappeared. Then the river wound in dizzying loops across bogs and wetlands, among reeds and groves of bulrushes, in and out of ponds. The Pathfinder never hesitated and never had to backtrack. Ahead, the glint of the Ice grew brighter, the sky above it a deeper, darker, richer blue. Mount Varakats swelled larger and closer, but never became impressively high and probably never would. In the thin air of the Edge, another conical blister showed very far away to the north. The Face was *flat,* after all. It was only because rivers flowed inward to Ocean that people spoke of going "up" to the Edge or the "High" Ice. The sun burned ever hotter, until about noon. After that rain and clouds and wind came to cool the sweating paddlers.

Dantio took over the task of pounding Florengian into Orlad, and Fabia started on Waels. The scrawny old Pathfinder knew some of the jabber, so he insisted on using it too. Orlad learned the Florengian word for "blood" when his hands started bleeding. That was just before Hermesk called for a brief rest, saying that they could go longer next time. Was revenge so sweet, or did he just hate men younger and stronger than himself? He certainly enjoyed giving orders to Werists.

At their second halt, as they sat on rounded boulders to wolf rations and quaff cold, crystal water from a pond—Hermesk had warned that drinking the Milky was a mistake no one ever repeated—Fabia demanded an account of the Nardalborg pass from Orlad.

When he managed to understand her sign language, he said, "Heth always estimates five days to First Ice, five to the Mountain of Skulls, five more—"

She scolded him in Florengian.

"*Anconti?*" he said. "What's *anconti*? Little? . . . Oh, *details*? You want details? Well, the Ice isn't continuous. First Ice is a wall, but when you've struggled up that, you still find lots of rock beyond it. There is nothing but rock at the Edge itself. Mountain of Skulls was where Stralg had his first big disaster, a sort of human avalanche. Nowadays there's a staircase there—part wood, part stonework, part hacked out of the cliff. Another five days gets you to Fist's Leap, and that's as far as I've been, that I remember. The Edge is about five days beyond that, but all those 'five days'es are rough guesses and wishful thinking. On the High Ice men can drop dead in their tracks. Storms can blow forever. Heth admits that nobody ever made it from Nardalborg to the Edge in only twenty days. He just likes to keep people hoping. Twenty days coming *down* is possible, if mammoths are waiting for you at First Ice."

Fabia chattered at the Pathfinder. He answered in Vigaelian, more likely because he did not trust his Florengian than out of sympathy for Waels and Orlad. "We'll reach our closest point in another three days. If we cut across country, we should—if the weather holds and we don't have any accidents— we should reach First Ice one day after that."

Fabia said, "So if Saltaja set out this morning, as we did, we should get there about the same time she does?"

"Depends how big an escort she has," Orlad said. "How many men and how many mammoths. It's crossing the rivers in relays that takes the time."

"How big an escort do you expect?" Waels asked.

Dantio said, "Very big. She doesn't have Therek and Horold lurking in the background to defend her now. She'll be well guarded."

"Then we should be able to travel faster than she can."

"As long as we can stay in front of her to Mountain of Skulls," Orlad said, "we'll be fine. There we'll rip out the stairs. That will slow her. After that we just stay ahead, sleeping in her shelters, eating what we need of her supplies, and burning the rest! We'll get to Veritano before she does!"

"Sounds good to me," Waels said. "Maybe we can even tip off the Mutineer's men that she's coming."

Fabia said, "No!"

Although puzzled, Orlad dared not ask what she meant. He had been inclined to trust his strange sister's motivations ever since a mysterious invisible force had aided the rescue of Witness Tranquility two nights ago, but there were times when Fabia made his blood run colder than the Milky, and this was one of them. Dantio was frowning. Waels and Hermesk just looked puzzled. Those two must never be allowed to suspect that they were traveling with a Chosen.

He changed the subject quickly. "When the Ucrist asked you to name your price last night, Pathfinder, you told him something about Yeti Pass. What did that mean?"

The weatherbeaten man shrugged. *"Om fornito presto orotinatori do happo alcuni."*

Orlad curbed his temper. Revenge was a fruit that was sweeter when ripe. After four more days he would not need this old grouch. Then he would see about mending manners.

Fabia took pity on him. "I asked Horth. There is no known pass between the Vigaelian Face and the Cignial-Zer Face, but there is a certain valley, far to the west, where strange apelike animals turn up from time to time. They're called yetis. They're always solitary, and always male. No one has ever seen a female yeti in Vigaelia. The males must wander in over the Edge from Cignial-Zer. Father once hired Pathfinder Hermesk to hunt for a pass, but withdrew his support because he was killing too many of his helpers."

"I am comforted by this information," Dantio said wryly.

"Half my life I have spent looking for Yeti Pass," the Pathfinder said. "And now I have a backer who never fails."

"That's right," Fabia agreed sadly. "If there's gold to be found, Horth will find it. He never fails. None of his ventures ever loses. And no success can ever make him happy."

♦

By evening, even grass had disappeared, and the Milky wandered through a land of rock and lichen. Mount Varakats glowed red against a cobalt sky. The travelers slept on the cold ground, their bedrolls huddled together for warmth and their heads tucked under the upturned canoe in case of rain.

The next day the Milky shrank to a brook and they had to portage around shallows. Waels and Orlad, as the strongest, were given the honor of carrying the canoe itself. Later Hermesk left the river altogether and took to the lakes—small lakes, big lakes, winding and twisting, portage after portage. Even when snow flurries blotted out the world, the Pathfinder never hesitated, guided by his goddess.

As the day grew steadily colder, though, he began to grumble about ice. At the noon break he suddenly balked. "We must turn back. The lakes are starting to freeze."

"We are not going back," Orlad said.

"Fool boy! You do not know what you are saying." The old man's voice grew shrill. "Ice will destroy the canoe, understand? If you step on a rock under the snow and twist an ankle, you will never be able to climb the pass. Would I tell you how to fight a battle? My goddess tells me we must turn back or we will die."

Orlad said, "My god tells me we must continue. We'll vote on it. Waels?"

"We go on, lord."

Waels had been a safe bet. "Fabia?"

She smiled wanly. "I yield to the authority of my brother."

Long may that last!

Dantio looked almost as worried as the Pathfinder. "He speaks the truth, Orlad." He leaned closer and touched his brother's cheek. "But you haven't lost your seasoning. I vote to continue."

"We go on," Orlad said. He removed one mitt and formed the bear's paw. Half a year ago, on an epochal first night in the chapel, the agony of battleforming had almost stunned him, but now he was ready for it and did not even flinch. It was Hermesk who cried out when the black fur and the deadly claws appeared in front of his face.

"We go on!" Orlad repeated. "Or I rip your precious canoe to shreds. You will deliver us to Varakats Pass at First Ice, as you swore to do, or you will die with us. If you cannot return to High Timber from there, you are welcome to accompany us to Florengia."

"This is madness!"

"Yes, but you will address me as your lord."

By nightfall the lightest pack seemed to weigh more than an ox, and even going back over flat ground for another required serious effort. Orlad decided he had underestimated the advantages of mammoth travel. He remembered to collect all the paddles and make sure they spent the night in the bedroll between him and Waels.

◆

By morning, snow was still falling and in places had drifted waist-deep. There was ice around the lakeshore.

Orlad awoke dreaming that he had been dreaming in Florengian. In reality he could ask some simple questions now and even understand some of the answers. He was certainly learning faster than Waels was, so his childhood memories might be returning.

They had hardly struck camp when the snow turned to rain. Later the sun came out. The weather changed faster than a weathervane could spin.

◆

Late on the fifth day, a long rainstorm lifted to reveal a landscape Orlad recognized. He was not surprised, because for some time the ground had been littered with old mammoth dung. The Celebres had arrived at First Ice and the Nardalborg trail.

That morning they had left the canoe wedged between rocks so it would not blow over. They had been walking ever since. Although he and Waels carried the heaviest packs, he had expected to walk the other three clean off their feet. He had not. The problem here was not legs and strong backs, it was lungs. And cold. He was soaked through. He felt as if he had never been warm in his life. It might be a long time until he was. All the others were in as much distress as he was.

In the far distance stood a cluster of barns and sheds, a lonely outpost of humanity in a rocky, barren hollow flanked on three sides by slopes of dirty ice. He looked around anxiously, afraid that the lifting of the rain might have left him exposed in full view of Caravan Six. Fortunately, the rolling slaggy landscape stretched off to the south as a desolation of rock, ice mound, and water, apparently empty of life.

"We've won," Dantio said. "We're here first. Nothing shows within my range. Those droppings are not recent."

Orlad sat down on the gravel and wriggled free of his pack. "Need a break." The others dropped beside him to do the same. "Pathfinder, you have amply fulfilled your side of the bargain. Fabia, give him the receipt."

"Of course." She fumbled in pockets and produced a small leather bag. She put five tiny pebbles in it, then passed it across to Hermesk. Horth would recognize the bag and five pebbles as the agreed signal from her that the contracted services had been delivered. "I am grateful, Master Pathfinder."

"You should be." He spoke sourly, but he did take the bag.

Orlad had given up dreams of teaching him manners. "Will you come with us, or try to find the way home alone?" If he could portage the canoe single-handed, he was a better man than Orlad.

"Finding the way is no problem," Hermesk said sourly. "Surviving the journey will be."

Dantio spoke up. "It is your decision, Pathfinder. If you choose to come to Florengia with us, and if our father still rules Celebre, then he will give you an immense reward for aiding our return. I swear this."

The surly oldster sneered. "Enough to buy a farm and put my feet up? Watch the weeds grow? Your father cannot reward me. Horth could—with Yeti Pass." He stared up at the lowering, darkening sky. "I will decide in the morning. At least we can sleep under cover tonight."

Orlad sighed. "I'm not sure we can. If Stralg's forces are anywhere near here, they'll certainly push hard to arrive by nightfall. We'd be sitting ducks in there."

"They can't travel in the dark, can they?" Fabia was staring at him in open dismay. She was exhausted—face pale under its windburn, dark shadows below her eyes, straggles of black hair escaping from her equally black hood. Why did she wear black furs when there were so many other colors available? Saltaja had worn black on the one occasion Orlad had met her.

"They could follow the mammoths' trail," he said. "They'd only need a single torch. We'll have to bivouac near here somewhere, far enough away that we won't be seen if Saltaja arrives with a horde." The glacier climb beyond the camp was an ordeal for tomorrow, and no place to be benighted.

"Saltaja may be dead," Dantio said quietly. "The Werists may have all switched sides, as Huntleader Karrthin did. We know that you killed Heth's father, but he may not. There may be no one coming up that trail at all."

"But there may be."

"We must dry off," the seer insisted. "Right now pneumonia is a bigger threat than the Queen of Shadows. Believe me, wet clothes are more dangerous than the dry cold of the Edge."

A prickle of alarm worked its way through Orlad's weariness and discomfort. Until now he had been leader. Dantio might have been deferring to him because of his local knowledge, or just to humor Baby Brother, but if the two of them disagreed, then the seer's age and experience must prevail. Orlad would be deposed.

He found a face-saving compromise. "Let's follow that gravel ridge. We'll be able to see a long way from the top of that, and if there's anyone coming, we can hide behind it real quick. If we don't see anyone by the time it gets dark, we'll go indoors and sleep in luxury."

"Good idea."

"You going to burn this place when we leave tomorrow?" Waels asked.

Orlad said, "They might still catch us. If we can stay ahead until we get to Mountain of Skulls, that's where we could really slow the pursuit."

"Makes sense."

"Does it?" Fabia muttered.

Dantio was staring at her with clear alarm. "What do you mean? You said something like that before. What do you have in mind? What are you planning?"

She shrugged. "Just something Orlad told me. I'll tell you later."

twenty-three

SALTAJA HRAGSDOR

was extremely unimpressed by mammoth riding. The howdah seating was sadistically uncomfortable and the weather perversely appalling. Lodging and food were as bad as any she had known since her childhood; even the river had been better than on her journey to First Ice.

She was more than seventy years old and even Chosen did not live forever. Without the power she could draw from the Old One, she would not have survived the first day. Although the sacrifice she had offered in Tryfors had brought her great favor, she must hoard that influence for the worse ordeal ahead. She now had Heth Hethson well Dominated, so he needed no further work for the time being. The girl, Guitha, was biddable without any Control at all. An angry word or a slap worked on her. But Saltaja did expend power on Cutrath Horoldson.

Shaping was her greatest skill and she had forgotten how enjoyable it was. She kept him at her side, sitting on the wind-swept howdah or rolled in a blanket next to hers in the shelters at night, completely unaware of her subtle prying in his mind. He was an excellent subject, being of her own blood and never having formed a character of his own. What personality he did have was totally dominated by fear of his father's displeasure and brutal discipline. She enjoyed whittling away Horold the ogre.

She needed something to replace him, though, and it took her a while to identify the vague shape lurking deep in Cutrath's dreams. She had expected his dead brothers or some other commanding young Hero. To her anger and astonishment, the mysterious idol turned out to Benard Celebre. He was strong, he was clever, he was Ingeld's lover. Even before that disaster happened, the young Cutrath must have sensed that his mother preferred the Florengian hostage to him, yet he dared not model himself on Benard when his father despised Florengians (wrong color), hostages (losers), and artists (sissies). But Benard was all Saltaja could find in there and he would have to do. She began to Shape a better Cutrath around his own view of the sculptor: physically strong, confident, courageous, popular with men, attractive to women. She was annoyed to think that the real Benard might not be too far removed from that image.

She had seen right away that the other men despised Cutrath. They snubbed and mocked him. She also knew that he would never be able to carry on the family business until he could command warriors' respect. Wondering if Werists could smell fear, as other predators could, she concentrated on erasing Cutrath's terror of his father. She knew she was making progress on the sixth night of the trek, when the expedition reached the shelter at First Ice. While she waited for hot water to be brought for her bath, she saw him talking with some other men. They no longer spurned him. They even laughed at some of his jokes. He was probably giving obscene answers to their questions about her, but she saw his flush of joy in the firelight.

Given time, she could make something of Cutrath.

◆

The next morning was the worst part of the trek so far. Heth's chosen assassins had disposed of the Nastrarians in the night; at dawn the mammoths rampaged. Some went off in search of vegetation, bulls began fighting over cows, still others tore open the barns to loot the last of the hay.

Saltaja's carrying chair had been unpacked and assembled. Heth had picked out the strongest eight men in the hunt to be her bearers, two teams of four, and she interviewed each of them briefly, imposing only a trace of Dominance, just lancing each man's venom enough that he would not be tempted to drop the Queen of Shadows over a cliff somewhere en route. She found the chair a tight fit with all her robes and cushions, but she would have taken to it sooner had she known it would be so much more comfortable than a howdah.

The path up the Ice was rarely wide enough for more than one man at a time. Foreseeing this problem, Heth had designed the chair with poles long enough that the bearers could walk between them, in single file. They took the weight on shoulder straps, leaving their hands free to hold the guide ropes. Her military aide fussed and fretted along close behind them, although Xaran alone knew what good Cutrath thought he could do.

At the top Saltaja saw a line of men heading off over a white plain toward a snowy ridge and the indigo sky beyond. The Edge itself was still days away. Westward the view was dominated by Mount Varakats and the wall of the world. Below her the buildings of First Ice blazed furiously and the last of the mammoths were disappearing over the stony desert. There was no turning back now, and no chance of pursuit. All she had to do now was live through the journey. Her eyes filled with tears, but it was the icy wind doing that, not sentimental thoughts of being reunited with Stralg after all these years.

It was cold! She closed the shutters against the wind and made herself comfortable.

✦

The road wound up and down endlessly. Wind and cold were their companions now. There was no real scenery, no mountains, only rock and ice. Even snow was rare. Stars shone in full daylight. She had nothing to do but endure, and yet she found herself growing weaker. Soon she could not sleep, she had no appetite. The constant cold was as bad as the lack of air, making her lungs ache and throat burn. She wished she had sacrificed more young men to the Mother of Lies.

Each night they came to a shelter that seemed smaller and cruder than the one before. The walls were built of local stone, without mortar. Everything else, from the doors to the roofing beams, had been carried up from First Ice on men's backs. The roofs were of slate or leather and the floors gravel or bare rock.

Every shelter had been provisioned with enough food and fuel for a two-night stay. Each morning the men were allowed to load up as much as they

could carry of whatever had not been consumed. Then the huts and their remaining contents were burned. At the fourth shelter the weather turned so
bad that they had to stay three nights, huddled together in fetid misery, listening to the wind howling through the chinks. The food lasted, just, but the
fuel did not. On the last night they could drink only if they sucked on fragments of ice.

Next morning the weather was little better, but now they must move on or
die. The march was resumed in a thick blizzard. Snow was drifting in a few
places, but mostly it just blew and the ground was scoured to bare rock. Fortunately the way was marked and led mostly downhill, in a long but easy slope.
When Saltaja judged that the day was near to ending, she passed the word for
Cutrath and he came to trudge alongside the chair. He was just another huge
man swathed in furs. It was not until he spoke that she could be sure it was he.

"Another pot-boiling to go, Aunt."

"Why do we keep going down? We are not over the Edge yet, surely?"

"No, Aunt. We are coming to Mountain of Skulls, they say. A big climb tomorrow. Stralg lost more men there than he ever lost in battle. So they tell me."

She thought it was also where his brothers, Finar and Fitel, had died, but
did not say so, not being sure. "I was not satisfied with my quarters, these
last three days. I want you to go ahead with the advance party and pick out a
place next the fire for me."

Cutrath sighed. "My aunt is kind." He disappeared into the mist. His father had used exactly that sort of impudence when he was young.

It seemed near two pot-boilings before she saw him again. The hut was
smaller than ever—absurdly small for four sixty men—and still icy cold. It
was also dark, full of grumbling, jostling shadows as the men filed in, but
there was a fire. Cutrath was sitting on a keg beside the hearth, and she went
to claim it. She sat and pulled off her mitts to warm her hands.

"I need Guitha," she said. "Find her."

Cutrath loomed over her, very big in his furs. "The huntleader is carrying
her. She has frostbite. She can't walk."

How annoying! "Then my military attaché will have to deal with my
chamber pot, won't you? I need the curtains put up."

Cutrath knelt at her side. "Aunt," he said quietly. "Listen!"

The front of his hood was open. Under the grime and stubble, he looked
scared, and that infuriated her. He should be beyond such weakness now.
She had been Shaping as fast as she thought safe. Must she resort to even
more drastic surgery?

"What's wrong?" she demanded.

"Sh! We mustn't start a panic. When we got here, I went to light the fire. Aunt, the hearthstones were still warm under the ashes! I swear it!"

Her first, unthinking, response was, "Late couriers coming from Florengia! We missed them in the snow."

"We couldn't have missed them! The road's too well marked. Aunt, suppose it's someone *ahead* of us?"

Fear ran through her like a peal of thunder. "You're imagining things."

"No! Aunt, I could smell the fire! The last supply party stocked this place a sixday ago. The fire wasn't that old. It was recent."

"That's im . . ." *Was* it impossible? "Ahead of us? We would have seen traces of them before now."

He shook his head. "In these pigsties? Who would notice? Nobody counts the pemmican. Outside . . . The wind wipes away footprints."

Her heart began to pound frantically. Cutrath was right to be frightened. Rebels? Celebres again? The Orlad one? It could be all four of the accursed Celebres, but the Werist was the one who knew the country. He could have killed Therek and then somehow gotten ahead of her. *And she had closed all the doors behind her!* She gasped for breath. *Holy Xaran defend me!* "Find Heth! I must speak with him!"

"I'll tell him when he arrives." Cutrath went away.

She crouched over the fire, shivering constantly. She must have a hot drink, something to eat. Then she would feel better.

Soon Heth dropped to one knee beside her. Evidently Cutrath had told him the news, because his eyes blazed blue, like chips of ice. "You think we may have cut our own throats, my lady?"

"It's the Florengians, isn't it? That Orlad?"

"It could be. He's a warrior to reckon with."

"You must send some fighting men ahead! Catch them and kill them! There can't be many of them."

Heth shook his big head. "No. I think that dizzy nephew of yours is imagining things. Even if he isn't, it's too late to worry about it. Tomorrow we climb the Mountain of Skulls, assuming the bridges and ladders are still there. If Orlad or anyone is ahead of us and wants to stop us, then this is where he'll try. He's had all day to break the staircases and cut the ropes."

"We can't go back!"

"No, we can't. But there can't be very many men ahead of us or we'd have found the rations short. I have lots of men! We'll need a few days to repair the damage, that's all. We may get hungry, but we can do it."

She peered inside his mind and confirmed that he was still loyal. He was giving the best advice he had. But she still had to ask, "You're quite sure?"

"Quite, my lady. The men are exhausted. They need food and rest. The worst thing we could do is start a panic!"

She could agree with that. "Are there other bridges after this?"

"A few. Nothing we can't repair or jump over if we have to. No, the place to close the trail is right here, my lady. If it's going to happen, it already has. We'll know in the morning."

twenty-four

MARNO CAVOTTI

heard the fighting before he saw it, but that was the whole point of his journey—this country was just made for ambushes. At first sight it seemed absolutely flat, but in fact it was dissected by a network of shallow channels. In the days before the Vigaelians came, the peasants had grown crops on the plain and planted palm vines in the lower, moister hollows. Now the level ground was mostly weeds or pasture and the vine trellises had collapsed into a sort of jungle tangle that could easily hide the entire population of Dodec. Every day without fail, the ice devil host camped outside Tupami dispatched foraging parties to rustle cattle, and that sort of dirty habit just cried out for a reprimand. Two days ago they had hunted north, toward Celebre, and yesterday east, so hopefully today south, to where Hostleader Vespaniaso was waiting with a couple of hunts.

Vespaniaso was quite capable of running a routine massacre, but a leader should attend a battle if he possibly could, just to show his men he cared. Cavotti had decided to make the effort. The chance to spend a night with Giunietta had helped. The fifth or was it six now? He had even started thinking of their relationship as a romance, until he had been quietly warned that he was far from her only partner. She almost never refused a Werist, he was told. Half the army knew Giunietta. But raw sex was better than nothing for a man without a home or family.

The six guanacos pricked up their ears nervously and hummed, but the wind was behind him, so they should not be smelling blood. Marno cracked his whip to warn them that he would not tolerate nonsense. The chariot continued to rattle and bounce along the dusty track. For the first time in ages, the wind felt cold. The sky was a lead plate and would likely drop some rain soon to make an official start of winter. Florengia had very little in the way of seasons, but very little rain could slow down a lot of war.

Stralg had been pulling back, concentrating his forces in the northwest of Florengia. So far he was avoiding towns and cities, having learned at Miona that they were flammable. At the moment the Fist's prime objective was undoubtedly to protect his supply lines and his road home. Cavotti had closed in around his perimeter and the rest of the Face was basking in the delusion that it had been liberated, that the war was over. It wasn't, but how long the present standoff would continue was in the lap of Weru Himself. A year of victories had boosted the partisans' morale enormously and they were collaring new men far faster than Stralg could bring in reinforcements. Another year should do it, two at the most.

Today, if all went well, the bloodlord would lose another sixty men. The bestial sounds of battle grew louder; then the road dipped and Cavotti saw evidence of recent carnage in the hollow ahead. The track was flanked on either side by jungle, an exemplary ambush site. Vespaniaso had chosen well. There were bodies in open view on the ground and thrashing shrubbery showed that the fighting continued on both sides. The vultures had not arrived yet.

The llamoids unanimously decided that they did not want to go any closer. Marno battleformed his throat to release the growl of a hunting catbear, a sound that never failed to curdle their blood. The chariot shot forward like an arrow, down the long slope. By the time he managed to rein in the team to a walk, he was in among the bodies—ten Florengians and four Vigaelians. That was a puzzling, bothersome ratio. If the ice devil foragers had been running along the road, they should have died on it when the jaws closed. How had the battle gotten into the shrubbery?

What he was hearing now, over the guanacos' terrified humming, was mostly just screaming. Werists roared a lot during a battle. When it was over, the surviving losers screamed. Heroes could recover from incredible wounds. With proper care, they could take an amazingly long time to die, and the winners were usually in no hurry. Butcher had been known to keep men dying for days, using nothing more complicated than a sharp stick. Something along those lines was going on in the shrubbery.

It didn't sound quite right, though . . . It took the Mutineer a moment to realize that the spectators were jeering in Vigaelian.

He yelled at the team and lashed out with his whip. The llamoids were happy to oblige. The chariot jumped forward, careering wildly along the trail, rocking wildly, zigzagging between bodies, gathering speed. For a moment, as the car cleared the last corpse and began to climb the long slope ahead, Cavotti could hope that he was actually going to get away unnoticed. The Vigaelians in the shrubbery had more amusing things to do than keep an eye on the road. Then an animal throat bugled. Three golden warbeasts scrambled out of the brushwood and came after him, closely followed by two more, all baying like hounds to summon more.

The chase was on. There was no hope of a chariot outrunning Werists, but he had about a fifty-yard start and might as well save his breath as long as he could.

What had happened? Had the consistent foraging pattern been a trap? Had the notorious ambusher himself been ambushed? Perhaps he had been betrayed, or Vespaniaso had. Giunietta? Or perhaps this was just the chance of war and the Mutineer's good fortune had run out at last. In ten years he had never been seriously wounded.

The luck stops here.

That had not been Vespaniaso's main force at all, just some of his scouts running into the ice devil foragers and dying for it, a minor skirmish. The main forces were elsewhere.

Cavotti kicked off his sandals and ripped away his chlamys, leaving himself wearing only his collar. He battleformed just enough to let the guanacos smell him. They hummed like a million beehives and increased their pace. The chariot raced up out of the hollow, onto miles of empty plain, in danger of flying apart from the battering it was taking on the ruts. He saw no cover, nothing much in sight anywhere except a few clumps of fruit trees, usually with a cottage and outbuildings nearby, now deserted. The roofs of Tupami were visible in the distance, across an empty plain that somewhere hid Vespaniaso and eight sixty men.

Having stayed biped, Cavotti could grip the rail with taloned, black-furred paws while twisting around to view the pursuit. He saw the same five yellow brutes behind him, all quadruped and more or less feline. Another three farther back had chosen to go more equine for greater speed. He had taken on long odds before, but eight to one was unthinkable. The three leaders were so close that he felt he was staring straight down their slobbering maws and had to struggle against an urge to battleform all the way; he must keep his wits working as long as he could.

He wondered if they knew who he was. After so many years of battle-forming, he had grown absurdly big, even for a Werist. Only Filiberno could match him for size, and Filiberno was so battle-hardened that he looked more like a bear than a man. Very few of the Freedom Fighters traveled by chariot and only Cavotti and Filiberno drove teams of six. If the Vigaelians knew that they were about to become famous, they would try not to kill him too quickly. His dying days were likely to be long ones.

The road swung north in a long curve. The right-hand ice devil cut the corner, which was clever for a warbeast and stupid by human standards. Cavotti waited, watching, judging distances . . . angle . . . and speed, be-cause the team was tiring. The two closest pursuers were almost close enough to stroke, keeping their eyes fixed on him but unable to board the speeding, bouncing chariot. The corner-cutter was moving in on the right, aiming for the team, being animal-stupid.

It closed on the lead right guanaco and everything happened at once. The team swung left to avoid the predator. The left-hand pursuer found it-self almost under the wheel and tried to come aboard. Gripping the rail for balance, Cavotti swung a killer back-kick to smash its head in. The chariot left the trail, such as it was, and the axle broke. He vaulted over the rail; cleared the tumbling wreck of llamoids, warbeast, and chariot with one gi-ant step off the pole; and hit the ground ahead going flat-out. One of the pursuers lay alone in the dirt, howling as it tried to heal its shattered skull. Distracted by the guanacos' screams and wildly flailing limbs, the other three had leaped in on the kill. Stupid! He would have gained a hundred yards before they realized their main prey was escaping.

Cavotti sprinted away along the trail on cloven hooves, gradually in-creasing the length of his stride as he went. Biped was his standard warbeast because it gave him an overview of what was happening on a battlefield. His front limbs were armed with claws, his mouth with fangs, and his forehead sprouted a conical horn about a handbreadth long. Being still fresh, he should be able to keep ahead of the pack for quite a while.

The problem was that he had nowhere to go. Eight sixty friends con-cealed somewhere along this road or one of the many other trails close by were absolutely no help when you had no idea exactly where they were and had—he risked a backward glance—a lot of enemies after you. Human-Marno would be able to count them. Now he just knew they were too many to fight. He had nowhere to hide and they could follow his scent anyway. Oh, *Weru's armpit*! The road was bending to the left for no reason. He went across country, cutting the corner, but the pack would cut it more.

Why stay on the road? Human-Marno had had a reason. Oh, yes, friends on the road maybe somewhere, if lucky.

Livestock ahead . . . from where? . . . more livestock . . . golden . . . They were warbeasts, Vigaelian warbeasts rising out of the ground. Many, many, many . . . Another Stralg patrol coming out of a hollow. They had seen him, were heading his way. Human-Marno would have been able to work out who they were but it didn't matter. He was between enemies. No escape.

He changed direction, heading for a lonely tumbledown shack under some spindly, unpruned trees, a farm abandoned when its owner died in the war, long ago. Peasants lived in villages now. Safer. Cover would not save him, but if he got his back against a wall he might take a few more of the brutes with him. He hurdled fences. He was slowing now, but he could still reach the ruin before the opposition reached him—conserve his wind for the fight.

He hurdled a last tumbledown fence into a wasteland of weeds and shrubbery. He was probably the first man to set hoof in there for fifteen years, nearly sixteen. He was thirsty. There was no defensible position, not even a stoop he could stand on to gain some height. He chose a barn wall where he would not have the sun in his eyes. Nothing to do now but wait.

The luck stops here. One more year and he would have learned how victory tasted. Now it would be Stralg who got Marno stuffed, not contrariwise. The devils might guess who he was. Biped warbeasts were unusual. Memo: Fight to the death.

He had little time to catch his breath before a long tawny beast came over the fence and without breaking flow gathered in its back feet and sprang at him like a golden flame. His hoof caught it full in the muzzle. He was slammed back against the wall and it went down in a splash of blood. Two came in together. He slashed and kicked. Something massive crashed into his groin, but his genitalia were retracted deep inside and covered by a bony plate. Jaws caught his right wrist and crunched it. They were all over him now. He clawed and jabbed and tried to kick, but they were too many, smothering him. Talons raked his chest, rattling off every rib like rocks on a washboard. He sank his horn in an eye socket and was blinded by blood. Teeth at his throat—

He had never imagined that there could be such pain. Some of the howling must be his, bubbling through blood . . . not all of it his. He'd hurt some of them. But his limbs were all twisted and broken and would not obey him. He was down in the dirt, howling and bubbling, writhing to try and escape the pain and only making it worse, bleeding . . . hurting. *Oh, Weru, help me!* Two naked Vigaelians were standing over him, mocking, laughing, and systematically stomping him so his bones wouldn't set. Another had found a pointed fencepost.

twenty-five

ORLAD CELEBRE

located the strip of pemmican he had dropped on the cave floor, gnawed off another piece, and went back to lacing up his boot. The boot had spent the night inside his bedroll and was warmer than his hands. The pemmican gritted on his teeth as he chewed.

"A hot bath," Fabia said, busily doing much the same things at his side. "I would give its weight in gold for a tub full of hot, scented water."

Waels looked up from folding his blanket. "It would freeze with you in it. How long did you say you spent here, my lord?"

"About a thirty. At least it's out of the dust."

They were in the Cave, a labyrinth under a mountain of rock slabs. Orlad had lived in there while helping to build the bridge at Fist's Leap, a short distance along the trail.

Fabia yawned. They all yawned a lot now. "How far to the Edge from here? In real distance."

"Less than a menzil."

"And that will take us five days?"

Orlad rolled up his blankets. "Heth always allows five days. It takes as long as you need. No more shelters. The Cave will seem like a palace."

"Wait until you get to the Edge!" Waels said. "There's a great marble gate with stone lions. And hot baths. The wine shop—"

"You talk too much. Heroes should be strong and silent."

"My lord is kind." Waels did not sound very repentant. "And this is the day we have been waiting for. Click! The trap is sprung."

"No!" Pathfinder Hermesk tried to yell and managed only a feeble wheeze. "You mustn't! Mass murder. Travelers do not do such things to one another."

At first the Celebre team had traveled by forced marches, bypassing some shelters to gain ground on Saltaja. The Pathfinder had started strong, but slowed as they grew closer to the Edge, his aging lungs laboring and wheezing. The dust of the last two days had been especially hard on him. Fabia could not have kept up any better with the two Heroes if she had worn a brass collar herself. Dantio, the weakest of the five, had done well until he sprained an ankle just before Mountain of Skulls. The team had waited there, giving him as long as possible to heal and keeping watch for pursuit, but since then they had barely managed to stay ahead of the Vigaelians. Most mornings they saw flames from the burning shelter they had left the previous day.

"We warned you what we were going to do when we began," Orlad said impatiently. "And now we have no choice. The wolves will catch us if we don't stop them."

"I agree that Saltaja must die," the Pathfinder whispered. "But how can you be certain she is there?"

"She is there!" Fabia took over the argument. "Who else would be burning the shelters? Werists wouldn't. They hope to go home one day."

"But all those innocent men with her?"

"We decided this back at First Ice, when we could still think straight."

Orlad could barely make out his sister's face in the gloom of the Cave, but her voice carried absolute conviction. It was she who had persuaded them that to try blocking the trail back then would be futile. The construction at First Ice would be too easily repaired and to interfere with it would just bring a troop of warbeasts after them. Fist's Leap, as Orlad had admitted when she cross-examined him, could be made completely impassable, and by then Saltaja would have closed off her own retreat. Fabia's arguments had carried the day then and she repeated them now.

"Saltaja and her foul brood have been a blight on the world for almost thirty years. This is the first real chance anyone has ever had to remove her. How many sixty-sixty more people will she slay in future? Will you have their deaths on your conscience?"

Orlad had hung back at Mountain of Skulls to watch the pursuit arriving, and his opinion was that it included the whole of Caravan Six. That meant four sixty men would die with the Queen of Shadows. More fool them for supporting the bloodlord. He finished lacing his pack and shivered. "Time to go," he said. "Don't be late."

He squeezed through the gap into the vestibule, past the high pile of bales of pemmican, and so out of the Cave. Into the wind. The sun was behind him, shining on the cone of Mount Varakats straight ahead, above a featureless gray landscape. Five days to the Edge, and then he would no longer have to stare at that mountain. That was the first sign that you had reached the other face, they said—Varakats disappeared. And the Veils of Anziel danced above you almost close enough to touch.

The Cave itself offered nothing flammable, not a joist or beam, but the cache there was the last food on the Face. Here travelers must load up with all they could carry and make a dash for the Edge. This supply was critical. As soon as all his companions were out of the Cave, Orlad spilled oil on the pemmican mountain and added a glowing ember. The wind caught the flames; he backed away quickly. Pemmican was dried meat and lard. Even here it burned. Oh, yes, it burned!

"Warmth at last!" Fabia said. "Where is the bathtub?"

Orlad hoisted his pack. He was bent almost double by it, for today it included a jar of oil as well as his bedroll and two sixdays' food. "Don't linger. When they see the smoke, they'll be after us like hungry catbears."

Hermesk was still grumbling that breaking bridges was an offense against holy Hrada, but the real trap was this bonfire. Without that food the caravan would have no hope of reaching the shelters on the Florengian side. If all went well, the Celebres would find those that had been provisioned from Veritano. First they must close the Leap and escape before the doomed men behind them arrived and took their revenge. No one had mentioned cannibalism yet, but that was part of the Stralg legend.

"Fabia, bring up the rear," Orlad said. That meant, *Look after Dantio.* "Waels and I will go and get started."

As the two Werists plodded off along the trail, Waels said, "Where does all this dust come from?"

"No idea."

Dust lay everywhere near the Edge, a curse and a torment. It burned the eyes and throat, it seeped into everything, stuck to everything. Whatever ice or snow there was lay hidden under dust. The landscape was a monotone gray, like a vast ash bed. Heaps and hollows hinted at boulders beneath, but the bedrock had been rounded and smoothed by the creep of infinite time. The sun was barely above the horizon, deadly bright in a sky whose blue was almost black, speckled with stars. Always the wind blew over this desert. It swirled dust along the ground, it lifted dust in choking clouds, and it even seemed to power the Dust River. In time it would bury the road too, but at the moment there was no need for signposts—the passage of many hordes had trampled a wide track through the maze.

"Tell me again," Waels told his feet, because he was doubled over as much as Orlad was, "why closing the trail here is better than at Mountain of Skulls."

Orlad paused to catch his breath. He could have carried a load like this all day at Nardalborg. Here he could manage only a few steps at a time. It was like walking in snow with only half a lung.

No need to waste breath repeating the story of the Leap for Waels. It was part of the legend of the first crossing. Stralg's horde had arrived at the Dust River and tried to wade it, only to discover that the Dust River was quicksand. The dust was as slippery as oil. Men fell, and then it filled their clothes and nostrils and pulled them down.

So the horde had searched out the narrowest place and tried to jump it— in battleform, of course. Three men in succession had fallen short, plunging to their deaths. Then Stralg himself had tried and done it. His men had thrown him a rock on a string. He had pulled a bundle of clothes over before he froze to death, then a rope. They had built a rope bridge. It had lasted many years, until constant gnawing by wind and dust rendered it unsafe. Last summer Heth had sent a construction gang up to replace it. When Satrap Therek refused to let Probationer Orlad try for promotion to novice, Heth had assigned him to the team. He had carried more than his share of the new bridge all the way from First Ice, and had stayed to help build it. Now he was going to destroy it.

"Stralg had ropes," he said. "They won't. No rope, no bridge."

"But if he could leap it, why can't other men? They'll come after us!"

"I'll show you." Orlad began to move again. "When we get there."

If they got there . . . He knew every up and down on that short trek, but he had never tried it with a mammoth on his back. Last year he had grown better acclimatized as time went on. Now he was still fresh up from Nardalborg. Black spots danced in front of his eyes and he paused until they went away.

"Want you . . . carry me," Waels gasped.

"I'll run . . . ahead . . . dump my pack and . . . come back."

"Take mine with you."

With a supreme effort, Orlad found enough breath to chuckle. Life was brighter when Waels was around. He liked the Orlad he became then.

✦

The Leap had not changed. The jagged gap of Dust River zigzagged across the rounded landscape, seeming completely at odds with it. The wind, the deadly cold wind, wailed constantly along the gorge. Its sides were vertical and polished to glassy smoothness. At the moment the low sun filled it with ebony shadow, but on the rare occasions when the bottom was visible you could see the surface of the river seething, faint clouds of dust rising and settling. Fall that far into water and you would probably be stunned or smashed, but if it were deep enough and you were an exceptional diver, you would have a chance of surviving. Not here. Dust was strange stuff—soft underfoot and rigid as solid rock when struck hard. No one falling into the Dust River had a hope.

The bridge came into view, looking just as Orlad and his fellow workers had left it a year ago, a simple deck of wooden slats carried by a dozen sturdy hemp cables anchored to bronze stakes hammered into the rock at either end. Hand ropes on either side gave an illusion of safety and were set just far enough apart for a heavy-laden man to hold comfortably as he crossed.

Two heavy-laden men staggered across and dropped their loads on the far side with gasps of relief. This was not yet the Edge, but somehow this crossing seemed more significant. Orlad looked back and cursed. A spectacular black cloud was unfolding above the vicinity of the Cave, dwarfing Varakats. He had cursed the wind up here a million times, but never for *not* being strong enough. The pursuit would see that cloud and know that it spelled their death.

"Better not dilly-dally," Waels said. "We cut it at the Vigaelian end, yes?"

"Of course." They must not leave anything on that side that might be useful or salvageable. "Move the packs a safe distance along the road."

Two puzzled eyes peered out of Waels's hood. "Safe from what?"

"They may throw things at us."

"Ah. I left my wits at First Ice. I'll run back and fetch them." He took up his pack again.

Orlad retrieved his jar of oil and returned to the Vigaelian side. Tools and coils of spare rope abandoned there a year ago still lay in the dust. He carried the tools one at a time onto the bridge and dropped them off. At Nardalborg he could have thrown them the whole distance. The rope he dragged all the way over to the Florengian side, just to make certain.

Despite that ghastly black plume in the sky, fire was hard to start on the High Ice and burned reluctantly. Ingeld Narsdor had blessed some tinder for Fabia to bring on the crossing, but it would have seemed wrong to use that for so deadly a purpose. Fortunately Orlad had brought the portfire from Hermesk's canoe. He confirmed that the coals were still glowing and laid it a safe distance away. Then he began soaking the ropes and slats with oil. It was awkward work with his hands in thick mitts and eyes peering out a slit in his hood, but he had built the bridge that way. He should be able to destroy it likewise.

He began to worry about pursuit. He had little knowledge of Zarpan Zarpanson, the leader of Caravan Six, but if Heth were in charge, he would react to that smoke in one heartbeat. Heth would have a flank of warbeasts streaking up the trail to see what was going on and stop it.

He felt the bridge sway as Waels returned to stand at his back.

"You haven't told me, beloved, why you think Saltaja's men won't be able to leap this."

"Could you jump this far?"

Waels said, "Um. Usually, easily. I'd carry you on my back. Up here, I'd rather not try. But Stralg did it, didn't he? Can I help you with that job?"

"Almost done. No, Stralg did not jump here. Stralg jumped at that wide spot over there." Orlad rose and tossed the empty oil jar into the abyss. It vanished into shadow without a sound. He could see almost nothing of Waels's face, but could guess at his incredulous expression. "Gzurg told me."

As one of Stralg's closest buddies, Hostleader Gzurg Hrothgatson had been here then. He had *seen* the leap. Last spring the old veteran had come home from the war, and his arrival at Nardalborg had coincided with one of Therek's visits. The two old-timers had plunged into an orgy of nostalgia and suicidal drinking, but Therek had taken the chance to appoint his crony examiner for the current crop of probationers. When Gzurg had chosen Orlad for the chain collar, he had also entertained him to a solid night's carouse and maundering reminiscence, just the two of them. The hangover had been memorable, the stories even more so.

"The River of Dust erodes," Orlad said. "It abrades. The reason the horde tried to cross there was that the river divided there. They could make two short jumps. There was a pillar. It was sharp at the top, Gzurg said, and its top was lower than the banks. The trick was to leap down to the pillar, land your front paws on a tiny area, pull in your back paws, and launch yourself up at the far side, all without slowing down. That was what the first three men failed to do. Stralg did it. But once they had a cord strung across, they moved downstream and built the bridge at the narrowest point. When Gzurg came back this way in the spring, he noticed that the pillar had disappeared. We were talking about the new bridge, and he told me. He laughed and said that the bloodlord wouldn't want to try his leap now."

"*Fry me!*" Waels said.

"Not here and now." That was a joke. Sometimes Orlad could even make Waels laugh, and that always felt good.

"But you're closing the pass forever!"

Not quite. Varakats Pass would survive. The bridge could be replaced, but only with a lot of planning, and with equipment Caravan Six did not have.

At last the others were coming along the track. The Pathfinder was out in front, but moving very slowly, shuffling and unsteady on his feet. Dantio was farther back, leaning on his sister's shoulder and obviously in pain.

"Here they come! Listen, my good buddy. My hands are all oily. I'd love to be warm, but not that warm. There's the portfire. As soon as we get everyone across, you light the oil and run, understand? And then—*Oh, Weru slay me!* Look at that!"

Warbeasts! Four golden shapes had crested the skyline and were racing over the gray, featureless landscape, their paws throwing up puffs of dust. They disappeared into a hollow and more came after them, at least a full flank. They weren't even following the trail, just heading straight for the bridge. Someone knew the area personally. Not Zarpan, certainly.

Orlad screamed "Fire the bridge *now*!" and took off like a spear.

He would not have believed that it was possible to run, and what he achieved was not much better than a fast stagger. How could those warbeasts keep it up? Either they were coming more slowly than they seemed, or they were going to kill themselves. He passed Hermesk, who had seen the danger and was making a gallant effort to go faster. Then he reached Dantio.

He gasped out one word, "Run!," to Fabia. Then he stooped, folded Dantio over his shoulder, and started carrying him back to the bridge.

That wasn't physically possible, but he did it anyway. He floundered like a drunk, feet sliding in the greasy dust, all off-balance, hearing his own breath howling in his throat; not listening to Dantio begging him to drop him and save himself. Up ahead, Waels had obeyed orders. Of course. Waels would cut his own throat if Orlad told him to. The near end of the bridge was streaming black smoke. But Orlad had not told Waels to go back to the far bank and save himself. No, no! Waels was coming to help. Idiot! Idiot!

Fabia had more sense. She was still heading for the bridge.

The warbeasts were faltering, all except one. One was well out in front of the others. That one would arrive before any of his followers, without support. There might be hope yet, if that one could be stopped. A fight? Could even Werists fight in this cold and without air? Black waves surged past Orlad's eyes. A noise of mammoths roared in his ears.

"My turn!" Waels said.

He did not so much lift Dantio off Orlad as slide under him when Orlad fell to his hands and knees. Orlad did not quite pass out, but he kept his head down, hauling air in and out of his lungs. When he could look again, Fabia had safely passed through the flames and was reeling across the bridge, pack and all. Hermesk had fallen to his knees on the trail, but seemed conscious.

Wrestling himself upright like a sack of rocks, Orlad went after Waels. *Family begins at home,* he thought fuzzily. No, that wasn't right, it was charity began at home, but he left Hermesk for later anyway.

Dantio was wasting air yelling, "I can walk! I can walk!"

Orlad said, "Let him!'

Waels let Dantio down. The Heroes laid his arms over their shoulders and the three of them staggered up the trail in a bizarre five-legged race. The leading warbeast was closer to the bridge than they were, but had collapsed in the dust. Perhaps it had killed itself. Yellow flames streaming from the near end of the bridge were starting to spread along the cables.

Waels plunged into the flames, hauling Dantio behind him. Orlad pushed them both ahead of him. The bridge creaked and rocked, but they went through safely. Almost safely—one of Orlad's mitts was on fire. He beat it frantically against his leg until the flames went out. Dantio and Waels were safe now, almost across. Fabia was watching from the far bank.

That left Hermesk, who was still on his hands and knees on the trail. One of the cables snapped; the bridge shuddered and tilted sideways. Orlad eyed the fire and decided he should have just enough time to rescue the Pathfinder, but not in oily mitts. He hauled them off and dropped them on the deck.

He took two steps and was sent hurtling backwards by the golden warbeast as it came bursting through the fire. Flat on his back, he looked up in horror at ivory fangs and drooling jaws. Claws pinned him to the deck, cutting into all his layers of fur. To battleform inside all these clothes would be suicide. He would never fight his way out of them. His face must be invisible inside his hood.

"Heth!" he screamed. He did not know how he knew, but he had no doubt. "Heth, it's me, Orlad!" Clothes or not, he could never fight Heth, who had helped him so much, trained him, saved his life from the satrap.

The warbeast hesitated, glaring at him with terrible, bestial blue eyes. Ropes of saliva hung from its teeth and tongue.

"Heth, it's Orlad. Don't kill me!" He was a Hero and he was begging for his life? And why was Heth hesitating?

A roaring black warbeast struck the gold one head-on as Waels came to the rescue. The bridge sagged under the impact, cables snapping with cracks like thunder. Snarling and clawing at each other, the two monsters reared up on their hind paws above Orlad. He felt blood spattering his face. The deck sank and twisted as the failing ropes stretched. Heth fell backward, and Waels came down on Orlad with a sickening impact that half stunned him, because he had not expected it. Then Heth was back, and this time all three of them roiled and raged, with Orlad at the bottom of the heap expecting them all to roll off to their deaths.

The bridge sagged again, weakly supported by burning ropes that stretched out impossibly under the tension. The last cables snapped. It fell with a strange lethargy. Roaring and tearing, the two warbeasts somersaulted downhill together toward the fire. Feeling himself slide, Orlad yelled, "Hang on! We're going!" He twisted over and grabbed the slats with fingers already numbed by the burning cold air. Still supported at the Florengian end, the deck folded downward to slam against the canyon wall and hang there like a ladder.

Jarred by the impact, Orlad almost let go. He saw his mitts fly past him, but if he had still been wearing those he would not have been able to squeeze his fingers between the bars. Waels had flashed out a paw and caught the tangle of burning ropes with his claws. Screeching in pain, he streaked up the net like a giant black cat. The pale warbeast that was Heth Hethson somersaulted down into shadow and was gone. There was no scream, no sound of impact. It was as if he had never been.

With the flames now directly below him and no purchase for his boots, Orlad hauled himself up the ladder by arm strength alone. At the top his wrists were seized by Fabia and a naked Waels. They pulled him to safety. For a moment the three of them coalesced in a great hug.

"Heth!" he said. "That was Heth! Get your clothes on, you maniac. Oh, Heth!" He tucked his hands under his arms and backed away from the smoke and fire. "Why did it have to be Heth?"

Dantio was helping Waels dress.

"I should have brought my seamstress," Fabia said. "But if we cut a couple of slits in your parka, you ought to be able to keep your hands inside and save most of your fingers."

Heth, Heth! I killed Heth!

"Can we salvage some of that wood?" Fabia said. "We could improvise a sled and pull Dantio."

Waels said, "You're pretty stupid not to have thought of that sooner."

"Did you?" she snapped.

"Of course not. I'm a Werist."

On the far side of the canyon, not as far as an athlete could jump in normal circumstances, Pathfinder Hermesk stared blankly across at his former fellow-travelers.

Not far behind him, four young Vigaelians wearing only brass collars stood in the dust field with their arms extended in some sort of impossible appeal, like children wanting to be lifted into their mothers' arms. They wailed their dismay in a wordless lament; the wind snatched it away.

Other warbeasts, farther away yet, were loping back to their caravan to retrieve their clothes and report the disaster. Waels Borkson and three Celebres were safely across. The Pathfinder was marooned. Saltaja Hragsdor was trapped, done for. Doomed.

All Orlad could say was, "Heth Hethson! Why was he here? Why did it have to be Heth?" Tears froze on his cheeks.

Part U

◆

THE END
IN
SIGHT

◆

twenty-six

OLIVA ASSICHIE-CELEBRE

walked alone in the Hall of Pillars. Expecting company, she had donned a simple, sober gown of forest green silk, the one her dresser tactfully insisted made her look "more slender" than any other she owned. She had never been a small woman. Grief and worry made other people fade away, but she only grew more massive. Not fat, just massive. It was her shoulders. Her one adornment was a double string of pearls, because the effect she was striving for was *competence and authority*. She must at all costs avoid *arrogance* or *presumption*.

Likewise, her choice of the Hall of Pillars. It was without question the largest chamber in Celebre, its huge colonnade rising giddily high to a frescoed ceiling. Beyond the great pillars lay the ducal gardens, sweeping down to the river, while the Bright Ones presided in a great mural on the opposing wall, above the doge's throne and his consort's ivory chair. For Oliva to receive the delegates while sitting on that chair would be rank provocation. Doing so in the throne room was—she hoped—a gentle reminder of who ruled and who was suppliant. Perhaps she was wrong. Perhaps she should greet them in the palace kitchen with flour on her nose. Or go to the other extreme and awe them with swordsmen and heralds and trumpets? She still wore Piero's seal on her wrist as well as her own. She still ruled in his name.

No, she ruled in his memory. She was not expecting company, she was dreading it. The charade was about to end.

Was she so evil, that the gods never answered her prayers? For years she had prayed for her children's safe return. By the time she realized that they must have made lives for themselves in Vigaelia and might no longer want to return, she had been praying instead for Piero's swift recovery. A year ago, she had begun to pray for his quick release. Now, she supposed, the limit of her supplication would be that he be allowed to die in dignity, as doge, not as a discarded husk. Was even that small boon to be refused her?

She paced over to the pillars and stared out at the drizzle, the gray weeping sky, the temples on the far bank. The rainy season had begun, but over in Vigaelia this was cold season, and the pass was closed. Few of the trees and shrubs were blooming now—only the exiles, red and white. They were called exile flowers because they bloomed when no others did.

Where were her own exiles, her three sons and her daughter? Where did they bloom today, if they bloomed at all? She would not know them if they walked in the door right now, and they would not remember her. It was a year since Stralg had promised to send for them, or some of them. She had not heard a word from the Fist since, but rumor said he and his horde were being driven ever closer to the walls of Celebre. There were constant rumors of Cavotti victories, Stralg defeats. She no longer cared which side won, if they would just leave the city alone. And give her back her children.

Faint sounds warned her; she turned and saw that her visitors had arrived, accompanied by a dozen or so flunkies. Surprisingly, they remained clustered around the doorway while the chief herald advanced toward her with a single companion, black-robed and black-hooded. Even at that distance Oliva could recognize Quarina Poletani, justiciar of the city. She had not been included in the invitation and her presence was ominous. Nevertheless, she must be shown proper respect. Oliva strode forward to meet her halfway.

She rummaged in memory for the laws Piero had explained to her half a year ago, when he began to fail in earnest. As senior judge in the city, the justiciar came first in precedence after the elders and would chair the council during the interregnum, when it chose the next doge. They couldn't declare Piero legally dead, could they? If Speaker Quarina said they could, who would argue? The political infighting had begun.

Female Speakers were rare and Piero had raised many eyebrows when he promoted Quarina to head the judicial bench. Unlike most Speakers, male or female, she did have traces of a sense of humor. She had raised two children and had two, perhaps three, grandchildren; she was spare or even frail. Oliva liked her.

Quarina arrived and was presented by the herald in a quiet voice, no trumpets. With the protocol so dubious, Oliva had forbidden excessive formality.

"A pleasant surprise, Speaker."

"No cause for alarm, though." Quarina did not smile, but possibly her eyes twinkled slightly. Did she dislike being used as a weapon of intimidation? "Since the matter that brings the honored councillors to wait upon your ladyship is an affair of state, they persuaded me I should be present as a witness. I agreed only upon condition that you approved."

"To witness what?" Oliva asked, eyes wide, brain racing. Then she caught herself. "But of course they will wish to tell me themselves. Your counsel and presence are most certainly welcome, Speaker." She nodded to the herald, who bowed and withdrew.

The moment he was out of earshot, Quarina said, "Also, I bring a message for you. I was not told who sent it, only that it was important."

Oliva felt every muscle tense. "It must be, to deserve such a messenger."

Quarina's smile was ladylike, not judicial. "As upholders of holy law, we Speakers are supposed to be sacrosanct, although I have never felt tempted to put that clause to the test." She was doing so now, if the sender was who he must be, Marno Cavotti.

"You had better relieve yourself of your burden, then."

"I was just told to tell you that the tholos urgently needs repairs."

Oliva let out a long breath. Yes, it was Cavotti. A scaffolding around the tholos atop the temple of Veslih would be a signal that his troops had her permission to enter Celebre. "I see."

"I admit that I do not. I was also told that there would be no answer."

"No," Oliva said. "There is no answer." Stralg was almost certainly on his way. Refugees were flooding in. One side or other would occupy the city whether she liked it or not, and the other would promptly try to raze it. Why had the gods chosen her to solve such problems?

The two elders who had requested this meeting were Giordano Giali and Berlice Spirno-Cavotti. Oliva had not convened the council in half a year, but she knew that its members had taken to meeting unofficially, in secret. They decided nothing, remaining steadfastly deadlocked, but sooner or later enough of them would die off to shift the balance of power. Meanwhile, this pair were unofficial leaders of the two main factions. Evidently the council had agreed to do something, but was either not sure what or did not trust any one of its members to do it unsupervised.

Berlice was a hard-faced woman of around sixty, leader of the pro-Stralg faction, the do-whatever-the-Fist-says-fast faction. She was also the mother of Marno Cavotti, the Mutineer. Piero had appointed her to the council to replace her husband, who had encouraged his son to rebel and for that had been publicly flayed while his wife and children were forced to watch. Berlice's face had a right to be hard. That incident had also lost the Cavotti family its standing among the very rich, so her sons and daughters had been forced to marry a few rungs down the social ladder. Whether her loyalty to Stralg was genuine or opportunist, only the blood-lord and his Witnesses knew, but she certainly had no love for Oliva Assichie-Celebre.

Giordano, on the other hand, was head of one of the greatest houses— old, bulky, silver-haired, and gloriously robed. His face, pouchy and florid, bedecked with bushy white eyebrows, wore an amiability that hid the ethics of a snake. He was a stout Piero supporter, leader of the traditionalists, rather stupid. Whatever his private opinion of Oliva, he would defend her against Berlice supporters because Piero would want him to.

"My lord Giordano," Oliva greeted him as he bowed. "How nice to see you. Councillor Berlice, you look well." *Considering your age.*

Then she shut up. This little get-together was their idea. Let them talk.

Berlice said, "Lady Oliva, we are all aware that the lord doge is most grievously sick and unlikely to recover. Is this not so?"

Oliva nodded. She had kept the elders away from Piero's sickroom for half a year, but to deny the truth any longer would be absurd.

"The council is concerned about the succession," Giordano rumbled. "We asked the Speaker to advise us on the law. She said—"

Quarina objected. "Not 'the law'! Holy Demern requires us to be obedient to our rulers and adjures them to rule justly. Never does He stipulate who is to rule. In Celebre the doge's successor is chosen according to custom. My guidance on custom I give as a judge, not as a Speaker."

Oliva awarded her a sliver of smile and said nothing. Holy writ could not be changed. Custom could.

"The doge is chosen by the council of elders," Berlice said.

"The day after his predecessor's funeral," Oliva added.

Berlice's smiles could be even thinner than hers. "At which meeting, the dead man casts the first vote. It is the most important vote, because few councils have ever overruled a doge's posthumous choice."

The justiciar said, "Five."

"And how many doges have there been?" Oliva asked.

"Thirty-two chosen by council. Customs were different earlier."

Pause.

Giordano coughed heavily. "The council has sent us to inquire of the lord Piero who has his dying voice."

Mostly they wanted to know just how ill he was. They would be shocked. Piero had not spoken or even known his wife in that last two thirties. Any breath could be his last. As soon as the elders had established that, they would appoint a more suitable regent than Oliva Assichie-Celebre, daughter of a very minor house.

Berlice said, "Custom decrees that the nearest adult male relative shall succeed, but there is no such man available in this instance—yet." Then she drove in the knife. "Because lord Chies is not yet of age."

Meaning, *Because lord Chies is not of the House of Celebre*. Anyone could tell just by looking at him that Chies was Stralg's. At the turn-of-the-year sacrifice, he would come of age—only yesterday Oliva had helped him choose the insignia for his seal, which was now being carved. He would be the youngest new man in the temple, for he had been born only hours before the end of his actual birth year, but such was the custom in Celebre. The council might not give a sixteen-year-old doge free rein, but he would be eligible to wear the coronet if the elders so wanted.

Had the honorable elders really come to ask if Oliva was ready to declare her youngest child a bastard and disinherit him? Chies would appeal to Stralg. The councillors must know that they were irrelevant as long as the Fist had a vote.

"The lord doge has given me no instructions," Oliva said.

"Has the bloodlord?" Berlice asked in a voice like an envenomed stiletto.

"No. A year ago we asked him to return the children he took as hostages, and he promised to bring back at least one, probably lord Dantio, our eldest."

Eyes turned to look at the drizzle and the sodden gardens.

"They cannot arrive before dry season now," Berlice said.

Oliva sighed. "No. And the doge cannot help you. Put the question to him if you wish. It will be only a formality. He will not hear you."

"Indeed? How long has he been in this condition?" Berlice meant, *When did you usurp the throne?*

"It happened gradually," Oliva spoke as civilly as she could manage. "The doge gave his seal to me and my authority stands until he revokes it or returns to the womb. Is that not correct, Speaker?"

Quarina nodded. "That is the custom of the city."

"You have done a fine job, my lady," Giordano said, jowls wiggling. "In very trying times, too. We are all in your debt."

Berlice made no sound, but her expression was expressive.

Oliva said, "My lord is kind. If you will come with me? I should prefer that we go unattended."

She led them across the great hall, out into windy, shadowed corridors . . . servants falling to their knees and bowing heads until the nobility passed . . . the sad stillness of a house in mourning . . .

"My husband directed that the state bedchamber not be used as a sickroom," she explained, in case the delegation assumed that this was her idea. In fact the state bedchamber was where the most valuable pieces of the ducal art collection were kept. It had been kept shut up for years and apparently Stralg had never learned of it. In accepting the surrender of the city, he had guaranteed no looting, but had he ever seen the treasures in there he would certainly have smashed the treaty tablets and helped himself.

Piero's sickroom was so small that there was little space to move around the tiny cot on which the dying man lay like a discarded rag doll—a skull face on a pillow, and a barely perceptible shape below the sheet. The air was hot and heavy with the reek of godswood braziers, plus a sour scent of death. On a stool at one side of the bed sat a brown-robed, hooded Mercy, holding the patient's hand, although for the last two thirties he had been unresponsive even to the Nulists. He was beyond pain. The woman looked up and nodded respectfully, but did not rise.

On the other side of the bed, arms on thighs and head bowed in sorrow, sat a large young man. He sprang to his feet as if startled, then hastily bowed to Oliva and each visitor in turn. He even got the order of precedence right.

Chies *never* came here! *How* had he known the elders were coming today? The reason his own mother had failed to recognize him for a moment was that he was draped in an adult chlamys, to which he was not yet entitled. A simple ivory pin fastened it at his right shoulder and the sheet itself was of unbleached linen, quite unlike the rich brocade he favored for his usual loincloths. The dagger at his side was plain bronze, without as much as an alabaster pommel to decorate it, and hung on a simple cord, not even a leather belt. When had she ever seen him wearing no jewelry at all, not even a ring?

She was staggered. Was this the rebellious adolescent pest she fought with every day? The hellion who threw up in corridors, who consorted with street girls and ice devil Werists? He was still slim, of course, but the drapery of the chlamys masked his skinniness, and he was much taller than lord Giordano, who was no mouse. The great hooked Stralg nose no longer seemed so absurd, now that he was gaining the chin and shoulders to justify it.

Her initial anger switched suddenly to pity, and even admiration. Stralg had never acknowledged that Chies existed, far less was his son, and yet who else could the boy use as a model? He had absolutely no right to the ducal coronet. He knew that and so did everyone else, but his real father was never one to worry about legality. Oliva could not blame him for trying. He was entitled to try. If he could get himself elected doge, even the Fist would be impressed.

Berlice Spirno-Cavotti was watching Chies with a completely unreadable expression. Had she put him up to this? Her faction might have concluded that Chies as a figurehead doge would be the best way to keep Stralg off their necks. Giordano Giali and his traditionalist faction might even have agreed with them, on the understanding that Chies would accompany his father to the Dark One's embrace when that happy hour arrived. Or Stralg himself might be behind this, having bypassed Oliva as irrelevant.

"A sad time for you," Giordano said, "—my lord."

Delight at the honorific flashed in the boy's eyes and was suppressed. He bowed. "I am young to lose a father, lord Giordano. I wish I could have been given time to be a good son to him."

Oh, really! Oliva made a note to find out who had coached him. She must congratulate him on his performance, provided he did not overdo it now. "The councillors are here on business, Chies. You may withdraw."

He bowed. "I do think, Mama, that this is one of his better days. You know how some nights I can't sleep, so I come and sit with him here. Just before dawn this morning I thought he knew me for a moment or two."

"Oh?" Oliva had given *strict* orders that she was to be informed if there was any change in Piero's condition. She hurled a ferocious glare across at the Nulist.

"He did stir a little about that time, my lady. It was nothing." The Mercy did not state who else had been present. Had Chies bribed her?

Chies recognized that his time was up and made a flowery departure. He had done very well, although Oliva doubted he had deceived this audience.

"Can you rouse him at all, Mercy? This is important."

The woman sighed. "I will try, my lady." She clasped the dying man's hand in both of hers and closed her eyes. After a few moments, she opened them again and said, "Be quick!"

Oliva said, "Piero? Piero, can you hear me? It's Oliva."

Did his breathing change a little? She looked to the councillors and shrugged.

Giordano said, "My lord Doge, this is Giordano Giali. The council sent us. Can you hear us?"

Nothing happened for several heartbeats. Berlice leaned forward as if to speak . . . and Piero's lids flickered. His eyes opened slightly. They stared up at the ceiling, motionless, but they were open.

"My lord," Giordano said, "the council sent us to ask you a question: Who is your choice to be your successor?"

The eyes did not move.

Berlice tried. "My lord, the council wants to know who is to be doge after you? Your children are not here. We need a doge. Who?"

The sheet over his chest lifted slightly . . . sank . . . rose . . . Doge Piero whispered something and closed his eyes again. They repeated the question several times, but he had gone, returned to whatever anteroom the Foul One used to store the near-dead. The delegates exchanged baffled glances.

"What I thought he said," Oliva said, "was 'The Winner.'"

Quarina agreed. Berlice nodded, thin-lipped. So, when asked, did the Mercy.

Giordano would not admit that he was deaf. "Winner?" he barked. "What winner? Winner of what?"

twenty-seven

MARNO CAVOTTI

handed the reins to one of his guards and lurched down awkwardly from the chariot. More guards opened the cottage door, releasing a blaze of firelight into the darkness; they peered inside to make sure it was safe for the precious Mutineer to enter. Cavotti detested bodyguards because they made him feel like a child, but ever since his near-death and last-minute rescue by Vespaniaso at Tupami, the Liberators' governing council insisted he go nowhere without them. He limped up the steps and pushed in past them. The door closed behind him.

Half a dozen men sat in a semicircle before the fireplace. Cavotti dropped his pack and hobbled over to them—his left ankle had not mended properly at Tupami and never would. He passed through the line without a word and knelt to warm his hands. Even in his alpaca cloak he was frozen, having driven for half a day over the wind-scoured, treeless moors of the Altiplano.

No one spoke. He could imagine the glances. The smoke was making his eyes water and he would not let this audience see his tears. Butcher's hand came into view holding a smoke-stained pottery beaker with an enticing odor. Cavotti took it and drank. He scalded his throat and shivered deliciously.

When he had drained the cup, he could delay the inevitable no longer. He stood up, shed his heavy cloak, and finally turned to warm his back and survey the company—Filiberno, Nuzio, Vespaniaso, Fangs, and of course Butcher. Big, black-bearded Werists all, as hard and ruthless a collection of killers as you would find on all Dodec, veterans of their lifelong struggle to rid Florengia of the ice devils. All were oversized from too much battleforming. Fangs and Filiberno were so brutalized that they barely looked human, while Nuzio was just a larger version of the fresh-faced boy who had ripped out his first Vigaelian throat eight years ago. They were permanently filthy and most of the time lousy. Even these days they often went hungry, but the very fact that they were daring to assemble like this showed that the bloody tide had turned in their favor. Including Cavotti himself, this was six-eighths of the Liberators' governing council.

They had shed their Altiplano cloaks and furs, and were sitting around in their usual chlamyses. Freedom fighters pinned theirs under their right arms instead of on the shoulder, either just to be different from extrinsics or perhaps to flaunt their brass collars—he could not remember why they had agreed on that. A chlamys would double as a bedroll, and for emergency battleforming could be removed just as fast as the Vigaelians could shed their loincloths. The boy rebels had been able to afford nothing better in the early days of the mutiny.

No doubt they had been well warned what to expect. Butcher knew what Cavotti had become, and so did Vespaniaso. None of the others had seen him since it happened. At least now he would be able to look Filiberno in the eye without shame. Filiberno had looked like a bear for years. Cavotti was like nothing the gods had ever dreamed of. Children fled screaming from him. The miracle was that he still lived.

This temporary command center was one of the few habitable buildings in Nelina. Once a prosperous ranching and mining town, it had been the first in Florengia to learn the folly of resisting the ice devils. Stralg had raped and slaughtered, and finally burned the houses. Before leaving, he had poisoned the wells by stuffing corpses down them—but that had been fifteen years ago. Now the water was sweet again and Nelina had a few inhabitants. They could be relied on to support the Liberators.

Lacking furniture, the Heroes were sitting around on their packs or stacks of firewood. At dawn the chariots would roll; they and their guards would disperse again. Rarely in the last ten years had Cavotti spent two consecutive nights in the same place. There should be a woman present, too. His eyes had failed to grow in again completely at Tupami, and he needed a moment to find her, sitting back in the shadows, wearing a dark brown wrap. It was Giunietta, and from habit his heart jumped. *Heart?* said his conscience. *That's not your heart down there.* He had known there would be a seer, not that it would be she. What must she think of the monster he had become? Still, sex was a complication he need never worry about again.

"What have you decided?" he asked. "I need something to eat."

Butcher said, "Nothing." He would never let anyone decide anything when his idol was not present. The others would have reached a consensus without his noticing.

"What have you discussed, then? Fangs?"

Fangs did have fangs, the right one badly chipped, but no nose. His smile was straight nightmare. "He was only a kid. Thought if he deserted as soon as he got here, we would forgive him. Spilled a lot of interesting stuff."

Fangs would take all night. Cavotti should have asked one of the others, anyone except Butcher.

"Was he telling the truth, Witness?"

Giunietta said, "Yes. The hostleader promised him his freedom if he would, and he kept his side of the bargain. Every word he spoke was true. And when he had nothing more to tell, the hostleader killed him!"

"Quickly?"

"Reasonably quickly," Fangs said. "He admitted he helped kill prisoners in his training."

"Then I hope he paid for it." Cavotti met the seer's accusing stare with one of his own. He must reassure the others that his own ordeal had not softened him. "It's standard practice, Witness. Standard on both sides. I don't care what oaths he swore, he could have betrayed us, whether he meant to or not. Stralg has seers, too, you know. Will somebody please tell me what the prisoner said that was worth my coming all this way?" Butcher handed him a leathery slab of meat, cooked but cold. He tore off a chunk without looking at it, still on his feet, lording it over them.

Giunietta said, "Vigaelia is in revolt. Recruiting is down to almost nothing. Most new initiates never reach Nardalborg. He said his hunt started from somewhere near Ocean and was down to a sixty by the time he got to Nardalborg. The deserters are massing, preparing a revolution. He didn't know where or when, but probably soon."

Cavotti nodded. Good news, but not urgent enough to call a council.

"The prisoner crossed in Caravan Five," the seer said. "He says there will definitely be a Six this year. Nardalborg was waiting until Five left to begin restocking the shelters."

Nuzio was smiling. He was the logistics expert. He could work numbers like a tallyman. "It must arrive within the next few days or it won't arrive at all."

"But we discussed this," Cavotti said angrily. He was tired—oh, gods, was he tired!—tired of the two-day race up here, tired of the endless homelessness, the slaughter, the whole Xaran-accursed war. He was already tired of being a monster, and he had the rest of his life to enjoy that. Meetings like this were still dangerous folly. Suppose Stralg had planted that informer? If the kid had not known he was being used as bait, the seer might not have detected the trap. "We agreed we wouldn't try campaigning on the Altiplano in the rainy season." The ice devils were far more tolerant of cold than Florengians, or so the Florengians believed, and a mere belief like that could tip a battle before it even started. "So we take out one caravan? We kill four sixty of the swine, but then we have to fight our way out again, past five times that many at Veritano."

He saw the leers. Especially Fangs's.

"You haven't heard the best of it, Mutineer," Nuzio said. "It looks like the Fist's been counting on us thinking that way. He *doesn't have* five hunts at Veritano, no more than five sixty men, the boy said. At the most. He was quite certain of that! They change stripes all the time, so our watchers think there's more of them."

"But the supply trains—Ah!" Now Cavotti saw the play. "Yes! Go on!"

More leering. "Yes! He's been shipping in far more food than the real garrison needs. He's stockpiling the fort so he can try a breakout in the spring, home to Vigaelia!"

Cavotti limped across to the door, fetched his pack, and found a place in the half-circle between Butcher and Filiberno, who was almost as good a strategist as he was himself. "So what do you want to do?"

"Depends how you are doing at Celebre," Filiberno said tactfully.

The agreed plan for the rainy season was to stay out of the Altiplano and keep nibbling away at the Vigaelians' perimeter. With both sides concentrated in the northwest and fairly evenly matched in numbers, the war had become one of maneuver. If Stralg let his forces get too dispersed, units could be cut off and wiped out. If he ever got too concentrated, he would be ripe for encirclement and starvation. But he had the inside lines now. He could concentrate his forces and break out at any time. It was a dance of scorpions.

"Nothing has changed," Cavotti said. "Stralg keeps feinting at Celebre. He wants us to move in ahead of him to defend it. He needs a victory, and storming Celebre with us in it would give him one, very likely. We'd like to see him make the same mistake."

He did not mention that a few days ago he had sent a message to the dogaressa, reminding her of the tholos signal. So far she had not fallen into the trap. Stralg would certainly have learned of the code from his seers, so if she had responded, the Fist might have stormed in to keep the Liberators out. That was not the sort of triple bluff to try and explain to Butcher.

"Famine, then?" Nuzio said. "We're going to see famine by the spring. If we stop the Fist's stockpiling, that would help a bit."

The opposing hordes were wasting the whole northwest, using up the peasants' surplus. When they had eaten even the seed corn, the only food left would be in the granaries of Celebre, and one side or another would be forced to take the city. And after that had gone . . .

Filiberno scratched a furry ear with a claw. "We could bring up half my host and feint at Veritano. If Stralg wants to keep his back door open, he'll have to divert forces up here to defend it. Or we can add some of Fangs's men and take it. Then he won't have a back door! He won't have any reinforcements next year to look forward to, either."

It was damnably tempting, so tempting that a tiny inner voice of caution kept whispering that it must be a trap. "When?"

"We figure we can have three to one in a sixday," Nuzio said. Those were the minimum odds for an assault on a defended position. "If the boy was right, and if we can get there before the caravan arrives."

"They'll be in no shape to fight if they've just come over the Edge." Cavotti spoke dismissively and noted the grins that followed this hint of approval. They wanted to do this, every one of them. It was risky, yes, but doing nothing was risky too. After a year of victories they were losing momentum.

Butcher handed him a wine jar and another greasy lump of meat. Butcher was as loyal as a hound, but some of these others were future rivals. The end of Stralg would be the end of unity. Already men were slipping away and heading home to other parts of the Face. That was another worry.

"Then what?"

Filiberno shrugged. "Stralg will try to take it back. Then we hit him in the rear."

And sacrifice the men left in Veritano? "How do you get those numbers there so fast?" Cavotti asked. "If we stick around, how do we avoid being pinned against the Ice?"

He was playing for time to think. To move a host into the Altiplano might be suicidal folly. The rains were already starting to wash out roads. The Fist would counter with his cold weather advantage—in fact this Veritano bait might be a trap like Cavotti's tholos message to the dogaressa. But if Veritano was lightly manned, they could certainly raze it in a lightning strike and make sure both the Fist and the Face heard about it. Stralg would have lost another battle and another five sixty men. The ice devils' morale would plummet even lower. But do not linger. Hit it, burn it, and run—safe but effective. *And do not stay!*

He explained. It took a while, but he brought them around without having to overrule anybody. "And if Caravan Six appears it can eat ashes," he finished. "So there go four sixty more at no cost to us."

They all grinned, excited at the prospect of another massacre. He did not point out that they would be stripping men away from the main theater, a force that might not get back easily if the weather changed, and would be badly missed if Stralg tried something. Nor did he tell them his hunch that Stralg would react by occupying Celebre and trying to use it as a bargaining chip to buy his way home to Vigaelia.

Always Celebre looked like the final prize in the war. It was the last big city left standing. If the Face was ever to be rebuilt, surely they must preserve it as a model of what civilization should be? Celebre was Cavotti's hometown and he secretly yearned to save it, somehow. He did not know how. He had not saved any of the others, every one of which must have been somebody's hometown.

"I want to do this one myself," he said. "I need some action."

"You can't battleform any more!" Butcher growled.

Cavotti gave him a glare. His glares were much more deadly than they used to be. In fact he could battleform again, but only once. It would kill him.

"You don't need to prove anything, Mutineer," Vespaniaso said.

"*I know that!*" Cavotti roared, although he didn't. "I also know that some of you find it a lot harder to give up ground than take it. I want to be certain there's no sudden change of plans. Fili, you go and take over at Celebre for me. Nuzio, it may be a trap; we must keep close watch that Stralg doesn't follow us up there. Can you get orders on their way by first light?"

Nuzio laughed. "Sound the trumpets!" He sprang up and departed, taking his pack. Quickly the others followed him, muttering about checking on their men. By the time Cavotti saw what they were doing, they had all gone, even Butcher, and when the door slammed he was left with what was probably the only really warm room in the town.

And Giunietta.

"You don't mind if I sleep here too?" he asked the fireplace.

"Of course not." Her voice in the shadows was low.

Not looking at her, he knelt and opened his pack to find the salt he used to clean his teeth . . . correction: his fangs. A thirty ago his arms had been smooth brown skin, like Nuzio's. Now they were matted with black hair. Just about all of him was. His fingernails were black claws. His face . . .

"They warned you, I hope?" he said.

"I knew." Her voice was closer. "It doesn't matter."

He looked up sharply. She was spreading a blanket in front of the hearth.

"I don't mean I'm not sorry for you," she said. "Of course I am. I am also enormously happy that you were rescued before they killed you. I'm relieved that I don't smell madness on you, after what you went through." She turned and stared at him. "In fact I don't even detect any bitterness."

"I've done my share of havocking. It was their turn, that's all. And Vespaniaso made sure they paid for it."

"You are a most extraordinary man! Hurry up. I'm waiting."

"You know that's impossible now," he said. "I mean, I am very grateful for the offer, but no, we mustn't and I won't. There's nothing more to discuss."

Her wrap fell around her feet. "I know that you still have everything necessary under that chlamys. Come on, lover. You can't deceive me."

He sat down and began to fight with his boots. She knelt at his feet and used human fingers to untie the laces. "You can't deceive a Witness, you know. You're extremely horny. So am I."

"Why don't you go and find someone human?" he said desperately. "Butcher, or Nuzio. Or one of the bodyguards. You can't want to have carnal relations with a beast!"

"Oh, don't I?" She hauled off his right boot. Each foot ended in two small hooves instead of toes, but of course she would have known that before he even entered the cottage. "Butcher's too quick, too eager to hump you and dump you. Nuzio keeps wanting to try odd things." She leaned over Cavotti's knees to unpin his chlamys. "I would try a bodyguard or two if you weren't here, but you are and I am, and I am going to lay you. Lie back and enjoy it."

He tried to push her away. She had stretch marks from childbearing. The fullness of her breasts showed that they had suckled. He knew nothing of her history or private life at all.

"Stop torturing me!" he said. "Stop torturing yourself. You know what would happen if I got you with child. You'd produce a monster. It would grow and grow until it burst you. You would die, Giunietta."

She smiled sadly. "Poor Marno. Yes, that's true. You can never have an heir now. But you forget I am a seer."

Despite himself, he could not keep his enormous hands off her. "What do you mean?"

"I mean that there are only certain times in a thirty that a woman can make a child. If I lie with every man in Nelina tonight I cannot conceive. Tonight is safe for me and I want you desperately."

"Then do it," he muttered. He clasped her to him and rolled back until he lay flat on the boards with her on top of him, like a child. She was not the most beautiful woman he had ever embraced, but she was a woman and willing; and probably the only woman who would accept him ever again.

twenty-eight

CHIES CELEBRE

was left cooling his heels in the corridor. He was very angry about that. Furious, in fact. He would see that the guards regretted this insult, if not right away then as soon as he became doge. Whether the council of relics elected him on their own or the Fist ordered them to wouldn't matter; it would happen. He was also very drunk, not sure which would come first, falling asleep or chucking up. The captain came out and said her ladyship would see him now. Chies snarled at him and marched into the ducal withdrawing room, staggering slightly as he rounded the door.

He had not been in there for years. It was a mausoleum of old junk. It seemed a lot smaller than he remembered, but all the paintings and figurines and pottery looked exactly as they had done then. Most of it should be melted down. The lyre! He wondered if she still played it sometimes. Old Oliva Ancient-Celebre herself was seated on her favorite chair, holding her sewing. She had *hordes* of women to embroider for her if she wanted. She was also giving him a very sour look, but this was long past her usual bedtime.

He bowed very carefully, neither falling down nor chucking up. "You sent for me, Mama?"

"I have been sending for you for days. You are not of age yet and even if you were, I am still effective ruler of this city." Old bat in bad mood.

"Been busy."

"So I've heard. You'd better sit down before you fall down. I was going to offer you wine, but I see that would be unwise. Can you still understand me?"

"Course. But you listen to me first! Those thugs of yours turned my friend away at the door. Sent her out in the streets alone in the middle of the night! You better send them to—"

"Yes, I heard. Babila Scarlatti has been rolling around those streets since before you were born, Chies, and I choose that verb for exactitude. A Nymph of Eriander is in no danger."

"She is not a Nymph!"

"Of course she is. And when I gave you the key to the private door, I never meant you to bring in women like her. I have many times told you not to wander the city without your guards, especially wearing a sword. Tonight I warned them that they will be punished if you get away from them again. Now, about the succession . . ."

If Babila was a Nymph, that would explain a lot . . . "What about the secession? Mean *succ*ession."

"You did very well the other morning. You impressed the councillors, I'm sure. You certainly impressed Speaker Quarina, because she told me so later. You even impressed me."

He let the words dog-paddle around in his brain for a while. Then he muttered, "Good."

"You don't impress me now."

"Nag, nag, nag. Why do you always nag?"

"You give me so much to nag about."

"Treat me like a man and I'll behave like one."

"I do and you don't. I wish you were still a child or already a man."

" 'Snot my fault I'm not."

She sighed. "Of course not. Let's try again. Your year comes of age next sixday. Normally your father would have a great celebration, involving the whole city. But we can't have a formal feast when he is about to return to the Old One. Are you following me?"

He grunted a positive.

"But I could invite the elders to an informal reception."

He thought about it. So what? "You asking my permission?"

She sighed in that martyred way she had. "I'm asking if you would like a chance to meet them, all of them. And for them to meet you."

That took longer. "You mean you *want* them to make me doge?"

She laid the sewing on a table beside her and met his eyes for the first time. "I'm not sure. They have to choose someone, and the only other male in the family is old Arnutho, a third cousin or something. He's senile and has no children. Chies, do you understand that you would be in great danger if they did elect you? *Very* great danger. It's no secret that the Fist is your true father. A lot of people might want to kill you as soon as they hear the news. Stralg is almost certainly going to lose the war, and then who wants his bastard ruling the greatest city of Florengia?"

"You want me killed?" he asked bitterly.

She shook her head. "No. You have more faults than the palace kennels have fleas, but you are still my son and I still love you. I swear that is the truth. You are all I have left. But *if* you understand the danger, and *if* you are brave enough to try, then I will support you."

Needing time to find the trick in this, he said, "How?"

"I will present you to the council. If you can impress them as a sensible, well-intentioned young man—a *sober* young man, in other words—then they will at least listen to what you have to say. And you can make a case that you are the logical candidate."

He blinked at her while this sank in, but she was still very fuzzy around the edges. "Why?"

She looked as if she were about to sigh, but didn't. "Piero always accepted you as his son. I would help you prepare a speech. Who coached you the first time? Who chose that chlamys you wore?"

"Babila."

"Maybe we should ask her advice, too." The old crow bent her wrinkles into a smile. "Go and sleep it off. We'll talk again in the morning. Or maybe afternoon would be better."

"Much better." He lobbed a smile back, maximum cute. It worked sometimes. This was one of the times. Her eyes glistened.

"Oh, Chies, Chies! It wasn't your fault, but what happens from now on will be." She stood up. "I couldn't talk you out of trying, could I?"

How small she was! He could bend his head, looking down at her. "No."

"Then I'll give you all the help I can, because you're my son and I love you. I certainly don't want a kiss, but at least give me a hug."

◆

A page lit the way to his rooms for him. The outer chamber was a mess. He'd been trying on clothes earlier and had left them all over the floor. He thought about having the boy pick them up and fold them for him, but his dresser would do that in the morning. He told the boy to leave the lamp and go.

Just as well Babila wasn't there. He had drunk a lot more than he realized. Feeling an urgent need for a chamber pot, he pushed through the bead curtain into his sleeping chamber.

"About time," a man said.

"Past time," said another.

Chies dropped the lamp and tried to draw his sword. The men stamped out the wick before the spilled oil caught. They stuffed a rag in his mouth before he got the blade free of the scabbard, then tied his arms behind his back. He protested, "Uuuungh!" If he vomited behind this gag he would choke.

"Don't mumble," one of them said as they hustled him out on the terrace. "Bad manners."

They were Heroes—he saw starlight reflected on their collars. But they were Florengian Heroes. And they were big. Huge. They tied a rope around his waist, then one lifted him over the balustrade and the other lowered him to ground level. It occurred to him as he went down, spinning around and around, that he was being kidnapped.

twenty-nine

INGELD NARSDOR

was confident of a safe homecoming and a warm welcome. She had been watching the mound that was Kosord draw steadily closer for several days, and now she could make out the palace itself. Even Oliva seemed to be kicking harder, as if anxious to be let out to survey her future domain. The crew promised that the aptly named *Joy of Return* would dock by noon. Every night Ingeld viewed auguries in the campfires, and lately they had shown her back at work, relighting the sacred fire on the apex of the pyramid, which was her most solemn public duty.

Deserters from the city had been joining her procession for days, for while Horold's original host had been outsiders, its younger Heroes were Kosord-born and news of the satrap's death had caused many of them to revert to their ancestral loyalty to the dynast. They reported that Daughter Sansya had done a superb job of substituting for Ingeld in her absence, and had recently taken to proclaiming the dynast's imminent return. Sansya must be seeing the same visions she was. Holy Veslih had things well in hand, then, and no doubt the star Nartiash would appear at tomorrow's dawn to proclaim the turning of the year, right when it would show to maximum effect.

So Ingeld herself would be safe, but the flames had shown her nothing of Benard. The gods gave no guarantees for his safety anymore, nor for old Guthlag's. If there was going to be fighting, those two were the most vulnerable and the usurper's horde must still outnumber her tiny force by a sixty to one. She might survive, but without Benard her happiness would not.

Those doubts she tried to keep to herself. She sat close to Benard in *Joy's* bow and watched the winter birds swoop low above the water. The day was cold, but sunny and not too windy. The half flank of Werists serving as today's guard of honor were all formerly Orlad's men—Jungr, Snerfrik, Hrothgat, Narg, Prok, and Namberson—and she was sure Hordeleader Guthlag had good reasons for that assignment. The other six boats that now made up her flotilla were following in close formation. Although river traffic was light at midwinter, once in a while some hardy crew would go past, struggling upriver against wind and current. Usually now they knew whose fleet this was, and cheered her.

Witness Tranquility was no doubt busily recording, but nothing of her was visible under her veils.

A head surfaced and disappeared again.

Snerfrik sang out, "Here comes another one!"

Something splashed alongside the boat. A whitish flipper slapped at the gunwale and became a hand. Snerfrik and Prok reached over and grabbed, hauling the man up until he could cling to the side, half in and half out of the boat, blinking water from his eyes. He wore a brass collar, naturally.

"Next boat behind!" Prok said. "Hordeleader Guthlag is aboard and will take your oath. There's a Speaker there to help you get out of the present one."

This happened all the time now, and usually that was the end of it as far as *Joy* was concerned, for she was a small boat and already crowded. But this time the newcomer stopped puffing long enough to say, "Got a message for the dynast from Daughter Sansya."

"He speaks the truth," Tranquility said cheerfully.

"I'm sure he does," Ingeld declared. "Bring Packleader Yabro aboard."

They had a procedure for that. She decorously studied water birds and shipping on one side of the boat, while Prok and Snerfrik helped the recruit over the other, Namberson handed him a pall to act as both towel and covering, and Narg went to the meat crock they kept for just this purpose. The clink of the lid going back on the jar was a sign that the newcomer was respectable and it was safe for Ingeld to look. Safe, except that Oliva did not appreciate her landlady watching men tear at raw meat.

She looked to Benard instead. "Packleader Yabro Yorgalson and I are cousins," she explained. Fourth or fifth cousins. Her foremothers had been dynasts for so many generations that hardly a family in Kosord was not related to her in some contorted fashion.

Benard nodded. "He has your ears. I thought he was only a flankleader?"

Yabro was a youngish man, not large by Werist standards, with hair and beard closer to red than gold; his good looks were not limited to the shape of his ears. His mother was a Nulist, and had been Palace Mercy for many years, so he had been a playmate for both Benard and Cutrath. *Ah, where was Cutrath?* Sansya had chosen a credible messenger.

He gulped down the last bloody lump, wiped his stubble with a brawny, furry forearm, licked his fingers, and said, "Flankleader, yes, my lady." He glanced longingly at the meat crock.

"Speak up, then."

"The Daughter says that Huntleader Jarkard, who now calls himself hordeleader, intends to force you to marry him, my lady. He's stationing men all along the waterfront and in all the boats he could commandeer. Everyone with you, all the Heroes, are to be put to death." He glanced apologetically at Benard. "Especially you, Hand. Congratulations, by the way."

"Kind of you," Benard said dryly.

"Did she say she foresaw this?" Ingeld had not.

"No, my lady. She learned it from men who don't like the orders they're getting. She say she sees you as dynast again, but she has not been shown your return." Yabro's plaintive interest in the meat crock paid off when Narg pulled out a leg of mouflon and passed it to him.

Ingeld was not at all surprised by Sanysa's news, for it only confirmed what they had been hearing for days. "He really is a nastiness," she said, more to herself than anyone else. News of the satrap's death had provoked the predictable power struggle in the city, and the winner so far was Jarkard Karson, leader of Vulture Hunt. The fall of the House of Hrag had left Kosord with far too many Werists, and the same would probably be true of all Vigaelia for years to come.

"Very well. I know I am in no danger, so I will go on alone. Flankleader, tell Master Mog to signal a parley, please."

Snerfrik pouted rebelliously, but scrambled aft to tell the eavesdropping riverfolk what they had just overheard anyway.

"Alone except for me," Benard said.

They had worn this argument to death over the last three days. Trouble was, she wanted his support. She hated to admit that she needed it.

"If you insist on that, my love, you will make it much harder for Guthlag and his men to stay out."

"Then they can kill me themselves right away and save Jarkard doing it. Otherwise, I will be at your side when you step ashore." He set his face in his most moronically stubborn expression.

The crew were turning the boat. It tilted, the sail flapped unhappily.

"Put away that snack for a moment," Ingeld told Yabro. "I need to think. Thank you. About three score Heroes have come to join us already. Not nearly enough for a pitched battle, of course. You say the rest don't like their orders. If the usurper tries to use force, will he be obeyed?"

The messenger squirmed. "Against you, my lady, no. Some might obey, but the rest would swat them. But . . ."

"But her mudface gigolo will be fair game," Benard completed helpfully.

Pink under his stubble, Yabro nodded. "He has a special flank picked out, hard cases who don't like, er, Florengians. Volunteers, all of them. They'll be right there on the waterfront, my lady, drooling blood."

Benard nodded. "My blood. But if you want to keep me as your husband, love, then I must come with you."

Ingeld wondered how many of Cutrath's childhood friends would be in that death squad. *Felicitous Memory* was coming alongside, bearing Hordeleader Guthlag, Speaker Ardial, and more than a dozen Heroes. Ardial had seemed quite happy—insofar as any Speaker could ever seem happy—to accept the post of justiciar and return to Kosord. He would be no help in a fight, though, unless he could bore the enemy to death with texts.

More than the horde would be waiting to welcome her. Most of the extrinsic population would turn out, too, wanting to cheer. She dreaded the possibility of them getting involved. But surely Veslih would have warned her if a bloodbath was likely? And if she put up no resistance at all, then Benard would be forever banished from the city, and she would be back to being the wife of a Werist. Oliva needed better than a Werist stepfather. Benard was right. For someone who normally seemed to drift along slightly above the ground, he was wrong surprisingly rarely.

The boats came together with hardly a bump and the crew held them there with boat hooks.

"Hordeleader," she told Guthlag, "Flankleader Yabro reports that Jarkard is certainly planning violence. You are too badly outnumbered to do more than throw your lives away. Speaker Ardial, I wish you to accompany me. Apart from the Speaker and my husband, I will go in unescorted."

It took a little while, but she eventually overruled Guthlag's protests.

◆

For the next pot-boiling or so, Ingeld just sat with her eyes closed and prayed. Praying to Veslih in an open boat was extremely difficult. The sense of warmth and comfort she normally experienced was erratic and intermittent there, but she could hardly ask the riverfolk to build a fire for her. She must return today, because the Festival of Demern had ended and the skies were clear. These were the Dark Days, unofficially regarded as belonging to the Evil One. She was convinced that Nartiash would rise tomorrow, and the city needed her there to declare the turn of the year as her foremothers had done for six sixty years. And then Consort Benard could proclaim the feast.

Even in the Dark Days, it was exceedingly rare to see the city frontage deserted, and yet *Joy of Return* passed not a single moored boat as she came in. There were people, more people than Ingeld could ever remember seeing. The entire population of the city seemed to be standing along the levee, starting well outside the city proper. They knew her robes and her red hair dancing in the wind, and they sang for her. It began unevenly, a single childish voice barely audible in the wind, completely unplanned, but at once other voices took up the refrain. It swelled as she passed the hovels of the poor on the outskirts. By the time she was level with the first of the great trading warehouses, it was a steady, unanimous choir.

They sang none of the great hymns to Veslih, neither a joyful welcome nor a triumphant victory song. Over and over they sang "Ambilanha," an old and simple folk song calling for a lover taken by the river, ambiguously vague as to whether the singer was man or woman, and the lover gone on a journey or simply dead. It seemed strangely inappropriate, and yet it filled her eyes with tears.

Captain Mog had no choice of berth. The river was at its lowest now, so only the main traders' docks were accessible to even the smallest riverboats. Moreover, there was only one place his passengers could easily disembark because the bank was everywhere walled with people except for a gap in front of the Temple of Ucr in the center of the trading district. In this gap, a decorated arch of welcome stood forlorn and pathetic with its feathers and gaudy bunting fluttering in the breeze. The steps below it had been kept empty for the dynast's return—some effort had even been made to wash them. Two boys stood ready to catch the lines and bend them to the bollards.

Ardial and Benard helped her disembark. Oliva was already making Ingeld unsteady on her feet, and the stairs seemed unnecessarily long. She took them slowly, leaning on Benard's arm. At their side walked Speaker Ardial in his black robes and permanently bloodless expression. A Speaker was safe enough. Even Stralg had been content to drive Ardial out of the city, when he would have put an extrinsic ruler to death. Witness Tranquility followed them up, carrying her distaff and spindle to record the dynast's return.

Still the people chanted "Ambilanha."

Ingeld paused at the top to catch her breath, to survey the enemy, and to smile at the crowd. The arch proved that someone had planned a public welcome. Beyond it, a band with trumpets and drums stood in glum silence, making no effort to overrule the "Ambilanha" dirge. And there was a wagon with a throne on it, all brightly decorated, the sort of contrivance the Lamb Queen rode in at the Festival of Nastrar. The ropes that would draw the wagon lay deserted on the roadway, and the children who would pull them were nowhere to be seen. There was no sign of Sansya or the senior priests and priestesses, the heads of cults and guilds and senior families, all of whom should have been here to greet her.

The great crowd was held back, upstream and downstream, by walls of massed Heroes, at least six deep, perhaps a mustering of the entire city horde. And in the center of the open space stood the self-proclaimed horde-leader, Jarkard Karson, backed up by a dozen Werists—presumably the Benard execution squad, Yabro's *hard cases who didn't like Florengians.* They were all smiling eagerly.

Benard's hand on her arm was steady, but icy cold. He kept it there as they walked forward and the chanting crumpled away into silence.

Ingeld stopped several paces back from Jarkard. "Return your men to barracks, Huntleader. They are not required."

Jarkard was big, of course, but more bloated than beefy. Either he had practiced long and hard, or his face had come with a built-in sneer. "They are here to witness our marriage. I see you brought a Speaker. How considerate!"

"He is here to administer your oath of loyalty."

"Then he will be disappointed." He pointed at Benard. "You, *boy,* will leave now. I will count to three."

"And I," Ingeld said, "shall count to two." No need to delay. Either the goddess would support her or She wouldn't.

"You can count anything you like, my sweet," the Werist said. Was there a hint of hesitation in his puffy eyes?

Nasty though he was, Ingeld would prefer not to kill him. "Do not provoke my wrath!"

Jarkard's sneer remained unruffled. "One!"

"One!" Ingeld echoed. "I warn you for the last time."

"Two!"

"Two!"

Jarkard opened his mouth to say "Three" and Ingeld laid the curse of Veslih on him. He did not so much burn as erupt, as if he had been struck by lightning. His pall and skin charred instantly. A tower of red flame hurtled upward, then his head and belly exploded in fire and steam. His escort leaped back in horror, and every throat in the city cried out—except Benard's, because he had been forewarned, but his grip nearly crushed Ingeld's forearm. The crowds, even the Werists, fell to their knees in the presence of the goddess. In moments Hordeleader Jarkard was reduced to a smoking, reeking litter of charred bones.

Ingeld was shivering with the relief of tension. She had never cursed a human being before. Once she had dealt with a mad dog, but she had not been certain that she could bring herself to kill a man. Her grandmother had done so twice, reputedly. The crowd was moaning and weeping.

"Dramatic!" Ardial said dryly. "Twenty-seven years ago you did not treat Stralg so harshly."

Ingeld bit her lip. What could she respond to that? *I love Benard but did not love you*? Or perhaps, *Horold was handsome and you were not*? Even, *I was only a child back then*? She said, "Oliva will need her father, Ardial." That felt nearest the truth.

"It is unfortunate you did not burn the Fist, though. The world has suffered much since then."

"I am sure you could quote me a number of texts about missed opportunities. Witness," Ingeld added quietly, "will there be more challenges?"

Behind her, Tranquility laughed. "Not a peep, my lady."

"You!" Benard bellowed. "Flankleader! Get those men back to barracks! All of them. Do you want to be next? Bandleader, play!"

The cheering began, rising to a roar and drowning out the brazen shriek of trumpets. Consort and dynast walked forward to the wagon. As they passed the cinders, Ingeld averted her eyes and met Benard' s loving gaze. Those artist's eyes—dark Vigaelian eyes—missed nothing, not her nausea, her relief, her shame, her joy. His great hand tightened around hers

"Well done!" he said admiringly. "You didn't warn me you were going to melt his collar."

"Horrible!"

"But necessary. And there won't be any more. Everything will be all right now."

thirty

FABIA CELEBRE

had never seen anything as flat as her first view of Florengia. The floodplain of the Wrogg at Kosord had been mountainous by comparison. Dantio called this the Altiplano, and it looked as if it had been raked and rolled, fine gravel stretching off in all directions forever, coated with brownish lichen, not one blade of grass anywhere. Behind them, a ruled white line below the indigo sky marked the Ice they had left two days ago, but even the Ice had been much smoother on this side of the Edge than in Vigaelia. Straight as a javelin, the trail ran ahead, a line of different color rutted by wheels and stained by many years' animal droppings. Beyond it the world ended in the usual mistiness of the wall, with just faint hints of very distant hills visible late in the day, when the sun was at Fabia's back. Every fresh heap of dung was a landmark, and proof that the pass was still being provisioned and patrolled.

A new world and a new year. This morning at sunrise, Dantio had pointed out the holy star Nartiash, whose heliacal rising heralded the turning of the year.

The constant eye-watering cold wind was one problem and Dantio's limp another, but the gravest concern was water. The shelter at First Ice had been stocked with shabby leather canteens, obviously left there so travelers would know to fill them at the seasonal meltwater pools. There had been nothing at last night's shelter except timber windbreaks and some jars of pemmican. Now the second day was drawing to a close and the canteens were running dry. The world ahead was flat gravel and more flat gravel.

"Are we nearly there yet?" Waels asked, yet again. The joke had worn as thin as the soles of Fabia's boots. If he weren't a Werist, someone would hit him.

"It is not *known*," Dantio said, "but it is suspected, that we are nearly *somewhere*. There's a dip ahead. I can't see it, but I can sense it, just barely."

Waels did something that briefly made his face twist out of shape and his eyes bulge. "Bless my fangs and talons! You're right."

Fabia wondered what they would they do when they got "there," wherever "there" was. Veritano, the Florengian equivalent of Nardalborg, was supposedly a smaller settlement. They had hoped to slip past it unseen, for it would be manned by Stralg's men, but on this terrain a mouse would be conspicuous.

"Has anyone thought up a good fable yet?" Dantio asked the landscape, tactfully not asking Fabia directly.

Xaran was the Mother of Lies. If anybody could think up a workable cover story, it should be the family Chosen. Fabia had prayed for guidance in the night, but none had come. She was in little danger because she could claim to be a hostage from some obscure place on the far side of the Face. Dantio was merely an escaped slave. But Orlad and Waels would have to talk very fast to convince any Vigaelian Werists they met that they were not Cavotti rebels.

"Not me," she said. "I can only suggest we tell the truth and call for a seer to verify it."

"Stralg can't have many seers left. I very much doubt that he'll have one stationed out here."

Waels sighed. "Pity to come all this way just to bleed to death."

"If the gods are kind," Orlad said, "there will be someone at Veritano who knew us back at Nardalborg."

"And what do I say when they ask why I changed color?"

"Look blank and say, 'I did?'"

From Orlad that was good repartee, so the others laughed.

"You had better start practicing," Dantio said, "because we are about to have company. Dust ahead."

This time both Werist faces deformed, their eyes swelling until Fabia turned away, unwilling to watch.

"Chariots. I make it six, my lord."

"Six it is. A flank on patrol." After a moment Orlad added, "But they're Florengians. We don't have to bleed yet."

♦

The chariots were low wickerwork structures on two wheels, drawn by teams of four furry things like long-legged, long-necked black sheep. Although smaller than onagers, they could move their little hooves to good effect. Each car carried two brown-skinned young men. They bore no visible weapons, but brass collars encircled their necks and their black hair and beards were close-cropped. Three chariots turned off to one side and two to the other. The leader pulled up in the road ahead, the driver turning the car at the last moment so his superior could look down at the strangers instead of having to stare along the length of his team.

These Werists wore what seemed to be wool blankets, draped over the left shoulder and pinned on their right side, so they left the right arm bare and covered the other down to the elbow. The leader's was blue and the others' brown.

The leader looked over the filthy, ragged, and hairy wayfarers with distaste. "What have we here? Deserters?"

"My lord," Dantio said, "you are a welcome sight! I am a Witness of Mayn."

The flankleader raised a skeptical eyebrow, but he tucked his left hand behind his back.

"Two," Dantio said. "Three. Thumb only. All five now."

"So you are!"

"And we always speak truth."

"So they say. Welcome back to Florengia, Witness. I am Flankleader Felice Serpanti, proud to serve in the Liberators."

Dantio was grinning all over, like a boy left to guard a sweetmeat stall. "It is good to be back! I am Dantio Celebre, eldest son of Doge Piero. Orlad Celebre, my brother, formerly a flankleader in the Tryfors Host, now his own man. Hero Waels Borkson, his liegeman. Lady Fabia Celebre, our sister."

"Welcome all!" Felice looked to his driver, whose eyes were wide with astonishment. "Know any of them, Dimo?"

Dimo was younger and slighter, his beard patchy. His steady stare at Fabia was flattering, especially considering how rumpled she was from her travels. "No, my lord. Before my time. But the doge did have four children taken hostage."

"Now we are back," Dantio said. "Three of us. I gather that Veritano has fallen to the, er, forces of freedom?"

"Last night. And the Mutineer plans to burn it tomorrow. Your timing is admirably chosen, lord Dantio."

"Praise the gods! How goes the war? Our father?"

"The war goes well, but the ice devils have not been brought to bay yet. The doge still lingers, I think. Right, Dimo?"

The boy nodded. "The girl looks very like Dogaressa Oliva, lord."

"The war goes very well beyond the Edge," Dantio said. "We bring wonderful news. Do I gather that the Mutineer himself is at Veritano?"

Felice laughed uneasily. "I did not say that. Is there anyone behind you?"

"No. We burned the bridge at Fist's Leap and closed the pass."

If a seer said so, it must be true. Fabia had not told the others about her nightmares.

The flankleader said, "Weru's b—buttocks! *Closed the pass?* I am going to take all four of you to Veritano directly." He took the reins from his driver. "Dimo, you can have the honor of reporting that we are returning."

"My lord is kind." Dimo turned and was gone in a swirl of cloth. He dove from the chariot, hitting the gravel with two front paws, and a black warbeast streaked off over the plain. The furry things shied, tossing their heads and humming oddly, but they did not panic as onagers would have done. Felice, who had caught the brown chlamys before it dropped, bundled it up and put it at his feet inside the car.

The tension had eased. Felice barked out commands to the rest of his men. Men sprang down from chariots when he named them. His dark eyes looked over the visitors and settled on Fabia with a smile that showed white, regular teeth and an invitation to flirt. Florengia must be full of young men with that glowing brown skin, although surely few of them would show it off as well as this one. For far too long she had been limited to the company of men who were not interested.

He offered a hand. "Lady Fabia? Will you honor me?"

Realizing that she had no further use for the smelly, dirty bedroll she had carried so long, she tossed it aside and accepted his hand up. She grabbed the rail as a flip of his reins sent the rig shooting forward. The car was small enough to be intimate and would be a tight squeeze for two big Heroes.

"All right?" He wrapped an arm around her, enveloping her in his chlamys.

"*Quite* all right, thank you, Flankleader. I am no stranger to chariots."

"Pity." He left his arm behind her, but gripped the rail instead of her, which was an acceptable compromise. Why did he bother? She had never felt so like a midden in her life. Her clothes were rotting off her. Her hair, her skin . . .

"You actually walked over Veritano Pass, all the way?"

"My boorish brothers refused to carry me." The chariot rode more smoothly than hers had, back in Skjar, although the flatness of the terrain helped. Three more teams were following, leaving two chariots and seven men stranded on the Altiplano until another party could be sent to pick them up. "Marno Cavotti is here, at Veritano?"

"I did not say so." His smile said so.

Incredible fortune! Or was it? Cavotti would soon devise his own plans for the Celebre hostages, and their own wishes might not carry much weight.

"He will be surprised to meet us."

"Yes, even Marno could not expect to find you here. Of course," the flankleader added mischievously, "he may have some surprises for you, too."

"What does that mean?"

"Wait and see."

"How long does it take to go from Veritano to Celebre?"

"About a sixday by chariot. The Mutineer can do it in less, but he needs many relays of guanacos."

"I must go to my mother," she said, feeling a sudden lump in her throat. Not that she could remember Oliva. It must be the idea of motherhood that affected her—that, and pity for a woman whose life had been so blighted. "I was only a baby when I was torn from her arms. And now my father is dying. This just doesn't feel real."

"Our news is a few days old, but the last I heard, the Liberators and ice devils were still feinting at each other near Celebre. So far neither has tried to occupy the city. I heard the . . . heard someone say just last night that Celebre could be critical. There will have to be one big battle before this thing is over."

"What will you do with the prisoners when it is over?"

Felice's face hardened. "I don't know that word. Prisoners?"

That was a chilling reminder that she was in a war zone, and not a mere bystander either, if Celebre was important.

The road dipped into a gully, which rapidly widened and began to wind, heading steeply downward. Side gullies merged with it. When the trail grew rough, Felice slowed the team, but not so much that he and his passenger would not be bounced together at every lurch. He wrapped his arm around her again, holding all the reins in one large hand and letting the guanacos follow the trail more or less by themselves, taking corners on one wheel. She knew he was showing off, but she was impressed anyway. The cliffs grew higher, sculpted into bizarre pinnacles and towers. Patches of green appeared, brightening the arid ground.

Soon huge black birds screeched and flapped, some fighting up into the air, others just cavorting along the ground. Vigaelia had similar creatures, although smaller. Whatever their names, they fed on carrion. As the chariot hurtled past the first kill, she caught a glimpse of a large, yellow-furred dead thing, ripped and bloody, a glint of brass. Then she saw more of them. Some of them were visibly human, some indeterminate. No black or brown ones, though. Those would have been treated with more respect.

"Last night's losers?"

"They tried to break out to the pass," Felice said carelessly. "Of course our leader had anticipated that and posted a full hunt here to stop them. You should thank the gods that none of them got past us."

Thinking about that, she did not speak again for a while.

The valley was still spreading out on either side, flat bottomland carpeted with lush vegetation and flanked by cliffs receding into the distance. She was amazed at how far they had descended. The air was gentle, wonderfully easy to breathe. Florengia was much warmer than Vigaelia, Orlad had warned her, quoting his friend Gzurg. According to Dantio, much of the time it was a steam bath. Thinking of which . . .

"Is that steam?" She pointed at the nearest of several plumes.

"Warm springs," Felice told her. "The source of the Puisa."

"Who?"

He gave her an odd look. "The river that flows through Celebre. Veritano is famous for its hot baths."

"Now I know I'm dreaming. Don't make any loud noises."

Soon they passed a string of chariots heading out to rescue the rest of Felice's men. He released Fabia long enough to make a hand signal that probably meant the situation had not changed since Dimo's report. The other leader waved acknowledgment.

Brown and black guanacos grazed in emerald fields. Obviously that was Veritano ahead, a complex of adobe buildings with red tile roofs and strange, feathery trees—and several lazy columns of steam.

"Finest place in the Altiplano," Felice said. "Used to be a sanctuary. Lords and ladies came here to enjoy the warm springs. When the Fist took it over, Sinura left."

"Smart goddess."

The car rattled through an arch into a wide courtyard. Along one side many chariots stood in rows, their shafts pointing skyward. A small paddock had been railed off on the other, and men grooming guanacos there stared in surprise at Felice's passenger as he drove past them, heading to a gate at the far side. She noted signs of neglect—tiles missing, walls crumbling, creepers and other greenery running riot. The chariot rattled to a halt.

At the gate stood a giant, fists on hips. Fabia had seen big Werists and bestial Werists, but this one was both, grotesquely misshapen and thickly furred with black hair. All of him, especially his face, seemed cruelly lopsided. A stub of horn the size of a thumb protruded from his forehead and massive brows overhung his eyes like the roof of a cavern, while his chin was lost under a toothy protruding muzzle. He wore the same sort of knee-length chlamys Felice did, but his was green, and linen instead of wool. Oddly shaped boots and a brass collar completed his attire. Could this monster be the celebrated Mutineer, the man who had outwitted and outfought Bloodlord Stralg?

He was the most repulsive parody of a man she had ever seen. Even Horold Hragson had seemed more human than this.

She liked him even less when he smiled, for that muzzle was all teeth, too many huge, onager-sized teeth. He stepped forward and offered a very large hand. Fabia had trouble not shuddering as she accepted it, noting black claws tipping the thick fingers.

Murmuring, "Thank you, Flankleader," to Felice, she stepped down.

"Lady Fabia? I am Marno Cavotti." He did not bow, and for her to curtsey in the rags she wore would be ridiculous.

"I used to be Fabia Celebre, my lord. I hope to be so again, once I have bathed and dressed. I am happy and honored to meet you. All Vigaelia knows your name and supports your cause."

He bore a strong animal odor—not as repellent as Horold Hragson's had been, but not human. He glanced over his shoulder. A woman emerged from the gate and came to stand at his side. Her simple wrap clung to an angular, bony figure. She was not young—white-streaked hair, care-lined face, penetrating eyes—but women aged rapidly during their bearing years. His wife?

She said only, "I am Giunietta, my lady."

"I am honored to meet you."

The second chariot had arrived. Dantio stepped down, favoring his gimpy ankle. He bowed—to the woman. "Witness Mist, sister."

She smiled as if caught out. "Witness Giunietta, brother."

Another bow. "Dantio Celebre, my lord Mutineer. I am greatly honored to meet you again."

Cavotti responded with a bend of his bull neck. "I would not have known you."

"Boys notice their elders more than their juniors. I remember you, but only dimly."

"Faugh! My own mother would not know me now. Welcome home, lord Dantio. You arrive at an interesting time." Again he glanced at Giunietta, and they exchanged the sort of looks that couples exchange. He was puzzled by this soft-spoken young man; she was saying she would explain later.

Orlad sprang down and saluted. He introduced himself and Waels in very stilted Florengian. Fabia noted Cavotti's manner cool. A Florengian who had been initiated in Vigaelia was suspect. "Piero had a fourth child, as I recall."

"Benard," Dantio said. "He remained behind, having just become consort of Kosord."

"Kosord? Why is that name familiar?"

Dantio grinned. "Because it was previously ruled by Horold Hragson. You want the news, my lord Mutineer? Brace yourself. Benard killed Horold with a little help from Orlad and his men. Orlad killed Therek Hragson with his own bare, er, teeth. Hordeleader Arbanerik and his New Dawn rebels took Tryfors and were poised to take Nardalborg when we left. Saltaja Hragsdor tried to flee over the pass with a large escort of Heroes. She closed the road behind her, but we closed it ahead of her, leaving her trapped near the Edge without supplies or a way out. She may be presumed dead."

"Hands of death!" Cavotti roared. "Is any of this true, love?"

"All of it." Giunietta clapped her hands. "Oh, most wonderful news!"

Cavotti bared teeth in a monster's leer. "You Celebres don't play for cakes, do you? Hero Orlad, I hail you as worthy of our god!" He grabbed Orlad in a bear's embrace, lifting him right off the ground.

Orlad did not like that. The moment he was set down he snarled, "And you likewise, Mutineer," and treated the giant likewise. Just to show he could, probably.

Cavotti laughed and thumped his shoulder. "The whole foul brood dead except for Stralg, then?"

Fabia did not want to reveal her suspicions yet, but she could not leave him misinformed. "A warning, my lord. I agree that Saltaja's position seemed hopeless, but you know that the Queen of Shadows has always been a tool of the Ancient One. When we burned down the bridge at the Leap, we inadvertently left our Pathfinder on the other side. No one knows any other way to cross the Dust River, but if there is one, he will have found it for her. You should post a watch on this end of the pass, my lord, just to be quite certain."

She had not mentioned that possibility to her companions, but their frowns were nothing compared to Cavotti's. He said, "I will do so, with orders to kill her on sight. What comes first, my lords and lady—hot water? Food? News? Talk? Sleep?"

"You have the right order exactly," Fabia said. She doubted they would have much time left over for sleep.

thirty-one

FABIA CELEBRE

was conducted to a bathing pool that would have held sixty women without a jostle. She had it to herself, in a courtyard so steamy and overgrown by feral garden that it would have been private even without the high wall surrounding it. Although paving, statuary, and stone benches were all cushioned in green moss, the water itself was clear, gushing up from a corroded bronze grating and trickling away through another. She sank into bliss, submerging totally until she had to come up for air. The gods knew that she had earned this! Nothing in her life quite compared.

Soon Giunietta came bustling in with a pile of clothes. "Try rubbing yourself with this paste, my lady. It cleanses and freshens the skin. These are the only women's garments I could find. I'll hold them up, and you can tell me what color you like and what you think will fit you . . ."

After that Giunietta dusted off a bench and sat down to chat while Fabia washed, soaked, swam a little, and generally luxuriated. Whenever her head was above water, she freely recounted the family adventures: how she had learned Florengian from Paola, why Orlad spoke it so badly, how Benard had risen so high so fast, how Waels had changed color, and so on. Some of it only a seer would believe, and Giunietta must know that she had an ulterior motive in telling it. After Fabia had dried herself off with the softest towels she had ever encountered—alpaca wool, whatever that was—Giunietta offered to rub her with lavender oil. That was an offer not be refused, and she stretched out on the bench, facedown. It was nice to feel kneaded.

"But now it's my turn. Tell me about the Mutineer. How did you meet him?"

Gentle fingers spread cool oil on her shoulders. "The rule our Goddess decreed for Her mystery here is not quite the same as She set out for Vigaelia. We do not go veiled, for example, unless we are testifying. Both cults are forbidden to meddle in events, but when Stralg perverted Her mystery in Vigaelia and then brought this evil over the Edge with him, our Eldest decreed that any Florengian Witnesses who wished to assist the opposition would be allowed to do so, within certain limits. I am forbidden to send men to their deaths, for example, but I may warn of ambushes. Very few of us can bear to do even that much. I fear I have more tolerance for brutality than most."

Unsure how to respond to that, Fabia said, "How long have you known Marno Cavotti?"

"About two thirties."

Oh. No children, no marriage.

"He broke into Celebre itself to appeal to the doge." Giunietta's voice was soothing, but she lacked skill at oiling and pummeling. Fabia longed for Lilin, back in Skjar. "Your father was incapable and your mother was ruling in his name. Marno spoke with her and then escaped by the skin of his heels. He takes absurd risks sometimes! I had agreed to help his men locate him, and that was when we met. One thing led to another, and . . . Later I discovered that his real purpose had been to lure the Vigaelians into a trap, and he won a great victory by it. When he says victory he means massacre, so my involvement was not as harmless as I had hoped, but that is typical of Marno."

She worked on Fabia's thighs. "We very nearly lost him a few sixdays ago. He got trapped between two Vigaelian squads and was horribly wounded and tortured, very nearly died."

"How awful!"

"Until then he could pass for an extrinsic—big, yes, but handsome as a god. Some of his men rescued him in time to save his life, but he could not heal all his injuries. He does not complain, but it must be hard for him."

Hard on anyone who had to look at him. That bestial face would give Fabia shudders even without the horn. "You are lovers?"

"Seers do not fall in love, my lady. Love is a form of blindness."

"I am sorry. It is none of—"

Giunietta chuckled quite crudely. "But we take pleasure together. You cannot imagine me coupling with that great unicorn bison? Well, I do, and eagerly, every time I can get him to take a moment away from the war. I confess I am sadly promiscuous where Werists are concerned. Sometimes we

Witnesses can be snared by our own powers, and I know that some of my sisters have become as addicted as I have. We have more talents than just sight, you know. One of our abilities is to detect the inner nature of things or people. We call it 'smell,' but it has nothing to do with noses or scent. We have to call it something, and it has about the same range as an odor. We can sniff out lies and liars, poison in a goblet, bad news in a letter, disease or rotting beams. I can tell boy babies from girls before their mothers are even aware of their existence. Will you turn over now?

"Many Werists are brutal all the way through. That type usually enlists voluntarily, seeking out the god. They can be handsome as maidens' dreams outside and solid monster inside. Marno wanted to be an artist and a patron of the arts, but he was snatched off the streets of Celebre and coerced into the service of Weru. Had the gods never inflicted the Fist on Florengia, he would have been a different person. Your brother Orlad is much the same. But all that is might-have-been, and gossamer for Voices of Anziel to spin.

"Deep inside Marno Cavotti I still sense the gentle boy artist, much like your brother Benard as you described him. Outside that sweetness is a crust of murder and ferocity that outdoes even Stralg. Between them rages a zone of fire I cannot describe. For a Witness to give herself to such a man is an experience at once terrifying and exalting. He could crush me, destroy me in an instant, as he has destroyed uncounted men, and yet he is so vulnerable, so in need of care and love . . . Only a Witness could understand the turmoil of fury and despair, of hatred and need. Marno is like no other man. I fear what will become of him after this war is ended. He will win it, if he lives, but then his life will be empty. He cannot go back. He can never have a normal marriage and children. What does he do? Invade Vigaelia?"

Fabia could not resist asking, "Does that horn get in the way much?"

Giunietta laughed. "No more than noses!"

"And he has seasoning, as I do?"

The hands kneading her thigh stilled. "Your brother told you about that?"

"Orlad has it also. Benard and Dantio did have it, but they have lost it."

"Four of you? That is incredible."

"So I am told. The Mutineer must have it, so how does a Witness react to whole-body contact with Marno Cavotti?"

"There are no words for it," Giunietta said. "I believe the food will be ready soon, my lady. If you care to sit up, I will comb out your hair for you."

◆

Once splendid, the dining hall showed the ravages of many years' neglect under the Stralg regime. Plaster had fallen from walls and lay in heaps in corners. The tables and benches were battered as if they had survived fights or very rough sport, and the windows looked out on a jungle where there should be a fine park. In among the tangle of lank vegetation shone flowers like red and white stars.

"Exiles!" Dantio said, leaning out to pick some. "Also called Outcasts. And they are blooming to welcome us!" He handed a sprig to Fabia.

"Can I eat it?" she asked. "Don't you feel drafty in that towel?"

The men were transformed, clean and curried, but all three wore brown Hero chlamyses, doubtless the only male garments to be found in this outpost.

"The man who wore this yesterday never came back for it," Dantio said bleakly.

"Oh." Who would be a seer and know such things?

Then Cavotti entered with Giunietta, plus a short, heavyset Werist who was presented as Huntleader Melchitte. Fabia lost interest in him almost immediately because servants followed him, bringing food. For about a thirty she had eaten nothing but pemmican and beans. Now she saw real food again at last, and more than enough of it for two women and five men, although she recognized almost nothing. There was no cutlery, only fingers to take what they fancied from steaming bowls being passed around. If these were proper Florengian table manners, not just crude Werist habits, she would have to learn a whole new code of behavior. She chose something like a roll of pastry; when she bit into it hot gravy spurted down her chin. Waels sniggered like an idiot. It was meaty and tasty, though. She passed on a bowl of mysterious paste and took a small fish on a twig from the next. At least the flagon of wine that was placed in front of her seemed to be for her own use, not for sharing.

"We do not normally eat this well," Cavotti said. "The Veritano garrison commander was a gourmet. Now his cooks work for us. They had brought in many delicacies for a year-end feast, which he unfortunately is not present to enjoy. He is treating the vultures. Try these curried lizard heads."

The Mutineer was a restless man, and not as famished as his guests. He soon began talking business. He wanted to hear—and wanted Melchitte to hear—all about Saltaja and the closing of the pass. Dantio obliged between mouthfuls.

"How many men did she have with her?"

"We do not know, although Orlad saw at least a sixty. Four sixty if she brought all of Caravan Six. We know there were about eight sixty in Nardalborg, but the pass was not provisioned for that many."

When a hefty elbow jabbed her ribs, Fabia realized that she had Waels on one side of her, Orlad on the other, and had been elected interpreter. She explained in a whisper as Dantio described the events at Fist's Leap.

"Surely," Melchitte said, "if they knew you had torched the last food cache, they would be more inclined to turn back than press on? Coming this way they faced a harder journey and a war when they arrived."

Dantio hesitated, eyed Fabia as if wondering what she knew that she had not told him, and then said, "I agree, my lord, and with anyone else I would not worry. But Saltaja does have chthonic powers and she would certainly want to press on to Florengia to join up with her brother. Only death waited for her at home in Vigaelia."

Cavotti was skeptical. "She was old. She had no food. Even if she had four sixty men with her, they would be more inclined to kill her in anger than help her escape. How long will you need to destroy the shelters, Melchitte?"

The huntleader smiled. "Two days should be more than ample, my lord. If we encounter any ice devils, they will be exhausted and starving."

Fabia could not let such folly go unchecked. Nor could she discuss her chthonic efforts to view the Queen of Shadows. She suspected that her attempts had been somehow blocked, for her dreams had revealed nothing except brief glimpses of Saltaja gnawing on bloody meat and crossing the Dust River on a bridge of corpses. She had no idea whether those were genuine sendings or the Mother of Lies plying her with nightmares.

"Lord Marno, I beg you not to underestimate Saltaja Hragsdor! She ruled all Vigaelia for fifteen years. No one has ever done that before. I will never be convinced that she is dead until I see her carcass. She *did* have food. She had four sixty head, on the hoof."

Into the angry silence, Giunietta spoke softly. "The lady may be mistaken, but she means what she says."

The Mutineer drummed fingers on the table. "I want to raze this place. If I leave a garrison here, I risk drawing an attack by Stralg's forces to retake it. If he gains any inkling that his sister may be approaching, he will certainly try to reoccupy the site. But I see your point. Huntleader, we will take this warning seriously. I will leave you here with blue pack for a thirty to kill any stragglers coming over the pass. They should be in no condition to fight back. When you are ready to withdraw, take enough from the food cache for your own use, and then burn the rest, and the buildings. Start your patrols right away."

Melchitte rose. "My lord is kind." He stepped over the bench and headed for the door.

"And when you come back, bring our prisoner." Something about Marno's smirk raised Fabia's hackles. She noted both Dantio and Giunietta looking at him strangely. She recalled Felice's warning that he might have surprises of his own.

He popped one of the round, green peppery fruits into his armory of teeth and spoke around it. "What are your plans?"

"We have no plans, only wishes," Dantio said. "First I must rescue the seers Stralg kidnapped. When he set out to invade Florengia, he ignored the Eldest's protests and took a dozen seers with him. We know that most have since died, but the survivors must be informed that the compact is now broken and their ordeal is ended. If we can rescue them, the Fist will lose his eyes."

Cavotti seemed curiously unenthusiastic at the prospect. "That will help in the long run, certainly. I agree that mercy requires us to release the poor women, but I must consider how best to use this turn of events. Giunietta, how can I inform them of the news?"

The three of them discussed seers. Fabia explained to Orlad and Waels, then began considering her own priorities. When Cavotti reached a long arm for a sweet roll, she was ready.

"My lord? Before we discuss what *we* want you to do *for* us, why don't you explain what *you* intend to do *with* us?"

The ogreish, misshapen eyes turned to study her. Seeing that she bore his gaze without flinching, he said, "Aren't we allies against the Fist? Don't you trust me, lady Fabia?"

"I hope we can be allies. No, I don't trust you."

He raised his eyebrows, snuggling them up around his horn stub. He was amused. "Wise of you, perhaps. I'm not sure just how I want to *use* you. Your arrival has changed things considerably." He pulled something out of the nearest bowl and crunched it with his millstone teeth.

"Ten years ago, Stralg controlled the Face, and we were a raggle-taggle pack of oath-breakers hiding out in the jungles around Ocean. Every year after that we grew stronger. Every year we grew stronger *faster*. Now Stralg is down to about three sixty-sixty and I have more men than he does. I need more, because I have been herding him this way, to the northwest. I knew he would want to keep his lines to Vigaelia open. He knew I knew that, and knew I would always leave this direction less defended than any other. We both have seers and know more or less where the enemy is. We are playing a gigantic game of *tégale*."

He paused to nibble while Fabia made a quick translation.

"The art in this sort of war lies in concentration and dispersion. Last rainy season Stralg occupied the town of Miona. He squeezed twenty sixty of his men in there, so we surrounded it and burned it. Few Heroes escaped, and almost no extrinsics. He hasn't made that mistake again. That is why he has not occupied Celebre yet. At the moment he holds roughly the area from Umsina to Veritano, including Celebre, but he has only a token force in the city itself. Even our advantage in numbers would not hold him if he wanted to break out, but he doesn't, because Veritano is his escape route, understand? He was stocking it, making ready for a pullout over the pass in the spring." The Mutineer grinned, which was a nightmare sight. "A Stralg pullout! He goes first and the Old One takes the hindmost."

Again Fabia translated for her neighbors. Waels was smiling, Orlad scowling.

"Armies never willingly give battle," Cavotti said, "unless they are sure of at least a local advantage in numbers. Eventually I will force Stralg into a corner, bring up all my reserves, and crush him. I came here because we learned that he had left Veritano vulnerable. He miscalculated, or else he hoped to trap me into a bad move. Either way, I took the bait. I planned to burn it, expecting him to rush in and take it back so he could restart his escape plan. Reinforcement here would shrink his perimeter elsewhere, understand, and make life easier for us. But I do not want to lose men.

"Now you bring news that there is no back door for my lord Stralg. Not only have you burned his bridges, but Vigaelia has turned on the spawn of Hrag. His brothers and sister are dead. He is alone. This makes a real change, and will require new strategy. Any beast is most dangerous when cornered. I can try to keep him ignorant of this development. Or I may let him find out. If I do that, what will he do? Break out to the south, and abandon hope of going home?"

Dantio muttered, "Open negotiations?," but Cavotti was obviously addressing Orlad. There was a crackling tension between the two Werists.

Orlad asked Fabia a few questions to make sure he understood. Then he said, in his accented Florengian, "He takes Celebre?"

Cavotti nodded his oversized head, leering terrible teeth. "I think he may do that! He could seize the city and hold it hostage as his price for peace."

Would the Mutineer then treat Celebre as he had Miona?

"So it seems that by returning we have doomed Celebre," Fabia said. "My lord, we wish most of all to visit our father, if he still lives, and to comfort our mother. We ask your help in this. Will you refuse it?"

The great wall of teeth showed again. "I wish to destroy Stralg. That is the only thing that matters to me. Your request must be judged against the demands of war. I will give you my decision as soon as I have made it. In this nightmare game of *tégale,* I have one more tile to show you, although one of very minor importance."

Cavotti was facing the door, she was not. She turned to see who was making that peculiar clattering sound.

Huntleader Melchitte had returned, chivvying along a prisoner who was at once taller than he was and about one-third the width. He was a Florengian, his ankles and wrists chained together so that he was forced to walk in a stoop, shuffling his bare feet. The only other thing he wore was a dirty loincloth, so narrow it would have barely made a sleeve for Cavotti. He was obviously only a boy, and Fabia felt a flash of anger that a child should be so maltreated.

She turned to say so, and was shocked by Dantio's horror-struck expression. She took another look at the prisoner. He, in turn, was staring at Cavotti with a truculent expression that failed to conceal an understandable fear. That face? She had seen a face like that in a vision. And in Benard's art. And she had spent half a year with Saltaja Hragsdor.

"My lord Cavotti," she said, since no one else was speaking and she disliked his sneer. "Obviously you have captured a Stralg by-blow, or a nephew, perhaps. But he is only a child. Must he be chained like that?"

The Mutineer turned his scowl on her. "He needed a lesson in manners."

"They're scared of me!" the boy jeered.

Fabia said, "If he talks back to you in his position, then I admire his courage, if not his wits. Are you frightened that he will escape? Cannot your warbeasts track down a fugitive?"

Cavotti smirked. She turned back to the boy and now he was the one showing shock. He was staring at her in disbelief. She had guessed who he was—and he knew her also? Just as Benard had known her the first time they met. That explained Cavotti's little game. Suddenly furious, she jumped up and went over to the boy.

"I am Fabia Celebre. What's your name?"

Even stooped, he was taller than she was. He hesitated. "Chies Celebre."

No—Chies Stralgson! She had seen a vision of Stralg dragging her mother away. "Then you are my half-brother."

He nodded as if he expected to be struck. "You are so like Mama!"

"I am flattered to hear it! You look much like your father. I am happy to meet you, brother Chies!" She kissed his cheek. "Here is your oldest brother, Dantio."

Dantio had recovered his poise and was apparently willing to follow her lead. He walked forward and gave the youth a hug. "Well met, brother Chies. We did not know you existed, but we shall not hold it against you that you do. How is Mama?"

Young Chies looked as if the sky had just fallen on him. "All right," he mumbled. "Or she was before I was . . . kidnapped. Kidnapped by these—"

"Don't poke sticks at the bears, Chies," Fabia said quickly. "Not when you're the one in the cage. And there—" She hoped this was going to work. "—is your youngest brother, Orlad. He used to be Orlando, but it's safer to call him Orlad."

For a moment Orlad glowered at the beanpole and the beanpole stared at the Werist in horror. Then Orlad said, "Why don't I just tear his head off?"

"Don't be snarly," Fabia said. Curiously, Chies seemed to have understood that remark. Had his father taught him Vigaelian, just as Paola had taught her Florengian?

Orlad switched to Florengian. "Welcome. The more family is the best. Better, I mean." But he stayed at the table.

Chies said, "Thank you." Surrounded by unexpected relatives willing to be allies, he lifted his chin and shot a look of triumph at Cavotti. He did not lack courage.

"Tell us, my lord," Fabia said, "how our brother came to be here to meet us?"

"First you tell me how you recognized him." Cavotti would not have survived so long had he been a trusting man.

Fabia was not about to confess to receiving visions from Xaran. "I know Stralg abducted my mother. Now I know why. Also, I knew his uncles, and his aunt, and my brother Benard used Stralg's likeness in a mosaic. Please can he be unchained? You know he can't escape."

The Mutineer said, "Loose the pup, Huntleader. Your father is dying, my lady. The council will have to choose a new doge, and this trash started mincing around like a prince of the blood. I didn't think the elders would be insane enough to elect him by themselves, but the Fist might force them. We removed the temptation."

"He wants to use me to trap my father!" Chies snapped. The boy's loyalties were a bit confused, perhaps. Understandably.

Cavotti said, "He has grandiose ideas of his own worth. He imagines his sire would bother to cross a street to rescue him."

"If you saw him as a political token, then the Fist may as well," Fabia said, aware that she was now the one poking sticks at bears.

Dantio intervened with the question that had to be asked. "Has our father named a successor, my lord?"

Cavotti chuckled. "Apparently he did. He was asked, not long ago. To everyone's surprise he rallied enough to cast the dead man's vote."

"And?"

"He said, 'The Winner!'" Thanks to his beetling brows, the big man's smile was more fearsome than most glowers Fabia had ever met. "Perhaps he meant Stralg. I doubt that he meant lord Chies."

"Then the elders will decide," she said. "Since we offer them a wider choice now, may our half-brother accompany us to Celebre?"

"Si' down, all of you," Cavotti growled. And, as Chies's chains clattered to the floor, "You, too, boy. Eat if you're hungry. My lady, Celebre is in the middle of Stralg country. You are escaped hostages. You realize the danger you will be in if you surface here?" He looked to Orlad. "You, especially. No Florengian enters Celebre now with a brass collar on. Understand?"

Orlad nodded. "I will risk this."

"We all will," Dantio said.

"Your necks are your business," Cavotti said, shrugging. "Your loyalty I cannot doubt, but the bastard I will not trust. He stays here. You can leave with me. I will turn you over to people who will try to get you into Celebre. No guarantees. If you do get in there, though, for gods' sake keep your heads down."

Chies, who was eating with both hands, found room in his mouth to say, "He wants to use you to lure my . . . to lure the Fist into Celebre so he can burn it down, like he did with Miona."

Fabia had wondered that earlier, but remarked, "I think your father is too clever to fall into the same trap twice, Chies." However, she suspected the Mutineer might be cleverer still.

thirty-two

CHIES CELEBRE

watched with mixed feelings as his new relatives drove away. In their place, he would have chopped his head off, but they seemed willing to accept him. Things were looking up. The accursed chains had been struck off. If Stralg lost, Chies Celebre was the doge's brother. If Stralg won, Chies Stralgson was the Fist's son. He would have felt happier being taken home, though. He had been allowed to overhear the Mutineer ordering Huntleader Melchitte to treat the prisoner well as long as he behaved himself and kill him otherwise, or if the Fist tried to retake Veritano. It was not fair to make him hostage for what his father might choose to do.

He went back to the dining hall and celebrated by eating up all the food left on the table—everything except the greenfish, which he disliked—and emptying the wine flasks. The world suffused with rosy well-being.

Melchitte peered in. "There you are." He surveyed the table. "Pig!"

" 'Waste not, want not,' my mommy always says."

Pigface sneered. "And a sweet, dutiful little lad you are, too. Well, bastard, I was told you are to be treated well. Mind your manners and we'll agree on what that means. Otherwise, I win the argument. Don't try to escape. You know warbeasts can follow a scent? And outrun a chariot? And you know what usually happens when a pack runs down its quarry?"

Chies tried cute. "Please, my lord! I've just eaten! Besides, why should I want to escape? The food here's better than the palace's. I'll need a girl in a day or two, but it's not urgent yet . . . unless you have a spare one lying around?"

Melchitte laughed and went away. Rebel Werists were much the same sort of louts as the Vigaelian ones Chies had cultivated for years. Talk dirty and they would eat out of your hand.

He decided to go and lie down. Thanks to the chains, he had not had a decent sleep in days, nor nights either, and he *was* very full. And drunk. But when he reached his room he was still sober enough to take the key out of the door and hide it under a loose floor tile.

✦

The next day, after his stomach settled, he mooched around the complex, had a swim, inspected the llamoid pens, and took a very brief look at the pile of corpses that the Heroes called the bird feeder. Bored, he began chatting up Werists. Among four sixty men some would be susceptible to the smiles of a winsome lad, and he soon located Sesto Panotti, leader of rear flank, blue pack. Sesto was not much older than he was and almost as good-looking— not that Chies had any intention of letting their friendship get serious. Girls were his preferred prey, but he would tolerate a grope or two for a good cause.

Sesto had lost a man in the battle, which meant eleven men for six chariots. There would be no harm in taking a passenger along on patrol, would there? *I could ride with you, Sesto.* Interested, Sesto asked his pack-leader, who shrugged and agreed. Staying on the lookout for Stralg forces approaching from seaward was serious work, but rear flank had drawn the evening patrol Iceward and that was a meaningless exercise. Nothing more was going to come over the pass at this time of year. Sesto told his new friend to find himself a chlamys and be ready one pot-boiling after noon.

The chariots were racing models, very light, made of bentwood and wicker, their four-spoked wheels rimmed with bronze. Sesto's had a quiver for hunting, although it held a long-handled ax instead of arrows. They were rigged with teams of four for the long climb up to the Altiplano. Even so, the guanacos went at a slow walk.

"Never drove a team of four," Chies said hopefully.

"Now's a good time to start." Sesto gave him the reins.

A chariot was cramped with two men in it, and a chlamys was a very loose garment, open down the sides. Being right-handed, Sesto had put himself on the left. Soon he said, "You're doing great, lad!" and gave Chies an encouraging pat on the butt. Oh well. Chies had known what the price would be and driving a rig like this was fun. He just wished the rest of the flank was not following so close, able to watch what their leader was doing.

After a while he said, "How far do we go?"

"How far would you like me to go?"

"Don't mean that. Not as far as you've gone already, please. I'd rather you waited until tonight so we can both play."

"Promise?"

"Oh, you bet! I need some lessons, and you're a wonderful hunk." Chies's door could be locked from the inside. "I meant, how close to the Ice?"

"Second shelter. We have to destroy the equipment there and burn it. That's what the axes are for. They burned the first shelter yesterday." Sesto chuckled. "Death to the ice devils! No escape."

Thinking of that disgusting pile of corpses at the bird feeder, Chies did not comment. He was half ice devil himself.

✦

The jaunt turned interesting again when they emerged on the Altiplano. After the guanacos had gotten their wind back, Sesto told him to give them their heads, and they took off like a sea storm. *Whee!* The wind whirled Chies's hair around and the wheels hardly seemed to touch the ground. Best of all, Sesto needed both hands to hang on. It was a shame that the road was so straight, and that a bank of cloud hid the Ice itself. But this was living! One day Chies would have his own racing stable.

In no time they went hurtling past the charred remains of the first shelter.

"Whoa!" Sesto said. "Slow down there, Killer. Looks like we have company. Two of them?"

It was three. Chies had excellent eyes, even if they were watering madly in the wind, but he knew not to contradict Werists.

In a few moments it became clear that there were indeed three men, and they were staggering—literally staggering—along the road toward them. They were muffled in furs, but obviously Werists. Sesto took back the reins and brought his flank to a halt about sixty paces away. By then the visitors had fallen to their knees.

"Mercy? They want mercy!" Sesto pulled out the ax and surveyed his men. "They should have thought about mercy sixteen years ago. Orders are to kill on sight. Volunteers?" Ten hands went up. "Raul, you missed out last time. Don't battleform unless you have to."

Raul jumped down from his chariot and trotted forward, grinning. He took the ax and Chies looked away. Even three against one would be no fight, for the Vigaelians were totally spent. Whatever Raul did was quick and undoubtedly fatal because the other Florengians cheered, but the victims did not sound dead when the patrol drove away.

Sesto jeered. "Squeamish, sonny?"

"We could have questioned them."

"You understand that gobble-gobble of theirs?"

"Some," Chies admitted. He was fluent.

"Then show me what you can find out from this next one."

Sure enough, there was another approaching along the road. He seemed very tall, but soon resolved into a large man carrying another on his back.

By the time the chariots arrived, the big man had knelt down to release his burden, and then collapsed altogether. The other just stood over him, hands out, as if to hold off the execution squad racing toward them. His white hair blew loose in the wind, his rags flapped, his nose had turned black with frostbite, and he had lost two or three fingers. Sesto pulled up close, so Chies could ask questions

But Werists never wore their hair long like that. It wasn't a Werist. Nor a man, neither. But whoever it was, she did have extraordinary eyes. Crazy eyes. Mad, mad eyes, staring up at him as if she knew him.

Part VI

◆

THE DOGE
IS DEAD,
LONG LIVE
THE DOGE!

◆

thirty-three

ORLAD CELEBRE

was much impressed by the famous Mutineer. He was everything a leader should be—decisive, quick-witted, successful, and adored by his men; a giant's physique never hurt, either. He had demanded no oath from Orlad, just offered a spade-sized hand and said, "Your foes are my foes!" That was how Heroes committed to each other when they were equals, so Orlad had been happy to agree. An oath would have been tricky, because obviously their priorities must differ if Marno thought killing Stralg required the destruction of Celebre.

Nor was Cavotti one to sit around and digest. If the Celebres wanted to go with him, they had to leave immediately. He had his own chariot, bigger than most and pulled by a team of six guanacos, and he usually traveled with a bodyguard of six Werists. He replaced three of them with Orlad, Waels, and Dantio, remarking that Orlad and Waels more than made up for Dantio's lack of fighting skills. This might be true normally, but was not necessarily so after a thirty or more crossing the Edge. He told Fabia she could squeeze in beside him as long as she promised not to breathe and she did not seem displeased by the suggestion. Orlad had hoped for a Hero-to-Hero chat with the Mutineer, but could see that there would not be room in the car for both of them.

His driver was Packleader Tabbeo, a five-year, tough-as-bronze veteran, who claimed to have slaughtered seven Vigaelians with his own hands—and teeth, of course. Orlad could claim a greater score than that, but the two that Tabbeo wanted to hear about were the sons of Hrag. He was also willing to learn about Saltaja and remarkably patient at correcting his companion's Florengian.

The countryside was lush, fascinating, totally different from the bleak Nardalborg moors of Orlad's childhood. The animals were different, the trees, the houses—everything! The weather was about the same, sun and rain alternating, except that the rain was warm here. Cavotti set a bone-shattering pace, changing llamoids frequently. This might officially be Stralg country, but obviously Cavotti had it well organized, and the inhabitants could not do enough for him.

He did not hesitate to travel by night; he rarely slept more than a couple of pot-boilings at a time. Meal breaks never lasted longer than it took the hands to harness up new llamoids. Fatigue settled around Orlad like a fog. He barely exchanged a word with the others for the next three days, although he dearly wanted to know what Fabia was learning from the Mutineer. He still hadn't managed a private chat with her when they came to a ranch outside Montegola, less than half a menzil from the fabled city of Celebre.

✦

Orlad awoke to the sound of wagon wheels and an unexpected scent of hay. Memory returned with a thump—Montegola. Celebre was visible from the ranch, he had been told; he would see it in the morning. The sun was up now, obviously, and what they called a winter day here already seemed hot to him. Waels slept on at his side. It was the work of a moment to turn a blanket back into a chlamys and slither down the ladder. By the time he paused in the barn doorway to take stock of the yard, he could hear Waels following.

There was the wagon that had woken him, with four guanacos hitched and a spotty-faced youngster slouched on the bench. Beyond it stood the house and a couple of other buildings, built of wicker and thatch, but seemingly well kept. And yes, even from where he stood, that gleam of white towers across the plain must be Celebre itself. It was much bigger than he had expected. His heartbeat rose.

"Could eat a mammoth," Waels said, stretching and blinking at the sunshine.

"Nice day, feels like summer."

"We are not in Nardalborg anymore, my lord."

Rain clouds far to the east suggested a change later. Dantio and Fabia were just emerging from the house, followed by their host. Cavotti had disappeared the previous evening on other business.

The rancher, Eligio, wore a peasant's loincloth and flaunted a brass collar in full view. That seemed like rank insanity in Stralg country. When Orlad had asked his rank he had answered merely, "Spy." He had good reason to be surly, for he looked no older than Waels but had lost an arm and one eye and would never battleform again. He ran thirty or so llamoids and a staging post for the Liberators. His wife, Carmina, seemed impossibly young to be the mother of the two children. She was an excellent cook, but Orlad reluctantly postponed thoughts of breakfast.

"You might have warned us that you were leaving."

Eligio barely looked at him. "You're staying here. Go back to the loft and keep out of sight." He greeted the driver with a fast twitter of Florengian.

Fabia said, "Or go and beg Carmina to run you up a stack of her onion pancakes. The gods dine here." She hooked a foot in a wheel and swung up to the wagon as if she had been doing it for years.

Dantio said, "Nice legs," and followed more circumspectly.

Eligio and the boy were still yammering away, both at once, with much hand-waving. Orlad stepped to within biting distance of Eligio.

"Why are they going? Why are we not?"

"Don't worry. We can trust them, Orlad," Dantio said quickly.

"I still want to know what's going to happen."

Eligio looked at him as if he were moronic. "*They're* going to a safe house in the city, and don't ask me what they're going to do there because I don't know. *You* stay here for now. No one enters Celebre without showing his neck to the scum on the gate."

"So how do Waels and I get in?"

"I'll tell you when it's time."

"Why not now?"

"The less you know the safer."

"Why don't they wait and come with us?" Orlad was surprised at how protective he felt toward his siblings now.

Eligio rolled his eyes. "Because they're not Heroes, stupid. You want my help or not? If you do, throttle your gullet."

"You're speaking Vigaelian!" Orlad said, realizing belatedly.

The Florengian showed a set of teeth as jagged as a saw blade. "I help interrogate prisoners. It's a hobby of mine." He looked up to Dantio. "Leave the stuff I gave you at the triple fountain after dark. Check if they've picked it up every pot-boiling or so. If they haven't arrived by dawn, try again to-morrow night. If they don't appear then, they won't be coming. If it isn't safe to meet up, try to leave a broken pot there instead. Then they'll come back here and wait for news."

Putting on the best face he could, Orlad smiled up at Fabia and Dantio. "Until tonight then. Twelve blessings on you. Give my love to Mama. Tell her I like my steak raw."

"Twelve blessings on you," Dantio said. "Raw it will be."

Fabia said, "Try and stay out of fights, you two."

Waels flashed her his heart-stopping smile and said, "Why?"

As the wagon rattled out of the yard, Eligio growled, "You want to eat?"

"Very much we do, my lord," Waels said. "And then we want some lessons in looking after guanacos. All I've learned so far is that they don't smell as bad as onagers."

Orlad had learned that they didn't kick as hard, either, but he wasn't going to mention that.

thirty-four

CHIES STRALGSON

had never been so frightened in his entire life. Not even on the night he was kidnapped, because then he had been falling-down drunk. But now . . .

Now the sun was setting and Chies was driving down the gully road at breakneck speed because he couldn't control the team. The car leaped and bounced and rocked, heading steadily closer to Veritano with Sesto following, yelling at him to slow down. The best thing that could happen now would be for him to tip the car and fall out and break his neck. Or throw Saltaja out, but he was certain that would never happen.

He had always known he had half-brothers and a half-sister somewhere beyond the Edge. No one had ever mentioned an aunt. Certainly not a foul, mad, murderous, gangrenous aunt. An aunt who invoked *Xaran!* An aunt who had cast the evil eye on him and murdered ten Werists.

Sesto had promised, speaking in his curious new singsong, that they could pass Veritano on a trail so far from the buildings that Witness Giunietta would not notice. But Chies couldn't control his rig. And Melchitte had at least two other patrols out, somewhere. And the dead Werists up on the Altiplano would be missed soon, so searchers would go looking. And warbeasts could outrun llamoids with one paw behind their backs and follow a scent for days. When they caught the killers they would tear them to pieces.

Saltaja was haggard and stank of rotting meat. She had lost fingers and toes and most of her nose. And teeth. She was so weak that Chies had to keep one arm around her to hold her in the chariot. He had tied the reins around his waist so he wouldn't fall out, but that was hunting technique and he had never practiced driving that way. He ought to head straight to Veritano and scream for men to bring ropes and spades to tether and bury a Chosen. He wouldn't, because she wouldn't let him. He would do exactly as he was told.

He would also tell Sesto to do whatever she said, and Sesto would obey, too. She spoke no Florengian, yet that had not stopped her using her evil eye. She'd first enslaved Chies and Sesto, then given her orders through them to the other men. She had made them line up so she could hobble along the line, muttering at them, one by one. Then they had been told to strip and kneel down. And then *they had just stayed there on their knees while their flankleader split their heads open with a wood ax and she chanted a hymn to the Evil One!*

If a Werist flankleader had killed his own men on her orders, what chance did a boy like Chies have of resisting her? But he was not proud of himself, even so. He had thrown up when the killing started, and lost control of his bowels when she kissed him. He must smell as bad as she did. Now he was terrified by the chariot's breakneck plunge down the hill and she did not seem worried at all.

"How old are you, Nephew?"

"Sixteen. Just turned."

"And so tall! Have you made your vows to the gods yet?"

He shivered, wondering why she wanted to know that. "No. The rebels kidnapped me before the turn of the year."

"That will help. What's that smoke?"

"Steam. Hot springs."

"Ah, I could use a good soak. So could you. Stop at a warm pond."

"I'll try," he mumbled. He could not turn the team of four with only one hand, but if he let go of his aunt she might be hurt, and he knew he mustn't let that happen, whatever he did.

"Tell me about the war," she mumbled.

"Dunno nothing. The Mutineer seems to be winning. All the battles are his victories."

"Then tell me about your father."

"Which father?"

"Don't play games with me, boy, or I'll curse the balls off you."

"I don't know!" Chies howled. "Stralg? I've never met him, not that I remember. He doesn't . . ." He was going to say "doesn't love me" but that would sound ridiculous. How could anyone love him now? He was in league with Xaran, helping one of Her Chosen. Murdering people.

♦

Sesto caught up with them and shouted instructions on how to turn the team. When the llamoids had been slowed to a walk, Chies told him they must find a hot pool. With Sesto leading this time, they reached a place where he said they could bathe. She told Chies to tell him to lift her down from the car.

"Undress me!" she ordered Chies, waving her mutilated hands, and of course he did. She was a horrible sight, the color of old bone, tufts of white hair, every rib showing, dried out dugs like empty meal sacks. "Help me into the water. You get in, too. And tell him to follow." Sesto had blood all over his hands and arms.

So the three of them sat in the steaming water as the stars came out. Chies had little chance to brood on all the dead men, because she kept mumbling questions and he had to answer, or find out from Sesto for her—the war, the assault on Veritano, yesterday's unexpected visitors. She listened eagerly to that part. She made Chies tell her all the things the Celebres had talked about with the Mutineer, so far as he had heard. It was a long agony. She was in no hurry, yet the warbeasts might be on their trail already.

"Now, how will you get your dear old aunt to Celebre?"

Chies translated. "We have to take her to Celebre. How can we do that?"

Sesto's face kept twitching strangely and he spoke funny. "We'll have to take to the river, or the others will track us."

"There are boats?"

"Small boats. It's a small river until we get near the city."

Chies hugged himself in misery. "Won't they just run along both banks until they find us?"

"Warbeasts can't run forever, boy. Boats can."

Chies told the hag about the river, and boats.

She cackled with satisfaction. "You will arrange whatever we need. He will obey your orders if you say they come from me. If you need anything from someone else, tell me and I will Control them just like I'm Controlling him."

"And me," he muttered.

She patted his shoulder with a ruined claw of a hand. "No, Nephew. I'm not Controlling you. I'm forcing him, I admit. He knows I'm doing it and he can't help responding. But you're helping your poor old auntie because you *want* to, aren't you?"

"Yes, Aunt." He thought he was just too frightened to argue.

"You want to punish the people who did these terrible things to me, don't you? You want to help your father defeat the Mutineer, don't you? You want to be doge, don't you?"

Had he heard right? "Is that possible, Aunt?"

"Bah! If I can send a flank of Heroes to Xaran, you think a ragtag herd of elders will stop me making you doge?"

Chies said, "No, Aunt!" *Holy Twelve!* That made a difference.

"You get me near this Marno Cavotti and there won't *be* any rebellion."

"Yes, Aunt. I mean 'No,' Aunt." Hello, Papa. Aunt Saltaja and I have tamed the Mutineer for you. I have his head in this bag. And the elders elected me doge . . .

"We children of Hrag stick together and help one another!"

"Of course I will do whatever you say, Aunt!"

"How will you get us into the city itself?"

Chies turned back to Sesto, whose twitch seemed to be growing even worse. Giving orders to a rebel flankleader was a heady sensation. "How do we get into Celebre?"

"I can't go in. The ice devils watch all the gates. They'll kill me."

"I can. How about her?"

Sesto blinked, chewed his lip, flicked eyebrows as if his face had gone crazy. "They'll question a Vigaelian woman. Don't see them around often."

Chies turned it into Vigaelian for her.

She was undoubtedly madder than a burning cat, but she was not stupid. "The Celebre boy is a Werist too. And had another Werist with him, you said. How will they get in?"

Translation . . .

Sesto whimpered, as if in pain. "The Mutineer was going to take the Celebres to Flankleader Eligio. He runs a ranch north of Cypress Gate. He has friends. He gets people in and out."

"You know this place?" Chies asked.

"Never been there, but it will be easy to find. Just south of Montegola."

The news made the Chosen cackle again. "Then we will go there and speak with Flankleader Eligio. We'd best be on our way. Chies, you will dress me. Now you see why I told you to collect the men's robes before Sesto got blood all over them?"

As Chies was helping her out of the pool, he said, "If you want to meet up with Stralg, Aunt, I don't think we should go to Celebre. He won't be there."

She turned and smiled at him. Her mouth was a foul-smelling pit of bloody gums and a few blackened teeth. "Good, good! Starting to be help-ful. Your father can wait, boy. What matters first is your sister."

"Um, Fabia?" He kept forgetting he had a sister.

"Yes, that one. Frena, she used to call herself. But I don't care what she calls herself. I do care, very much, how she dies. Understand?"

"Er, yes, Aunt."

"Very horribly, very slowly. Because of what she's done to me."

"Of course, Aunt." Chies finished drying her scrawny carcass with one chlamys and reached for another to drape her. "And her brothers, too?" He didn't want a contested election.

✦

Not far off dawn, they stole a boat. Two dogs started to bark, then had second thoughts and ran away into the darkness, whining in terror. Their owners were either asleep or had enough sense not to interfere. The hag made Sesto release the exhausted llamoids and push the two chariots off the scruffy little jetty into the river. They floated away upside down, wheels plaintively turning. How soon until the Veritano warbeasts arrived?

Chies gave Sesto his orders, then collapsed in the bottom of the boat and went to sleep.

✦

Before noon they left the river and commandeered a wagon.

That night, Chies found himself eating a hearty meal in a farmer's hut. Several hearty meals, in fact, one after the other. The farmer was a heavyset man, almost big enough to be a Werist, but he was Controlled as tightly as Sesto, wearing the same mindless expression, answering questions in the same singsong. He had a fat wife, a hulking adolescent son, and a remarkably pretty daughter. They were all Controlled, too. Sesto was a walking corpse, barely able to speak, but he had probably not slept since leaving Veritano. Chies repeatedly had to order him to keep eating.

Aunt Saltaja was starting to look better already. Her mouth bled less and she was steadier on her feet. Yet her mind seemed even more twisted than before. She rarely spoke of anything except the atrocities she was going to inflict on Fabia Celebre. Also the brothers, but mostly the woman. Fabia was another Chosen, apparently. Chies was sorry to hear that, because he had quite liked her. She had kissed him and gotten his accursed chains taken off.

He finished eating at last, picking a few last treats out of his teeth. He yawned. A comfortable rug and a blanket were in order now. The lamp was flickering, its oil almost gone, and the fire had shrunk to embers. The hut was built of bamboo, wicker and palm-leaf thatch, so all the rooms were tiny, but there were several of them. He assumed Aunt Saltaja would take the best sleeping platform, and hoped he could steal a place by the fire. Or just steal away? He had very good night-sight. If the stars were out, he might manage to escape.

"You want her?" his Aunt said suddenly, leering her black stumps at him.

"What?"

"You've done well. You deserve a reward. You want her for the night?"

He gulped. He realized he had been staring at the girl. She was certainly pretty. He was very tired, but a man had to look out for his reputation.

"I would enjoy that, Aunt."

She beckoned the girl over to her, pulled her head down close, and stared very hard into her eyes. She mumbled something.

"I don't think she understands Vigaelian," Chies said uneasily.

Saltaja released the girl. "Doesn't matter. I spoke to the Mother, not her. Take her. She'll do whatever you want."

The girl was staring at Chies. He nodded. She blushed furiously and beckoned for him to follow.

The room was tiny and the sleeping platform was a narrow frame full of sand. He closed the door, wishing it had a bolt, which it did not. Ignoring the girl, he examined the window, but it was fitted with stout bars of bamboo, which he could not budge. The night was cloudy, anyway, and the farmer had dogs out there. So no escape tonight.

The girl slid her arms around him. She was not merely willing, she was eager. She had no clothes on. But . . .

But Saltaja was going to get caught sooner or later, probably sooner.

He could not help doing what she told him when she was there, fixing him with the evil eye. She had made a flankleader murder his own men, so a boy like Chies could not be expected to refuse her orders *when she was there*. But if he refused this girl, that would show he wasn't really cooperating with the Chosen the rest of the time, wouldn't it? If it came to a trial, that would save him, wouldn't it?

The girl had a hand at his crotch already, so he had better decide this quickly.

She whispered "Love me!" in his ear and tried to kiss him.

Fortunately, she had very bad breath, which made the decision easier.

He said, "No!" He squirmed loose. "Don't touch me. You sleep on the floor. Lie down!"

She obeyed. He couldn't see her face in the dark. He heard her snivel. "But I want . . ."

"Be quiet! Don't speak. And don't come near me."

He stretched out on the sand, wriggled a hollow for his hip, and turned his back on her. It wasn't as hard as he expected. In fact, the thought of what they did to rapists was quite enough to dissuade him. *Big softie!* he thought. Little softie, in fact. He went to sleep.

◆

He had worried that his aunt might not leave any witnesses behind when they departed in the morning. She didn't, but not the way he had feared. She hexed the farmer and his family to forget that they had entertained visitors—also to forget that they had owned a chariot and two guanacos. The car was very cramped with three on board, but they soon met a man driving another one. They left him sitting by the wayside in a daze. Sesto handled the second team.

Three days, two nights, and two more women later, they saw the spire of a temple that Sesto claimed marked Montegola. Sesto was almost imbecilic—drooling constantly and barely able to drive a team. When Saltaja said to stop, Chies had to yell at the top of his lungs to make him understand. He would chew food only when ordered to and forget to swallow.

"Why are we stopping here, Aunt?" Chies could see nothing of interest in the farmland, just the distant temple, stubbled fields, a few hedges, and a forlorn clump of trees. They looked somehow ominous, drooping and stark against the sunset. It was to those that she pointed.

"Why don't they plow there?"

"I . . . have no idea, Aunt."

"It's probably accursed ground. If it isn't, it will have to do. You ready?"

Finding his throat suddenly dry, Chies just nodded. He had trouble finding enough spit to order Sesto to follow, suspecting that the dolt would just stand there in his chariot on the track until he died of thirst. They drove slowly across the stubbled field to the copse. Chies lifted Saltaja down again, told Sesto to follow. The weeds were long and unkempt between the rain-wet trunks. He kept stumbling on the uneven ground, and Sesto fell several times.

"Old battlefield, I think," Saltaja said. "Smells of evil." But when they reached the center, she peered around and frowned at a group of four or five cottages in the distance. "It's not as private as I had hoped. We had best be quick. You are ready?"

He was shaking like a palm frond in a sea storm. He said, "Of course," but it came out as a croak. He didn't have any choice, did he? She would never trust him otherwise, never release him. No, she'd mush his mind and turn him into a pudding like Sesto.

She leered, knowing what he was thinking. "It has to be of your own free will."

"Oh yes. I really want to do this, Aunt." Didn't he? Power? Girls?

"Well, I told you what to do. You brought the knife?"

He nodded and started taking his clothes off. He told Sesto to do the same and kneel down. He thought for a horrible moment that something like fear showed in the man's eyes, but he obeyed Chies without argument. Soon everybody would!

Chies stepped behind him, and whispered the words of the oath she had taught him, all the terrible promises *by blood and birth, death and the cold earth.* He pricked his own arm, shed a few drops of his own blood on the cold earth and a few more on the sacrifice to mark it as coming from him. Then he took Sesto by the hair and put the knife to his throat.

Sesto moaned and reached up to stop him.

"Let go!" Chies said in sudden panic. The strong fingers opened for him. "Now keep still!"

The knife was not as sharp as he would have liked. He had to saw with it. When he reached the artery, he was amazed at how far the blood spurted. He closed his eyes and was taken by surprise when Sesto collapsed at his feet. So it was done, and Chies felt no different, just very shaky and a little ill.

He turned to look at his aunt.

She cackled. "Well done, my little man. You made a wise choice."

He did not ask what his alternatives had been. He forced himself to go to her and give her a kiss. "Thank you." He wondered if he could kill her too, now. The Old One—*Xaran!* He could say the name now—Xaran might like two sacrifices. Chies could go home and claim that he had escaped from her, and who would be the wiser?

On the other hand, he had a lot to learn and Saltaja could teach him.

"Time to go, Aunt," he said, throwing down the knife and wiping his bloody hands on the grass.

He unharnessed the two unneeded guanacos and released them to gladden the heart of some fortunate peasant. He lifted his fellow Chosen back into the chariot and drove off with her in search of Flankleader Eligio and his llamoid ranch.

thirty-five

ORLAD CELEBRE

and Waels Borkson ate again as the sun was setting, although their host told them to eat sparingly. Then he led them out to the pasture.

"North." He pointed, although few stars were visible yet and much of the sky was shrouded in clouds. "That's Hrada's spire in Montegola, very nearly due north, see? We're going this way."

"Got it," Waels said. "A tenth west."

They plodded off over the rain-slick fields and came to a wide river, flowing surprisingly fast for such flat country.

"This is the Puisa." Eligio pointed upstream. "See that bridge? That's your landmark. It's the fourth bridge up from the city."

Counting up to four in battleform would be tricky, Orlad thought.

"Then we come back to you?"

"Two-fifths east. Follow the guanaco smell."

"We can backtrack," Waels said. "Nothing in the world smells like Orlad's feet." He added a faint *Oof!* sound as a fist impacted his ribs.

Eligio had no sense of humor. "When you reach a pool," he said, "you're at the city, so keep your heads down. The river enters through five tunnels under the wall. They're closed at the city end by gratings, and the current is strong enough to pin an extrinsic against them to drown. Understand now why I wouldn't let your sister come with you, my lord Orlad?"

"You are starting to make sense."

"Middle grating has been cut. Can you imagine what that cost? Dive, rasp until you're close to drowning, then battleform to swim back out against the current, surface, recover, repeat. Again and again, all night long, every night for a thirty. Don't betray this to the Vigaelian scum!"

"Brave men. Were you one of them?"

"No. Had friends who drowned doing it, though. Now, listen! The *middle* one of the five! At the *bottom* of the grating! Retroform, because the gap is narrow and there are sharp edges that can rip you. You'll need your head more than flippers there. We don't call this the Heroes' Gate for nothing. After you're through, float until you see the triple fountain on the *right* bank.

It's an easy landmark, in the grounds of the palace. Can you tell right from left in battleform?"

"Half the time," Orlad said.

"Then you'd better be human. If your brother hasn't left clothes at the fountain, you'd best come back here and try again tomorrow. Do *not* try to leave downstream. There's knives on the weir there. Leave by the same way you got in. Broken pot at the fountain means danger. Any questions?"

Waels said, "How many men have entered Celebre this way?"

"How should I know? None from here ever came back to tell me."

"I was afraid of that."

Orlad removed his sandals and chlamys, handed them to Eligio. Not ready to enter the river, he sat down in his collar and studied the dark rushing water. Excitement and disbelief fizzed through his veins. He was certainly going into extreme danger, but he was also going to change his life. He was going to lay claim to the coronet wearing a rebel's collar, while Stralg was still in nominal control of the city.

He realized that Eligio had gone when Waels sat down close and put an arm around him. The night was far from cold, but the contact was welcome.

Orlad said, "I've never been so scared in my life."

"*You,* scared? Never!"

"Scared peeless. This is not like King's Grass. Then I knew I was going to die because my lord had set the hunt on me. I was just so bloody-eyed mad that I had no time to be frightened. I wanted to kill as many as I could before they killed me. This is different. If we have to fight at all, we'll have failed."

"A man about to meet his mother for the first time is entitled to feel nervous," Waels said tactfully.

"You not scared?" Orlad asked.

"I'm always scared. I just follow you and trust you. If you can do it, whatever it is, then I must do it to be worthy of you. Much easier."

That made it worse. How could he drag Waels into mortal peril just to further his own ambitions?

"Buddy . . . I want to say . . . if this doesn't work out for both of us . . . I'm very grateful. You've taught me so many things—love, loyalty, friendship."

"We discovered them together."

"You don't have to come with me tonight."

"Yes I do."

"That's what I mean. Thanks." Pause . . . "Waels?"

"Orlad?"

"You do *not* have to come with me! I'm only doing this because I don't want Fabia staking her claim while I'm not around."

"Nonsense. You're taking me home to meet your parents."

Orlad exploded in laughter. Waels returned the punch he owed him. The laughter turned into a wrestling match and they rolled down the bank together into the river.

✦

No Hero had ever managed to swim up the waterfall at Nardalborg, although many had tried. (In winter it froze and the garrison held climbing races on it instead.) The Puisa seemed pleasantly warm by comparison. A standard amphibious warbeast was shaped much like a seal, a black seal in the Florengian case, but it would be folly to waste so much energy when they had a long way to go. Orlad contented himself with webbing his hands and feet and closing off his nostrils. He adopted a leisurely stroke that he could keep up for a couple of pot-boilings if he had to. He could feel Waels moving in the water at his side. Once in a while their heads would break surface together and flash toothy smiles.

He was surprised when the current changed. He surfaced and looked up at the towering walls of Celebre. The pool, already? Then a hand caught his arm. Waels retroformed beside him, with a finger on his lips for silence. He put lips to Orlad's ear.

"We have company!"

For a moment they drifted together and then Waels pointed downward and sank. They submerged together, holding hands, moving as little as necessary until they reached the bottom and could take hold of weeds as tethers, to stop them floating back up. Starlight failed to reach down there, so far as human eyes could see, but a Hero's eyes were negotiable. In a moment Orlad made out the faint glow of the surface. He saw fish . . . driftwood . . . and then a line of dark shapes heading toward the city. He wondered how Waels had known.

Soon after that the two strangers surfaced in some reeds near the shore. "Florengians?" Waels whispered.

"Think so. Yes. Not Stralg, then. Mutineer didn't tell us he kept a force in the city."

"Maybe it's new."

"Maybe it is." Orlad wondered about treachery, but he could have been captured much more easily at Montegola. "Let's go and see what's happening. If we're parted, we'll meet at the triple fountain. If you find a broken pot there, head straight back to Eligio's."

thirty-six

OLIVA ASSICHIE-CELEBRE

hurried along Wheelwrights' Alley with her cloak clutched tight so that the hood concealed her face. Every day she came to the Vigaelians' barracks close to sunset, because Huntleader Purque was almost always there at that time. None of the other ice devils would speak civilly to her. He would, although he would not answer her summons. She had to come to him.

She uncovered her head as she stepped through the open door. The room was dingy, stinking of urine and dogs, just a vestibule with a few ramshackle benches and a barred window. Three ice devils were sitting there, growling in their guttural speech and gnawing on meaty ribs. The floor was half covered with mangy street curs waiting for their turn at the bones.

One Hero looked up at her and said something he thought was funny.

Another, wearing a flankleader's sash, gestured at the inner door. "Go in. He wants you."

Her heart jumped—she would have said it leaped and sank at the same time, were that possible. Purque had news for her? Good or bad? She stepped carefully between dogs. The hall beyond was where the Werists exercised, and she was relieved to see it deserted, because they usually did so naked and used that as an opportunity for more coarse humor at her expense. She crossed to the huntleader's room and found him there, talking with a couple of his men. In contrast to the general squalor of the rest of the barracks, his quarters were clean and fully furnished with fine-quality chairs, no doubt looted from their legal owners. He gestured and the men jumped up and left. Oliva closed the door. He did not suggest she sit down.

"You have news of my son?" she demanded.

He shook his head. Sitting with his half leg propped up on a second chair as if it hurt, Purque looked wearier and older than usual, but certainly no wearier and older than she felt. It was almost two sixdays since Chies had disappeared. If he lived, she should have received a call for ransom by this time.

"No," the Werist said. "But I have heard from the bloodlord. He was displeased. He clawed my messenger, almost tore the man's eye out. He talked of sending a Witness here to find out what happened and who was responsible."

Considering her son's disappearance an affair of state, Oliva had sent for Speaker Quarina right away. She, in turn, had summoned a Witness to investigate. Purque himself had heard the woman testify that two Werists had kidnapped Chies, lowering him from the balcony. Purque had set Werists to track the kidnappers. They had followed the scent across the city, then lost it just outside the wall, where the fugitives had boarded a boat. Stralg must have been told all this, so whom did he disbelieve? He reputedly never let his Vigaelian Witnesses out of his presence, so if he wanted one of them to investigate, he would have to come in person. That might explain the huntleader's worried look.

But there was worse. "He also talked of reprisals."

"What sort of reprisals? Against whom?"

Purque sighed. He was basically a decent man, the only Vigaelian she had ever met she could imagine growing to like. No longer a combatant, he had allowed his hair and beard to grow in, and their original flaxen had turned to a deader sort of white. Years of Florengian sun had crinkled his pale Vigaelian skin into a red, wrinkled brick. A man missing half a leg could neither fight nor cross the Edge, and his chances of finding some bucolic haven to coddle him in his old age here on the Florengian Face seemed poorer by the day. The best future he could hope for now was a quick death. He did keep his Hero rabble under some sort of control, unlike the callow louts who had preceded him.

"Against anyone. My lady, the boy is the Fist's son also, and has been abducted or . . . or worse. Stralg is not the sort of man to accept that."

"He has never cared two grapes for Chies!"

"But he values his reputation. I don't know what he has in mind. He may have just spoken in the heat of anger."

"Or not?"

"Or not. He has been known to order random killings. This time he hasn't, so far." As his regent, Purque would have to see such an order carried out. He studied her face. "Any change?"

"No, but the Mercies are confident that it will be very soon. They can no longer get him to swallow." The sooner the better! Why did the Bright Ones not take pity on Piero and end his suffering? How long would they let the Evil One torture him?

"Tonight, you mean?"

"Probably." And she should be sitting with him at the end, not wasting time with this Vigaelian hoodlum.

"You will send word here?"

"The trumpets will sound."

"Before that! I'll pull my patrols off the streets. I don't want trouble."

"Neither do I. Thank you. And in turn you will warn me if you have any important visitors? I don't want him bursting in on me unexpectedly."

Purque smiled wanly. "I will warn you if I can. If he does come, he will burst in on me unexpectedly, too."

She went away. As she was passing through the vestibule, the thugs sitting there threw bones down ahead of her, so she was almost bowled over by the dog pack. She waited until the winners had bolted out the door with the losers in hot pursuit. She followed the losers.

Head covered again, she hurried back along the darkling alley to the private door. As she fished the heavy key from her pocket, she realized that she might be doing so for the last time. The moment Piero died, the last trace of her shadowy authority vanished. She would not even have the right to live in the palace. For generations, Piero's ancestors had succeeded one another on the throne, so the problem had never arisen before, but now his line was ended. Even Chies, whose claim had been a polite fiction, was no longer available to serve as a puppet for the elders, had they ever managed to accept that solution. A dynasty was falling.

She had just reached the stairs when she heard someone calling for her to hurry.

✦

It was not quite over. For a short while she sat holding his hand. His death throes were barely visible, just a few bubbling gasps, but at least she was there when the royal physician proclaimed that they had ended. Her eyes stubbornly refused to shed tears. The Piero she had known and loved had passed through the veil a long time ago. She shooed away the remaining Mercies, declining their offers of comfort. Yes, she would allow a couple of them to remain in the palace and would call on them if she needed them, and yes they could give solace to any of the servants who wanted it.

When she was alone with him, she knelt by the bed and repeated the prayer for the dead as a personal farewell. Its ancient sonorities comforted her. Then she stepped outside to where the senior palace officials had gathered. She told them to begin doing all the innumerable things that must be done, everything they had been planning for so long. Piero's body must be washed and taken to lie in state in the Hall of Pillars. Notifying Huntleader Purque was already on the list. But the first and most important message must be advance warning to the justiciar. Only when Speaker Quarina had formally declared the reign of Piero VI ended could the real wheels began to turn.

It was a relief. His sufferings were over; Oliva's burdens were lifted. She had no one left to worry about except herself. Even Chies had gone, and what happened to the city did not concern her now. She would almost welcome Bloodlord Stralg roaring in on her. Then she could ask him what he had done with her other children, and he could claw her eyes out for impudence.

✦

She bathed and dressed in the black of mourning. She prayed briefly in the palace chapel before going to inspect the Hall of Pillars. The catafalque stood in the center, a lonely block of carved and gilded wood. The throne was draped in black silk and everything else had been removed. Beyond the giant columns the gods wept, rain pattering on leaves and puddles. Tomorrow the citizens could come and pay their respects, filing in at one end of the long hall and out at the other. How many would come? For years Piero had been despised as a loser who had given away his birthright, but lately she had sensed the mood changing as the war growled ever closer, as city after city was wasted, as tides of refugees flowed over the land. The people were being reminded just what they had been spared sixteen years ago, and if they had wits at all they must mourn the loss of the faithful doge who had stood between them and the evil, sacrificing his own children.

Around the bier stood twelve great silver candlesticks, each one as high as a man and holding a tall black candle, which the chamberlain's men were just lighting. Piero had never been big, but he had seemed big when Oliva married him; now he was tiny. Only his head was visible; the rest of him lay hidden under a shroud of golden cloth pulled up to his chin. His hair and beard had turned completely white during his sickness. He wore the ducal coronet, and the jeweled sword of state lay at his side. As the candle flames brightened, the catafalque began to glitter in sad majesty.

The chamberlain solidified out of the darkness.

Oliva handed him the ducal seal and spoke the words she had been told tradition required: "Deliver this to the justiciar, Speaker Quarina, and inform her that the gods have placed the city in her hands." The man bowed and disappeared as gently as he had come.

Bats wheeled high overhead. The rain grew louder beyond the pillars. Servants bowed and departed, leaving Oliva alone with memories. It was over. She had completed her duties. Soon Speaker Quarina would take charge. No doubt she was already rounding up a seer and her scribes and anyone else she needed for the formalities . . . And then what? *The Winner?* Those last words from Piero seemed more and more like a sending from the gods. He had shown no signs of awareness for a thirty before or after that moment, but Celebre had been his life, and why should They not let him name his successor? Except, he hadn't. It still made no sense. Why not a name?

Something moved in the north doorway—*thump, thump*—and Oliva turned to glare at the big man limping toward her. Purque leaned heavily on the spear he used as a staff, the impacts of its butt syncopating with the lighter tap of his ivory stump. His striped smock was soaked, his white hair all rat-tails. At least he had had the decency to leave his escort outside, but she still half-turned from him to show that his intrusion was an insult to the dead.

He halted at the far side of the bier, studied the corpse for a moment, then looked across at her. "He was one of the bravest men I ever met, my lady."

She thought he was mocking and snapped, *"What do you mean?"*

"Exactly what I said. He did not just go into danger himself, he took you and his children as well, because he had to. Most rulers would have long since fled. I have never seen such dedication. It was duty beyond the limits of courage!"

"You were there?" She felt her face flame scarlet. To mention that day of her shame was unspeakably cruel. She had not thought Purque was that sort of Werist. Bah! All Werists were scum, animals, dregs.

"I was the Fist's driver that day. I know what happened after, too. I helped guard your prison. You were not without courage yourself, my lady."

She turned her back on him. Chies was what had happened. Now even Chies had gone.

They were alone in the great chamber, and yet Purque dropped his voice. "What you asked me earlier . . . I have had no official word, but my scouts report a column of chariots approaching the Meadow Gate."

"Stralg?" she whispered.

"It could be, my lady. The force is about the right size to be his bodyguard. It may bypass the city, of course. He never forewarns of his coming."

She nodded her thanks, her skin crawling at the thought of seeing the monster again. He had visited Celebre twice since his conquest, but the last time had been almost ten years ago. Both times he had publicly mocked her, reminiscing about her days of slavery. Surely she need not endure that again, and on the very day of Piero's death? Intolerable! As soon as these last formalities were completed, she would flee to the Refuge of Nula. Even the Fist's seers would not find her there.

More movement and voices, this time at the south door. The chief herald led in a parade: the justiciar, the high priest, a blindfolded Witness, two scribes with their satchels, the chamberlain . . . and Berlice Spirno-Cavotti! What right had that awful woman to be here so soon? Certainly the elders would assemble to pay their respects before anyone else did, but why should that sour-faced woman have precedence over all the rest of them? And she had even had the gall to bring an attendant with her, a girl in servants' dress carrying what looked like a bundle of laundry.

The priest went to the bier and covered his eyes to pray.

Speaker Quarina frowned at the Werist, then extended the frown to include Oliva. "Stand back, please."

Oliva took a few paces backward. So did Purque—*thump, thump*—deliberately ignoring the hint that he should withdraw completely.

The justiciar bit her lip, but did not comment. She began the ritual. "Witness, who is that?"

The seer was male, surprisingly—a youngish man wearing a simple black robe and a white blindfold. When he spoke the formal reply, his voice was high-pitched and quavered with emotion that Oliva had never heard from a Witness before.

"This is our doge and he is dead."

Quarina turned to the herald. "Let the trumpets sound."

The scribes were already sitting cross-legged under the candles, producing clay and boards and styli.

It was finished. Oliva could leave. But when she turned to go, her path was blocked by scrawny Berlice Spirno-Cavotti wearing a strangely sly expression. Oliva and the Mutineer's mother were definitely not on intimate terms and never had been, yet now the woman moved as if to embrace her. Oliva was too startled to dodge.

And even more startled by the whisper in her ear. "We bring wonderfully good news, my lady!"

Oliva recoiled. *Good* news? On this day, of all days?

"Oh, what is that stupid girl doing?" Spirno-Cavotti said loudly, gripping her arm and turning her. "Do go and speak to her, my dear."

Her dear? Her servant was furtively heading for the columns and the rain-washed darkness beyond, still clutching her washing. Speaker Quarina was dictating something utterly incomprehensible to the scribes. The Werist was watching the proceedings. Berlice's eyes were urging: *Do as I say!*

Too bewildered or battered to argue, Oliva said, "You, girl! Where are you going? Come here!" She strode toward the girl, who edged away from her instead of responding to the summons. Oliva caught up with her in the shadows near the columns and found herself looking at eyes full of tears, set in a face strangely familiar. Her long-dead sister Pina? No. Just a chance resemblance. It could not possibly be—

"Mama!" A whisper. Then brazen trumpets began to wail from the palace roof, strident screams in the night. Echoes rang back from the temples and mansions of Celebre. The air in the hall seemed to tremble as the city itself cried out its loss. Now the girl could speak louder. "I'm Fabia, Mama! The Witness is Dantio. Chies is safe. Benard is well, but chose to stay in Vigaelia. He's a wonderful sculptor. And Orlad, I mean Orlando—he's probably out there in the grounds, but he's a Werist, so that ice devil mustn't see him. I must go and warn them, er, him!"

Fabia? Chies? Benard? . . . *Werist?* Now Oliva recalled Piero's strange rambling discourse on the night Marno Cavotti had broken into the palace: *Remember we used to say Orlando was the fighter?* he had said. And that Fabia had looked just like her. Had the gods been speaking through the dying doge? *The Winner.* He had said that much later. Their children had been returned to her, but not to him.

It seemed to Oliva then that the hiss of rain swelled to a roar and the floor tilted under her feet. The Witness sprinted across the hall and caught her before she fell. The candles faded for a moment, then came back. She stared in disbelief at the two young people holding her. The girl, so like her younger self. The boy had lifted his blindfold and was smiling, yet his eyes were bright with tears. She knew him now.

"Dantio! My son!"

"We're back. We're all well, all your children."

Too late! she thought. Just a pot-boiling too late. No, half a year or more too late. Piero would not have known them had they come even in late summer. Their arrival now would do little good, but at least they were home, safe. The priest and the herald arrived to help. Dantio replaced his ritual blindfold. They carried her to the black-draped throne and sat her on it, ignoring her protests. The priest went back to mumbling prayers. Berlice smirked surreptitiously from the far side of the catafalque: what sort of double game was she playing? Trying to find the winning side? Quarina was still dictating her gibberish to the scribes, but she kept flicking amused glances toward the group around the throne. She must be in on the secret too; she had brought the Witness.

"Must go and warn Orlad," Fabia whispered.

"No," Dantio said. "They're watching from the bushes. That Werist is suspicious. They won't come in while he's there. He's worried, too. Why is the Werist so worried?"

"Stralg," Oliva said. "He thinks Stralg is on his way."

Dantio groaned. "Oh, is that who I keep seeing on the periphery?"

thirty-seven

CHIES STRALGSON

would never have found the Eligio place by himself—not without going to cottage doors and asking directions, and he was very reluctant to do that with Aunt Saltaja at his side. She was too memorable, too unpredictable, too unscrupulous. There would be dogs, perhaps even the sort of violent men who would kill strangers to steal their chariot, and he certainly did not trust his chthonic powers to defend him. Not yet, at least.

As it turned out, Saltaja knew exactly where to go. "How do you do this?" he demanded. He had much to learn.

"I asked the Mother, of course. Sleep on the cold earth or near it, and pray Her to send you the right vision. Shed a little blood first, if it's important. She will teach you. Turn left after the ford."

It was dark when they arrived. He did not see the buildings until he almost drove into a rail fence. He reined in with a yelp of surprise. No dogs barked.

"You're not trying," the hag grumbled. "Chosen can see in the dark. Go and fetch the man. Control him and bring him."

Chies squeaked, "I can't do that! I don't know how."

"Yes, you do. You'll never learn until you try. I'll hold the reins. Go!"

He peered down at where the ground must be but saw nothing. It was a murky night, with rain beating on trees overhead, black as tar under them. Chosen could see in the dark? Not this Chosen. He tried a quick prayer. *Holy Mother Xaran, let your servant see in the dark.* Still nothing. *So that I may serve you? Please?* Ah, that was better! He did not understand. No spooky goddess-light shone around him, yet he could now see the ruts and puddles and heaps of dung. He jumped down and headed for the house. Now he knew it was true. Sesto had not died in vain. His death had made Chies one of Her Chosen—able to prowl the night, control people, cast the evil eye. Also, liable to be buried alive. Better not to think about that bit.

Still no dogs. Sesto had said this Eligio man was a rebel agent, so he might not want dogs barking in the night to alert neighbors. Faint candlelight showed through grass cloth shutters. Chies began to raise a fist and was suddenly frozen by terror. Who would answer his knock? A gang of huge horrible hulking Werists? Cavotti himself could be lurking in there! Chies could imagine what would happen if he tried to put the evil eye on someone like the Mutineer. A giant like him would break his neck with one hand. He felt ill.

Yet a worse danger was waiting behind him, out there in the chariot. Maybe he should just run away from both of them? He could be home by morning. No, he did not think that would work. His aunt was not a very patient woman. He must do this!

Holy Mother give me courage . . . to serve You. Serve Her how? He had given Her Sesto. But that had been the admission fee. What else would She want? He drew a deep breath. *Holy Xaran, tonight I really will take the woman. I will Control her myself, or them, if there's more than one. I'll get it up and bounce them, I swear. Let me control the men in here and I will rape the women, to your honor. I will be worthy of my father, mighty Stralg!*

That thought gave him a great surge of excitement, and he rapped his knuckles hard against the planks. *Evil comes calling.*

The chink of light under the shutter disappeared. He heard a step, a rattle of chain. The door opened a crack. No light showed. He could see an eye looking at him, and suspected an extrinsic would not see even that. The homeowner spoke first.

"Is that you, Gievo?"

Eeee! Gievo? Who was Gievo? Gievo was a password, that's what! And Chies didn't know the other half of the code. Again he almost panicked. His knees trembled with an overpowering urge to run. How could he put the evil eye on someone he could not see? *Oh, Mother!* But probably the man could see him.

"My chariot has a loose wheel . . ."

"Go away or I'll call my brothers." The door slammed shut.

In a panic, Chies uttered a silent scream: *Open that door!*

Chain rattled. The door swung open. The man who stood there wore a Hero collar, but he was young and had only one arm and one eye. The eye was blinking rapidly, as if he did not know why he had just done what he had just done. A man with one arm couldn't be too dangerous. He couldn't even battleform.

"You will obey me."

"Evil One take you if I do! You pox-faced, squint-eyed, overgrown little turd, you can stuff—"

You will obey me!

"I will obey you," the man agreed. Then, even louder, "Why should I? What are you doing to me?"

"Be quiet!" Chies squeaked.

Silence.

"Call me 'lord.'"

"My lord is kind."

"You will not speak unless I tell you to. What is your name?"

"Eligio Lomotti, my lord."

Enjoying himself now, Chies said, "Who else is in the house, Eligio?"

"Only my wife and children, lord."

"Tell her to light some candles, and then you come with me."

Chies headed back to the chariot. A moment later he heard a crash behind him as the man stepped in a rut and fell headlong. An outburst of lurid oaths ended abruptly. When he scrambled up, covered with mud or worse, Chies took his wrist and led him the rest of the way to the car.

"You deal with this and the guanacos and then come back to the house."

"My lord is kind."

"Come, Aunt, I'll carry you myself." He would not have tried that even yesterday—he had been making Sesto do all the heavy work—but he was a Chosen now and thought his abilities ought to include some manly strength. Saltaja did not object when he went to lift her, and was no great burden to carry to the cottage. *Aha!*

The house was a better peasant kennel than others he had seen on his travels. The first room boasted a table and stools, a big stone fireplace, and two doors leading to other places. Metal pots sat in with the crocks on a shelf, and nets of roots ands dried fruit hung from the beams. Lingering food scents made his mouth water. Tiles on the floor were a real luxury.

The girl had lit half a dozen candles, probably about two sixdays' normal usage. She was cowering in a corner, hugging a weepy infant. Another brat clung to her leg. Chies set his aunt down and went to the girl. She glanced up in fear and he had her.

"You will obey me, no matter what I tell you to do."

Her eyes glazed. "I will obey you."

She was a lovely thing, with curly hair and milk-swollen breasts. He felt tremors of excitement under his chlamys, the sort of reaction Babila produced in him. He'd never had any trouble bouncing her! Yes, tonight would be good. This one's husband was a rebel. He deserved to have his wife raped. He deserved to have to watch.

"Call me 'darling.'"

"Darling?"

"As if you meant it. Better. Now kiss me like you kiss Eligio."

She put down the brat, clasped Chies's face between her hands, and pushed her mouth on his, exploring with her tongue. Mmm! Wow! Eligio was a lucky man. When she paused for breath, Chies debated priorities, then decided he was too hungry to enjoy anything else before he ate. Sex could wait. "I want food, lots of it. The woman needs soup and help eating it."

Saltaja had found a seat by the hearth and was leering horribly. "Think you can get it up this time, sonny?"

Oh, gods! He should have guessed that he had not been fooling her.

"She's going to make up for all the others."

"No reason why not, if that's what you want. There's not much you can't do now, lad, as long as you keep pleasing the Mother."

"Would a good rape please Her?"

"Of course. And a dead rebel in the morning?"

Gulp! "Why not?" Chies preferred to think about the first part of the program, but Papa would expect him to kill a rebel.

While he ate, he learned that her name was Carmina. If she was one-sixth as good in bed as she was as a cook, then he wasn't going to get much sleep tonight. Eligio returned and put the two brats to bed. One of them was colicky. Chies told it to shut up and it stopped wailing instantly. Growing tired of the hatred blazing in the Werist's eye, he ordered him to go out and stand in the rain until the mud washed off. The man obeyed without a word.

When Chies was done eating and about ready to take Carmina to bed,

Saltaja told him to call Eligio back in, they had business to attend to. The rancher was soaked, of course, and grinding his teeth with fury, although he did not say anything. Sesto had been much more subservient. Chies still had much to learn about Control.

"Question him," his aunt said.

"Right." Chies left Eligio standing and pulled Carmina down on his lap to fondle her. "When was the last time you saw Marno Cavotti?"

The Werist bared his teeth. His arm trembled violently. He made choking noises, but he had to answer. "Yesterday, lord."

"When?"

"About this time."

"Where did he go?"

"I don't know, lord." He smiled triumphantly.

"Who was with him?"

"A woman, a man, five Heroes."

Chies translated.

"Their names!" Saltaja shrieked. "Where did they go?"

Eligio snarled, but Chies dragged out answers. Orlad and Waels had left at sunset to swim to the city. Fabia and Dantio had gone that morning by more conventional means, to be delivered to an agent in Celebre.

"What agent?" Chies demanded. Father would want to know. So would he, when he was doge. Traitors!

Eligio had chewed his lower lip bloody, watching where Chies's hand was straying. "Berlice Cavotti."

"You're lying! She's head of the Stralg party on the council."

"I am not lying, lord."

Chies looked doubtfully at Saltaja. Was it possible for the Mutineer's mother to play a double game and deceive Stralg's seers while doing it? Or had she deceived her son and betrayed the Celebres? Something to worry about.

"Do you know who I am?"

"Lord, you are the Fist's bastard from the palace."

Ah, he would certainly have to die. "Correct. My companion and I need to get into Celebre without being questioned by ice devils. How will you arrange that for me?"

Eligio snarled. "Just go. Now, tonight."

"The gates shut at sunset."

"Not tonight. You go outside and listen. The trumpets are blowing. The doge has died. No curfew tonight."

Puzzled, Chies translated.

Saltaja uttered a shriek and staggered to her feet. "Blood! Blood!" She stared in the direction of the city. "I can smell blood!"

Chies could not imagine how she could smell anything at all with that oozing, rotting stump of a nose. She was crazy. "Um, do we want to go there now?"

"Yes! Yes! They're fighting! Stralg may be there. And Fabia Celebre almost certainly is! And the next doge must be there to claim the throne. Tell that one-eyed idiot to harness up a chariot for us."

Drive in the dark? . . . "Yes, of course, Aunt. Eligio, we need your best car and best team. Now!" He sighed at Carmina. He would have to postpone his enjoyment until another day. "You go and help him. Aunt, we won't kill them, will we? That would leave a trail from Veritano to here and then to me, when I'm doge. Show me how to make them forget us, Aunt."

Saltaja sighed. "Softie! But I suppose you're right."

thirty-eight

DANTIO CELEBRE

was overloaded, losing detail. Whole areas were disappearing from his vision. Fighting had broken out in Pantheon Way. He knew that men other than Orlad and Waels were invading the palace grounds, but he could not identify them. If any were Werists, he hoped they were Marno's. They might just be town youths scrambling over the palace walls to view the action, stimulated by the near-riot spreading through the city. Roused by the doge's death, Celebre was bursting out of its long sleep.

Like all Witnesses trained in the Ivory Cloisters, Mist had been repeatedly warned of the fate that befell the seers of Jat-Nogul. Trapped in the city during the sack, they had been driven raving mad by the horrors, and so had any other Witness who went near them thereafter. Even some tough survivors of Stralg's massacre at Bergashamm had succumbed to the emotional storm of Jat-Nogul.

Celebre was not at storm level yet, but winds were rising to dangerous levels. The trumpets had proclaimed the news of Piero's death, and Celebrians were notoriously demonstrative mourners. Defying curfew, citizens poured into the streets, wailing at the tops of their voices and hammering cook pots, drowning out even the trumpets' ear-torturing wail. One of the city gates had been opened to admit a cavalcade of chariots bearing at least a full hunt of Vigaelian Werists. All those llamoids and ice devils were trying to force their way through a grief-maddened mob, and there just was not room. Soon they would start hurting people, and then violence would erupt like a volcano.

One host—four sixty—was a strong force, but a very small part of the Fist's horde. That it might be Stralg's personal bodyguard made sense. But Marno Cavotti had both excellent sources of intelligence and extraordinary cunning. He had been smuggling men into the city all day, pod after pod of black seals swimming in through the secret gap in the siphon. He had set up Celebre as a trap. Stralg would never walk into a trap as long as he had his Witnesses to warn him, so Cavotti must have managed to pass along the news that Dantio and the others had brought from Vigaelia, that the notorious compact was broken and they were free to deceive the monster they had served so long. Dantio himself had set this pot a-boiling.

Whether Stralg himself had arrived or not, Liberators scattered in safe houses all over the city were gradually learning of the Vigaelian incursion and emerging to slake their bloodlust.

All of this was bad enough and promised to get infinitely worse when the fighting and arson began, but Dantio was also personally involved in the drama around his father's bier. Orlad and Waels had found their way to the palace grounds and were lurking, naked and wet, in the bushes outside the pillars. They could see the ceremony under way, could see Oliva and her two newfound lambs struggling to restrain their reactions, could even see the bag of clothes lying just out of their reach within the hall. They could do nothing about that glowering, suspicious Huntleader Purque, Stralg's commandant in Celebre, short of charging in and killing him. Purque had guessed that something significant was happening right under his nose and was trying to learn what it was.

Oliva was gamely fighting against hysteria, stressed almost beyond endurance by the events of the evening and the continuing threat of the peg-leg Werist. Their plans for a secret, confidential reunion had collapsed into this turmoil. Dantio was being pummeled by joy and grief, fear and frustration, from all directions.

Just as he braced himself to go and tell Purque that Stralg was looking for him—which must be true to some extent—he sensed agitation outside the north door, where the huntleader had left his escort. With an effort, Dantio unearthed the psychic clues of a Hero having just brought a message from the barracks in Wheelwrights' Alley. After a moment's hesitation, the ranking flankleader opened the door and peered in. The commandant frowned and stumped off toward him, thumping along on his spear. Saved! Sure enough, in a moment the Werist was gone, leading his troops back to the barracks.

Everyone else present smelled trustworthy.

"All clear for now, Mama." Dantio trotted over to the bundle of clothes and hurled it out into the darkness. Waels saw it eclipse the candlelight, leaped up, and grabbed it.

Wiping sweat from his forehead, Dantio turned back toward the catafalque in its lake of candlelight. Completed or not, the ceremonial recording of the doge's passing had obviously come to an end. The scribes were carrying away their tablets to be baked. Fabia and Mama were locked in a tearful embrace—which was wildly out of character, because neither was naturally demonstrative—and everyone else was staring in bewilderment either at them or at him, the eccentric bag-throwing seer. Neither Quarina nor Berlice had been told that Orlad might attend this meeting also.

But Dantio Celebre, heir presumptive, was home in the hall of his ancestors. This was the day he had dreamed of. He raised his voice and let it ring back from the vaulted ceiling.

"My lords and ladies! I am Dantio Celebre, eldest son of the late Doge Piero. This is my sister, Fabia. We have just returned from our exile in Vigaelia."

The resultant rush of joy almost knocked him over. The elders curtsied, bowed, and cheered, all at the same time. He detected no hidden reservations at all, not one. Oliva came sweeping to meet him and they embraced. She was sobbing. *Holy Mayn, so was he!*

"Dantio! Dantio! . . ." she exclaimed. Then came the shock of finding unbearded lips on a man nearing thirty.

Before either of them spoke, someone cried out in fear. Two Werists came striding in through the pillars—Florengian Werists, unarmed and barefoot. Dantio led his mother forward to meet them.

"Mama, this is Orlad. And this is his liegeman, Waels Borkson."

The dogaressa ignored the liegeman. She just stared in disbelief at her Hero son, as if petrified by that sinister collar. Orlad stared back with his emotional defenses higher than mountains. Since leaving Nardalborg, he had begun to shed his crust of enforced brutality. Hints of a decent human being were starting to emerge, but he did not know how to respond to a mother. Or any woman, for that matter.

"So big!" she whispered.

"You think that's big, you ought to see Benard!" Fabia said. "Orlad, you chump, hug her until her ribs creak."

Orlad forced a smile and did more or less that. The tension broke, if not the ribs. Oliva said "Oh, Orlando, Orlando!" about fifty times, kissing him as she did—his face did not lack stubble. Dantio and Fabia exchanged relieved smiles. Had there ever been so much joy at a lying-in-state? Were Benard there, he would be blubbering like the triple fountain. Somehow Dantio did not think his father would have regarded this celebration around his bier as disrespect.

"Oh, Orlando, my baby!"

Dantio caught Fabia's eye and they exchanged grins.

The dignitaries were pushing forward to greet the revenants, giving Dantio precedence as the eldest, of course. He would certainly not be the heir, but he could not explain that now. It was all he could do to withstand the waves of riot and emotion washing in from the city. The first fires had started. Mobs of enraged extrinsics were savaging golden warbeasts but paying a terrible toll for their presumption. Black warbeasts were swarming out of hiding to aid them.

More palace officials streamed into the hall. So the news had escaped: The children are back! Elders of the council, summoned to the palace by the trumpets, were shoving to the head of the line to pay their respects. Heads of families famous in the city's history: Giordano Giali, Ritormo Nucci . . . The temple of Ucr was burning. A seer was running along the corridor outside, and Werists were coming too. Vigaelian Werists.

Screaming gods!

Only one man could emit that fearful stench of death and evil. Dantio dithered in panic. Had he miscalculated? What if the Fist's seers had not heard about the broken compact after all? Perhaps it was not a hunt for his Chies bastard that brought Stralg to Celebre this night, but a craving for revenge on the legitimate children! Therek, Horold, Saltaja all dead, and their killers gathered here?

"Out!" Dantio yelled at Orlad. "Stralg's coming. He's almost here! Hide!" The rest of what he tried to say was lost in screams of alarm. Half the assembly thought he was addressing them. They bolted for the pillars and disappeared into the night and the rain. Then the rest had second thoughts and followed.

Oliva remained, with Dantio and Fabia beside her. Speaker Quarina, the high priest, Berlice, ancient Nucci . . . yes, the elders and only the elders, eight of them so far. They were more than a little flustered, but they were standing their ground, gathered around the catafalque.

"Fabia, you should leave, too!" Dantio said, but he was too late and knew she would not have gone anyway.

The north door flew open, shedding light that was immediately blocked by the bloodlord himself. He strode in without bothering to have his bodyguard inspect the hall. He had no need to, because a white-shrouded seer scuttled along at his side like a dog on a leash. For thirty years Witnesses of Mayn had kept him safe from harm. Incongruously, and unknown to anyone but Dantio, the stooped little woman with him was blazing joy like the sun. She *did* know that the compact was ended. She could smell the trap awaiting him. She luxuriated in it, savoring her hate.

Stralg slammed the door behind them, thundering rage like a sea storm. Out beyond the pillars, a steady thumping drumbeat of fear from the onlookers in the rain failed to hide one great bugle call of hatred. Dantio knew that emotional note as well as he knew his brother's voice. Orlad saw the cause of all his troubles at last, *and he had left his bodyguard outside.* With his faithful Waels to help him, Orlad would never resist this temptation.

The bloodlord had been a handsome man in his youth. As he advanced into the candlelight, Dantio recalled faint memories of him on the day of the fall, mostly of how big he had seemed. He still did. While he was not battle hardened into bestiality as his brothers had been, he was not a normal human, either, standing over eight feet tall and massive in proportion. Wearing only his brass collar and a black loincloth, totally hairless, with skin as white as granular ice and a head like a boulder with ears, he resembled some oversized statue come to life.

He had not visited Celebre in ten years. The elders shrank away from his glare. He peered down at the doge's corpse and spat on it. Then he located Oliva.

"So, now you're a widow. Want to come back to me?"

"Never," she said, with admirable calm, but her internal hate was almost unbearable.

"Wouldn't want you anyway. But *you,* now . . ." He had just noticed Fabia. "Who're you?" He licked ice-white lips with a long red tongue.

"Fabia Celebre."

Amazingly, she was almost as calm as she looked. Oh, sister! Was she counting on Orlad to protect her from the monster, or relying on her own chthonic powers?

The Fist glanced at his attendant seer, who stayed silent behind her veils. There were, Dantio noted, definitely some Florengian Werists coming over the palace walls now, Cavotti's men. How could he let Orlad know that help was on the way? Would that information make him wait for reinforcements? No, it would just drive him on. He would not want to share the Fist's death with anyone.

The bloodlord had realized that all was not right. "When did you get here? Who brought you?"

"I arrived this evening." Fabia's voice rose. "My brothers brought me. Your sister tried to, but she was on the wrong side of the Fist's Leap when we burned the bridge, so I wouldn't wait up for her if I were you."

"She is lying, isn't she?" Stralg asked his Witness.

The answer was a shriek of triumph. *"No, she's not!"*

He roared and swung a fist to smash her, but the old woman anticipated the move and dodged back.

"Stralg Hragson!" Compared to the great pillars, Orlad was only a tiny shape against the fires in the city behind him, but he had amplified his throat and lungs so his bellow carried even over the roar of riot and trumpets. "I am Orlad Celebre, Doge Piero's son and heir. I killed your brother Therek on the hills above Tryfors. I helped kill your brother Horold on the Milky River. And your sister, also, trapped in the Edgelands without food or shelter or any way to escape. They are *dead,* Stralg, all dead! You stand alone, last of that vile litter, and you are about to pay for your crimes."

The elders would not have understood the Vigaelian words, but the smell of challenge was obvious. They quickly shuffled around behind the catafalque, clearing the battlefield.

"True!" screeched the seer, scampering to safety also. "He speaks the truth, monster!"

Stralg turned his great head to look at the north door. His bodyguard was out there. He started to move that way and Orlad ran forward, with Waels at his heels. Stralg stopped and spun around to face them again. They stopped also. It was a standoff. But they were closer to Stralg than he was to the door.

"Coward!" Orlad yelled. "When I was three years old I had more courage than you have now. You held out your hands to me and I went to you! You lifted me up and threatened to smash my brains out, I'm told. Try that now; I'm bigger." He stretched out his arms. "Come to me, coward."

Stralg must weigh more than the two younger men put together, but he had not lived so long by accepting personal combat against odds. They would certainly be on him before he could reach the north door and open it.

Orlad moved one pace closer. "Therek is dead!" he mocked. *Pace . . .* Waels followed, still his shadow. "Saltaja is dead! Horold—"

Stralg blazed rage and hatred. He lowered his head like a bull as he watched the two of them come. It seemed to Dantio that the man's legs were growing and his arms shrinking.

Pace . . .

"Hostleader Arbanerik!" Orlad chanted. *Pace . . .* "Remember Arbanerik? And Nils Frathson?" *Pace . . .* "They've been stealing your recruits, Stralg!" *Pace . . .* "They have forty sixty now, the largest horde in Vigaelia. They killed Horold, Stralg, with a little help from us Celebres. They took Tryfors, Stralg. The garrison switched sides rather than fight."

Orlad stopped his slow approach. "You've lost Vigaelia, Stralg! And Cavotti has taken Veritano, Stralg. The game is ended, Stralg!" He beckoned mockingly. "Your turn now. Come to me, coward."

Stralg charged. As he moved, he battleformed, ripping off his covering. His face bulged into a huge fanged muzzle, his legs stretched. He leaned forward to balance the thick tail he was growing, and his arms shrank to white claws.

"Speed," Orlad said.

He and Waels threw off their chlamyses and shapeshifted. As Stralg's monstrous jaws slammed shut where Orlad's head had just been, Orlad was landing a dozen paces away. Waels slashed at Stralg's ribs and vanished before Stralg could turn to deal with him.

Then Orlad leapt to the attack.

The contest pitted one giant white biped against two smaller black things shaped like frogs. The bloodlord spun and dodged on great taloned feet, swinging his tail like a club and snapping giant jaws. Two identical warbeasts leaped around him, all legs and black fur, bouncing up and down, making yattering noises and waving their front limbs at the giant. Soon even Dantio lost track of which was which. Their hands and feet were clawed and they moved in blurs, but their blows failed to penetrate the Fist's scaly hide. It was as tough as chain mail and he was too enormous to wrestle.

The battle was a stalemate—he could not catch them and they could not hurt him.

Being the only other man of fighting age present, Dantio grabbed the sword of state from his father's bier and ran forward to see what he could do to help. The first problem was going to be getting close enough. He was restricted to human speed, while the three contestants were a single black-and-white whirlwind. Waels and Orlad kept trying to come at Stralg from opposite sides, but he was armed at both ends, and his talons tore the floor tiles as he pivoted and dodged. To a seer's senses the two smaller men were consumed with bloodlust, solely intent on the immediate fight, great waves of hatred and little else, but the wily veteran Fist retained enough tactical sense to keep edging closer to the north door.

Dantio hovered on the outskirts, seeking an opening. Again and again Stralg snapped and grabbed and failed to connect. The youngsters were everywhere except where he was, bouncing, mocking, dodging, occasionally slashing. At last Dantio thought he saw his chance and dove in, driving his sword hard into the Fist's ribs. It slid off without making any impression at all. Stralg's tail caught him with a glancing blow and hurled him halfway across the hall. His sword clattered away across the tiles.

He could not have been stunned for more than a few heartbeats. When he came to, Oliva was kneeling beside him, wiping blood from his face and making anxious noises in Florengian. He seemed to be thinking only in Vigaelian. He struggled to sit up and screamed at the agony in his left shoulder. It was shattered. Some ribs were cracked, too.

Witnesses should not meddle in events.

"Lie down!" his mother said. "We'll send for Healers."

No! Every Sinurist in town would be overloaded already, and he was going to see the end of this battle if it killed him. His mother stopped resisting his struggles and helped him sit up.

The fight was slowing. The younger men might wear Stralg out eventually, but he was perilously close to the north door now. Did they even remember that danger? Dantio tried to locate the Florengian warbeasts he had detected in the grounds earlier, but his head was spinning too fast to register anything beyond the pillars. There was a fight of some sort going on out in the corridor, too.

Disaster! One of the Florengians either dropped low to come in under the monster's guard, or just slipped . . . and in that instant Stralg closed his great reptilian jaws on the man's skull. Growling triumph, the bloodlord jerked him clear of the floor and shook him as a dog would, snapping his spine like a biscuit. His buddy, whichever he was, leaped up on the Vigaelian's back—and promptly started to slide off again, unable to find purchase on the scaly surface.

The Fist reared, spitting the corpse away like a grape seed and simultaneously trying to dislodge his burden. In the nick of time his assailant managed to stretch one front paw high enough to hook claws into Stralg's collar. Unable to reach back with arms that had shrunk almost to nothing, the bloodlord twisted violently, swinging his passenger out like a flag and very nearly catching him with a snap of his great jaws. But then the Florengian had both front paws on the collar and could pull himself up and brace his back feet on Stralg's shoulders. Holding the collar like reins, the rider heaved. The metal stretched and stretched again. He worked his feet inside it, and still he pulled until he was standing almost upright, cutting ever deeper into the bloodlord's throat.

Strangled, Stralg dropped to the floor with an impact that made the candles flicker. If he hoped to crush the Florengian by rolling on him, he was too late. Stretched out to wire, the brass collar snapped with a twang. The younger Werist fell clear, still holding it. Deprived of his god's blessing, Stralg gagged and thrashed and went into convulsions. And died. And retroformed.

The black frog was suddenly Orlad, dancing around him like a mad thing, whirling the brass string overhead in bloody hands and yelling his triumph. "I won! I won! I am the winner!"

thirty-nine

FABIA CELEBRE

knew how to bandage a broken shoulder, for she had watched while they took care of Paola. She grabbed a black sheet from the throne and ran to aid Dantio, arriving at his side just as yells of triumph from the north end of the hall told her that Orlad had won.

"Lift his arm!" she told her mother.

Dantio screamed, but that was to be expected.

Then another scream echoed through the hall, a howl audible over all the rising babble.

Oliva said "Oh, dear! What's that?" in the tones of someone who could not stand any more surprises.

"Orlad." Fabia was concentrating on working the sling under her patient's arm. "He's found Waels, I expect. They were very close."

When the bandaging ordeal was over, she helped Dantio to his feet—this was definitely not the sort of night to be sitting around immobile. Only the gods knew who or what might invade the Hall of Pillars next. The elders were fussing around Stralg's corpse. Other people were oozing in between the pillars, reluctant to enter the hall but being pushed by the press behind. The news of the Fist's death would be everywhere in no time, so which horde controlled the city?

"We'll sit you on the throne for now," she said, supporting his good arm as much as she could. "This is an exciting homecoming, isn't it? Is Celebre always this busy, Mama?"

Her mother blinked and sniffled, half-laughing, half-weeping. "No. I haven't come to terms with it yet. I feel old and confused."

"I'm young and more confused. We were told you've done an incredible job of running the government for the last year."

"Oh, how I wish your father could have been here to meet you!"

"We all do. But we just put on the funeral games, didn't we? Orlad slew the dragon and we can lay it at Papa's feet as an offering. Celebre will survive and the Hrag horrors are over—thanks to your children! We got our revenge, Mama. We won in the end! Everything . . . *oh, bless my fangs and talons!*"

That had been one of Waels's sayings. It was provoked in this case by the sight of his body, which Orlad was carrying in his arms toward the catafalque. No one spoke as he solemnly laid the corpse alongside his father. One of the elders—Somebody Giali—had retrieved one of the dropped chlamyses, and now handed it solemnly to Orlad, who snatched it from him with a bad grace and wrapped himself to hide his nudity. Candlelight shone on his tears.

But Waels had not retroformed, so what lay beside the dead doge was a furry animal, something between a frog and an ape, its head mangled and bloody. Where was his beauty now?

Oliva saw desecration and protested. "No!"

Fabia said, "Let him be, Mama. It was Waels who won the victory. He let Stralg catch him, so that Orlad would have his chance."

"No!" again.

"I saw it." In that battle of instant reflexes, the momentary delay needed to kill Waels had made the difference. She helped Dantio to the throne, the only place to sit. He was very pale and obviously in great pain.

"We must find a Healer," Oliva said. "Or a Mercy. You should be in bed."

He grimaced. "And miss all the fun? I think the Good Guys have won the palace, at least. I can't tell what's going on out there . . . the city, I mean."

Fabia hugged Oliva again. "All these years with only one of us to mother, and suddenly you have four. We did tell you Chies is safe, didn't we? It will take years to explain all this!"

"You met Chies? You've seen him?"

"Yes, Mama. The Mutineer had him kidnapped, but he's been well cared for and he was being very brave. They had not broken his spirit. You would have been proud of him!"

"Oh." Oliva seemed to be at a loss for words. She was not as tall as Fabia, but broad and imposing. Care lines marred her face and her hair was streaked with silver, yet the resemblance was strong enough that Fabia could almost believe that she was viewing herself in a poor quality silver mirror.

"Chies certainly looks like Stralg," she said. "But that isn't his fault, is it? And it wasn't your fault. You and Papa raised him and he's a credit to both of you. We made him welcome, Mama, all three of us did."

Oliva stared hard at her, searching her eyes for evidence of false comfort. "You are very kind. He was all we had, you know—after you had gone. He has been difficult these last few years."

"What boy is not, at his age? His position cannot have been easy. Look after Dantio while I see to Orlad." Fabia started in his direction, but Orlad was striding back to the bloodlord's corpse. He pushed some gawking elders out of the way, took it by the ankle, and began to tow it. Evidently he had the same idea she had, of laying the carrion at Piero's feet. More and more people were plucking up courage to enter the hall. Both doors were open, admitting Florengian men wearing brass collars— and in some cases nothing more, save bloodstains. Cavotti must rule the palace, as Dantio had said. She wondered when the Mutineer himself would appear.

There were at least four big fires burning across the river and she had a view of less than half the city. What an incredible day!—the drive from Montegola, entering Celebre by the Cypress Gate, the cloak-and-dagger meeting with Cavotti's mother and later the justiciar; the news that Piero had just died. She had walked with Dantio along Pantheon Way and Goldbeater Street and other great avenues that he had told them about during their crossing of the Edge. She had admired buildings far grander than anything Skjar or Kosord had to offer. Some of them would be gone by morning, although the rain should help limit the fires' spread. It was the Day the Lost Returned. The Day Doge Piero Died. No, history would remember this day as the Fall of Stralg.

Servants were trying to clear the hall. One accosted her officiously. "You, girl! You must leave now."

She told him who she was and he fell to his knees, stammering a horrified apology. She wandered back to Oliva and Dantio at the throne. They had serious company—senior-looking Werists, some priests, palace officials wearing black robes of mourning and carrying staffs of office. The woman barking orders at them all was Speaker Quarina. She was being obeyed, men scurrying to do her bidding.

Order was being restored. Flunkies were replacing the mourning drapery on the throne, stools had been brought for Dantio and Oliva.

"Speaker!" barked the old Giali man. "What is going on here?"

Quarina said, "Pray take a seat, my lord. I am about to explain."

What was going on, or about to go on, Fabia realized, was a meeting. Servants were setting out stools in a horseshoe facing the catafalque, ringing them with tall silver candelabra to lift the darkness. Eighteen stools and one chair? Quarina was convening the council. *Curse of Xaran!* Fabia had not expected this to happen for days yet. She was not ready.

A portly herald began bellowing. "My lords and ladies!" He bade elders draw nigh and all others disperse. Now a double row of stools was being laid out facing the mouth of the horseshoe; Dantio and Oliva were going there. The four in the front must be intended for the family, so Fabia went to join them. She sat next her mother and a moment later Orlad slumped down at her side and put his face in his hands.

"I am very sorry about Waels," she whispered. "He was a wonderful man and a great Hero."

Orlad paid no attention. There had been so little love in his life! Small wonder if he felt the gods had betrayed him in his moment of victory.

Palace officials were still jostling for places in the row behind, with angry whispered arguments about precedence. Behind Speaker Quarina, cross-legged scribes were hastily laying out their tools. She did not wait for them.

"Honorable elders, by the authority of custom and in my office of justiciar, I hereby convene this meeting. I see fifteen of you present. There are eighteen elders on the council, so any vote of ten or more carries the weight of all."

"Protest!" The big old man was on his feet, face scarlet.

"Lord Giordano Giali?"

"No meeting of council should be held without the doge except the meeting to elect the next doge, and that is never held until the day after his funer—"

"You are overruled. I can quote at least nine instances where the election was held on the day the doge died, or even before he died. The city is in flames, there is fighting in the streets, the bloodlord's corpse lies at your back with his death unavenged, and a hostile army lurks outside the walls. We must have a doge!"

She stared menacingly around at fifteen faces—twelve men, three women. Werists had cleared the hall, herding the onlookers back to the line of pillars. Fabia caught the knowing eye of Berlice Spirno-Cavotti and they shrugged in mirror image. This sudden election was not a possibility they had discussed that afternoon. It was improvisation time.

"Very well," the Speaker said as Giordano subsided. "I testify to this company that the invariant custom of Celebre is to elect as doge a close adult male relative of the doge most recently deceased, to the farthest extent of first cousin twice removed, excepting that female relatives within such degree have been recognized on two occasions by the election of their husbands. It is likewise custom for a doge on his deathbed to recommend a candidate to the elders. Although that recommendation is officially given the weight of one vote, I know of only five occasions on which the council did not accept it as binding.

"You have been previously advised that, on the first day of the Festival of New Oil, two honorable elders here present waited upon Doge Piero and prayed him to disclose the name of his preferred successor. As they will confirm, he responded by saying, 'The Winner.' Yes, lord Ritormo Nucci?"

The peppery little man was on his feet. "What *winner*? Who decides who that is?"

"You do. The council does. Or the council may ignore that report, as it pleases." The Speaker squared her shoulders, as if glad to be done with the preliminaries. She smiled across at the row of spectators. "As president of this meeting, I call for any eligible relatives of our dearly mourned Doge Piero the Sixth now present to identify themselves and declare their willingness to serve."

Dantio tried to stand and failed. He raised his good hand. "May I speak seated, Speaker?" Even his voice trembled.

"You may."

"Honorable elders, I am Dantio Celebre, eldest son of Doge Piero. I have only today returned from exile. I take myself out of contention on the grounds that I am a sworn Witness of Mayn and am therefore committed to observe the doings of the world, never to influence them." He forced a pale smile. "My present discomfort was caused by an attempt to interfere in the execution of Stralg Hragson and may therefore be regarded as divine punishment."

The elders' chuckles swelled into a round of applause. The mood of the council was visibly changing, as if they were just realizing that they did have a function after all, that Stralg would not be appointing a governor over them. Clouds were rolling back from the sun, revealing a world they had almost forgotten, Florengia without the Fist.

"Question!" said a fat, oily-looking man. "Speaker, cannot a cultist be released from his vows under such circumstances?"

Having discussed that during the afternoon planning session, Quarina knew Dantio's views. "If lord Dantio were to apply to the Eldest of his order in Vigaelia, she might agree to release him. Do you wish to make such application, lord Dantio?"

"I do not. I will not serve as doge."

"Then I declare you removed from consideration. You may present any other candidates present." That, too, had been agreed beforehand.

Dantio's face was slick with sweat, but his voice was steadying.

"I will first mention two who are not present. Our brother Benard, next in line to me, has remained in Vigaelia, having won office as consort of a great city, Kosord. As the honorable elders can see, breeding will tell!"

Laughter, more applause. They were enjoying this new authority.

"Our youngest sibling," Dantio continued with tactful irrelevance, "lord Chies, is also not present." That name provoked dark looks from the elders. "He unavoidably missed the turn-of-the-year ceremony. Consequently he is officially not yet an adult, therefore not eligible."

Smiles. That neat way out of the Chies problem had been arranged by the Mutineer, of course, but no one was mentioning him. Again Fabia caught Berlice's eye. Marno, wherever he was, could not know about this precipitate election. He might be menzils away or putting out fires in the next street. He had not been present during the afternoon planning session;

Fabia had not seen him since the previous evening. No one had known that Stralg would die, the city riot, the Speaker stampede the election.

Dantio said, "I have one more brother to offer, my lords and ladies. Lord Orlad tonight slew the monster Stralg. He is not only the sole candidate eligible under the terms outlined by Speaker Quarina, he must be the Winner foreseen by our father. Stand up, Orlad."

Eyes still red, cheeks still damp, Orlad rose and scowled at the elders. They sprang to their feet also, clapping and cheering. He had won the prize he had wanted more than anything, and it must taste as bitter as alum. And now he was going to win the battle for the succession by default. Fabia was not ready to make her play.

Speaker Quarina called for order. When the elders resumed their seats, she said, "Are you able and willing to serve as doge, lord Orlad?"

"I am."

Two words he could manage. If they wanted a speech, he would flounder.

And he was very young. This was the first time the justiciar had met Orlad, and the doubt showing on her face was reflected on many of the others'. Fabia could damn his candidacy just by pointing out that he had never even seen a great city before today, let alone lived in one. Instinct warned her that she would antagonize not only Orlad but the council as well. She would seem like a mere spoiler. And yet what else could she do? . . .

"My lords," the Speaker said, "you appear to have a choice of one candidate. Doge Piero has already cast his vote in favor of the Winner, and you may make up your own minds whether he had been granted foresight by the gods . . ." Marno's mother was on her feet. "Councillor Spirno-Cavotti?"

"Justiciar, I do not belittle Hero Orlad's magnificent feat in killing the evil Fist tonight, but it is common knowledge that the tide of war has been turned and the utter defeat of the ice devils is only a matter of a season or two. There is another winner the honorable elders should—"

The council erupted. "No! No!"

The loudest was little Ritormo Nucci. "Traitor!" he screamed. "You supported Stralg. Every meeting for years you voted for whatever might please him! For years you and your jackals ran with the Vigaelian pigs and now you want to put your son on the throne? You should be evicted from the council, you and all the other snakes!"

Dantio murmured, "Muddled zoology." He had his eyes closed and should be rushed off to a warm sleeping rug.

Roars of agreement and disagreement filled the air. Half the council wanted to expel the other half and vice versa. Beside Fabia, Oliva was laughing—nasty, tight, silent laughter all for herself, not shared, perhaps not even conscious. Politics were no longer her problem. Quarina was yelling for order and not being heard.

"*ELDERS!*" Orlad's superhuman roar would have silenced a thunderstorm. The hall rang with it. "Sit down!"

They sat down, but he had not helped his cause.

The Speaker smiled, thin-lipped. "Thank you, lord Orlad. It would appear, Berlice, that the council does not wish to consider your son as a candidate."

More angry growls and murmurs indicated that some of the council did.

Berlice bounced up again. "That was not what I was going to propose! May I be heard?"

"Very well. You have the floor."

"Elders, one child of Doge Piero has not been mentioned. May we hear from her?" Berlice sat down.

The Speaker hesitated. She had not been forewarned of this. "Unless the council objects?" Most elders were frowning, but no voice was raised. "Lady Fabia?"

Fabia lurched to her feet and faced the assembled glares as bravely as she could.

"My lords and ladies, I am Fabia Celebre, fourth child and only daughter of the late doge. I am aware that women are not elected doge." She glanced sideways. Orlad was still on his feet and his incandescent glare showed that he had guessed what was coming.

"Continue!" Quarina snapped.

Fabia waded deeper into the crocodile pool. "How could my father have known my brother would fight Stralg tonight, let alone win such a battle? I ask the honorable elders to consider my fiancé as a candidate for the office of doge." The only difficulty was that she did not have a fiancé. "Had this meeting been held after the funeral, as we—"

Now the Speaker had guessed also, and was angry that she had been kept out of the secret. "Will you deign to tell the council the name of this fortunate betrothed, or have you yet to choose one?"

"My lords, ladies, I have the honor to be engaged to marry lord Marno Cavotti, the Mutineer, the Liberator. He is a native of this city."

She was lying. They were not engaged. They had discussed the possibility on the journey from Veritano. They had agreed it had merit and they would think about it. They had expected to have more time. But fortune favors the swift—Marno had told her that.

Everyone tried to speak at once, and in the confusion Fabia saw salvation over by the pillars. Civilians were fleeing in terror. A bodyguard of a dozen or so Werists was opening a way through the crowd, making room for the twisted, ogreish figure of Marno Cavotti, looming head and shoulders over even the largest of them. With the fires at his back, he was a troll's nightmare. But a very welcome sight for Fabia. At last!

Oliva screamed. "What is that?"

"The Mutineer, Mother. Marno Cavotti."

Both Oliva and Berlice cried out in horror.

Orlad muttered, "*Trollop!* So that was what you were up to in that chariot!"

"Celebre needs him, Mama. Orlad, I am truly sorry. I was going to tell you, but there was no time."

Dantio muttered "Nicely done!" under his breath, but did not explain what he meant.

"*Slut!*" Orlad sat down. "You would bed down with *that*?"

"Mama?" Fabia said, but she was addressing the council. "Papa was in a coma for a long time. How much did he know about the war, I mean the last time he could understand the news?"

Oliva tore her gaze away from the nightmare Mutineer. "What? Oh . . . I see what you mean. Yes, he knew Stralg was losing. I remember how he smiled when he heard about the victory at Reggoni Bridge."

"So he knew that Cavotti was going to be the winner? He must have known he was a native Celebrian. He knew nothing of his own children, let alone how Stralg would die here tonight." Without a glance to see how Orlad was reacting, Fabia walked over to meet Marno. He was obviously exhausted, eyes sunk even deeper into their caverns, face and chlamys smeared with ash and blood. It was only a day since she had said goodbye to him at Montegola, and yet she had already forgotten just how huge he was. And, of course, the smell, a sort of heavy musk. It was not obnoxious. She had grown used to it in the chariot, and it was certainly male. She could live with it.

His great paws closed around her shoulders and he bent to touch his lips to hers—she had not had a proper kiss from him yet. He folded one fist around her hand, but instead of going back to face the elders, he limped on past them, toward the catafalque. She felt like a child beside him.

"What's been happening?" he asked quietly.

"I just announced our engagement. Two speeches later and they would have elected Orlad."

"I have been busy." He halted within the ring of candelabra and bent his head in respect to the dead doge. "Who's that?" he whispered. Obviously he did not mean Piero.

"Waels. Stralg killed him, but he was distracted enough by it that Orlad could take the advantage. Waels and Orlad were very close."

"So Giunietta told me." The bizarre, lopsided eyes stared hard at her. "You really want to go ahead with this?"

"I do, certainly. You can have the coronet without me, if you prefer," she admitted. "They shouted down your mother as a traitor, but they will give it to you if you demand it, rules or not."

"All I need do is whistle over a dozen warbeasts?" He sighed. There were unexpected depths to Marno Cavotti—as both Dantio and Giunietta had told her, and as she had discovered for herself on that hectic chariot journey. "Forget the coronet. Leave it out of the discussion. You would take a monster like me as your husband?"

"Happily. But my dowry depends on the coronet."

His big mouth twisted in a rare smile. "So I don't have to choose between you and it? You know the problems, my lady. It cannot be more than a political match."

"We can settle the details later." Would all authority rest in the doge consort, or would he share it with the dogaressa of the blood?

Marno was a clever man—he detected her duplicity and eyed her carefully, but time was running out. "I can't believe you will willingly share an ogre's bed, even to share his throne. Won't you have nightmares?"

"I'm tougher than I look."

He considered that reply for a moment, then shrugged. "Then let's go and do it."

Still hand in hand, they went back to face the horseshoe of elders, who were sitting just as she had left them, as if petrified. Perhaps it had not occurred to them until now that Florengia had another bloodlord, one who might impose his will on them just as easily as Stralg would have done. Probably none of them except Berlice had ever seen the Mutineer before, and it had been ten years for her. This hulking grotesque was not the boy she had known, the son she had reared.

He was ten years older than Orlad, a native of Celebre, a victorious general. He spoke the language and knew the city. His men controlled it as completely as his presence dominated the hall.

He bowed first to Oliva, who glared at him. "My deepest sympathy on your loss, my lady. Celebre owes more to Piero than she has ever owed to any doge in her history. And it owes much to you, for piloting it this last year. I wish he could have lived to see our victory." He held out a hand to Orlad. "Your foes are my foes."

Orlad, ignoring the hand: "That much we already agreed on."

"So we did." The Mutineer turned and bowed to the elders.

With admirable calm, Speaker Quarina said, "Will you report to the council on the condition of the city, lord Cavotti?"

Marno uttered a deep bark of a laugh, the sound of a large and hungry carnivore. "Celebre will survive. Extrinsic casualties will probably not exceed two sixty. I have sent runners to neighboring towns appealing for more Healers. Our Hero losses were heavy, but not as bad as I feared. The ice devils are dead or fled, all but a few stragglers we are still rooting out. My men have secured the gates and are organizing teams to fight the fires—thank Weru for this rain! We have started digging mass graves for the enemy." He glanced around at Oliva. "Your rose garden may need replanting, lady, but it will be well fertilized."

"You know why this council is gathered," the Speaker said. "You are engaged to marry lady Fabia?"

"I have that honor and pleasure."

She pursed thin lips. "The custom is that husbands are eligible, but there is no precedent for electing a fiancé."

Berlice began, "A quick wedding would—"

"I object!" lord Nucci screamed. "An elder should not vote to elect her own son!" Rumbles of agreement and disagreement . . .

"Elders!" Cavotti did not battleform his throat and lungs as Orlad had done, but his sepulchral roar was impressive enough. "It is true that my mother supported the Vigaelians. She had seen her husband skinned for encouraging me and she had other family members to defend. She knew that the Fist's seers were watching her. It is also true, as only I and a very few others know, that for years she has worked tirelessly and fearlessly behind the scenes for the cause of liberty. If there are to be recriminations, then I can bring charges of collaboration against many of you. It will be my policy, if you elect me doge, to let bygones be bygones. No reprisals, no settling of scores. You have my word on that. Speaker, in the last two sixdays I have

fought two battles, driven about forty menzils, and had very little sleep. I ask that you bring this to a speedy vote."

Quarina looked over the council. "Are the honorable elders ready to vote?"

"No!" Orlad jumped to his feet. "I am not . . . I will . . ."

" 'I withdraw,' " Dantio murmured without opening his eyes.

"I withdraw." Orlad sat down and went back to staring at the floor. He had accepted the inevitable.

Fabia reached over to him and squeezed his shoulder in thanks. He pushed her away.

"At the moment, then," Quarina said wryly, "we seem to have no eligible candidate at all. Lord Marno Cavotti, are you and your betrothed willing to declare yourselves man and wife before the gods and this company?"

Cavotti looked down—a long way down—at his bride-to-be. Or bride.

Fabia murmured, "Fortune favors the swift."

"We are," he told the Speaker.

"And who gives this woman in marriage?"

Dantio said, "Orlad, say 'I do.' "

Orlad said, "I do."

"Turn to face holy Veslih," the Speaker said. "That one, up there. Marno Cavotti, repeat after me . . ." She ran through an extremely brief ceremony of marriage. "I declare you husband and wife. Honored elders, if you accept lord Marno as doge, pray stand. Unanimous. Doge Marno, you are elected according to the customs of the city. You may also kiss your bride."

Forty

MARNO CAVOTTI

had learned how to make speeches, as he had learned so many other skills. First, he assured his new in-laws that they would remain honored members of the ducal family.

"This palace is your home," he said, "and always will be, as much as you want it to be. My lady, my lords, you will be granted estates to support you in a style befitting your rank. I count on all of you to help my wife and myself bear our great burdens. The war is won, but the troubles will continue for years. From now on Celebre must stand guardian on the passes, forbidding invasions in either direction." And so on. Oliva and Orlad nodded. Dantio smiled politely.

Marno thanked the elders and dismissed them. He ordered the palace officials to go away and plan a service of thanksgiving for the city's deliverance, a state funeral for the doge, a state wedding, and a coronation. He gently assured Orlad that Werist Waels would rank as the first of the heroes of the liberation, but that his corpse must now be removed from Doge Piero's lying in state.

Then he excused himself to go and sleep.

In all the years of struggle he had never felt wearier than he did now, balanced precariously on the brink of victory. He had the city under control and could trust Butcher and Nuzio to pursue the war until morning. Stralg's corpse was to be delivered to the ice devils as proof of his death. Runners were on the way to Melchitte with orders to burn Veritano and abandon it. No doubt the headless Vigaelian horde would shatter and spread like a plague all over the Face, but many would head for the Edge and might be pinned in the Altiplano to starve. The rest would have to be hunted down and slaughtered, every last brute of them, but that would not be a job for him. Hordes of Florengian Heroes were going to need employment for the rest of their lives.

From guerrilla to hordeleader to ruler—the ducal sleeping chamber was a jarring surprise, an unwelcome warning of the new state he had just accepted. It was larger than most temples, with two rows of columns supporting the ceiling. He could have bivouacked a host in there. The sleeping platform in the center would have held thirty men. Why did he need a score of tree-sized candelabra with two dozen candles apiece when he just wanted to sleep? Why five flunkies to escort him to his quarters? This was not where the late doge had died, they assured him, and certainly he could detect no odors of death or sickness. A bit musty, was all. They had not expected a new doge so soon. He was too tired to bother asking for a smaller room.

"It will suffice," he said. "Leave me."

Did my lord want the candles snuffed?

How ever long would that take? "No, no!" he said. "And no. I wish to study the ceiling frescoes. Go. Go away! Go now."

They closed the door—one of the doors. There were three doors and sixteen high windows, draped in silk brocade. If he were in his right mind he would have had Butcher or some other trusty search this entire wing for lurking ice devils, but he was too tired to care.

He sat on the edge of the platform to remove his boots—and stopped with one off and one on, distracted by what he was seeing. This was a treasure house. He had known from childhood visits that the ducal palace was luxurious, but he had never been in this hall. There was enough lapis lazuli and gold leaf in the wall frescoes alone to finance a major war. The candelabra were studded with jewels. At first glance the chamber had seemed vast and empty, but he started to count the chairs, tables, and chests, and gave up after a score. No doubt every one was a masterpiece. The floor was covered with rugs of the finest alpaca wool, woven in brilliant colors, and the platform was heaped with them. Then there were the ceramics and statuary and tapestries. How had Stralg been kept from looting this hoard? Marno's brothers would be coming around with wagons to collect compensation for the hardship his revolution had caused them.

Brothers? He had not seen them in sixteen years. They were just one of sixty-sixty headaches that would afflict him in the near future. He sighed, knowing that he was not going to sleep. Too many problems were building nests in his brain. He had met this condition before, when exhaustion passed beyond sleep, and knew of only one cure for it, short of waiting for physical collapse. What he needed, ironically, was a woman. Giunietta, especially, would know exactly what he needed and wanted.

"Holy Ucr!"

He jumped and twisted around. His wife was there, closing a door he had overlooked. Problem Number One, she stared around with disbelief, then mockingly raised a hand to shade her eyes, as if peering across a landscape.

"Is that you over there, husband?"

He forced himself to seem pleased. "It is. Shall I send a chariot for you?"

She headed in his direction. "Orlad accused me of being a slut. For selling my body for the crown, I suppose. I had no idea I had made such a good bargain."

"You should see the silver pots in the servants' latrines."

She wore a white wrap, filmy and clinging. Her hair hung loose in black ringlets that fell to a handbreadth below the nipples that so clearly raised the fine cloth. He watched her stroll across the rugs toward him, fascinated in spite of his exhaustion. He had wanted a woman and yet he must not accept what the gods sent.

Her grin seemed both childlike and genuine. "I am informed that a wife is expected to sleep in the same room as her husband. This is big enough for both of us, is it not?"

"I am afraid my snores will echo and waken me," he said, "but it will do until we find a better. But, Fabia, we agreed that ours would be only a political match."

She sat on the edge of the platform, not close, but within reach if he changed his mind. "A pretend marriage, you mean?"

"You know what I mean. We discussed it. If I get a woman with child I am as good as murdering her. I sought out a Healer I know and trust, and she confirmed that it is a Werist problem, so holy Sinura will not help. To the world I am your husband, and I expect you to keep up the pretense. In practice, you will have to find a discreet young man to father Piero's grandchildren. I won't care or ask who he is." He smiled as well as he could without uncovering his fangs. "Preferably one man at a time, but even that is your business as long as you create no scandal."

Her face gave away nothing. "While you install Witness Giunietta as palace seer?"

He laughed trying to imagine what Giunietta would say to the invitation. "Now, *there* would be scandal! I like and admire Giunietta very much, but she is blatantly promiscuous. She would be marching the palace guard through her chamber in no time. A Witness is a possible playmate for me, because she knows when it is safe, or a Nymph, because they do not conceive. But at the moment, wife, I have far more urgent problems, of which the most urgent is sleep. If you will forgive me?"

She nodded. "It has been quite a day. Whatever your wishes, my lord, your handmaiden will most humbly agree." She fingered the rugs as if marveling at their softness. "There is certainly enough space for us to sleep here without disturbing each other, isn't there? Perhaps in the morning—" She looked around, frowning. "I asked Dantio to scan these chambers to make sure no one was hiding anywhere, and he said they were safe. I also asked a steward for some wine. I think that must be it over there, beside that door. Marno, my lord, it has been a heavy day for both of us, but I have two brief requests. I want to drink a pledge to our lifelong partnership, and I want one real kiss from you."

"Real kiss?"

"I told you two days ago that I was a virgin and nothing has changed since then, but I have spied on enough hanky-panky on riverbanks to be certain that you can manage a better kiss than the one you gave me tonight in the hall. As soon as you have attended to that, sleep by all means. If you need me I will be here. If you don't, I shall not sulk, I promise." She rose and held out a hand. "Come and drink a pledge."

He replaced the boot he had shed and waded across the rugs with her.

Any woman who was prepared to consider intimacy with an animal like him was either incredibly brave or insanely greedy for power.

She said, "Giunietta is an unusual woman."

"She is a free thinker."

"Is that a polite version of what my brother called me?"

Obviously that remark had hurt her. "In Celebre many marriages are arranged just to seal commercial or political unions."

"And in Skjar also."

"So? If you are a trollop for marrying a title, then what am I for marrying all this loot? As I see our arrangement, your family needed a man to run the family business, Celebre. Dantio refused and Orlad lacks experience. I saw myself being out of work very shortly. We are an excellent match."

She laughed and slid an arm around him. "I never doubted the *quantity* of husband I am acquiring. I am just beginning to appreciate the *quality* as well."

"The ugliest bridegroom in the history of the city."

"I was put off when I first saw you," she admitted. "But looks matter less than honor and courage and kindness. Muscles are cute, and you qualify in that department. Also, in Vigaelia, the word 'horny' means, er—"

"It means the same here, too. And it is irrelevant. Please do not keep mentioning the matter."

"I am sorry. That was inconsiderate of me. Consideration is the most important thing in a marriage, isn't it?"

He had never had time to learn to understand women. She was barely more than a child and yet she baffled him.

"Respect first, I think," he said. "Consideration certainly second. Understanding that nobody is perfect and everyone has faults. Patience. Compromise. If we can bring all those to our marriage, it should prosper."

"That's lovely! Let that be our pledge."

They had reached the table where six wine jugs stood, swathed in damp cloths. He unwrapped a couple and chose one.

"A star and two swords, see?" he said. "Means this is from the hills above Quiloni, a fine wine, not tart, but not too sweet." He broke the seal.

"These goblets!" Fabia said, using both hands to lift one. "These are . . . incredible!"

He lifted the other to inspect it. Each stood half a yard high, depicting a youth and a maiden supporting the cup itself in their raised arms. "They are called lover cups, made of rock crystal from the mines of Ritorni. This set was undoubtedly carved by Pecculli of Samercci, the greatest master of this form. My parents had half of a pair, much smaller, which they treasured as one of the finest pieces in their collection. Yours is the man's, though. This is the woman's."

She set hers down and took the other from him to inspect. "I was told you once had ambitions to be an artist."

"Only a connoisseur. I have no talent of my own."

"How can you tell which cup is which?"

He chuckled as he poured the wine. "The boy and girl touch in only one place, always. In the woman's the two are kissing, see? In the man's their contact is lower and more intimate, although the portrayal is discreet. It is almost impossible to place two bodies in such postures and still make them seem graceful, as these are. This pair would buy twice sixty acres of prime farmland, perhaps more. And you haven't even mentioned the mosaic table. That is a genuine Ragottilo, worth much more than the goblets." He laid down the flagon. "Now, will you offer first?"

She was reaching both hands for the cup when the door beside them opened and Chies walked in, wearing an ominous smirk.

Forty-one

CHIES STRALGSON

could not only see in the dark better than a cat, he could even drive a team in the dark. It had been a *very* instructive day! He could Control even a Werist. Saltaja said he might risk as many as three people at a time once he'd had some practice, but he should never try more than that; mobs were deadly. If Sesto's men had had their wits about them, they would have struck her down. From now on he could enjoy any woman he wanted with as much or little cooperation as he fancied, and then make her forget all about it. He could steal anything he coveted. And his aunt had not finished her instruction yet! None of Master Preceptor Dicerno's lectures on etiquette and court protocol could compare with this.

He drove into the city through Cypress Gate without challenge, mingling with country folk rushing to join in the mourning. Blazing buildings threw flames high in the night, filling the rainy streets with golden reflections. The trumpets had stopped, but the city was still a madhouse, with riots and looting mixed in with wild celebration, and even some local panics as bands of ice devils were hunted down and destroyed. He had never seen Florengian Werists in Celebre before, and they were everywhere, even some in battleform. The guanacos hummed with fear, but he kept them under control—using mostly real skill and only a dash of chthonic power.

"Aunt," he said. "There's something wrong here! They should be mourning Pap—I mean the doge. They're not! They're celebrating!"

She did not answer. All the way from Montegola she had been mumbling and maundering about revenge and curses and finding Stralg. She seemed crazier some times than others, and this was one of those times.

He tried to turn into Wheelwrights' Alley, but it was plugged full of people singing at the top of their lungs, and the Werist barracks was ablaze. He went on to Fishhook Lane, still skirting the palace walls. Getting inside those was going to be tricky. By this time of night the palace was usually sealed as tight as a virgin priestess. He turned to consult his passenger.

"Aunt? *Aunt!*" Gone! He was alone.

"I'm here."

He felt her claws grip his arm. "Invisible?"

"Veiled. I'll show you how to do that. How do we get in?"

He had lost his key to the private door. "Can you open a lock?"

"What's a lock?"

He explained. No such things as locks in Vigaelia, she said. He could not advise, not knowing how their insides worked. As he pondered, the problem solved itself. The Fishhook gate had been torn down and people were scurrying in and out of the grounds, mostly in. He halted and put down the brake with a sigh of relief. No need to worry about the rig. It wouldn't stay there long.

He found his invisible aunt by squinting against the light of the fires. He could detect her as a faint shadow, but only because he knew she was there. He lifted her down.

"Now I show you how to veil yourself," she said, and took his head between her claw hands. "Think!"

Images swirled. Ropes of darkness? "Oh! I understand."

"Ask Her for that. Just a little! All you need do is blur yourself a bit so people won't recognize you. If you disappear like me, they'll walk into you. That's plenty!"

He had barely started, but he would have to trust her judgment. He strolled toward the gate, knowing she was there by the feel of her talons on his arm. As they turned into the palace grounds, the chariot and team went rattling by them, being driven by a stout, white-haired woman. Lucky lady.

"Too slow!" she muttered. "Men your age walk faster. Here!"

He stumbled as pain shot through his right knee. "Ow!"

"Now you limp. That looks better."

Depending on one's point of view! He failed to see the merit in a red hot knife under his kneecap. What he would really like, now that he was safely home, was just to go upstairs to his chamber and lie down and sleep. It had been a very hard day.

Saltaja muttered angrily under her breath all the way through the sculpture garden, across the court of palms, along the river terrace. Once or twice a passerby would look twice to see who was talking, but nobody roused any hue or cry. A major crowd was gathered in front of the Hall of Pillars. That would be where Papa was lying in state, but the crowd was buzzing with good cheer, even breaking out into snatches of drunken song. This was not funeral behavior! Some of the snatches he was hearing suggested that ice dev . . . that Vigaelians had attacked the city and been beaten off.

The crowd had concentrated at the far end of the hall. He could see candlelight within, and guards between the pillars, men with swords. He headed that way and soon recognized fat Luenzi, deputy head of the palace guard, known to his men as the Stomach of Splendor. He was standing between two pillars with his arms crossed, but Luenzi was no threat to anyone unless he fell on them. Chies noted the man's affable drunken smile and the untidiness of his white hair. Luenzi had served in the doge's guard for a lifetime; he ought to be prostrate with grief, not celebrating. Chies shed his veiling.

It took a moment. Then—"Lord Chies! You're back! You're safe!"

"I escaped. Killed a couple of my kidnappers and climbed out a window." Four stories up? Sprained my knee? No, better leave it at that.

"But this is wonderful news! What a marvelous night!" Luenzi looked around to see who might want to share.

"Is it? Tell me what else is going on." Chies applied just a trace of power.

Possibly too much. Luenzi started to gabble. "Well your dear father, of course . . . the Evil One got . . . I mean he passed through the veil at last, poor man. But the other news . . . The children are back! Lord Dantio, lord Orlando, lady Fabia! All safe and grown-up. Then the Fist himself invaded with a horde. Stralg in the flesh! And he's dead! Lord Orlando killed him right here in the hall! Ripped his collar off."

Saltaja uttered a shriek that should have turned every head in the palace grounds. Luenzi paused, looked around him with a puzzled expression, then continued.

"But the Mutineer, I mean lord Marno, was here with his men, and they tore up all those ice devils in short order. So the elders assembled right here in the hall and elected him doge!"

"Marno Cavotti?"

Luenzi bared all fifteen teeth in a wide grimace of delight. "Yes, and he married the lady Fabia, so she's the new dogaressa! Oh, what a wonderful night!"

The night was not over yet. Saltaja would not stand for that.

"Fascinating!" Chies said. "Forget that you have seen me or spoken with me. You will not notice me leave."

The animation in the fat man's face faded to boredom. He scratched his belly and turned his head to watch what was going on farther along the hall.

Rounding the great pillar, Chies noted two things of interest. A bier stood in the center under a dozen candelabra. That was Papa, no doubt, but he was almost being ignored. Everyone else was at the far end, where a score of men were gathered around a two-wheeled cart, arguing noisily. Even from here he could see reflections off collars, so at least some of them were Werists. He could not imagine what a cart was doing in the Hall of Pillars, but he intended to find out. Someone started hammering.

He replaced his veiling as he walked. Squinting down at his gimpy knee, he made out a shadowy thing like a purple crab on it. He flicked it away with a mental twitch and the pain stopped. Pleased, he speeded up to his normal long-legged stride. He paused at the bier and pushed through the mourners to gaze at the corpse. Life had been hard on the old man. He had been sick so long that Chies had grown accustomed to not having him around, but he had mostly happy memories of his foster father. None of the usual prayers seemed appropriate for a Chosen to utter. *Holy mistress, treat him well! Please.*

He moved on to investigate the shouting mob around the cart. Half a dozen men were standing on it and the rest were steadying it as those above raised something onto a jury-rigged chair. Chies had to wait until they had it roped in place and started jumping down before he got a proper look at it. It was large, a sickly white color, and barely human; even bigger than Marno Cavotti. Ice devils were always pale and he had heard of the pallor that corpses acquired, but that *thing* was a horrible, fish-belly shade. The only color on it was the pale pink tongue that hung from its mouth and a purple necklace, a dark gash where the flesh had been crushed and cut by a garrote. The men were going to parade this corpse through the streets of Celebre for everyone to jeer and pelt it with garbage. *Oh, Father!*

His father. The Fist. Now he would never meet his father, never speak with him, offer to help him, hear stories of his conquests. All his glory had come to this? He felt his shock turning to anger. This was Orlad Celebre's doing. Back in Veritano Orlad had wanted to tear his head off.

Claws grabbed his arm again, his other arm this time.

"We must avenge your father, boy!"

"Yes, Aunt. Yes!"

"Where will she be?"

"She? Luenzi said Orlad did it."

"Oh, yes, we'll get the Werist too, never fear! And that eunuch. And the Mutineer! All of them. Chosen look after their own, boy, I've told you that, haven't I? And when we can't defend them, we avenge them. But we must start with the girl. She's the dangerous one. Where is the girl? Make her wish she had never been born."

"Let's go and find her." He would not argue with the old bat when she was in this sort of a mood.

◆

It was easy. Four Werists sat outside the doors to the family wing, which meant that Cavotti must be in there. Fabia would be with her husband, learning the joys of married life. Chies strengthened his veiling until the candles were barely visible. Curiously, his aunt became more visible to him, not less. The Heroes were busily fighting the evening's battles all over again and paid no heed as he opened the door and ushered her inside.

There was even a Werist on a chair outside the state sleeping chamber. Chies shed his veil. The man leaped to his feet with an oath.

"You will obey me! Do not shout. Do not battleform!" This godlike power was very enjoyable. "Is the new doge in there?"

The Hero nodded, flapping his mouth like a fish. He was a veteran, older and well scarred, and his eyes were as blank as glass beads.

"Is his new wife with him?"

"I do not know."

"Lie down and sleep. Sleep until dawn, no matter what happens."

Chies turned to smile at his aunt and couldn't find her. The door swung open by itself. He followed her in.

The hall was so huge that he was startled to find Cavotti and the woman right there, just inside the door. He was wearing a badly stained green chlamys and she a white silk web. Chies had barely had time to decide that he wanted to study her at leisure when his aunt blasted them both. The Mutineer hurtled back against a chair, which collapsed in a mess of kindling. The woman landed on her back several paces away.

Chies closed and bolted the door.

Cavotti was half sitting on a litter of firewood, half reclining against the wall. Only his eyes were moving. Fabia raised herself on her elbows and stared at Saltaja, who was now fully visible in all her mutilated horror.

"You're too revolting to be a nightmare."

"You don't know what horror is, child. I am about to teach you."

"I don't think you are." The dogaressa climbed to her feet with a fascinating revelation of legs. She dusted herself off and adjusted her wrap, frowned at Chies. "What have you done to the boy?" She seemed strangely unworried. Did she not understand that she was being threatened by a Chosen?

Cavotti made grunting noises and twitched. Deciding that the giant was out of commission and posed no danger, Chies turned his attention fully to the two women's confrontation. His sister was a real stiffener in that filmy, flimsy thing. He did not think his help was going to be needed.

"Nothing," Saltaja said, drooling and slobbering. "And if you think I'm ugly, wait until you see what I do to your pretty face. I will not kill you. That would be too easy. Belly worms. Tumors. Suppurating sores. Madness, so they lock you up. You will have years to sit in your cell, suffering and mourning your folly."

"Your time is over," the girl said calmly. "Your brothers are all dead, did you know? I assume Cutrath Horoldson was with you in the Edgelands.

Did you manage to rescue him as well as yourself? If not, then you and this boy are the only two left out of the whole disgusting brood. The Mother has tired of you. She has withdrawn Her favor." She had not so much glanced at her petrified husband yet, keeping her attention on the hag.

Who chuckled. "No, dearie! I am much more in her favor than you are. Remember those guards I set over you at Tryfors? The Heroes who let you escape? I sacrificed them to Her glory. Fifteen strong, healthy young men bleeding into the cold earth!"

"Yes, I know. I saw."

"You lie!" Saltaja shrieked. "She would not let you spy on me. Then there were two score I marched into the Dust River so I could walk across on their bodies. There were others we ate. And the Werists on the Altiplano—another ten! What have you offered Her that would compare with that?"

Fabia grimaced. "I do not believe that the Old One values Her Chosen by tallying their murders, but if you want to keep score by body count, then I counter with the whole escort you took on the Nardalborg Pass trail. It was my idea to let you close it behind you all the way to Fist's Leap and then slam the gate in your face. I had to talk even my Werist brother into that! All those deaths—a whole hunt, wasn't it? They were already dead men when you started eating them. They count to my credit, not yours."

Saltaja screamed and hurled a bolt of black fire at her. Fabia must have been expecting something like it, for she countered with one of her own, and they coalesced in a wall of black flame midway between them. It crackled and flared—and slowly advanced toward Fabia. The two Chosen were locked in a trial of strength. Chies could hear his aunt wheezing with the effort it cost. Then Fabia started to back away, and at once the flames leaped at her. She went down, screaming and writhing in an unholy blaze.

Saltaja laughed and released the evil. Fabia lay naked on charred and smoking rugs, struggling feebly to rise. She had apparently saved herself from harm so far, but she was clearly the loser of that round.

"Now that we've established who is the stronger, dearie, we can begin the entertainment. I think those pretty breasts first."

Chies decided he did not approve of this. Even if Saltaja was winning this battle, she had lost all the others and he had his own future to consider.

Fabia had befriended him at Veritano. How could he favor a horror like Saltaja over her? Watch her be tortured and mutilated? No! He lifted one of the rock-crystal lover cups from the table and swung it with all his strength. The impact threw wine over Cavotti and shattered the carving into a shower of hail. It didn't do much for the old bat's skull, either.

Forty-two

FABIA CELEBRE

felt as if she had just been dropped from the palace roof onto a gravel path and the palace was about to fall on top of her. Marno's eyes were bulging. So were Chies's, although for different reasons. Saltaja was probably not dead.

She said, "Thank you, Chies. Bring me a couple of sheets, quickly!"

He reluctantly dragged his eyes away from the scenery and strode across to the platform. The carpet was sharp with slivers of rock crystal, so she stayed where she was, but now she could concentrate her attention on Marno. She ripped at the vile shadowy net that entrapped him. It came away easily and disappeared.

"You all right?" she asked hoarsely, voice quavering. Her marriage was ended before it started, of course, and she would be very lucky if he did not hurl her into an open grave beside Saltaja.

He sat up, wincing. "I took a few splinters in places I won't show you. You?"

"Shaken, is all. I don't think she's dead." She saw Chies returning, clutching two silk sheets. His eyes were all over her again in that very un-brotherly way. "Give me one of those. Now tear the other one up and blind-fold her quickly!"

She wrapped herself. Marno flowed to his feet, shedding fragments of chair and crystal, then picked his way through the gravel and helped her stand. He did not stun her or break her neck, at least not yet. She was start-ing to shake with delayed reaction.

Chies said, "She's coming round. I can't tear this, my lady!"

"Cut it, boy! You're standing ankle-deep in broken glass!"

Marno took the sheet and ripped it. "There!" He used the first strip to bandage the Chosen's eyes, and two more to bind her wrists and ankles. "Will that hold her?"

"I think so," Fabia said. She finished adjusting her new sarong. "For now. Watch where you're walking."

"Here, let me!" Chies had shoes on. He hauled a rug in from nearer the center of the room, where no glass had landed.

"That's quick thinking, too," Fabia said. "Chies, I am forever grateful for what you just did. Did she harm you?"

It was story time. He shook his head solemnly. "No, my lady. But I was forced to do whatever she told me. She did something to me so I had to obey her! It was horrible." He stared down at her with eyes as big and innocent as dark forest pools. But forest pools were notorious for harboring water snakes.

Mother of Lies, have you enlisted a new pupil? Fabia remembered Witness Mist warning her that there was never any way to tell.

"You saved the day, lord Chies!" Marno proclaimed. He pumped the boy's hand and thumped his bony shoulder so he staggered. "Let's drink to a very narrow escape." He handed Fabia the remaining lover cup and Chies the flagon. Then he opened another for himself. "Is that the end of the Hrag farrow?"

"Except me," Chies said.

The Mutineer had the grace to look abashed. "I wasn't counting you. You're my brother-in-law now."

"So I am!" Chies smiled shyly. "A great honor, my lord. Congratulations on your election. And on your marriage. You, too, my lady."

"I want to hear what happened at Veritano," Marno said, "but first, what do we do with the Chosen?"

Fabia wondered, *Which Chosen?* "The traditional treatment is horrible, but she has more than earned it."

"We can arrange that very easily tonight. They won't have finished filling in the palace rose garden yet. Can I just carry her out there?"

All Fabia knew for certain was that Saltaja Hragsdor knew a lot more tricks than she did. "It would be safer to carry her in a sack, I think. If we roll her in a sheet, then you could hold one end; Chies and I could take the other." She would not dare let Chies out of her sight until she knew how safe he was. Marno must be feeling the same way about her. Whose funeral was this to be?

Saltaja moaned and twitched when they tried to move her. Her head wound was bleeding copiously. Marno gagged her. They rolled her in another of the incredible silk sheets.

"I think I can manage this end by myself, my lady," Chies said earnestly. "She's not too heavy. At times she made me carry her."

"You must be very strong. How can we get out to the rose garden?"

"This door. If you would be so kind as to open it?" Chies knelt, pulled one end of the cocoon over his shoulder, then stood up. Marno raised the other and they went forward with Saltaja slung between them.

Fabia drew the bolts and almost fell over a Werist snoring on the floor outside.

"It's not his fault, my lord," Chies said. "She commanded him to go to sleep. This way . . ."

A heavily bolted door at the end of the corridor led outside, to a paved terrace overhung by a leafy trellis. Rain pelted down harder than ever, making the fires in the city glow golden through clouds of steam.

They rounded a corner and came to what must once have been the rose garden and was now a wasteland of muck, a macabre scene lit by a hissing bonfire, smelling of wood smoke and wet loam. Two men stood chest-deep in a pit, hurling out shovelfuls of mud, while a third leaned on a spade, watching them. Light shone on their brass collars and wet skin; also on a stack of Vigaelian corpses waiting on a cart nearby. From the number of spades and picks she could see, Fabia guessed that the total workforce must be at least a dozen, so finding only three men here was good luck. None at all would have been even luckier.

The watcher jumped in alarm, recognizing the Mutineer.

Marno said, "I just killed an ice devil hiding in the palace. We'll bury him here."

The Werist took one look at the draped bundle, which was definitely starting to writhe. Then another, at Cavotti.

"My lord is kind. You two—out!" He offered each workman a hand in turn to haul him out of the pit. Marno and Chies swung their load and let go. Saltaja dropped into the grave with a splash. There was enough water in there to drown her. Fabia braced herself, waiting to see if she was going to be thrown in there also, and perhaps Chies as well. She knew very little about her husband, except that he could be utterly ruthless. She doubted that she could Control four Heroes at the same time. Whose side would Chies take?

Cavotti single-handedly lifted a corpse from the cart and tossed it on top of Saltaja. "Now fill it in."

"My lord is kind."

Holy Xaran, accept back Your faithful servant Saltaja Hragsdor and deal with her as she deserves, according to Your wisdom.

All three workmen shoveled vigorously. Chies eagerly grabbed a spade and lent a hand. In moments the hole was half filled and a great evil had gone from the world.

"You will not mention this to anyone," the Mutineer told them. "I do not wish people to be alarmed."

Fabia could have ensured the men's silence more certainly, but did not offer to do so. Marno put an arm around her and they headed back to the palace, feet squelching in the mud.

✦

In the morning, servants would wonder about the muddy tracks they found in the hallway, not to mention bloodstains and burned rugs in the state bedroom, but doges need not worry about trivia like gossip. Fabia was starting to appreciate the power in the man she had married, the radiant authority of Marno Cavotti. She had put herself and the city in the big man's hands and he had taken charge of them without a moment's doubt or hesitation. He would not loosen his grip until he, too, was summoned by the Oldest God.

Ignoring the reek of burned wool in the sleeping chamber, he set three chairs in a triangle, handed out wine, and told Chies to sit down and speak up. He interrupted only once, when he heard how Flankleader Sesto Panotti's men had let themselves be enslaved by Saltaja while on patrol. He said "Idiotic," paired with a noun Paola Apicella had not taught her foster daughter.

Fabia could not detect a single wrong note in the boy's story. Probably most of it was true, because a good fiction should be based on as much truth as possible. *Mother of Lies, you found an apt pupil!* What was she going to do about Chies? Was he or wasn't he? Could one palace hold two Chosen?

At the end, she asked what had happened to Sesto.

"She killed him, my lady. It was horrible! In a small wood not far away from the city. I think I could lead your men there, my lord. I know the area. I would like the poor man to have a decent burial."

"And how did she kill him?"

Chies hesitated for just an instant. "She cut his throat."

Not she. He. *Blood and birth; death and the cold earth.* An initiation.

Cavotti glanced inquiringly at Fabia. He probably just wanted her comments on Chies's story, but she deliberately misinterpreted, because she wanted to tell her brother the Chosen a few things.

"Now it's my turn. Yes, I am a Chosen. When Stralg took Dogaressa Oliva hostage—ostensibly hostage, but really as slave plaything—he gave me to a wet nurse, Paola Apicella. She had lost her husband in battle and her baby had died. But she was a Chosen, and Mother Xaran provided for her." Her husband winced when he heard the forbidden name, but so did Chies, equally. The boy was good! "She was my foster mother until four years ago, when Saltaja Hragsdor had her murdered. I heard that from a Witness, so it is true. Paola was a gentle, loving, caring person. She was nothing like the Queen of Shadows' triple-distilled evil."

Cavotti was a monolith. Chies was wide-eyed innocence.

"I could have refused to accept the Old One as my goddess. I did not. Had I wanted to be like Saltaja, I could have joined her gang, her family. She wanted to marry me to her nephew Cutrath. I refused. I have tried to use my powers to promote justice. I slew the man who killed Paola. I rescued an innocent woman being held captive by Horold Hragson, although I knew he would punish her guards. I did persuade Orlad and the others to trap Saltaja and her escort on the Edge. It was the only way I could see to end her career and stop her meeting up with Stralg. I honestly believed that fewer innocent people would die in the long run." She shrugged, wishing she could read the thoughts moving behind her husband's bestial face. "I do not intend to commit any more murders. Of course, if I or my loved ones are ever threatened by violence, I will respond."

"You worship the Evil One," Cavotti said.

"The goddess of death. She is the oldest and greatest of the gods. She is the Mother of Lies because we all lie about death. It is the one thing we all fear and fear most, so we lie about it. We say that people have returned to the womb, or passed through the veil, or feast in the halls of Weru. We tell stories about what happens after death as if we knew, but we don't."

"You are sworn to the Evil One!" he persisted.

"She chose me. I do not know why. Do the gods ever justify their decisions to mortals? I thought a lot about this while we were crossing the Edge. Mother Xaran is goddess of *blood and birth, death and the cold earth*. Death is not always evil. It can be a release, or a judgment. Birth is also Hers, because without birth there could be no death; without death we could not have birth, else we should fill the world, shoulder to shoulder."

On the Edge, Fabia had been very close to death. The Mother had taught her much, speaking clearly.

"She grants enormous powers to us, Her Chosen, but She also lets us choose how we use those powers. Saltaja treated other people like weeds, to be trampled. I truly believe that Paola used hers for good. So far as I know, the only violence she ever committed was in self defense. Power is not innately evil!"

She wondered how Chies was taking this lecture, but she kept her eyes on her husband, who continued to stare straight at her. "The uses of power may be," he growled.

"They often are, but that is the fault of whoever wields that power. All power can be used for good. All power can be abused. Absolute power can be abused absolutely."

Cavotti yawned and stretched, flexing his great muscles. "It cannot be far from dawn, and we have much to do these next few days. Where do you normally sleep, Chies?"

"Directly above here, my lord."

"Then you will not meet any guards on your way there. Go and sleep, and in the morning you can thrill your mother with a dramatic story of your escape from Veritano. Do not mention Saltaja to anyone!"

"Oh, I won't, my lord! I mean, they might think I had helped her and then they would want to bury me, too!" Grinning, he jumped up.

So did Fabia. "Wait! Chies, you have wonderful night vision."

He looked puzzled. "My lady?"

"I watched you when we went outside. You dodged branches that lord Marno did not see. You avoided rocks and holes. You must learn to be more careful, Chies!"

He smiled cheekily. "Careful about what, sister? I've always had wonderful night-sight. Ask Mama. She's always nagging me to carry a lamp, but I never need one."

Fabia stepped close and kissed his cheek, just as she had when they first met at Veritano. "I mean, 'Do not serve evil.' It is a terrible temptation, I know. If you are found out, you know what will happen, and we will not try to save you. But welcome back. Mama has been out of her mind with worry about you. You are one of the family and I hope you always will be. Thank you again for . . . *distracting* Saltaja."

"Sorry I broke the pretty goblet." He bowed. "Good night, my lord, my lady."

The door closed. *If that young lout ever starts asking for a bedroom on ground level I will personally—*

"Will we regret this one day?" Marno murmured behind her. "Is he?"

"I think so, I don't know. Never trust anything he says."

She turned and looked up at her bridegroom's face with the shadowy ceiling above it. Could *he* ever trust *her* was more to the point. "I did mean to warn you before we were married. I thought we would have much more time after Papa died."

"Tonight, did you turn Chies on Saltaja? Were you the reason he suddenly changed sides?"

She hesitated. "I don't think so. Just holding off Saltaja was taking everything I had. Let him have the credit. And, Marno, I swear I did not use any power on you earlier! In the chariot, I mean. When we talked about what was going to happen after Papa died and who would be doge, I did not put the idea in your head!"

He clasped her shoulders in his enormous hands. "Of course you didn't. I had been thinking for a long time that Florengia would be in turmoil for years and Celebre would need a strong doge, one who could employ a Werist horde for defense without being deposed by it. My mother is an elder. I saw no need to suggest my name to her. I knew she would think of it all by herself. And then, when Hero Dimo came streaking down off the Altiplano in a lather to say that the doge's children were back . . . No, you did not put the marriage idea in my head."

"And you did not just arrange for the doge's children to disappear at Veritano. You could have done."

A Cavotti shrug was an impressive sight. "Never thought of it. But Chies is not the only one who must learn to be more careful."

"What do you mean?"

"I did not notice your night-sight, but I did wonder at your courage." His smile did not reach his deadly eyes. "You told me you were a virgin— which Giunietta had already Witnessed, by the way. I am a killer, a Werist, and three times your size. I could inflict serious injury on you in a moment's carelessness. Just being playful I could crush you. Yet you showed no fear of me. Tonight you came frolicking to my sleeping platform as if you had no cares in the world. You repeatedly hinted that you wanted to consummate our marriage. You are either incredibly ignorant of what men and women do together, or you trust in some special defense."

She could feel herself blush. "If you tried to hurt me, I . . . Yes, I would stop you."

"Just tell me. It will never be deliberate."

So here it came. "I trust you. Can you trust me?"

"I will. How can I prove it? Like this?" He scooped her up bodily, as if she were a child, and kissed her. It was an extraordinary experience, lips and tongue. Her eyes snapped shut to let her concentrate on it. She had never realized that a lovers' kiss was not like any other. It went on and on, somehow growing in intensity, sending tremors of excitement tingling in her breasts and deep down inside her. Her one free hand pawed at Cavotti's massive arm, hard as a tree trunk. Her heartbeat soared incredibly. When he took his mouth away and set her feet on the floor again, her knees buckled.

He clasped her tight against him. His chlamys was still wet, and her ear was level with his heart, which was thumping almost as fast as hers. His distinctive musky scent was overpowering, intoxicating.

"I will trust you, Fabia."

She gasped until she got her breath back. "You said you had consulted a Healer of Sinura since we first spoke. I asked my goddess directly."

"Blood and birth, you said?" His voice echoed deep inside his chest.

"Yes," she admitted. "Ingeld . . . Horold Hragson's wife told me how he impregnated a woman to see what would happen. She died giving birth to his child. It was human, but as big as a two-year-old. I will not be trapped like that. The Mother has authority over birth. I will be able to insist that your sons vacate the premises at the end of a normal lease." She had asked for confirmation of this the first night after she met Cavotti, and Xaran had reassured her.

"You bribe me. I thought I had lost the chance of children."

"I want children also."

The big man sighed in wonder. "You are prepared to trust the Mother of Lies?"

"If she plays me false I will die, but we all die, Marno." She twisted her neck to stare up at him. Yes, he was incredibly ugly. But he was a lot of husband. "Why else would I have come here tonight? Are you willing to be married to a self-confessed Chosen?"

One of his precious smiles brightened the room. "In your case, yes. And you want me to prove it now? Be warned, all your chthonic powers will not be enough to stop me once I get going!"

"You talk too much," she said. "Let me see some action."

Forty-three

LORD DANTIO

spent most of the next five days exhuming his childhood. He attended his father's funeral and the service for the fallen, but mostly he just walked the halls of the palace and streets of the city, wallowing in nostalgia. He avoided Fabia and Orlad, being heartily sick of the timbre of their emotions after spending so long in their company. They did not remember Celebre, and even he found it much less familiar than he had expected. He encountered few people he knew and escaped their vicinity before they noticed him, but he could not avoid the mind-numbing emotional tumult. Night and day the city reverberated with joy and sorrow in unholy counterpoint until his head ached. On the fifth morning, when the Healers had begun to recover from their treatment of the wounded, he went to a sanctuary and let them mend his shoulder. They refused any gift in return, because the new doge had already promised a huge donation to reward treatment of injuries sustained on the night of the liberation.

The new doge was extremely popular. Dogaressa Oliva had done her best, no doubt, but it was good to have a doge in charge again. *And Marno Cavotti himself!* The Mutineer ranked just below the Bright Ones in his birthplace now. "Poor man, how he has suffered for us . . . but he killed Stralg in the end." Despite the generous tribute Cavotti had paid to both Orlad and Waels during the service for the fallen, neither was being given credit by the Celebrians. The local lad had done it all, won the war single-handed.

That afternoon, while inspecting the fire damage to the temple of Weru, Dantio saw his half-brother Chies skulking amid the slums near the abattoir. Why in the world would he go there? No Witness could resist a mystery, and this one was only a few blocks away. Dantio arrived just in time to see Chies emerge from a doorway, accompanied by a grubby old man who looked seedy to human sight and duplicitous to the Goddess's. The man locked the door and handed the key to Chies. They nodded to each other and parted. Chies went only as far as the next corner, then doubled back, unlocked the door, and dived inside. He did not see Dantio inspecting cups in a nearby potter's shop.

Most curious!

Chies had given the man no money that Dantio had noticed, but it very much looked as if Chies had bought or rented whatever lay behind that ugly, warped little door. Or could he be going to meet someone there? Dantio left the store and strolled past the door, but all he could sense inside it was a squalid little room, mostly below grade, with a tiny barred window and plentiful roaches. Its only furnishing was a sleeping platform. Chies was in there, but Dantio's sight could not determine what he was doing, which was ominous.

What could a boy who lived in the palace want with such a pesthole? Not to take girls to, surely? The temple of Eriander was still in business and male adolescents worshiped there fervently. If it were a shrine to the Old One, Dantio would not be able to see inside it at all, but it certainly looked like the sort of obscure crypt She favored. No doubt a Chosen could conse-crate it to Her, although the Witnesses were almost certain that the ritual re-quired human sacrifice. *Chies?* Was he? Could he be? Did the ducal family now include two Chosen?

He had not been a Chosen in Veritano, or Marno's men could not have kidnapped him so easily. So what had happened since then? The story of his escape and the wild ride down the Puisa on a stolen boat, all the way to the city—was that credible? Dantio had heard it from people who believed it, not from any who knew the truth of it. It might be worth dropping a hint to Fabia.

✦

Toward dusk on that day, Dantio was tracked down by a Witness as he stud-ied the ducks in the river park. He sensed her approach and went to meet her. She was a bony, aging woman, unveiled in Florengian style.

"Brother Mist, I am Sister Edviga from the palace." She smiled as she read his annoyance. "The doge has called a meeting and requests that you attend."

"What sort of meeting?" He fell into step beside her.

"Your family," she said. "He received his own family this morning, his mother and brothers." *(amusement)*

"And?"

"And I am astonished you did not feel it, brother. He practically threw his brothers out bodily."

In fact Dantio had picked up a trace of that rage and ignored it. "Greed? They want their cut?"

"They are all Ucrists."

He laughed aloud. How long had it been since he did that?

✦

The Council Chamber was a pentagonal room on the second floor, with three great windows overlooking the grounds and a huge fireplace, which was making the room unpleasantly warm. It was furnished with a single low wheatwood table in the center, also pentagonal, surrounded by cushions. Dantio surveyed the scene with nostalgia, recalling how his father had brought him there once, treating him as an adult when he broke the news that he would have to go as hostage to the ice devils.

His mother stood there alone, staring out a window. Hearing him clear his throat, she spun around, then came rushing to him, arms open. She almost drowned him in a torrent of emotions so turbulent that he could barely distinguish them. He hid his revulsion as best he could.

"Where have you been? I was so worried. Why didn't you come and see me. . . ." And so on.

"I needed time to recover and I knew you had the others. We have years ahead of us, Mama!" In fact, he had decided he must leave the city very shortly. He had not been struck down, so either the Eldest in Vigaelia had decided to overlook his sins or her anathema carried no weight on the Florengian Face. Next sixday he would set off to visit the Florengian mother lodge and offer to add to its Wisdom, revealing what he alone knew about the war and Saltaja's death in the Edgelands.

Oliva was shaking her head. "I don't have Fabia, Marno has. Maybe in a thirty or two she will find some time for the rest of the world. Orlando is lost forever. So cold, so hard! Oh, what did they *do* to him, Dantio?"

"They made a monster out of him, that's what. They dehumanized him. But he's much better than he was, Mama. Give him time. Give him love, but not too obviously. He is trying, I promise you. He will recover. Mothers all over Florengia have the same problem, or soon will have."

She bit her lip and made an effort to smile. "Marno praised him so generously yesterday! And he is going to give you all rich estates to support yourselves and raise fam . . . live in proper royal style."

Chies was approaching. He paused outside the door, flashed some hypocrisy at the guard, who responded with a flicker of distrust—Dantio could not hear the words, only feel the emotion. Chies lifted the latch and entered silently, barefoot. *(fear, anger)* That reaction must be to Dantio himself, for the undercurrent of uncertainty and resentment was the easily recognized response of an adolescent male to his mother. Why fear? And what was behind the anger? It was not just from the demotion in status he had taken when his half-siblings returned; that was chronic, this was acute. He wore a youth's loincloth, although that morning in the town he had been sporting an adult chlamys.

Dantio greeted him and was rewarded with a bow, sweet words, and a blast of manly contempt for a gelding.

Next came Orlad with brass collar and a red chlamys pinned under his right arm. Only the seer could sense the abysmal despair hidden behind his cheerful greeting. He was taking Waels's death very hard. At the memorial service yesterday he had been close to tears, which was unthinkable for a Werist. He addressed his mother in quite passable Florengian. Even if he had memorized the words beforehand, his accent was improving.

Oliva embraced him. He registered disgust at his own hypocrisy. Chies bowed to him. (detestation) Orlad nodded back. (contempt) Then Fabia arrived. In the resulting social gavotte, Dantio managed to draw his brother aside. He was careful to exaggerate his smile, for Orlad was slow to pick up signals.

"Congratulations on your promotion, packleader!"

"I killed Stralg for him. He couldn't make me anything less."

"He didn't have to take you into his horde at all."

Orlad scowled. "On probation! I have three thirties to learn the language and show that men will follow me."

"You're doing well on the language, and I bet they're all eager to kiss the Stralg-killer's, um, ankle already."

The Werist shrugged (satisfaction), then smiled. It was a good smile, not deliberate. "You're not so far off at that. But a season isn't long for a language."

"You have ten years to wait, I'd say," Dantio said softly, provoking the avalanche of suspicion that was Orlad's inevitable reaction to any remark he did not understand. "Even Therek wasn't as battle hardened as Cavotti. He won't live to anything like old age."

Orlad nodded, and now the smile was genuine (ambition). "True."

"So no matter how many sons Fabia gives him, the next conclave of elders will have only one candidate to consider."

(pain) Orlad turned away. He had no interest in sons. It took very little to remind him of his lost lover.

A Hero opened the door wide and peered in. Then Marno lurched through, leaving it to be closed by his guards, who remained outside. He wore a chlamys of royal purple, pinned on his shoulder in civilian style, and belted with a silver cord. It did little to hide his ghastly scars and twisted bones, and his half boots could not possibly contain human feet. He glanced around the company from under brows like eaves. How was he ever going to manage to get the coronet over that horn?

As the giant limped over to the table, the other men bowed and the women curtseyed. Ruling families were more formal than most, and this one had stronger emotions than most, too, so many that Dantio could not analyze them all. That was why he must leave Celebre—seers went crazy if they let themselves become entangled in family ties.

Fabia's disposition interested him most. Five nights ago in the Hall of Pillars, her attitude to Cavotti had been one of calculation and resignation, mixed with some Ucrist-type greed, undoubtedly—how could she not think that way after being raised by Horth Wigson?—but also a surprising amount of sexual interest in the monstrous hulk, tempered with a virginal dread very reasonable in the circumstances. Fortunately Fabia had seen long ago that Orlad could not possibly wear the coronet. Even if the elders gave it to him, the city and Freedom Fighters would rise and impose a change of dynasty. Cavotti was Piero's only possible successor, and it was up to her to make it happen in a way that would preserve the family line. Privilege brings responsibility. Responsibility needs sacrifice.

And now? Much had changed in five days; much more in the intervening five nights, likely. Cavotti took her hand to steady her as she sank down on a cushion. Then he dropped nimbly at her side and they exchanged the knowing smiles of lovers: *First my relatives, now yours.*

The old mating magic was working again. Dantio would never experience it, but he had seen it happen many times. Two people could not shed their clothing and normal dignity, embrace each other in the most intimate ways possible, rollick like small children while performing the most adult of actions and exulting in the most potent of pleasures—not without being changed and bonded by common memories. Two personal walls had been breached and joined, so that now a single wall enclosed them both, shutting out the world.

The others instinctively spread around the table, choosing a side apiece. It was a very large table, able to seat the whole council, and with a mere six people they were spread far apart.

Cavotti looked very tired. He smiled his ogreish smile. *(contentment)*

"I apologize for taking so long to find time for you. This get-together should have happened much sooner, but you know what has delayed me, or some of it. I have promises to make to all of you. You, Oliva, will have equal precedence with my mother, and your children will outrank my brothers. That includes you, Chies. Second, a new doge must confirm his predecessors' land grants, meaning your appanages, although I expect most of you don't even know about those. Wife?"

Smiling happily, Fabia took over. "Mama, on your marriage you were granted an estate at Lacema, a short distance down river from Celebre, so we understand. Is it sufficient for you? Have its revenues suffered from the war?"

"I honestly do not know, dear," Oliva said. "In the last year I have had no time to visit it or talk with the tallymen."

"Please do both and let us know your wishes. Marno will grant whatever support you need to maintain yourself in proper state. Celebre owes you that and much more. Also, choose suitable quarters in the palace to be your city home."

Oliva expressed gratitude, while emitting waves of alternating happiness and loss.

Marno was enjoying himself, sharing out the spoils of war. "Also, my lady, I am appointing you to the council, as deputy-president. We need your wisdom and experience. Is there anything we have overlooked?"

"No, no! You are most generous."

"Dantio, your appanage at . . ." Fabia saw him shake his head. "No?"

"No. My lady, my lord, I cannot own land. The use of a room in the palace when I am in the city—that I would appreciate. Possibly a small pension if the Eldest does not accept me into the Florengian cult, but no more than that. I am very grateful for your offer and for your generosity to my mother."

Cavotti frowned. "You could be invaluable to me and my government."

"I betrayed my oaths once, but I am still bound by them, my lord. I must witness and not meddle."

(annoyance, disappointment) "Very well. Carry on, Dogaressa."

Fabia turned to Orlad *(caution)* and spoke in Vigaelian. "Packleader Orlad . . . You wish to remain Orlad or revert to Orlando? Orlad, then. You were granted an apanage called Guiniama. Go and visit it, then come and report to me or Marno. If it is insufficient, or has been wasted by the Vigaelians, we shall find you another."

Orlad said, "Thank you." *(envy—that should be me wearing purple)*

"Marno very much wants to have you as leader of the city host, a job he feels should be held by a member of the family. He promises to promote you as soon you have proved yourself, and to appoint you to the council at that time."

"My lord is very kind," Orlad growled in Florengian. *(distrust, pleasure)*

"You amply earned it all." Marno turned to look at Chies. *(abhorrence!)*

Dantio was startled by the intensity of the doge's hatred. And Fabia, too? Her smile at their half-brother concealed intense distrust and suspicion. Judging the situation only as a Witness and not as a family member, Dantio would conclude that Chies Celebre was in grave danger of his life.

What had changed? At Veritano Cavotti had been openly contemptuous of the boy, while in secret regretting the need to bully him. Indeed, his hidden sympathy for Chies had been the most startling of many startling things Dantio had noted about him, qualities unexpected in a Werist. At Veritano Fabia had not faked her support for her half-brother. Why had he suddenly fallen so drastically in their estimation? How had he alienated them both so quickly?

He obviously knew whatever was going through the ducal minds, for his polished, boyish smile hid screaming terror and murderous hatred. *Mother of Lies!* How was a boy like him managing to dissimulate so skillfully?

"Lord Chies," Fabia said with careful formality, "you should have been sworn in as an adult citizen last New Year. The person responsible for your absence—" She shot a smile at her husband. "—regrets the inconvenience. He has ordered the chief priest to arrange a private ceremony, for you alone. Congratulations on reaching your majority, brother."

Chies thanked doge and dogaressa profusely. *(contempt, distrust)*

"Congratulations," Orlad said.

Chies turned the same false smile on him. "Thank you, too, packleader." In perfect Vigaelian, he added, "Does this mean that you don't want to tear my head off any more, brother?" *(detestation)*

"Not as much, anyway." *(scorn)*

"Stop that, both of you!" Oliva shouted, but she was registering *(fear)* in addition to *(anger)*, so even an extrinsic could sense the festering distrust.

Her outburst stopped the sniping. Everyone smiled as if they had been joking, and yet the emotional firestorm raged unabated. Orlad disliked the youth, both personally and as evidence of his mother's abuse by Stralg. His feelings were nothing compared to the hatred of Fabia and Cavotti. Chies, however, seemed to hate Orlad most, the man who had slain his real father.

So?

So there was no proof and never could be *proof* as the Maynists knew it, but adding up what Dantio had seen that morning, plus whatever had aroused such emotion in Fabia and that peculiar story of the escape from Veritano, there was good reason to suspect Chies Celebre of being a Chosen. Less evidence than that had sent many to living graves.

"Doge Piero," Marno told the boy, "deeded you an appanage at Fauniani. You know it?"

"No, my lord. Papa never thought it safe for me to visit it."

"It isn't safe now, but I am sure that won't stop you, so ask one of the huntleaders for an escort. And you may keep your present quarters, here in the palace."

Chies was being treated with astonishing generosity—most people in Celebre would agree with Orlad's first thought on meeting the Stralg bastard, that his head should be removed right away. Chies was thanking the ducal pair, and so was Oliva, and all was sweetness and light on the surface. Underwater the sharks still circled.

Dantio shivered. It was past time that he left. He had broken his oaths once and could not expect a second forgiveness. *Never meddle, never warn.* He must leave Fabia and Orlad to fight their own battles, or rather he must leave Fabia to fight them. Orlad was a spectacular killing machine, but he wouldn't have a hope against a Chosen, no matter how weedy and harmless the brat looked.

Forty-Four

THE STRANGER

disembarked late in the day, when the shadows were long and the summer heat lay heavy on the city. Young and powerfully built, he leaped ashore even before the riverboat tied up. His bundle of possessions was notably slim, his loincloth frayed, and the rag around his neck was grubby and sweat-stained. Even his golden hair and beard could have benefited from some attention.

No one questioned him or contested his arrival, although most cities had rules for dealing with young men who wore scarves like his. Usually the authorities would send them packing right away. He might be given the option of removing the scarf, but only on condition that he immediately swear allegiance to the city and its horde.

The stranger barely glanced at the busy frontage, with its hawkers and stalls, its traders and porters, and all the cargoes being moved between boats and carts. He headed straight to the nearest alley and vanished into its shadows. Thereafter he kept to the right-hand wall and carried his bundle on his left shoulder, shielding his face. Although the streets were merely gaps between a jumbled maze of mud brick buildings, he strode along without hesitation.

Other pedestrians mostly moved out of his way. The few men who did not, and came face-to-face with him in contested passage, took sudden note of the scarf and his scars and the look in his eyes; then they, too, stepped aside, muttering apologies. It was the eyes, mostly.

At last he came to a turning he did not remember, a wall so obviously fresh that it must have been built within the last year or two. He had antici-pated an open space there, but no space stayed open long in a heavily popu-lated city. He tried bearing right, then left, and eventually found himself below a flight of marble steps and the facade of a large stone building. He had forgotten how big it was. He remembered other things, though. With a snort of annoyance, or possibly disgust, he strode up the steps and entered.

He stood, then, within a single large, circular chamber that resembled a giant birdcage. The entrance he had used was one of twelve, all very high, separated by twelve walls like elongated, curved pillars that supported a domed roof. On this sweltering day in late summer the interior was shad-owed and cool, but it would be wildly uncomfortable in winter. The floor was notably devoid of furniture, a total waste of space, but there was a shrine at the base of each wall. Above each shrine stood a god or goddess, shaped from honey-colored marble. This was the Pantheon, home of the Bright Ones. Their images were so lifelike that the stranger could almost imagine Them stepping down at the end of the day and strolling off in laughing groups to Their carefree homes in Paradise.

One quick walk around and he could leave. If he could return to the riverbank before sunset he might find passage on a boat out; otherwise he would spend the night at the temple of Eriander and go as soon after dawn as possible. A dozen or so other people were at worship, mostly elderly women and attendant priests. Since they all happened to be to his right, the stranger turned to his left, feeling the marble cool and smooth underfoot.

The first idol was neither male nor female, just an ambiguous youth clutching a cloth in front of Himself or Herself. His or Her arm obscured His or Her breasts and the cloth covered His or Her groin. Yet why so sad? If the deity in charge of lust could not look happy, who ever could?

The stranger bowed his head and muttered the briefest possible prayer: "I honor You, holy Eriander; give me Your blessing."

A fat, shaven-headed priest came shuffling over, rubbing his hands. Then he noticed the stranger's neckcloth and cringed away from his glare. "If I can be of help, my—"

"No! You cannot."

The priest offered a meaningless smile and limped away on very flat feet.

The stranger strode on to the next shrine. He had seen this statue before. Hiddi! He knew the model intimately and had many happy memories of tumbling her in Eriander's temple. Even for a Nymph, she had been an incredible rollick. Here she depicted holy Anziel, holding a hawk on Her arm—goddess smiling down, bird turned to peer up at Her. Every feather on the bird was as perfect as every curl on Hiddi's head. Just looking at her image was enough to arouse him. He felt certain that the statue's leg would feel warm and supple to the touch.

Resisting that sacrilegious temptation, the stranger mumbled the same curt prayer and went on to the next god, a naked young man with a dove on his shoulder, smiling down at a fawn held in the crook of his elbow. Oh gods! That face! That smile! Was it Finar? Or Fitel? His brothers had looked exactly like that early in their Werist training, before their teeth and noses got smashed in the roughhousing. Finar, probably, but even their mother had been mistaken sometimes. The sculptor must have known which twin he was depicting, but how could he possibly have remembered them so well? "I honor You, holy Nastrar, give me Your blessing."

Seething with fury now, the stranger strode on. Beyond the next entrance was the idol he especially wanted to see. Or not to see. But there He was, holy Weru Himself, holding a sword, His emblem. He differed from all the others in that He was shown seated. Seated, and yet the same height as all the others! The implication took a moment to register—that Weru was twice the size of all the other gods.

That was what Satrap Horold had ordered. But Horold had died long before that statue was made. Why had the artist obeyed a dead man's instructions at the cost of spoiling the symmetry of the Pantheon? Why should a Hand so honor the war god?

The Terrible One deserved a longer prayer. "I honor You, most holy Weru, my lord and protector, mightiest of gods. I will live in Your service and die to Your honor."

"I promised I would be generous," said a quiet voice behind him.

The stranger's fists clenched into mallets of bone. He knew that voice. It was the last voice he wanted to hear. The face he would see if he turned around was the very face he had been trying so hard not to meet.

"Go away!"

There was no reply. He continued to study holy Weru. Weru studied him. The god's nose had never been flattened, his ears had not been bloated out like tubers. Otherwise their faces were the same face. The god was perhaps a few years older. Wide shoulders, thick calves . . . everything as it should be. More or less. More, probably.

"You were not stingy," the stranger admitted, just to discover if his unwelcome companion was still there.

"I was sent to fetch you."

The stranger turned around.

The Florengian was still big and hairy and dark of hide. He wore a leather smock smeared with clay and paint. If anything, he had grown even broader in the last three years or so. Life had left marks on his face, and robbed his smile of some teeth, but it had also given him more confidence—possibly even arrogance. Werists did not take kindly to extrinsics putting on airs.

Not even homeless hungry Werists didn't.

"It's wonderful to see you, Cutrath! We thought you were dead. Where have you *been*?" Benard whipped his great stonemason's arms around the stranger and crushed all the breath out of him. "Thank the gods!"

Cutrath tried to break free and was dismayed to find that he couldn't—not without using a wrestling trick or two, and that was not proper behavior in a temple. Masterless Heroes who disturbed the peace by brawling soon found themselves in serious trouble.

"Let me go," he whispered in the sculptor's ear, "or I will tear out your guts and strangle you with them."

Benard released him with a puzzled look. "Only trying to be friendly! I really am overjoyed to see you. Ingeld has been going out of her mind for days, staring in the fire day and night. Half a pot-boiling ago she started screaming, 'He's here! He's here! He's going to the Pantheon!' So we came to get you."

Dismayed, Cutrath said, *"We?"* Not his mother here too? Then he saw that the third person present was very small.

The Hand bent and raised her. She was another Florengian, with dark curls and very large, dark eyes. Thumb in mouth, she stared at the stranger from the safety of her father's arms.

"Your sister Oliva. This is your brother Cutrath who Mommy's been telling you about. What do you say to him?"

Oliva thought for a moment, then took her thumb out of her mouth. "Twelve blessings!"

"That's very good. Cutrath?"

"Twelve blessings on you too, Oliva. Now, why don't you run outside and catch pigeons while I break your daddy's neck?"

Benard set the girl down. "Pardon me," he said, and brazenly reached out to untie the rag hiding Cutrath's collar. "You don't need to wear this in Kosord—not you. You are not a masterless out-of-work unwanted Werist here, you are the dynast's son. You are also—if you will pardon my mentioning it—her consort's stepson. Old Guthlag is too old and I need to find a new hordeleader. Cutrath Horoldson is the logical man."

If Cutrath did not hit this mucker soon he would explode. He must smash him into rubble or die of frustration. Unfortunately the priests were nosily watching this encounter between the vagrant Werist and the consort, not to mention the dynast's heir apparent.

"*You* need a hordeleader? Oh, isn't that kind of you! You killed my father. You raped my mother. And now you have the gall to offer me a job? To work for *you*?"

The Florengian raised heavy black eyebrows. "Work for *her*, actually. Kosord belongs to your mother. I was not the one who raped her, Horold was. Repeatedly. I rescued her and took her away where he could not abuse her. And yes, I led him into the ambush that killed him. He came two eyelashes short of beating me to death while I was at it."

"My ambition is to finish the work my father started."

Benard sighed. "I should warn you that Ingeld forbids me to travel anywhere outside the palace without a bodyguard, a full flank of Werists. They are an accursed nuisance. Or have been up until now. Suddenly they feel sort of useful to have around. Why didn't you come straight home to the palace? Did you find religion? Develop a sudden interest in art?"

"I'm not staying. I won't go to the palace. I'm leaving as soon as I have walked around this craft shop of yours."

Infuriatingly, the Florengian laughed. *Laughed* at a Werist!

"That won't make my life any easier. Ingeld will order me to order the hordeleader to run you down and bring you back. What's the matter, really, my lord? Whatever it is, you're safe here in Kosord. How can we help you?"

Cutrath swallowed a mouthful of bile. A *Hand* offering to help a *Hero*? The world had gone mad. "You can't. I've been having bad dreams is all, terrible dreams. I keep dreaming I've become your Weru idol. I dream that instead of carving my likeness, you somehow turned me into stone, and there I am, sitting here in the Pantheon in Kosord, and people are going in and out and worshiping me—worshiping Weru I mean, but offering me the sacrifices. And nobody can see that it is really me! I can't cry out or move or anything. I finally went to an oneiromancer. He said the dreams were a sending from holy Cienu. Don't ask me how he knew that. His job to know. He said they meant I should come to Kosord and pray in the Pantheon. And when I had done that, the nightmares would stop."

Benard shrugged. "Go ahead and do it, then. If we keep your mother waiting too long, she'll spoil all your fun by strangling me herself."

Cutrath turned and strode on to the next god. "Holy . . ." The figure wore a robe and held a deck of clay tablets in his hand, but he was far younger than the Lawgiver as traditionally represented. Color him brown instead of pink . . .

"You are getting mighty uppity, aren't you, showing your own brother as holy Demern?"

"Orlad's a fine figure of a man," Benard protested, but he looked a little guilty at Cutrath's accusation. "He feels very strongly about oath-breaking. I had to use mortal models, you know. Gods don't do modeling. I used you, and your brother Finar, and my other brother, and Hiddi . . . and Orlad looks the part!"

His expression certainly looked stubborn enough. "I honor You, holy Demern, give me Your blessing."

"And here's Cienu!" Benard said eagerly. "I love His smile! I'm prouder of that than anything else in the whole temple."

Cienu, god of mirth and chance; Cienu as a naked young man holding a wine jug and wearing a mischievous, knowing smile. It was another masterpiece, of course. Oh, that face! Cutrath's fists balled, his arms and shoulders flexed. He thought he was going to burst.

"What's the matter?" Benard said, not looking a fraction as worried as he should. "Did you know him? Waels Borkson? Wonderful man!"

Cutrath swung around to stare at him. No, it was not deliberate. Even Benard could not be so suicidally offensive deliberately. He had always been a genius at blundering into trouble by accident.

"I met him at Nardalborg."

"He and Orlad were very close, so—"

"I *know* that," Cutrath said through clenched teeth. "I had barely walked in the gate when that Waels came over and said he heard I'd insulted a friend of his."

Benard said, "*Oo!* Ahem! *Oh!* I mean, he never told me this, Cutrath, I swear he didn't! If you would rather not talk—"

Cutrath looked again at the image. "He smiled at me just like that. Exactly like that. I thought it would be fun to rearrange his pretty face. So I told him what I thought of his mudface friend. In detail."

Pause.

"Surprise?" Benard said warily.

"Yes, you could say that." Why in the world was Cutrath telling this stonemason about it? "Like fighting a stampede of mammoths." The worst beating of his life. After he came to, he'd had to ask permission to battle-form so he could heal his broken ribs and fractured jaw. The man to ask had been the commandant of Nardalborg, Heth Hethson, and Heth Hethson had not only been the one person who could possibly have told Waels Borkson about Cutrath's wrangle with Orlad at Halfway Hall, but had later turned out to be Cutrath's cousin as well. Cutrath hadn't known that at the time, but Heth must have.

The sculptor avoided his eye. "Didn't know that. Waels died. Killed by Stralg, if it makes you feel any better."

Much better. "Tell me!"

"Don't know any details, just what my sister wrote. She said that Waels and Orlad took on Stralg in the throne room at Celebre. It was a standoff until Waels deliberately let Stralg catch him, so Orlad could get inside the Fist's guard." The artist hesitated. "Then Orlad killed Stralg."

"And Therek too, I heard. Earlier."

"Yes."

Curiously, Cutrath felt less worked up now than he had been at first. Trying to pick a fight with Benard Celebre was totally unsatisfying, somehow. "You and your brother really thinned out my family tree, didn't you? What happened to Fabia? At one time I was supposed to marry her."

"She's fine! A healthy son and another due about a thirty ago."

"Married to?"

"Marno Cavotti. Doge of Celebre."

Cutrath did not comment on that. He glanced up again at the haunting face of Cienu-Waels. How could even a Hand of Anziel make a lump of rock look as if it was trying to *tell* you something?

"Where have you been all this time?" Benard asked. "We thought you died on the Edge with Saltaja."

Cutrath shrugged. "Hoeing fields, chopping wood, digging irrigation ditches. People only hire Werists as Werists so that they can hold killing matches with them."

"I know," Benard said. "It's Horth Wigson and some of his cronies. After your uncles died and the war ended, he hired most of their men and just about all of New Dawn. He rents out hordes to towns, and that frightens their neighbors into renting larger hordes, and so on. Sooner or later two or three get together and hold a war. That reduces the supply and also makes the towns want even larger hordes. So the price goes up."

Cutrath had never heard it explained that way. It would be believable if it didn't came from Benard Celebre.

"How do *you* know all that? You're a stonemason."

Benard scratched his head. "Your mother explained it to me last night in . . . in a discussion about your coming home."

"Dada, I wanna come home too!" Oliva announced.

"Come along, then. How did you escape from the Edge?"

"You don't want to hear that," Cutrath said, and told him anyway, to see how he reacted. "Some of us headed back west. We'd agreed we'd draw lots at mealtimes, but then we discovered there were other groups going the same way and we had better keep our numbers up. We preyed a lot."

The sculptor pulled a face. "Don't tell your mother. What I heard was that you collected the largest band of survivors, disciplined it, and led it out without losing a man to the other gangs, and they all were hailing you as their bloodlord, but you disappeared. Why didn't you come straight home after that, for gods's sakes?"

Cutrath swallowed the last dregs of his pride. "Because I knew you would laugh at me. Because I knew I would rip your head off and that would upset Ingeld. Because I was Horold's son and the people would hang me. They still will, won't they?"

"No. You're Ingeld's son, so they won't." The Florengian stared at him with a puzzled expression. "You are home again and most welcome."

"*Shut up!*"

That worked. Cutrath prayed his way around the rest of the Pantheon without being interrupted, the priests carefully keeping well away. Benard followed in silence, with his daughter skipping alongside, clutching his finger.

When they came to Eriander again, Cutrath looked back. Weru was ignoring him, staring across at holy Veslih. So He didn't care.

But Cienu was still smiling at him.

"What are you looking at?" Benard murmured softly.

"Damn you! That smile."

"And what do you see?"

"I see Waels Borkson saying, 'Remember how you screamed when I stomped your kidneys?'"

"But what you are supposed to see," Benard said, "is holy Cienu, Who called you here. And what He's telling you is, 'Waels Borkson is dead and all that remains of him are memories and this block of stone; but you're still alive, so go and enjoy life while you can.'"

He started down the steps, holding Oliva's hand so she could jump each one. "Come on!" he called back cheerfully. "Now you've done what the oneiromancer said, everything will be all right. Cienu is god of parties, remember. Wait until you see what Ingeld's planning."

Cutrath shrugged and trotted down the steps after them. One chariot stood there, with a grinning urchin proudly holding the reins.

"Um?" Cutrath said. "Where's the bodyguard you mentioned?"

Oliva took her thumb out of her mouth. "Dada sneaked out without them," she said solemnly. "Mommy said she'd spank him if he did it again."

Benard swung her up into his arms. "So you'd better not tell her. I'll hold you, and brother Cutrath will drive the chariot."

"Is Cutrath a good driver?"

"He's a very good driver." Tossing the urchin something shiny that made him whoop with glee, Benard stepped up into the car.

Oliva said solemnly, "Mommy says you'll kill someone someday."

"I know. That's why Cutrath will drive. Come along, Hordeleader."

In spite of himself, Cutrath climbed aboard and took the reins. "I really should try that gut extraction on you. I'm sure I won't rest until I do."

"Messy," Benard said. "I'm cutting a statue of your father that's going very well. Hiddi's back in town, by the way. You must see the new temple of Nula I'm designing." He grinned happily. "Veal for dinner tonight! Ingeld says it's your favorite."

"Fat one?"

"Fat and greasy as they come."

Cutrath's mouth started watering fit to drown him. He sighed. "All right. Feast tonight, murder you tomorrow."

Appendix

THE WORLD

Fantasy worlds are impossible by definition. As I warned you at the beginning of *Children of Chaos,* the Dodecians' view of their world cannot be even remotely correct.

A regular dodecahedron is a solid enclosed by twelve identical pentagons. The twelve faces share thirty edges and twenty vertices. Regular dodecahedrons do not occur in nature, although the crystal form called pyritohedron comes close. A polyhedron cannot be scaled up to planet size, because no irregular solid is strong enough to resist the crushing force of gravity. Asteroids can be nonspherical, but only the smaller ones. For example, Amalthea, an almond-shaped moon of Jupiter, measures 167 by 93 miles (268 by 150 km), but density measurements show that it is a pile of rubble. Rubble or not, any body much larger than that must collapse into a sphere under its own weight.

Even if the core and mantle of the planet were so impossibly rigid that they could hold their shape against gravity, erosion would strip the crust at the edges and wash the sediment into the oceans. This happens on Earth, too, and tectonic movements push the sediment piles up into mountains in a never-ending cycle, but the scale of vertical movement does not come close to what would be needed to turn the planet into a polyhedron.

To prove how absurd the Dodecian view is, consider what Dodec would be like if it had the same mass and volume as the Earth. Every edge would be 3,250 miles (5,200 km) long, and each face slightly larger than Asia. That is *big*!

For simplicity, assume that the north pole is located exactly at the northernmost vertex of Vigaelia. Three faces must meet at every vertex, so there would be an arctic region of three "polar" faces and a matching triplet of antarctic faces. The remaining six, "tropical," faces would form a chain around the middle, pointing alternately north and south. Vigaelia is therefore polar, and Florengia tropical.

Because a plane presents a uniform angle to the sun, the faces would lack the north-south insolation gradient we take for granted on a spherical planet. Each face would show a *radial* change in climate, because the atmosphere would be much less dense near the edges. There would be *edge* ice caps.

The six tropical faces would be inclined at an average 10° to the "equator," equivalent to the latitude of, say, Panama. The six polar faces would have a tilt of 52°, about the same as London, England. Since Dodec is known to have seasons, its axis of rotation must be tilted with respect to the ecliptic, but all we know about the amount of tilt is that it is less than 38°, for otherwise Vigaelia would have no daylight at midwinter. The changing tilt would cause seasonal effects, but the hours of daylight would remain the same year-round, so seasonal climatic change would be much less than we are used to. Seasonal variation would be negligible on the tropical faces— but note that midwinter on a tropical face would coincide with midsummer for its neighbor on either side.

We are rarely aware that the Earth is round. We do not see large bodies of water as dome-shaped, and yet if you look at a calm sea or large lake, standing with your feet at water level, your horizon is less than three miles (five kilometers) away. In other words, we perceive the globe as flat. I suspect that a flat world would seem to be concave. On Dodec the center of each face would be much closer to the center of the planet than the edges are, so water would tend to run to the middle and pile up. If you stood at an edge and looked across that enormous plane, you might well feel you were looking down into a bowl with a heap of ocean in the center. Dodec has no moon, because the mere thought of tides gives me the willies.

On polar faces, such as Vigaelia, the dominant climatic factor would be seasonal variation acting on the central ocean, which would warm up and cool down more slowly than land would. In summer, when the ocean was relatively cool, air would rise over land areas and sink in the center, giving an outward radial flow at the surface. In winter, when the ocean was relatively warmer, the flow would be reversed. Coriolis forces would make the prevailing winds blow clockwise in summer, counterclockwise in winter.

Not only would tropical faces, like Florengia, lack much seasonal variation, the small angle they would subtend to the planetary axis would make their Coriolis forces weaker, although not completely ineffectual. (Note that the "equator" would have no direct significance to those forces. On the Florengian Face, the southernmost vertices would be the farthest points from the axis and thus have the greatest rotational velocity. Fluids would move as if the entire face lay in the northern "hemisphere.") Florengian weather, like Vigaelian, would be controlled by heat exchange between the hot, humid maritime center and the cold, dry uplands. Coastal areas would be jungles, racked by cyclonic storms, while the rims would be cold desert. The "fertile circle" in which Celebre is reported to stand must be a benign temperate zone in between. Such a zone could be relatively narrow but still enormous in actual area.

The weirdness goes on. Because the oceans would be domed, the sun would be able to set behind them, or reflect off them. It would be nice to think of the horizon flaming up bright green like an iceberg, but water on such a scale is not transparent. The domes would be opaque.

Air is not perfectly transparent either. From the window of a commercial jetliner in flight, the horizon is a blur, and yet it is only about 200 miles (300 km) distant, which is a trivial vista on Dodec. Rising hundreds or thousands of kilometers away from you, the sun would have to climb over the limit of transparency of the atmosphere, the "wall of the world."

Where water goes, so goes air. The maximum topographical variation on Earth, from the top of Mount Everest to the bottom of the Mariana Trench, is 12.4 miles (20 km). By coincidence, the deviation of the terrestrial geoid from a perfect sphere is of similar magnitude—ice floes at the terrestrial north pole are 13 miles (21 km) closer to the center of the planet than a surfer at the equator. The mean radius of the Earth is 3,966 miles (6,378 km).

On a polyhedral Dodec the ocean bed at the midpoint of each Face would be 3,600 miles (5,800 km) from the center. Sea level would depend on how much water the planet had, how much was tied up in ice caps, and how equitably it was distributed between the twelve faces, but if Dodec had about the same amount of water as the earth, the ocean would dome up roughly 50 miles (80 km) deep at the center and be 1,200 miles (1,900 km) across. Nardalborg Pass would then lie 600 miles (960 km) above sea level, and each vertex would be 350 miles (560 km) higher yet. Breathing would certainly be a problem.

Even if the planetary mass and volume were the same as the Earth's, nowhere on the surface of Dodec would gravity be as strong. This conclusion is counterintuitive, but a sphere is the most stable shape simply because it maximizes gravitational force at its surface. Lesser surface gravity would produce a lesser density gradient in the atmosphere. Furthermore, those enormous vertex "mountains" would produce complex gravity fields of their own, dragging some air away from a purely spherical shape. Even so, holding your breath long enough to cross the Nardalborg Pass would not be advisable.

I hope such technical quibbles did not spoil your visit.